Slummy Mummy

Slummy Mummy

Fiona Neill

RIVERHEAD BOOKS

A member of Penguin Group (USA) Inc.

New York

2007

RIVERHEAD BOOKS
Published by the Penguin Group
Penguin Group (USA) Inc., 375 Hudson Street, New York, New York 10014,
USA • Penguin Group (Canada), 90 Eglinton Avenue East, Suite 700,
Toronto, Ontario M4P 2Y3, Canada (a division of Pearson Penguin Canada
Inc.) • Penguin Books Ltd, 80 Strand, London WC2R 0RL, England
• Penguin Ireland, 25 St Stephen's Green, Dublin 2, Ireland (a division of
Penguin Books Ltd) • Penguin Group (Australia), 250 Camberwell Road,
Camberwell, Victoria 3124, Australia (a division of Pearson Australia Group
Pty Ltd) • Penguin Books India Pvt Ltd, 11 Community Centre, Panchsheel
Park, New Delhi–110 017, India • Penguin Group (NZ), 67 Apollo Drive,
Rosedale, North Shore 0745, Auckland, New Zealand (a division of
Pearson New Zealand Ltd) • Penguin Books (South Africa) (Pty) Ltd,
24 Sturdee Avenue, Rosebank, Johannesburg 2196, South Africa

Penguin Books Ltd, Registered Offices:
80 Strand, London WC2R 0RL, England

Library of Congress Cataloging-in-Publication Data

Neill, Fiona.
[Secret life of a slummy mummy]
Slummy mummy : the secret life of Lucy Sweeney / Fiona Neill.
p.   cm.
Originally published as: The secret life of a slummy mummy.
London : Century, 2007.
ISBN 978-1-59448-944-0
1. Motherhood—Fiction.   I. Title.
PR6114.E55S43   2007   2007001595
823'.92—dc22

Printed in the United States of America
1   3   5   7   9   10   8   6   4   2

BOOK DESIGN BY AMANDA DEWEY

For Ed

Every woman is a science, for he that plods upon a woman all his life long shall at length find himself short of the knowledge of her.

John Donne

You can dream different dreams while sharing the same bed.

Chinese proverb

Slummy Mummy

1

"A deaf husband and a blind wife are always a happy couple."

I leave my contact lenses to soak overnight in a coffee cup, and wake up in the morning to discover that Husband on a Short Fuse has drunk them in the night. For the second time in less than a year.

"But I told you they were in there," I protest.

"I can't be expected to remember that kind of detail," he says. "And I'm not going to try and make myself sick this time. Wear your glasses."

Tom is sitting up in bed, hair standing on end, wearing a pair of crumpled striped pajamas with the top button done up, arms crossed defensively. I am wearing a pair in tartan, buttons missing. When you both start wearing pajamas in bed, does it represent the beginning or the end of something in a relationship, I wonder? He reaches over to stack three books on his bedside table in order of size and to line up the mug that once contained my contact lenses equidistant from the table lamp on the other side.

"I just don't understand why you put them in a coffee cup anyway. There are millions of people up and down the country who perform this ritual each day and they never resort to using a mug to store something so integral to their daily routine. It's a form of sabotage, Lucy, because you know there is a risk I will want a drink in the night."

"But don't you sometimes want to live a little dangerously?" I ask. "Tempt fate a little bit, without harming anyone you love in the process?"

"If I thought there were unanswered philosophical questions behind this, rather than an empty bottle of wine and consequent amnesia, I would be worried about your mental state. I might be more sympathetic if you showed a little concern for me. It could be a medical emergency," he says petulantly.

"But it wasn't last time," I interject, swift to stymie the inevitable slide into hypochondria.

I resist the urge to tell him that there are bigger priorities right now, involving the need to get our children to school at the designated hour on the first day of term. I fleetingly recall dropping a contact lens onto the carpet a couple of months ago and start a painstaking examination of the floor area on my side of the bed. In a semi-fortuitous discovery I find in no particular order: a lens that the toddler had removed from my glasses last week; a half-eaten cream egg from so long ago that it has petrified; and an unpaid parking fine, which I swiftly stuff back under the bed.

"You need systems, Lucy," says Tom, unaware of what is being uncovered just a few feet away from him. "Then life will become so much simpler. In the meantime, why don't you wear your old glasses? It's not as though you need to impress anyone." He gets out of bed and moves into the bathroom for the next part of his early-morning ritual.

A decade ago, in the foothills of our relationship, this kind of exchange would have qualified as a full-blown argument, one of those violent eruptions that had the potential to capsize the entire affair. Even five years ago, roughly halfway through our marriage, it would have constituted a significant disagreement. Now it is no more than a footnote to the narrative of married life.

As I walk up the stairs to the top floor of the house to wake our sleeping children, I decide that relationships are like pieces of elastic, where a little tension is permissible, even desirable, if the two ends are to remain bound together. Too slack and everything falls apart, like those marriages where people say they never argue and which then overnight dissolve into nothing, not even recrimination. Too much tension and they snap. It's all about equilibrium. The trouble is, generally there is no forewarning when you are about to lose balance.

I curse as I trip over a LEGO model on the stairs and it breaks into tiny bits, joining forces with some toy cars and an arm that used to belong to an Action Man. My chin comes to rest on the top step and, tucked into the side of the carpet, I spot a tiny lightsaber, no more than an inch long, that belongs to one of Joe's *Star Wars* models. It vanished a couple of months ago in suspicious circumstances after our mercurial toddler, Fred, mounted a covert operation into his brother's bedroom in the early hours of the morning.

How long have I wasted searching for this lightsaber? How many tears have been shed over its disappearance? For a brief moment I rest my head on the carpet, feeling something close to satisfaction.

I stop outside Sam and Joe's bedroom and gently push open the door. Sam, the eldest, is in pole position asleep on the top bunk, Joe on the bottom, and Fred on the floor underneath. Like a club sandwich. No matter how many times I return Fred to his own room during the night, he has an innate homing device that leads him either back to his brothers' room or to the end of our bed, where we often find him asleep in the morning.

I stare in wonder at my sleeping children, their limbs casually strewn across beds and floor, and my restless thoughts fade. During the day they are in perpetual motion, and it is impossible to freeze any moment for more than a few seconds. Asleep, there is the chance to observe the exact tilt of a nose or constellation of freckles. I touch Sam's hand to wake him up but instead his fingers curl tightly around my own. Their body clocks are still on holiday time. I am instantly transported back to that first moment shortly after Sam was born, when he did this for the first time and that surge of untapped maternal love spilled over and I knew that nothing would ever be the same again.

Sam is almost nine years old. I stopped being able to lift him about two years ago. He is too big to sit on my lap, and I am no longer permitted to kiss him farewell at school. Soon he will be lost to me entirely. But all that warmth of early childhood will have been stamped upon him.

Surely there will be reserves of affection that he can draw on during the dark teenage years when he sees us with all our flaws. As he lies on the bed, his long-limbed body already clumsy with impending adolescence, I realize that I am looking at the last vestiges of childhood. I am sure this is why some women go on and on having children, so there is always a willing receptacle for their love.

Joe stirs first. He is a light sleeper, like me.

"Who will help Major Tom?" he asks before his eyes open, and I feel my heart sink slightly.

Playing David Bowie on our way to Norfolk during the summer holidays had seemed like a huge step forward in the fraught world of in-car entertainment. The narrative quality of his lyrics would appeal to the children's imagination, we thought. And they did. But we never moved beyond the first track of *Changes*.

"Why did the rocket leave him?" he asks now, peering from beneath the duvet.

"He got detached," I tell him.

"Why wasn't there another driver to help him?" he asks.

"He wanted to be on his own," I say, stroking his hair. Five-year-old Joe is made in my image, with his wild brown curls and dark green eyes, but his temperament is inherited from his father.

"Does the rocket leave him behind?"

"It does, but there is part of him that wants to escape," I explain. Joe pauses.

"Mummy, do you ever want to escape from us?" he asks.

"Occasionally, but only into the next room." I laugh. "I have no plans to go into outer space."

"But sometimes when I talk to you, you don't hear, so where are you then?"

Sam has climbed down his ladder at this point and is already putting on his school uniform. I urge Joe to follow suit. Two-and-a-half-year-old Fred will remain undressed until the last minute, because the moment our backs are turned he will simply remove his clothes. I go back to our bathroom in search of Tom—the husband, not the major.

❀❀

There was a time when Tom's ablutions fascinated me, but even though they are still remarkable in their fastidiousness, familiarity has tempered the novelty. In brief, he goes into the bathroom and prepares everything he needs for shaving: Brush, foam, and razor sit on a small table beside the sink. He turns on the cold tap in the bath for exactly three minutes, and then switches his attention to the hot tap. That way, he says, no water is wasted. I have always argued that the arrangement should work better in reverse but he has never taken up the challenge. "If something works, why would you want to change it, Lucy?" While the bath is running he puts on the radio and listens to the *Today* program.

The washing process is only interesting inasmuch as he spends an inordinate amount of time rubbing the soap with the sponge. Often during this part of the proceedings he chats. Even after we had been living together for a couple of years, I still sometimes misjudged that moment when banter became acceptable. Interrupting prematurely could lead to moods that were difficult to diffuse. But impeccable timing made him expansive and generous. And so the slow dance of marriage was perfected.

As I rifle through bathroom drawers, I try to explain that pale blue National Health glasses from the eighties are not the kind of accessory worn on the school run, but he has already retreated into the next phase, which involves submerging himself, apart from the tip of his nose, and shutting his eyes in a meditative underwater pose from which no amount of children shouting can rouse him.

Now he is out of reach, and I am left sitting on a chair with my legs crossed, elbow resting on my knee, palm of my hand on my chin, talking to myself, a metaphor for our relationship.

I am briefly transported back to the first night I spent with Tom at his Shepherd's Bush apartment in 1994. I woke up in the morning and decided to make a swift exit and crept around the bedroom, looking for my clothes. When I couldn't find them, I retraced my steps to the sitting room because I could remember with some clarity that we spent a longish period on the sofa before finally making it to his bedroom. But they weren't there. I was completely naked and recalled mention of room-mates.

Running back to the bedroom on tiptoe to avoid waking anyone up, I began to wonder whether this was an amusing diversion for him. Or whether, despite recommendations to the contrary, there was a dark side to his character that involved holding captive women who slept with him on a first date. When I went back in the bedroom he had disappeared, and then I really began to panic. I called out his name but there was no reply, so I gingerly put on a shaggy dressing gown that I found on the back of the door to make a logical search of all the rooms.

When I went into the bathroom, I screamed. He was underwater with his eyes shut, completely still. I thought he had fallen asleep and drowned. I felt a real sense of loss that I would never have sex again with this man, because it had been very good. Then I imagined phoning the police and trying to explain what had happened. What if they thought I was involved in some way? All the forensic evidence would point in that direction. For a moment I thought about running. Then I remembered that I didn't have any clothes. So slowly, trying to keep my breathing under control, I went over to the edge of the bath, stared at him for a few seconds, noting the waxy hue of his skin, and pushed my index finger very hard into that soft cleft between the eyebrows to see if he was conscious. Relief at the force of his head pushing back against my hand was quickly replaced by shock when he grabbed my upper arm so hard that I could see the skin going white between his fingers and shouted, "God, are you trying to kill me? Because I thought it was a pretty good night myself."

"I thought you had drowned," I said. "I couldn't find my clothes."

He pointed to a chest of drawers on the landing just outside the door, where they lay in a neatly stacked pile. Yesterday's knickers, lovingly folded in half on top of a bra that had seen better days and an old pair of Levi's 501s.

"You did that?" I asked nervously.

"Attention to detail, Lucy," he said. "That's what it's all about." And then sank back under the water.

The conversation was over, but no one could say that I didn't know from the outset what lay ahead. And yes, we did go back to bed.

Now, as he sprawls in the bath and I brush my teeth, I run through a critical inventory of his body, starting at the top. Hair, still dark, almost black, slightly receding but only to the expert eye. Laughter lines and worry lines fighting for supremacy around his eyes. A slight frown between his eyebrows that ebbs and flows depending on the progress of his library project in Milan. Chin area a little jowly because he eats more when he is worried. Fewer sharp angles all around, his stomach and chest softer but surprisingly lovely. I must remember to tell him that. A reliable man who promises comfort and conventional lovemaking, drawing on a well-practiced repertoire. An attractive man, so my friends tell me. His head pops out of the water and he asks me what I am staring at.

"How long have we known each other?" I ask him.

"About twelve years," he replies, "and three months."

"At what point in our relationship did we both start wearing pajamas in bed?"

He considers the question carefully. "I think it was the winter of 1998, when we were living in west London and we woke up one morning and the window was frozen on the inside. Actually, you used to borrow mine."

He was right; in the early days I had adopted an intimate and easy approach to sharing that I felt reflected the depth and breadth of our relationship. But after the first year together, he sat me down at the kitchen table and told me it wouldn't work unless I stopped using his toothbrush. "Do you realize how many germs we carry in our mouths? Any self-respecting dentist will tell you that there are more in your mouth than in your arse. Saliva transmits all sorts of illnesses."

"I just don't believe that," I said, at a loss to say anything else.

"Hepatitis, AIDS, Ebola, they can all be transmitted orally," he insisted.

"But you would catch them anyway, because we are having sex," I rationalized with him.

"Not if you use condoms. When you lick your contact lenses before you put them in your eye, you might as well stick them up your arse and then put them in."

It was apparent that this conversation had been brewing for some time. I acquiesced on both issues, and it was never a problem again. I still borrow his toothbrush and lick my contact lenses, but never in front of him, although occasionally he runs his finger over the bristles in the evening and eyes me with suspicion, wondering why they are damp.

"What were you thinking about underwater?" I ask him with genuine curiosity.

"I was calculating how much time we would save in the morning if we put Rice Krispies in bowls the night before. Could be as much as four minutes," he says before sinking back under.

But he reemerges after a few seconds to announce, by way of apology for his earlier outburst, that he will take Fred to his new nursery school. "I'd really like to," he says. "Besides, you might not find the way." And I am glad, because although I should feel relief that Fred is starting nursery, and for the first time in eight years I will have time for myself, the day is tinged with a heavy sense of loss, and I know that I might cry.

❧

And so it is that I find myself, half an hour later, meandering along the pavement with my hand on Sam's shoulder, in what I hope is a motherly fashion, on our way to school.

"Are we late?" he asks, already knowing the answer because just at the point when we were about to walk out the door, Joe scurried past the kitchen table and knocked a carton of milk all over his school uniform and my jeans, causing a critical ten-minute delay in proceedings. Despite the best laid plans, packed lunches prepared the night before, uniforms stacked neatly on chairs, shoes lined up in pairs by the front door, breakfast already on the table, toothbrushes sitting beside the kitchen sink, you cannot mitigate against unforeseeable disasters. Getting to school on time is as finely tuned as air traffic control at Heathrow. Any slight change in plan can throw the whole system into chaos.

"Nothing disastrous," I say. It is utterly baffling to me that I used to be able to put together the lead package on *Newsnight* in less than an hour but am so singularly unable to meet the challenge of getting my children

ready for school each morning. It seems unbelievable that I could persuade cabinet ministers to come to the studio late at night to be grilled by
Jeremy Paxman but cannot convince my toddler to keep on his clothes.

"Is God bigger than a pencil?" asks Joe, who worries far too much for a
five-year-old. "If he isn't, could he be eaten by a dog?"

"Not the kind of dogs that wander these streets," I tell him reassuringly. "They are too polite."

And it is true. We are roaming through upper-tax-bracket territory in
northwest London. There are no pasty-faced chisel-headed boys walking
pit bulls here. No OTB. No beef jerky. No teenage pregnancies. We are in
the heart of dinner-party land.

It is the first day of term and already standards have slipped. As they
walk along the pavement, the children are supplementing bits of toast
with fistfuls of cereal from a couple of those variety packs.

෧෧

My vision is reduced by myopia to the most impressionistic strokes, and I
recall a moment two weeks ago on a beach in Norfolk, when I stood
before the North Sea with a woolly hat pulled down over my eyebrows
and a scarf wrapped around my neck just below my eyes. An easterly
wind, uncharacteristic for the time of year, blew into my face, making my
eyes water. I had to keep blinking to stop the view from blurring. It was
like looking through a prism. No sooner had I focused on a seagull or a
particularly lovely stone than the scene fractured into a spectrum of different shapes and colors. It struck me then that this was exactly how I felt
about myself. Somehow over the years I had atomized. Now, faced with
the prospect of my youngest child starting nursery school three mornings
a week, it is time to rebuild myself, but I can no longer remember how
all the pieces fit together. There is Tom, the children, my family, friends,
school—all these different elements but no coherent whole. No thread
connecting everything together. Somewhere in the domestic maelstrom I
have lost myself. I can see where I came from, but I'm uncertain where I
am going. I try to cling on to the bigger picture but can no longer remember what it is meant to be. I gave up the job I loved as a television

news producer eight years ago, when I discovered that thirteen-hour days and motherhood were an unstable partnership. Whoever suggested that working full-time and having children equated to having it all wasn't very good at math. There was always something in deficit. Including our bank balance, because there wasn't much change from what we paid the nanny. And besides, I missed Sam too much.

What I should do in the here and now, with the playground looming in the distance, is think up a few stock replies to those friendly inanities that mark the beginning of the new school year. Something sketchy, because most people aren't really interested in the detail. "The summer was hard work, culminating in a disastrous holiday at a Norfolk campsite, because we are short of cash, during which I slid into my current introspective mood, reappraising key areas of my life, including—in no particular order, because my husband is right, I can't prioritize—my decision to give up work after we had children, the state of my marriage, and our lack of money," I imagine saying, miming the words and using my right hand to illustrate my depth of feeling. "Oh, and did I mention that my husband wants us to rent out our house and move in with my mother-in-law for a year until our financial situation is more secure?" The holiday was a watershed, we both knew that. But its repercussions were less immediately obvious.

"Mum, Mum, can you hear me?" demands Sam.

"Sorry, just dreaming," I tell him, and he asks me if he is like a guide dog. "Something like that," I say, squinting down the road.

I spot the blurry outline of one of the fathers from school walking down the road toward us. He is talking on his cell phone and running his fingers through his thick, dark hair in a gesture familiar to me from the previous school year. It's Sexy Domesticated Dad, with his disarming opinions about what constitutes a nutritional lunch box and a penchant for mothers' coffee mornings. But it's not those characteristics that fix him in my mind. It is the way he looks and the way he moves. Something much more primeval. In fact, the less he says, the greater his appeal.

Even from a distance I can recognize his shape. In that strange juxtaposition of random thoughts, it suddenly occurs to me that in appearing at this moment, he has inadvertently become part of the bigger picture I was just thinking about. I curse my hastily thrown-together second choice of outfit: tartan pajama bottoms under a long, grungy coat in what I'd hoped would pass for casual chic in underwear-as-outerwear fashion. But it's too late to hide in the hedge with my pint-sized sons, so I surreptitiously check for yesterday's unremoved eye makeup in the side-view mirror of a stationary 4 × 4.

I jump as the automatic window slides down and someone looks over the passenger seat to ask what I am doing. "My God, you look like a panda," says Yummy Mummy No. 1, my sartorial nemesis. She opens her glove compartment to reveal spalike contents, including a half-bottle of Moët, a Jo Malone candle, and eye makeup remover pads.

"How do you do this?" I ask her, wiping my eyes gratefully. "Do you have systems?"

She looks puzzled. "No, just staff," she says.

"Good summer?" I ask her.

"Wonderful. Tuscany, Cornwall. How about you?"

"Great," I reply, but she is already glancing down the road and tapping her fingers on the steering wheel.

"Must go or I'll be late for my astanga class. By the way, are you wearing tartan? How directional."

Sexy Domesticated Dad ambles down the street toward me. I can see him waving one arm in the air and have no choice but to speak to him. Then I notice the other arm is in plaster. Oh happy fate, an obvious subject for conversation.

"You've broken your arm," I say, a little too enthusiastically.

"Yes," he says. "I fell off a ladder at a friend's house in Croatia." He looks at me expectantly.

Then he smiles and I hear myself say in an unnaturally slow voice, "That must be really . . . relaxing." Except I say it in a slow, throaty way that makes me sound like Orson Welles.

His smile fades slightly. This doesn't conform to the predictable pattern of social niceties among parents that he was expecting.

"What could possibly be relaxing about breaking your arm? Especially in Croatia."

Sam looks at me, equally perplexed. "He's right, Mum."

"Actually, Lucy, it's really . . . painful." (Sexy Domesticated Dad is mimicking my intonation.) "And I don't think that my wife would agree that it's relaxing. I'm not much use at the moment. Can't get any work done, it hurts too much to type." He smiles. I suddenly think about the chance encounters of premarital existence and their infinite possibilities, and images of a previous life gate-crash my thoughts. Striped knee-high socks with individual toes, Sony Walkmans, leg warmers. I remember buying a copy of an album by The Cure in Bristol from a boy who wore really tight black drainpipe jeans and a mohair jumper and smelled of patchouli oil. I can even remember the words of most of those songs. I remember a flight to Berlin when a man asked me if I wanted to go back to his hotel with him and I agreed, and then his wife turned around from the seat in front and smiled. I remember being in love with someone at university who never unpacked his bag and had three pairs of identical Levi's jeans and three white shirts, which he rotated each day. Tom would have approved of him. Why have these memories stayed with me while others are lost forever? If this is what I remember now, will that be what I remember in twenty years' time?

Mention of Sexy Domesticated Dad's powerhouse wife brings me up short, because I have never considered him in the plural, and I arrange my features into friendly but businesslike mode. "How is she? Did she manage to unwind?"

"She's never very good at doing that, she's got too much energy. Look, do you want to grab a coffee after you've dropped off the kids?"

"Great," I say, trying to appear composed in the face of this unexpected incursion into my daydreams. Then I notice him looking suspiciously at my feet.

"Are you wearing tartan pajamas under that coat?" he asks. "Maybe we should do coffee another time."

2

"Coming events cast their shadows before."

Despite the mixed messages and tiny humiliations of that encounter, it causes some geological shift inside me. Plates stirring after a long, dormant spell. How else can I account for the renewed feelings of excitement that I experience over subsequent days? This is how natural disasters happen, I think. A series of imperceptible movements at the core, culminating in a catastrophe way down the line. I feel the way I do when I smoke a cadged cigarette while the children aren't looking, reconnecting momentarily with feelings of liberation associated with a different period in my life, when pleasure was there for the taking.

Over the next few days, I set off in the morning in the hopeful anticipation of chancing upon Sexy Domesticated Dad and then berate myself for feeling unreasonably disappointed when he doesn't emerge. Perhaps he is working again and his wife is doing the school run, although I know she has a Big-City Job that means she has to be at her desk by eight o'clock. Maybe they have an au pair, who is taking their two children to school.

I allow myself to indulge in a harmless flight of fancy and imagine him in the British Library doing research for a book he's writing. He could do that with one arm in a plaster cast, but he almost certainly couldn't type. He could dictate to me, and I could type it up. Him sitting in an old comfortable chair, his forearms resting on the arms, fingers pulling out bits of stuffing during silences while he contemplates me. We could spend long days shut up in his office (the children are out of the picture here), with me offering pithy advice and shaping the structure of his biography. Then I become indispensable, he can't work without me. Not that I know what he is writing until I Google him one evening after the children have gone to bed and find that he is late delivering a manuscript on Latin America's contribution to the international film world. Very niche. And a subject about which I know nothing. So there the fantasy ends. Benignly.

"Excuse me, madam, would you like a drink, would you like to order something?"

I am aware suddenly of a waiter gently tapping me on the shoulder. He is wearing an impeccably clean and wrinkle-free long white apron tied around the waist several times, with a neat bow at the front just above his stomach. I think of the war of attrition being waged back home in the washroom, where the piles of unironed sheets and shirts are threatening to besiege the kitchen. Our Polish cleaning lady, who is meant to come one morning a week, is now too arthritic to manage more than a cursory dust and abandoned the laundry pile to its fate months ago.

I consider asking him where he gets his laundry done or even whether he would do it for me. Would sleeping on sheets as smooth and cool as ready-made icing restore my equilibrium? I resist an urge to rest my head on his apron and shut my eyes. These are the kind of domestic issues that used to send my mother's friends reaching for the Valium. They are not important anymore, I tell myself. In any case, there are new weapons in the household armory: easy-iron shirts, disposable nappies, and quick-cook pasta. Laundry starch has long been banished, along with soda streams and carpet beating.

Besides, domestic chaos is a genetic condition. My mother cleverly turned it into an intellectual statement, and I grew up being told that a tidy home was antifeminist. Women should spend more time fine-tuning their brains and less time ordering the linen cupboard if they wanted to break the domestic shackles that prevented them from achieving their intellectual potential, she used to say to me as a child.

The waiter urges me to look at a long and confusing list of cocktails. They all promise a better tomorrow and have names like Sunny Dreams or Rainbow of Optimism. There are none called Uneasy Truce or Gathering Storm. I feel like a stranger in a foreign land and ask for a ginger beer, partly because it feels familiar but mostly because the writing is so small that I can't read the list of cocktail ingredients. Another year and I will need bifocals.

I am waiting in a private members' club in Soho for a rare evening out with my last remaining single girlfriends. Inside the old Georgian dining rooms, the walls are painted a deep crimson, and even in the dim light they cast a warm glow, inviting intimacy and whispered indiscretions. People flutter around like moths, looking for familiar faces. Buoyed by alcohol, they seem to have no doubts about the quality of their happiness.

I sit alone in the middle of a large faux regency sofa with wooden arms and faded velvet covers. Periodically, people come over and ask me to move up so that they can sit down, but my urge to be alone transcends any desire to be affable, and I tell them that I am waiting for friends. I know it will be a while before anyone turns up, but I wanted to escape the chaos of bathtime and bedtime and told Tom that I had to be here by seven-thirty, just to catch up with myself. Sometimes I play so many roles in a day that I think I am suffering from a form of maternal schizophrenia. Cook, chauffeur, cleaner, lover, friend, mediator. It's like being in a pantomime, unsure whether you are meant to be the back part of the donkey or play the leading role. Looking at my watch and calmly sipping my Luscombe organic ginger beer, I consider the major systems failure likely to be taking place at home. I imagine Fred refusing to get out of the bath and wriggling out of Tom's grasp like a slippery eel. His brothers will hold on to Fred's legs and shriek like banshees. Tom will swear under his breath, and then the oldest two will repeatedly taunt "Daddy said the f-word" until Tom loses his temper. Tomorrow he will no doubt hold me responsible for the anarchy. But there is a whole night between now and then. Even though this is the first time that I have been out for almost a month, I still reproach myself. Guilt is the bindweed of motherhood, the two so inexorably entwined that it is difficult to know where one ends and the other begins.

My brother, Mark, who is a psychologist, says contemporary mothers are the innocent victims of the nature-versus-nurture debate. According to Mark, we are burdened by recent trends in psychotherapeutic thought, which reject the idea that children are born with a unique set of traits and instead place full responsibility for every aspect of development fairly and squarely on our shoulders. "So mothers blame themselves for any shortfall in their children's personality," he says. "Flash cards, Baby Einstein, pencil grip, it's all part of the belief that you can model your children like clay, when the truth is, as long as you avoid extremes, the outcome for the child will be pretty much the same." I want to believe him, but when I consider the chaos of his own personal life, I always look back to our childhood for answers.

"Do you mind if I sit here?" asks a tired-looking man carrying a pile of loose papers under his arm. "I'm only going to be half an hour." When I look doubtful, he says exasperatedly, "I just want to be here long enough to avoid putting my children to bed." And then I know he is telling the truth. A fellow deserter from the domestic front line. I get out a newspaper from my bag to give him the illusion of privacy and a chance to rest with his own thoughts.

I decide, almost on impulse, to take up smoking again properly and ask the man whether he would keep my seat for a moment. He nods wearily without saying anything. It has been so long since I bought a packet of cigarettes that I am left fumbling in my coat pockets for change, when I see how much they cost. Then I can't remember how to use the machine. Do you put in the money first or choose the brand? In the end, I press the wrong button and end up with a packet of John Player.

I light up the first one, and even though it tastes vile and I feel so light-headed that I think I am going to pass out, I doggedly continue as if to prove a point to myself. It should be like riding a bicycle, but it isn't. I really need to get out more. Like a schoolgirl trying to finish a cigarette before the teacher spots me, I find myself smoking it so fast that the end becomes unpleasantly hot and the smoke billows thickly around my head. I start to cough and splutter. Through the fog I can see Friend with Improbably Successful Career circling the adjacent room, looking for me. Instead of waving or calling her name, I watch in wonder as she drifts from table to table, peering at faces and occasionally stopping to greet someone. Emma's ease amazes me. She is wearing a pair of black low-slung Sass & Bide drainpipes, knee-high leather boots, and a fantastic silver top with tassels that are so long they form a kind of slipstream behind her. But it is not just about what she is wearing, although certainly the general effect demands attention. It is more the way that she occupies the space around her with such authority, the same way that it is not simply the smoke that makes me invisible. Nor the fact that I am wearing a velvet jacket the same color as the sofa so that I merge with the furniture.

"Lucy." She beams, sitting down beside me. "I've found you at last." The tassels finally calm down as she looks at the empty glasses in front of me. "What are you drinking?" she asks.

"Ginger beer," I tell her.

"Lashings, I can see. Very Famous Five." The waiter comes over immediately and effusively greets her, in a way that is gratifying to them both, and she orders a bottle of champagne. It is fair to say that Emma is now so high up in her news organization that most parts of her life qualify as expenses, so I do not wince.

As I sip champagne from a tall, thin glass with a long, elegant stem, Sexy Single Mum appears and makes me, as the guest of honor, move into the middle of the sofa.

"Lucy, it's so great to see you. I can't even remember the last time we all went out together," enthuses Cathy, hugging me tightly.

"How's my lovely godson?" I ask her.

"Great. He's with his dad for the night," she says.

The springs are weakest here, and I sink into a dip, securely wedged between two of my closest friends, feeling something akin to contentment. Then a friend of Cathy's from work appears. As she sits down, I marvel at a world of such spontaneity where people are unaccountable to anyone apart from themselves, free from complicated arrangements involving third parties and lists of phone numbers and instructions on what to do if the children wake up.

Suddenly I am no longer a lonely married person on day release from the suburbs but part of an attractive group of nominally single thirtysomething women having a very good time, thank you very much. I imagine people looking at us and wondering how we fit together. Except that at a place like this, other people are too involved in the small print of their own lives for ours to warrant much attention.

There was a time in our twenties, although it seems fantastical now, when we lived parallel existences, carving out fairly successful careers and rather less consequential relationships. Then I met Tom at a party held by Emma, because he was one of the architects involved in designing the new offices for her company, and Cathy met the man we now refer to as Hopeless Husband on an ad shoot. We both got married and Emma nearly did several times.

After Ben was born, Cathy went back to work three days a week as a copywriter. For a good few years we traipsed around the same toddler groups together on her days off. We shared weak cups of tea out of polystyrene cups. We had half-conversations with our husbands on cell phones as we wheeled strollers through playgrounds we had never noticed before, despite their proclivity for primary colors. We lovingly checked sandpits for old syringes, as other mothers warned us to do.

While the tedium of my own conversations with Tom often left me numb, revolving as they did around subjects domestic, such as how to release Action Man from the u-bend in the toilet, Cathy's got ever louder and more acrimonious.

Her husband veered between trying to establish himself as a furniture designer and working on building projects, neither of which generated much income. So she had to go back to work full-time and shortly afterward became a company director, making him feel ever more inadequate. Of course, it was more complicated than that, because it always is. Her husband found a therapist who told him his wife was holding him back and decided to dispense with wife and child and move back in with his parents. Now Cathy lives a dual existence, as responsible mother of a five-year-old and wild party animal, depending on when her ex-husband has their son on weekends, with a full-time nanny organizing the bits in between.

Downing a third glass of champagne, and now more than perfectly happy with the quality of my own happiness, I start to review private clubs to which I belong.

"Of course there's no waiting list, and if you want to drink, you have to go into the loo with a hip flask, but in order of descending importance there is (1) Little Dippers swimming club, (2) Munchkin music group, and (3) Fire Engine playgroup."

"That one sounds good," says Cathy. "I could do with a bit of rough."

Then Emma shrieks. "Something tried to ladder my tights." The four of us bend down to look under the table.

"Forget the local wildlife," says Cathy. "It's Lucy's hairy legs."

Everyone demands to examine them, by running their hands up and down my calves in amazement. "God, Lucy, you could cause serious carpet burn with those," she says. I try to explain that having three children demands a minimalist beauty routine. Having a three-minute shower counts as major pre-party preparations, with anything from deodorant to a quick pluck of the mustache as bonuses tacked on to the end. Leg waxing has become a biannual luxury, after late-night attempts at home waxing ended in disaster involving hairy bedsheets. Incredulous looks all around.

"But what do you do all day?" asks Emma. "Isn't it all yoga and Cath Kidston floral prints? And what about home baking?"

So I relay key developments of the day from the domestic rearguard. "I got up at six-thirty, made two packed lunches, listened to Joe read, rushed to school to drop the eldest two, arranged a date for Sam's best friend to come for tea, looked in lost property for Joe's sweater, and then raced to nursery with Fred," I tell them, leaning forward for dramatic effect. "And this was all before nine o'clock."

"No," they say in awe.

"Do you really want more?" I ask. They nod.

"I went to the shops, raced home to unload everything, lowered the clothes mountain by about a foot, dealt with the discovery that Fred has been using the bin in our bathroom to pee in for two weeks, and then ran to his nursery to get him. Fred had a friend to play, so I phoned my mother while they were upstairs. Then I discovered they had taken out all of Sam's clothes from his chest of drawers, so I had to tidy up the mess. By then it was time to go back to school to pick up Sam and Joe. Then there was homework, tea, bathtime, and stories. Oh, and I forgot to mention that I played 'I'm Jens Lehmann' for half an hour after tea." More puzzled looks. "He's the Arsenal goalie. He's almost a member of the family."

"But it can't be like that," says Emma. "You are living our idyll. Don't spoil it for us."

Actually, this was a good day, and I quite enjoy role-play as Jens Lehmann, but I don't tell them that. There were no injuries. No illness. No breakages. Nothing to derail the status quo. I don't mention the things that I do routinely, the endless cycle of cooking, cleaning, washing, and ironing, partly because it has become second nature but mostly because even I can't quite believe that the contours of my existence have become defined by this domestic treadmill.

Besides, I am almost certain that Emma is too busy enjoying her own life to covet mine. She has a flat in Notting Hill and visibly winces on our infrequent visits with the children, when they leave tiny fingerprints all over the stainless-steel counters and run their tractors up and down the pristine oak floor.

The conversation quickly turns to more straightforward subjects, including analysis of a new boyfriend. "Tell me if this even approximates normality," asks Cathy's friend, the lassitude in her voice belying what is coming next. "He'll only have sex with me if there's a pillow covering my face or I'm lying on my front. And he doesn't want any physical contact afterward."

"You mean he's into asphyxiation?" says Emma.

"Could it be a cushion, or does it have to be a pillow?" I ask, adding quickly, "He might have an interiors fetish."

"Do you mean it would be all right if he was depriving her of oxygen with that gorgeous Lucinda Chambers cushion from the Rug Company?" asks Cathy.

"I don't know the one you mean, but there's something less sinister about a cushion, perhaps," I say. "There are more colors, for a start."

"Look, he's probably just gay," says Emma.

"Just gay," says Cathy's friend, her voice slightly trembling. "But that's even worse, because then there's no hope. I can be a lot of things, but never a man."

Emma confirms that she is still road testing hotels in Bloomsbury with a married father of four with whom she has been having an affair for the past eight months. They met during a dinner organized by a financial PR company to promote relations between bankers and journalists. "He says that he has had a sexual epiphany since he met me," she says gleefully. "For the first time in fifteen years, he is capable of having sex more than once in a night."

"I bet Tom could do that, if he was sleeping with you," I say. "It's not really about you, it's about the novelty of having sex with someone who isn't his wife, and there's nothing very profound about that."

"I think I am making it easier for him to stay married," she says, as though she is working in a soup kitchen on Christmas Day.

Cathy reveals that she has had unprotected sex with someone she met at a party and then starts pondering even more exotic sexual practices.

"Oh my God," I say, a little taken aback by her unusual lack of caution.

"You should save that for treats," says Emma. I have little to add to the conversation, since I don't think I have even had sex since we last met up. But sometimes, just sometimes, particularly at moments like these, that doesn't feel like such a bad thing.

"I think I fancy one of the dads at school," I say on a whim. Even as I speak, I wonder whether I have accidentally picked up the script of someone else's life, someone sitting at the table next door perhaps, because this is not what I intended to say. However, I do expect it to be treated with reciprocal equanimity by my friends. Instead, there is a stunned silence.

"Lucy, that is absolutely awful," says Emma. "It's shocking. Indecent."

"Ignore me, I'm just attention-seeking," I joke. They look at me with serious expressions. I start backtracking immediately.

"Nothing's happened. In fact, I've never been alone with him. Haven't even reached the sexual fantasy stage. Don't have time for that." I laugh with forced cheer, waiting for someone to join in with me. "Actually, I have barely even spoken to him." More looks of dismay. This is so hypo-critical. Friends are worse than parents in expecting you to conform to designated roles.

"Look, it's not all Peter and Jane up in northwest London," I say. "I am allowed to daydream."

"Does anyone else know?" asks Cathy disapprovingly.

"Know what? There's nothing to know. He does the school run," I say, hoping that will explain everything.

"I think we should come and check him out," says Cathy. "A whole new pulling zone."

3

"From the sublime to the ridiculous is only a step."

When I get home, I don't go straight to bed. Instead, I wander around the house, wrapping the darkness and silence around me like friends. The light is on in Sam and Joe's bedroom and I go in, relieved to find all the children asleep. I can tell by the train track on the floor, with its labyrinthine network of bridges, switchbacks, and tunnels that only Tom could have created, that bedtime was a protracted affair. Putting the children to bed alone is always a sobering experience for Tom, calling into question his belief that there is a magic formula for conjuring order from the essential chaos of domestic life.

Fred is asleep in the middle of the track, on his front, bottom in the air, his nose almost touching a level crossing. Sam and Joe have kicked off their covers, and I tenderly tuck them in again, then roam around the room, picking through the paraphernalia of childhood. Scraps of material so precious they cannot sleep without them, which I have to wash in secret because they love the smell so much. A muddle of bears, books, and trains. I carefully tuck these beloved treasures under their duvets and promise never to do anything that will disturb their untroubled sleep, although there will be no reciprocity in that arrangement. Over the past eight years, an undisturbed night has become a thing of note, a talking point, like sighting a badger in London.

I gently lift Fred and he makes reassuring noises, snorting and grunting into my chest like a small burrowing creature. I remove a cricket ball from Sam's hand and take Fred back to his own room.

Back downstairs in the kitchen I turn on the light, make myself a cup of tea, and sit down at the table. I look up to find myself staring straight at a painting given to us by my mother-in-law, Petra. It is a portrait in oil by an artist whose family moved to Morocco just after the end of the Second World War. Tom says that his mother was briefly engaged to the artist, he is unsure for how long, but refused to move abroad with him. This explanation seems to satisfy him. I have often tried to press Petra for more details, using the painting as an excuse, but she never engages. It is unfinished, and the green background is painted so thinly in parts that you can see the grain of the canvas. Petra says she doesn't know who sat for the picture, although to me it seems obvious that it is her. "If you don't take it, Lucy, I will give it away," she said when she handed it over during a visit. It was then that I asked her whether she was in love with the man who painted it. After all, she got engaged to my husband's father only a few months later, which I would describe as a classic rebound relationship. "If you imagine hard enough, you can love anyone, Lucy," she replied, looking at me intently.

I go up the stairs barefoot, zigzagging from one side of each step up to another in a well-rehearsed maneuver to dodge loose floorboards that might give my presence away. In the bedroom, I avoid switching on the light and put out a hand, knowing that I will find the corner of the chest of drawers four paces into the room on the right-hand side. I carefully open the wardrobe door and hide the cigarettes I bought earlier in a pair of leather boots.

I whisper soothing words to Tom when he mutters, "You're back already," although it will soon be getting light outside. I listen to the radiators gurgling disapproval and forgive them their inability to heat the house properly.

Then I edge into the bed using a technique of slow, imperceptible movements, remaining absolutely still when I sense any reaction across the other side so that I don't wake Tom. When I am close enough, I put an arm across his chest and lie there on my front, feeling his warmth, allowing sleep to come to me just at the moment that I want it most. Only a true insomniac or a mother with years of sleep deprivation under her belt knows the pleasure of that.

There is no logical reason why a combination of lack of sleep and too much alcohol should add up to anything more than a day of mood swings and a tendency toward weepiness. Yet somehow it doesn't happen that way. The following morning, I attend an assembly in the overheated gym to celebrate the new school year. Skittery Joe is always alarmed if he doesn't spot my face in the crowd, so I forsake my own breakfast in order to get to school on time, to grab a good seat near the edge.

"Somewhere midfield on the wing, you mean," Joe says, looking up at me hopefully as we walk through the school gates. I know what is coming next.

"Can we play 'Jens Lehmann' when I come home?"

I try to explain to him that a school afternoon consists of cooking tea, clearing tea, making sure homework gets done, bathtime, stories, and bedtime, and that it is a miracle that all this can be condensed into four hours already. Then I relent when I see his little face start to scrunch up.

"Shall we do cricket instead?" I gently suggest. "I can be Shane Warne, and you can be Freddie Flintoff. Just for ten minutes." He jumps in the air excitedly. It's so easy to please a five-year-old.

As Fred and I walk into the playground with my stroller loaded up like a packhorse, I pause, as I always do, waiting for silent applause for once again having made it before the nine o'clock watershed. I see the busy headmistress greeting parents on the steps. "Congratulations, Mrs. Sweeney," I imagine her saying. "Well done, not just for making it here this morning on only four hours' sleep and a hangover, but also for bringing two fully fed boys in the correct uniforms, and your toddler, still eating toast but nevertheless dressed and partially fed, two nut-free packed lunches, and one pair of named gym shoes. You and all those other mothers and some of those dads—although I know it's the mothers that remember everything really—are true heroes." Although no one cheers, I feel a strong sense of elation.

Feeling the worse for wear, I long for early-morning anonymity but soon find myself flanked in the gym on one side by Yummy Mummy No. 1 and then unexpectedly on the other by Sexy Domesticated Dad. I try to work out whether there are other chairs that he could have sat in and note there are plenty of spaces elsewhere. My heart starts to race and I feel myself blushing for the first time in years. I think I am suffering from a combination of premature menopause and delayed adolescence.

I try to focus on the gym equipment. Ropes, vaults, horses, wall bars. Not much has evolved. Schools have escaped interior makeovers. There is no shabby chic, no minimalist aesthetic. And the fetid smell of stale socks and sweat is so familiar that, when I close my eyes and forget the small child sitting on my knee, I am back at school myself. When you take your children into school, you too regress. So Alpha Mum seated behind us, former head girl and hockey captain, predictably sits on parent committees and looks on disapprovingly. The bullied have a nervous restlessness that diminishes only when they leave the school gates and their shoulders finally relax. And those of us who were busy appreciating boys, like, I suspect, Yummy Mummy No. 1, well, here we are, still busy appreciating boys.

Then I remember Simon Miller. My first boyfriend. When Simon Miller asked if he could walk me home after an A-level English class in October 1982, we strode in silence, our feet in time, to a shed beside the gym that I had never noticed before. There was not a girl in my class who would have turned him down, and yet he apparently never had a girlfriend. Even back then, we recognized that Simon Miller was the real thing.

Until we shut the door behind us, we barely touched. I don't think we even talked much. The only thing he said to me was, "I want you to be my girlfriend, but I don't want anyone to know because then my friends will want to know exactly what it is like having sex with you and it will be more exciting to keep it secret."

I nodded in assent, and he put out his hand and stroked the side of my face, and I felt a shiver run up my body and struggled not to cough in the whirlpool of Aramis aftershave.

The clumsy tangles on the cold plastic gym mats, which occurred weekly throughout that term, were the usual mix of half-clothed adolescent lust and endeavor. The possibility of discovery, the need for subterfuge at all times, and the revelation of mutual attraction were a heady and irresistible combination. To my surprise, neither of us had had sex before. The equality of this situation made us generous, and Simon Miller must have gone on to give a lot of women pleasure, because even at age sixteen he had an innate understanding and love of oral sex that few subsequent boyfriends ever got close to. It was only when I left school and discovered that at least three of my girlfriends had been engaged in similar clandestine relationships with him that the sophistication of his modus operandi was uncovered. But he had set a standard, and that is of lifetime importance.

And I knew from that moment on the benefits of keeping a secret. I never felt the need to share my curdled adolescent emotions with anyone. I just knew that one day it would all make sense. Whatever happened to Simon Miller, I wonder? If I logged on to Friends Reunited, I could probably e-mail him by the end of the day and find out that he had become a dentist in Dorking with two children and a wife with perfectly straight teeth. Some things are best left as memories.

Fred fidgets on my knee and I get hotter and hotter.

"Hungry, Mummy," he says. I pull a packet of raisins from my jacket pocket.

From the seat behind, Alpha Mum leans over so close that I can feel the collar of her wrinkle-free white shirt tickle my neck.

"Do you know that they contain eight times more sugar than grapes?" she whispers in my ear.

"Er, no," I whisper back.

"Do you know that she is eight times more acidic than the average mother?" whispers Yummy Mummy No. 1 conspiratorially.

I remember with a jolt that I have forgotten to bring "a taste of autumn" for show-and-tell and rummage around my bag in search of anything that might qualify. In a stroke of luck I find a rotten apple core, which seems to sum up perfectly the season of mists and mellow fruitfulness in all its decaying glory. All I need to do is tell Joe that it is a crab apple. In newfound good humor at my resourcefulness, I turn to speak to Yummy Mummy No. 1. "Have you brought anything with you?" I ask her, wondering whether she ever forgets show-and-tell days.

She points to an obviously attractive, twentysomething man slouching at the back of the hall and he waves back at us. "New term, new personal trainer," she smiles. "Kickboxing, he swears by it."

"He's too big for the autumn table," I tell her. "He might slip on a conker."

"Oh my God, I've forgotten show-and-tell," she says lazily. "I'll send my housekeeper with a bag of chestnuts from the tree in the garden later."

I ponder the fact that I have never seen her with her youngest children or her husband. They might be the nuclear family, but the molecules are spread quite thinly.

"The thing is," she says, choosing her words carefully and looking back across her shoulder at the personal trainer, "you need a good incentive to go to the gym every day, and there is something sublime about working up a sweat for this man, even if all he talks about are muscle groups and the importance of porridge. A dose of sublimity every day is very important, don't you think? And as you get older, it matters less and less what a man says."

"Do you think about him when you're not with him?" I ask, curious to gauge the breadth and depth of this relationship.

She looks at me, bemused. "Only when I'm reaching for a packet of biscuits and I imagine him wagging his finger at me and saying, 'That is *very* naughty,' and then I don't eat them."

I try to sit up straight and suck in my tummy, but it refuses to cooperate. Instead, the relief of relaxing the shriveled muscles that struggle to maintain some kind of decorum causes a ripple of flab to escape over the top of my jeans. Of course, no one can see it, but it is an act of rebellion nevertheless. There is a lot of tucking in to be done once you have had children, and your body is never loyal again.

"You should come, too, it would be lots of fun," she says in friendly rather than critical fashion, although she is most likely being insincere. I would like to explain to her that we live in a different financial stratosphere and that apart from an arthritic cleaning lady who can no longer reach the floor, I am the staff, but it would all take too long and, besides, she is a woman who likes to live in a rosy world where people can avoid rucksacks on the underground by taking cabs everywhere and Third World debt can be solved by a biannual three-course charity dinner with free champagne.

Fred falls asleep on my lap, pushing my lower leg to rest cozily against the calf of Sexy Domesticated Dad, and I am suddenly grateful for the imprecision of Tom's bedtime routine. Be grateful for simple, cost-free pleasures, I think to myself. I try to live in the moment, but my mind starts to wander, and to my disquiet I find myself hoping that he will press against me with the full authority of his upper thigh. Then I can't stop looking at his right leg. For minutes his foot rests still, the rubber sole of his Converse trainer firmly stuck to the floor. But as the piano teacher strikes up he starts to tap his foot, and then it seems as though his leg moves closer to my own. At least I can feel its warmth. When the music ends, his thigh is definitely closer than it was at the outset. At this point, it starts to get complicated. I think that I should move my leg in deference to his, just in case he thinks that I am responding, but then decide that it might look rude if in fact he hasn't consciously moved his leg closer to mine at all. As if I am accusing him of too much physical intimacy.

I try to peer over his knees to see whether his other leg is equally snugly pressed against the father who sits on the other side of him and then feel dispirited when I note that it is. Perhaps he swings both ways. That brings me up with a jolt: How have I reached this point? I think about Tom at work, trying to resolve his bureaucratic impasse with the Milanese planning department. I imagine standing beside his desk, using my middle finger to iron out the furrow in his brow as he speaks to a colleague in Italy about the latest stumbling blocks to plans finally being approved. But he wouldn't want me there. I know because when I call him at work, he can't get me off the phone fast enough. I sympathize with his stress but resent the way his work has consumed him. At least thinking about Tom brings back a restored sense of reality.

Just as I start to behave like a sensible adult again, contemplating what to cook for lunch and whether to go to the park with Fred on the way home, Sexy Domesticated Dad completely repositions himself and crosses his left leg over his right knee, and suddenly I find that I am joined not just with the top part of his thigh but with a large part of his buttock, too.

He leans and says sotto voce in my ear, "Just as well you didn't wear your pajamas today, it's really steaming in here." I look at him and for a moment wonder whether he is thinking about illicit pleasures in hotels in Bloomsbury, which Emma tells me are full of people having torrid affairs.

"Must be all those little teapots." I look for sexual innuendo in the word "teapot" but can find none. I am now up to speed on iPods, Rabbits, and wireless zones, but there could well be something that I have missed in the intervening years. The children in year one, including our own, have stood to sing very sweetly about being short and stout and do a rendition of "I'm a Little Teapot." Then it is straight into "Dear Lord and Father of Mankind Forgive Our Foolish Ways," and any incipient fantasy quickly unravels.

After the hymn, the headmistress asks for volunteers to accompany the class on a trip to the London Aquarium.

"I'm doing this one," whispers Sexy Domesticated Dad.

"Could anyone interested please put up their hand and then come to the front for more details?" says the headmistress, waving an envelope.

I leap from the seat as best I can with Fred in my arms, and wave.

"Lovely to see such enthusiasm," she says, and everyone turns around to stare at me, attempting to gauge whether I am a guilt-ridden full-time working mum trying to compensate for never being there, or one of those overearnest pushy types who give their children alphabet pasta for tea so that they can practice their spelling. The truth is far more shallow: I am going simply because Sexy Domesticated Dad is, and I think he knows it, too. What could be the harm in that?

I lean forward and start to get up to go to the front when I glance down to check whether I am wearing the jeans that promise to lengthen your legs or the ones that lift your bum. I note with horror that it is not my leg resting against Sexy Domesticated Dad but a large bulge protruding from my left calf. Yesterday's knickers. I feel my breath quickening, but there is no way I can extricate myself from this unforeseeable turn of events. I inwardly curse the return of skinny jeans—not even a pair of tweezers could remove these through the foot hole.

"What is that?" asks Yummy Mummy No. 1, who can deconstruct an outfit like a flock of vultures stripping a carcass. She looks down at my leg with suspicion.

"It's a device," I hear myself say, beads of sweat forming on my brow. I wipe my forehead on the back of Fred's coat.

Sexy Domesticated Dad looks interested. "Not one that you can detonate, I hope," he says.

"To reduce stress, Robert. If you feel anxious, you squeeze it," I counter, frantically squeezing yesterday's knickers.

"Like a stress ball?" he says dubiously.

"Exactly," I say confidently.

They both lean over Fred to have a feel, Sexy Domesticated Dad's plaster-cast arm resting heavily on my knee. In any other situation, this invasion of my personal space would definitely qualify as a moment of sublimity. "Well, I feel more relaxed already," says Sexy Domesticated Dad, his voice laced with sarcasm.

"I'm not sure I do," says Yummy Mummy No. 1.

"Mrs. Sweeney, would you like to come and get this?" says the headmistress, emphasizing each word slowly and shifting from side to side to get a better view of us. Hundreds of eyes bore into me. Then redemption. All the manhandling has shifted the offending knickers down toward my ankle and the M&S label is beginning to show. I bend over, feel the blood rushing to my head, and carefully grip the edge of the label. With skill I pluck them out in a single pull, get up, put them in my handbag nonchalantly, and move down through the row of parents, holding sleepy Fred in one arm, to go and pick up my envelope. I am dizzy from leaning over for too long and steeped in sweat, but the thought of a whole day at the aquarium with Sexy Domesticated Dad fills me with optimism.

But when I walk back to my seat, I see him looking at me with an expression familiar from the early years of my relationship with Tom. His eyes are wary, his mouth half-smile, half-grimace, taut with the tension of maintaining the inherent contradictions of such confused emotions. His body has folded in upon itself. His legs and arms are crossed and he is leaning forward over his knees, taking up as little space as possible. An air of quiet disbelief hangs around him. He doesn't say anything. Instead, he gingerly lets me pass, taking care to ensure that no part of his body touches my own.

"That is the stuff of nightmares," Yummy Mummy No. 1 whispers in my ear as I sit down. "I mean, a pair of M&S knickers, not even my mother wears those anymore. But don't worry, I'm sure no one else noticed. Besides, they might have thought the M was for Myla." She is trying to be comforting, which is gratifying, but I have no idea who Myla is.

When we stand up to leave the gym, I am impressed by how neat she looks in her wraparound print dress and calf-length boots with impossibly high heels, as she picks her way along the row of chairs. She does a graceful sidestep when it gets too narrow, and I note that she is so paper-thin that she has almost lost any three-dimensional quality. She bobs along confidently. No danger of her capsizing, despite the weight of a long brown sheepskin coat, which she has kept on throughout the proceedings.

"Joseph. It was a present from my husband, to say sorry for being away so much over the summer," she says when we come to a stop, recognizing envy. But actually what I covet isn't the coat but its cleanness. There are no marks on it, nothing betraying what she gave the children for breakfast, no jam stains, no leaks from pens left without lids in pockets, no rips or blemishes of any kind. Her lipstick and mascara are applied to understated perfection. She even smells polished, not in a glossy kind of way but with a timeless elegant formula perfected over the generations. She is untouchable, encased in perfection. Oh, the effort that goes into looking effortless. And Sexy Domesticated Dad. Well, he rushes away in the opposite direction, even though it is a more circuitous route. The last I see of him, he is cycling as fast as you can with a broken arm down Fitzjohn's Avenue.

4

"One man may steal a
horse while another may
not look over a hedge."

At five o'clock in the morning the following week, I abandon all hope of
any more sleep and lean over Tom to look at one of his clocks. The one
on the left of his bedside table is electric and wakes us up by saying
repeatedly, "Tom, get out of bed," in a slow, mechanical voice. The one
on the right he took from Sam, when he was too young to notice, and
runs on batteries. It has a rabbit's face and if left to ring for too long will
rock to the edge of the table and fall on the floor, such is the force of
the bell.

It is fair to say that since we have been together, we have never over-
slept. Neither of the clocks has ever failed, and on the rare occasions that
our children allow us to sleep beyond seven o'clock in the morning, we
are awakened by a chorus of alarms. There have been times when I have
been tempted to turn the clocks backward by an hour, to show Tom that
the world won't end if we do everything an hour late.

Insomnia gives you a lot of time to run through old arguments. Of
course, in the morning, any conclusions are forgotten and all that is left is
a bad taste in your mouth, but those dogged disputes that never give up
on you make great nocturnal replays. Today I return to an old favorite,
the dowager aunt of disputes, which revolves around my lateness and

Tom's belief that all is well in the world if everything is done on time. A great quality in an architect but less appealing in a husband.

The most recent round took place in the pantry at my parents' home in the Mendips, a few weeks before the ill-fated camping trip to Norfolk. If you were plotting a chart of significant events in my family, the pantry would feature disproportionately as a backdrop. It is where, years ago, I'd told my mother I was marrying Tom and she had congratulated me with tears in her eyes before saying, "You do realize that if you were a chemical experiment, you would explode." And my father had come in at that moment, muttering about unstable elements and the value of explosion over implosion as a recipe for a stimulating marriage. "There's no attraction without reaction," he had said sagely.

I can't remember exactly how the row between Tom and me had started, but I can recall that the tiles underfoot were so icy that my bare toes started to go numb, and yet even through the cold I could smell the festering odor of an old piece of Stilton abandoned there the previous Christmas. We were looking for a jar of coffee.

"I can't understand how your parents could run out of something so essential as coffee," said Tom, jumping out of the way as a mousetrap sprang at his shoe. "It should be a staple of any pantry, especially one of this size."

"They have other things on their mind," I replied, in an effort to distract him.

"Like their inability to do anything on time, even at our wedding," he said.

"There are so many worse things in life than being late," I told him, unsure whether I should feel gratified that the discussion had moved beyond coffee or dispirited at its new direction. Because I knew that criticism of my parents was ultimately about me and not them. Then, when he ignored me, I added, "Actually, it's rude to be early. Why don't we live a little dangerously and for the next four weeks, as an experiment, start arriving half an hour late?"

"You talk about living dangerously, Lucy. We are not at a stage in our life where that applies anymore. We are creatures of habit that should embrace the familiar. Like old sofas." I must have looked skeptical because he became more expansive.

"The sofa in our sitting room has a loose spring in the right-hand corner. There is a sticky patch at the back in the middle, from a sweet that got stuck there years ago—I think it's a lemon drop—and there is a hole on the side that gets bigger and bigger because one of the children is using it to store money." I could not believe that he noticed all these things.

"Even though all this should be mildly annoying, it isn't, because the familiarity of these imperfections is comforting. Don't you notice that I no longer say anything when you lose your credit card? Eyes face forward. Breathing normal. Eyebrows stationary. All facial tics under control."

"I thought you'd begun to understand that losing your credit card is simply not a big deal," I muttered, but he was impervious.

"Once you realize that you're not immortal, there is reassurance in routine, Lucy. Think how upset you were when Cathy's husband left her. Floored. You never complained about being early then. In fact, Lucy, you really don't like change. You would hate it if I suddenly started being late."

And, as usual, I ended up agreeing with him. Because he was probably right.

@@

Tom has slept the entire night in exactly the same position, on his front, legs splayed and his arms hugging the pillow. I, on the other hand, have dealt with the usual nocturnal visitations. Lying in bed, my ear is roughly at the same height as Fred's head, and at around one-thirty I awoke with a jump, to hear a deep, raspy voice whispering in my ear. "Want my cuddles. Want them now."

Then, roughly an hour later, Joe came in to announce tearfully that he was shrinking.

"I am smaller than I was when I went to bed," he said, gripping my arm so hard that there are still tiny finger marks in the morning.

"I promise you are the same size," I replied. "Look at your hand, it fits into mine in exactly the same way it did when we walked to school yesterday."

"But I can feel that my legs are shrinking," he said with such conviction that I wondered momentarily whether he might be right.

"It's growing pains," I said, the stock response for any inexplicable nighttime aches. "Daddy and I used to get them, too."

"How do you know it isn't shrinking pains?" he insisted. "Granny is smaller than she used to be. By the morning, I will be so small you won't be able to see me anymore," he said, his voice getting quieter and quieter. "And then I might get eaten by a dog on the way to school."

So I got out of bed and took him downstairs to the kitchen door, where Tom periodically records the height of our children.

"Look, you are even taller than when we last measured you." I showed him.

He smiled and hugged me, and I took him back up to bed and managed to fall asleep until the early-morning insomnia kicked in.

I make the mistake of starting to calculate exactly how many hours of sleep I have had during the night and then give up at five and three quarters. Caught in that nether land between deep sleep and being fully awake, I am conscious of a pit in my stomach, a reminder of anxiety that I carry in my body without being fully aware of its provenance. I start to run systematically through the usual scenarios that creep up at this time of day. I haven't missed my period. I know where I have parked the car. I have hidden my cigarettes. Yesterday's knickers lurk, but I have already managed to file that particular debacle away in the deepest recesses of my subconscious. Some things are so truly dreadful that there is nothing to be gained from analysis.

Then I remember what it is I have forgotten. Sam's "Six Great Artists of the World" project has to be handed in this morning. Three down, three to go. I spring from the bed in a single motion, surprising lazy muscles with unaccustomed intent.

Bad but not irredeemable. To avoid disturbing Tom, I rush into the spare bedroom and pull on the dressing gown that is hanging on the back of the door. It is the same one that I wore the first time I met him, the dressing-gown equivalent of a shag carpet, long, hairy, and impossible to clean, given to my husband by my mother-in-law when he was a teenager. Its presence therefore predates even my arrival on the scene, and it is now called into action only during times of great uncertainty. Thinking of Tom before he met me used to make me feel jealous of all the things we never shared together. Now it is something I relish. Because there is a point in a marriage when the unknown becomes more interesting than the known. I try to persuade him to take me through sexual exploits with the women who preceded me, but he is too honorable to indulge my prurience.

There are stains and rough patches down the side of this dressing gown, which I imagine are the residues of furtive adolescent skirmishes, and bits of unidentifiable food stuck deep inside the pile, and inexplicable bald patches. It is a better record of Tom's teenage years than any of the endless slides and blurred photos taken by his mother.

It hails from an era of Laura Ashley prints and records by Status Quo. I feel something in the pocket and half expect it to be a crumpled and stained page of a favorite big-breasted model torn from a 1978 edition of *Playboy.* But I couldn't be more wrong. It is a page from an old edition of *Mrs. Beeton.* I skim-read a couple of sentences: "I have always thought that there is no more fruitful source of family discontent than a house-wife's badly cooked dinners and untidy ways. Men are now so well served out-of-doors—at their clubs, well-ordered taverns, and dining houses—that in order to compete with the attractions of these places, a mistress must be thoroughly acquainted with the theory and practice of cookery, as well as be perfectly conversant with all the other arts of making and keeping a comfortable home."

Mrs. Beeton has a lot to answer for, I think to myself, moodily stuffing the piece of paper deep into the pocket of the dressing gown. How it came to be here I cannot understand, and I try to remember when the dressing gown was last called into commission. My mother-in-law stayed in this room most recently. I make a note to myself to reflect upon this discovery later, wondering whether Petra is trying to send subliminal messages to me, but right now there are other priorities. Within minutes I have forgotten its existence.

Outside the spare bedroom I bump into Fred, stumbling along the passage and rubbing his eyes. At this stage, he could be persuaded back into bed. But he senses my stress level and notices that I am swaddled in an unfamiliar, floor-length ensemble, and protests that he wants to come downstairs. Down in the kitchen I assess the situation while searching for paintbrushes and paint, opening and shutting cupboards forcefully and muttering under my breath, "Degas is done. Goya is done. Constable is done."

Fred repeats each phrase, excitedly appreciating that this unexpected change in his early-morning routine might prove favorable to him. I seat him on the stool beside Tom's drawing table and hand him scissors and pots of paint and other forbidden treats. Whatever it takes. Whatever it takes, I repeat to myself. For there are many times, even in households where television is allowed only on weekends, that mothers resort to dirty tactics to claw back those few minutes that will define the success or failure of not just the rest of the day but even the rest of their lives, because sometimes tiny things seem to have enormous resonance. It's the butterfly effect.

I must be making more noise than I think, because during the course of this flurry of activity, Tom wanders into the kitchen.

"I've got to do van Gogh, Jackson Pollock, and Matisse," I say, waving tissue paper in his face, "all by eight o'clock."

"What are you doing, Lucy? Go back to bed, both of you. You're having some kind of nightmare about abstract painting," he says. Then he notices Fred wielding a pair of large scissors. "Why have you woken him up, too?"

"Of course I didn't wake him up. It would be much easier to do all this on my own. He's cutting bits of tissue paper to do a Matisse collage," I explain.

"That might sound logical to you, but from where I'm standing that does not qualify as any rational explanation for all this."

"Sam has an art project. He's done half of it, but luckily I have remembered that the rest has to be handed in today. And if Sam doesn't finish this, then it is me who will be held responsible."

"But Sam isn't finishing it, you are doing it for him."

"It's quicker and less messy this way. If he were involved, it would never get done. Most importantly, if he doesn't hand it in, that means I have failed as a mother."

"Lucy, that is ridiculous. Nobody judges you for something like this."

I put down the paints and take a deep breath.

"That is where you are wrong. If Sam fails, it is a reflection on me. It's just the nature of mothering in the new millennium," I say, jabbing a paintbrush in the air to illustrate my point.

"Put that down, Lucy. Look what you've done to my pajamas," says Tom. They are covered in tiny spots of red paint. Fred puts his hand over his mouth and giggles in that way children do when they sense a parent is losing control.

"There are people, mostly mothers but some fathers, who will arrive today with their child's artists of the world project already turned into a PowerPoint presentation on a CD-ROM."

"But it's not the parents' project," he says, taken aback. "Anyway, you could never do that. Actually, nor could I."

"Precisely. So the very least I can do, the minimum, is to ensure that Sam finishes the project."

"We'll have verisimilitude, because this one here is about to cut his ear off," he says, pointing at Fred, who is engaged in some dangerous air cutting.

Then Tom sees the blotches of paint all over his table and on the wall.

"How did that happen? How do you make such a mess?"

"We were trying to do Jackson Pollock," I explain. "Actually, it looks quite good." I present him with an earlier work. "It could have been worse. Sam could have chosen Damien Hirst."

"Pickling the goldfish would have been less messy than this. Lucy, if you wrote these things down, it would all be so much easier."

"You don't realize how many things I remember in a day, you only focus on what I forget."

"We're not living in a state of siege, where it is difficult to plan ahead because we might be under attack at any moment, and our food and water supply has been cut off."

"You are not, but I am," I say. "I'm besieged. That's how it feels."

"Surely you are doing the same thing day in, day out? I know it's a bit of a treadmill, but isn't it simply a question of repeating the same formula every morning?"

"You can't imagine how many things need to get done in a single day just to tread water. You know that you won't achieve everything and that at any moment the whole thing could tumble like a house of cards."

"In what way?" he asks warily.

"Fights break out like wildfire, there are spillages, inexplicable illnesses, breakages, losses, eventualities that you can never prepare for," I explain. "Things that set you back months. Like chicken pox. Remember that? I couldn't leave the house for weeks. Even worse, there is a part of me that relishes the unexpected, because at least it breaks the routine and adds a bit of excitement to my life."

He looks taken aback.

"You mean that an element of latent chaos is appealing to you?" he asks, struggling to understand what I am saying. "There is no hope then."

He stares at me with this funny sideways look, mouth slightly open as though he is making an effort not to say anything else. This is not something that comes naturally to a man who enjoys having the last word.

Sam wanders in. He is fully dressed in his school uniform and carrying a cricket ball, which he repeatedly throws in the air and then catches. His pockets are stuffed with football cards. I make him toast—jam, no butter—and tell him at least five times to stop throwing the ball while he is eating. Then I wonder whether it is perhaps a good thing to encourage a boy to multitask in the hope that he will grow up to be the kind of man who can cook broccoli, change a nappy, and have a conversation about work all at the same time. After a couple of slices of toast, he obligingly writes a short piece to go with each work of art. I read the one closest to hand.

"Vincent was a man of great passion," it reads. "If he had followed the cricket, he probably wouldn't have cut his ear off. Matisse undoubtedly was a cricket fan."

I decide to drive to school so that the paintings can dry on the heater, and because there is comfort to be drawn from being enclosed in a cozy space after the exertions of the morning.

"Does getting this finished qualify as a small step for man but a giant leap for mankind, Mum?" Sam asks from the back of the car.

"Is Sam talking about Major Tom?" asks Joe.

"Something like that," I say, in response to both questions.

"Why do you always say something like that? Aren't things either right or wrong?" asks Sam.

"Life is largely gray," I tell him. "There are few moments of black and white."

"Unless you are a zebra," says Joe. He pauses, but I know there is something else he wants to say. "Maybe Major Tom made it onto the moon and it was so beautiful, he stayed there."

I notice the roads are very quiet. Sealed in the car with the heaters blowing wildly, it is easy to feel cut off from the rest of the world. When I stop at the next junction, I see a large number of parents walking their children to school with unnaturally cheery expressions of bonhomie and collectivism. I remember with a sudden lurch that I have forgotten it is Walk to School Day. I will have to suffer ignominious associations with childhood obesity, global warming, and congested roads. I switch down the heating and explain the situation to the children.

"By driving to school, we are releasing bad chemicals into the atmosphere. Today, lots of children in London are walking to school to show that they care about this. I have forgotten, we are late, and so we are going in the car. But if you crouch down and lie on the floor until I tell you to get out, we might be able to get away with it."

I pull on Joe's Spider-Man hat and shrink below the level of the dashboard to drive within two hundred meters of school. Then we all sit there, quietly waiting for a break in the cloud of parents wafting along the pavement.

I note Alpha Mum, striding down the road in a pair of heavy walking boots and wearing a rucksack. She lives miles away. She couldn't have walked here, but judging by the zealous look on her face, she has. Just as she is level with the car, Fred gets up and starts banging on the window. "Help, help," he cries.

I try to pull him away, but he is rubbing the steamed-up window with his tiny hand. A nose appears, pressed against the glass, one of those turned up, slightly superior noses that never has freckles because it is always protected from the sun with wide-brimmed hats and factor forty. Then a pair of eyes, wide open and blinking, tries to focus on the tiny face inside. The overall impression is ghoulish, and Fred starts to cry louder. It is Alpha Mum. "Someone has left a child locked alone in this vehicle," she shouts loudly down the street. Clearly she is a woman who enjoys taking charge in an emergency. "I'm going to inform the school. Will you stay here and try and comfort it?"

I hear Alpha Mum's walking boots stomping along the pavement out of earshot and shut my eyes, practicing deep breathing techniques that I hope will keep the car steamed up. Then I hear another voice on the side of the car facing into the road. "Look at that rubbish on the front seat, there's apple cores, melted chocolate buttons, clothes, plastic plates, it's unbelievable. And what are all those weird paintings on the dashboard?" It is Yummy Mummy No. 1. Another voice, male and under different circumstances now generally welcome, joins the conversation.

"I recognize some of these things. Isn't this Lucy's car?" says Sexy Domesticated Dad.

Alpha Mum rejoins the group with the headmistress. "Mrs. Sweeney, are you in there?" I open the car door and step out with flourish. "We were practicing a Tracey Emin installation for the 'Great Artists of the World' project. It's called 'An Unmade Car,' " I say excitedly. The headmistress claps her hands in joy. 'How clever of you. We must arrange for some photos so that the whole school can see it. Well done, Mrs. Sweeney. That is so imaginative."

She takes the two eldest children by the hand and leads them toward the school. Then Sam comes running back. "Mum, remind me what I mustn't say," he whispers.

"Don't tell the teacher that I did three of your paintings, and don't tell anyone that the car always looks like that. I'm not asking you to lie, I'm asking you to be economical with the truth."

"Is this a gray situation?" he asks.

"It is."

As I stand on the pavement, holding on to the hood of Fred's coat, I shut my eyes briefly and hope for a moment of reprieve. It is not even nine o'clock. When I open them, Fred has his trousers down round his ankles and is peeing against the wheel. "My wheel," he says proudly, and I bundle him back into the Peugeot.

I look up to see Sexy Domesticated Dad sitting on his bicycle beside the car. He is leaning back, legs splayed and slightly bent at the knees, to stabilize him on the pavement. His helmet hangs from his broken arm. He is wearing a pair of jeans and looks satisfactorily disheveled and wild, a white T-shirt hanging below a slightly too small green straight-cut jacket. I would like to say that he is unconscious of the overall effect, but I think there is a hint of vanity there, because he always is careful to remove his cycling helmet and run his fingers through his hair before he goes into school.

I notice the suggestion of a paunch where the coat doesn't do up and the T-shirt wrinkles over his stomach.

"It's my wife's," he says apologetically when he sees me scrutinizing him and smoothes down the jacket over the ripples. But despite all this, and despite his north London obsessions with Borlotti beans and cycling as a replacement for religion, there is something inescapably raw and dirty about him.

"You're good at thinking on your feet," he says, getting off his bike by lifting his right leg over the bar at the front. I'm unsure whether it is a compliment or a challenge, and I know that I should go home right now, because even that small comment will resonate much longer than it should until, by endless replay, it is invested with meaning that he never intended. And then I realize that my mother-in-law has it slightly wrong. The imagination involved in loving your husband is less than the imagination involved in elaborating an unreciprocated fantasy. Attempting to end rather than begin a conversation, I reply, "Years of practice," in what I hope is a dry, laconic tone.

It is one of those early-autumn mornings when it is cold enough to see your breath, and he is now so close that when I speak, our breath becomes entangled. I am not wearing any makeup, and I feel my cheeks go red in the chill.

"I'm sorry I had to rush off yesterday," says Sexy Domesticated Dad. "I'm having a bit of a work crisis. Can't seem to find the right structure for this book, and the Americans want to launch it before the Sundance Film Festival next year."

It could sound as though he is showing off, but he isn't. He is trying to engage.

"At the moment I'm writing about Zapata Westerns," he says. "Those are the ones that were set during the Mexican Revolution, like *A Fistful of Dynamite,* but although they were inspired by Mexican history, there wasn't much other Latin American involvement. . . ."

I nod knowingly, but I am exploiting this unusual verbosity to make a thorough appraisal of his right forearm, which has suddenly been freed from his wife's jacket as he uses his arm to emphasize a point.

To my mind, there is no other part of a man's body that so perfectly summons up the promise of what lies within than the forearm. In fact, I would go so far as to say that if you see a man's forearm, you can define pretty accurately what the rest of his body will look like, and he will have no idea how much can be extrapolated from even the briefest glance. You can gauge tone, texture, length of limbs, how much time he spends in the gym, whether he has been abroad recently. Sexy Domesticated Dad has a near-perfect forearm, medium-range, strong without being chunky, enough hair to seem manly but light enough and thin enough to pretty much guarantee no back hair. I smile at him.

"What do you think?" he says.

"Promising," I say emphatically. "I love Sergio Leone."

"Good," he says, pushing the sleeve of his jacket back down, "except that is not what I was asking. I changed tack when I could see your eyes glazing over. Doesn't matter. It happens all the time, unless I start talking about Benicio Del Toro, then women generally pay attention. I was asking whether you are going to put yourself up as class rep. I'll help you, but I can't run it myself because of deadlines. I want to do my bit to help the school." He pauses. "You look surprised."

I couldn't be more astonished if he had asked me to lick his forearm.

"Well, of course I'm considering it, my youngest one has just started nursery and it would be a good time to do something like that. But I don't want to look too pushy." It sounds so credible, I almost believe myself.

"I'll vote for you," he says good-naturedly. "So will Isobel. She was saying that it would be really entertaining if you won."

"Oh, did she?" I say, entirely mistrustful of Yummy Mummy No. 1's motives.

"I told my wife what happened yesterday. You know, the, er, imbroglio with the underwear. She thought it was very funny. Simpatico. So did I."

I wonder in what context it was discussed, what adjectives he used, whether he told her that we were sitting so close together I could feel the heat from his thigh. After he had cooked dinner, or when they were in bed? What were they wearing in bed?

"Pajamas," he says. "I told her about the pajamas, too." I know that I should feel gratified that he has shared this with his wife, because it hints at the promise of friendship. I imagine cozy foursomes sharing dinner, family picnics on Hampstead Heath, even holidays abroad. But I realize that I don't want anyone extraneous intruding on my fantasy because they could dilute its escapist potential.

๑๑

In the evening I lie at one end of the sofa, watching Tom at the other end reading last week's copy of *The Architects' Journal*. After almost a year's delay, building work is finally to begin on his library in Milan, and his mood is buoyant. Our feet are touching. The witching hour is over. The children are in bed and a bottle of wine has been consumed in lieu of dinner.

He will be traveling to Milan in the next couple of weeks. He tells me this apologetically, at pains to demonstrate awareness of the burden this will place on me. But I know he is excited because tonight there have been no searches in the fridge for food that has exceeded its sell-by date. No forensic examination of bank statements, looking for evidence of parking fines and other misdemeanors. No questions about new scratches on the side of the car.

"I'll leave an alarm clock, so that you aren't late in the morning. I'll put one hundred pounds in cash in the chest of drawers, in case you lose your credit card. I'll babysit for you when I come back. I'll buy my own socks at the airport."

The less I say, the more extravagant his offers, so I keep quiet.

"We won't ever go camping again. Next time, we'll rent a house. We'll never have such an awful holiday again. And we might even be able to afford to have a cleaning lady twice a week."

I make all sorts of rash promises in return. "I won't lie about little things. I'll put out the school uniforms the night before. I'll look in the fridge before I go shopping."

Then the phone starts to ring. After swift negotiations Tom answers on the fifth ring, as a quid pro quo for my opening another bottle of wine.

"It's for you," he says. "One of the dads from school." He raises an eyebrow and holds the phone just out of reach.

"Tell him I'm busy," I whisper, but Tom pushes the phone into my hand.

"Hope I'm not interrupting anything," says Sexy Domesticated Dad. "Are you in the middle of eating?"

I slap my cheeks in a desperate attempt to sober up. "No, no, we've just finished dinner actually," I slur. "Some vegetable stew my husband rustled up. Delicious."

Tom looks at me in astonishment. "Why are you lying? Tell him you put the wrong month on the Internet order and there's only an onion and a jar of marmalade in the fridge," he mutters bemusedly, starting to lurch toward me with lust in his eye. "I love it when you try to dissimulate; you are so bad at it."

Not now, not now, I think, pondering the complex dilemma that's unraveling: to end the sexual fast of the past two months or to risk alienating Sexy Domesticated Dad at the outset of our friendship. I start to push Tom away with my foot.

"The thing is," Sexy Domesticated Dad continues obliviously, "I put your name forward to be class rep." All thoughts of sex with either man fade rapidly. "But a competitor has already emerged, and she is phoning around other parents to warn them off you. Sort of a smear campaign." I struggle to digest this information. "In essence, she is saying that you don't have any experience running anything and that your exotic domestic habits are no recommendation."

"It's Yummy Mummy No. 1, isn't it? I knew she was untrustworthy," I say in full slur. "What does she know about my domestic habits?"

Tom is taking off his shirt and pointing to the sofa.

"Look, we could talk about this another time," says Sexy Domesticated Dad, obviously disturbed by my tone. "And, actually, it's not Isobel. It's the one whose children are learning Mandarin."

I hear my voice rise into a wail. "Alpha Mum. That's it, the truce is over," I yell into the phone.

"Look, don't shoot the messenger," says Sexy Domesticated Dad shirtily. "I was calling to offer to be your campaign manager."

The phone goes dead and I reconsider my options. Then the doorbell rings. It's the Internet shopping man, looking a little worried.

"Where do you want us to leave all these onions?" he asks Tom. "We thought we were delivering to an Italian restaurant." He brings three large sacks into the kitchen.

Tom starts rifling through the bags. "Explain how this is possible," he asks, baffled.

"I thought I was ordering by unit, not by kilo."

"But why did you want to order thirty red onions? I'm off to bed."

5

"The mother of mischief
is no bigger than a
midge's wing."

Winter is drawing in, this much I know, because the annual war of attrition over the heating has begun. I turn up the thermostat when Tom leaves the house, and then occasionally remember to turn it down before he comes home. But even on the good days, he uncovers any subterfuge by putting a hand on the radiator that runs along the passageway from the front door.

"We had an agreement. And the warmth of the radiator is exactly proportionate to the scale of deception," he says one Friday evening in late October. Downstairs in the kitchen, Emma has opened a second bottle of wine and is reluctantly nibbling Little Bear potato chips for want of anything else. The children are upstairs, asleep in bed.

"I know we said November, but the weather is not subject to your will. This is going to be the coldest winter ever recorded, colder even than the great freeze of 1963, and I think we will have to suspend hostilities until spring," I tell him, speaking a language I know he will understand.

There is a knock at the door. As he walks along the passageway to open it, I quickly turn the thermostat up a couple of notches. He turns around. I stand motionless, hand in the air a little north of the dial. We are playing an adult variation of grandmother's footsteps.

"All right, Lucy, you're in charge of heating until spring," he acqui-
esces. I think he is relieved to have the responsibility taken away from
him, although he would never admit this.

There are secrets in every marriage. There are large-scale acts of deception. Then there are the smaller, more innocuous kind. Despite being
married for almost ten years, Tom still hasn't uncovered the following:
(1) I have five sources of credit-card debt; (2) the car got stolen shortly
after I lost the spare key; and (3) I have an unconfessed infidelity dating
from the second year of our relationship. The last one might qualify as a
big one, except that I know he has one of similar magnitude.

He opens the door and is genuinely pleased to see Cathy standing there.

"Cathy, what a lovely surprise," he says with unaffected feeling, as
though her arrival is completely unexpected.

While some men might resent their wife's friends, Tom has always rel-
ished mine, and consequently they reciprocate with ill-thought-out adulation. Cathy kisses him enthusiastically and sweeps through the narrow
passage to go downstairs, hugging me on the way down. Cathy is perpetually in motion. She is one of those people who take up a lot of space
even though she is quite small, like a centrifugal force sucking people into
her wake. She comes with baggage: handbags, groceries, and a laptop
computer. Tom is immediately pulled into the slipstream and follows her
downstairs.

"God, it's hot in here," she shouts up to me.

When I get down, she has already opened the computer, removed our
phone from the socket, and sits down, tapping away without even taking
off her coat.

"Have you got a work crisis?" Tom asks.

"No, no, no," Cathy says excitedly. "I have to show you all a photo of
my next Internet date."

Emma is lying languidly on the sofa.

"Will you bring him over here, Cathy, so I don't have to get up?"

"Sure," she says. "That's the beauty of the Internet, men delivered to
the comfort and privacy of your very own sofa."

"I really can't imagine why you need to look for men on the Internet. Can't you meet enough through the normal channels?" Tom says, opening the door of the fridge.

"The men you meet through the normal channels are fatally flawed," she says.

"Well, there are several single men in my office. They seem normal enough."

"Why don't you introduce me to them, then?" Cathy demands. "I am doing multiple dating at the moment."

Scores of tiny faces the size of postage stamps appear on the screen. She points to one.

"What do you think?" she asks. "It was a tough decision. There's so much choice."

"Difficult to tell. I mean, he has all the key features in the right places, which is always a good starting point," I say, squinting at the screen.

So she starts to enlarge the photo, until frame by frame his face takes shape and we observe a well-calibrated if slightly large nose; short, almost spiky, brown hair; and challenging brown eyes.

When he is life-size, we sit in a row and silently stare at the stranger before us. There are a few wrinkles on the forehead and around the eyes.

"Absolutely your type," says Emma.

"Well, he's definitely walked on the wild side," I say after a long silence.

"How can you tell that?" shouts Tom from inside the fridge.

"Just something about those wrinkles on his forehead. They're not from laughing too much or being too anxious, they are the kind that appear when you wake up too many mornings and you can't remember where you are or who you are with."

Tom snorts and continues his tour of the fridge.

"Actually, Lucy's generally right about these things, Tom," says Cathy. "She was right about my husband long before the fault lines appeared. Anyway, isn't he gorgeous? He's a lawyer, thirty-seven years old, lives in Earls Court. What could be more perfect? The only sticking point so far is that he thinks I should cut my hair into a 'neat little bob.' "

"That's so disappointing," I say. "He doesn't look the type."

"What does a man who likes women with neat little bobs look like?" asks Tom with genuine curiosity.

"Well, sartorially speaking, he's never left the eighties. He probably wears trousers in primary colors and brogues, even on a beach holiday," says Emma. "In the winter, he puts on those thick Norwegian sweaters with loud prints. He has a sensible job with a reliable salary and enjoys a round of golf on the weekends. He's never done a line of coke. He reads the *Telegraph*. And he doesn't like to talk dirty in bed, at least not to women."

"But that's such a massive generalization," says Tom.

"No it's not, it's a truism," says Emma. "Does he want you to accessorize with a Labrador?"

Tom strolls over and takes a look.

"More likely a Reservoir Dog," he says enigmatically. "Write to him and ask if the name Mr. Orange means anything to him, because the other sticking point is that's not what he looks like. That's not a west London lawyer, it's the actor Tim Roth, and he lives in L.A. The man who wants to date you is an impostor."

Cathy pauses, looks at the photo again, then says, "I'm dating a film star. I'm prepared to move to Hollywood if it all works out."

"What about schools?" I ask.

"We'll live in Palo Alto, I'll give up work and do home schooling."

"But that would be a nightmare," I say. "Especially if you decide to have another child."

"I think we need to rewind a little," says Tom. "For a start, Tim Roth is married."

"Don't let that hold you back," says Emma. "Those fortysomething men are like wild animals when released from the purdah of marriage. They want to do everything they haven't done for the past ten years in less than a week."

Tom looks interested.

"I thought we were off-bounds. Fellowship of women and all that. And what about this?" he asks, patting his stomach so that it makes a hollow sound.

"There are other compensations," says Emma knowingly. "You are generally at the peak of your professional success, and money and power are powerful aphrodisiacs. Also, you are more emotionally coherent than twenty-year-old men. And actually, as soon as you rediscover your old sex drive, the weight just peels off."

"Then I shall look at those attractive young single women in my office in a whole new light," says Tom.

"Which attractive young single women?" I ask.

"You haven't met them," he says. "But none of them could compete with you for excitement, unpredictability, and all-around gorgeousness." And he comes over and puts his arm around my stomach. "Especially around gorgeousness."

"If he's advertising on the Internet, then I think it's fair to say he is up for grabs," says Cathy.

"The point is that Tim Roth doesn't need to do Internet dating. He probably has women throwing themselves at him the whole time," says Tom, losing patience, although I am the only one to pick up on the subtle change in tone.

"But that's like saying Hugh Grant didn't need to pay for a blowjob on Sunset Boulevard," says Cathy.

"Look, this man might be a west London lawyer, but this is not what he looks like. At best you'll be dating a five-foot-tall liar," says Tom. "At worst . . . well, you should definitely take someone with you in case it turns nasty. I'll come if you like."

Cathy shrugs and says, "Back to the drawing board," in the kind of way that indicates the subject is closed for further discussion. Tim Roth shrinks, click by click, until he is just another face in the crowd.

"Look, there's another one," I say, pointing to another stamp in the top left-hand corner. "Snap."

Cathy enlarges the image and, sure enough, it is another man masquerading as Tim Roth, albeit using a later photograph that even I recognize is him playing a robber in *Pulp Fiction*. This time it says he is a civil engineer based in northern England. Then Emma finds David Cameron.

"How can this man be so stupid to think that women won't recognize the leader of the Tory party?" says Tom. "Besides, I can't imagine that many women find him attractive." Silence.

"I can't believe that you all fancy David Cameron," says Tom incredulously. "Sometimes I find women completely incomprehensible. I think you should ask for a refund, Cathy. Or some free dates. Or at least a couple of discount dates, if they stretch to that. I can't believe that any man would go to those lengths to get a date. What can be wrong with them?"

"Actually, they do very well out of it. My last date was sleeping with five different women," explains Cathy. "What do you think, Lucy?"

"I think you should investigate the men in Tom's office first. And avoid married men, if possible. Although sometimes I know it's difficult to tell or resist."

"I wish you could come out with me, Lucy, and use your radar to sort out the wheat from the chaff," she says.

"Well, I owe her a couple of nights babysitting, so why don't you take her with you?" says Tom.

"Isn't he so lovely," they chorus. "What a great husband."

I don't mention the fact that men rarely pay back the babysitting debt and that with the Milan project back on track, he will be traveling backward and forward to Italy for much of the foreseeable future. Tom basks in the adulation. In fact, I think he panders to their expectations. There is no level playing field in the domestic point-scoring game. Women always start in the foothills, with higher to climb and farther to fall. A man who changes a nappy bounds ahead, while a woman who performs the same task in half the time, using three economic movements and a quarter of the wipes, barely registers progress. Consider the phenomenon of men glory-cooking for dinner parties, with guests falling over each other to find adjectives that adequately sum up the sumptuousness of the spread and the inventiveness of the cook. But the reality is that they learned two recipes from the River Café ten years ago and recycle them shamelessly when there is a chance for plaudits, while children's meals are considered beneath their dignity.

No one bothers to score the blushing spaghetti Bolognese, the diffident baked potatoes, or the humble shepherd's pies that mothers peddle to the table twice a day every day. They don't find their own way from fridge to table. And there is a fluency in their repetition that is as ancient as those leaf-cutter ants carrying bits back to their nest, doggedly fulfilling their genetic job description without any fuss.

I look at Tom talking to my friends and try and see him as they do: a man at ease with himself, confidently negotiating his way around the shared intimacies of this group of women, in a manner that is neither too intrusive nor dominating. A man who enjoys his midweek football with friends and manages to live off the pleasures of a hat trick for at least a couple of months. A man who goes to the pub for a few beers and then consumes only that. Reflected back to me through my friends, I know that I should consider myself a lucky woman. But no one can dissect a marriage except for the two people involved, and even then it is difficult to see around the corners. And there are always lots of angles and points of view. For example, the lightness of heart after three children have successfully been bedded for the evening has to be measured against the bone-aching tiredness that comes with the end of the day. Is it a good moment to mention that you have lost the house keys again? Does the relief of silence compensate for the irritation of nine o'clock feeling like a late night out?

I ponder on the impossible vagaries of relationships, whereby things that were once attractive evolve into negative qualities or become obsolete over time. For example, I used to love watching Tom roll cigarettes. He could do it with one hand, using his long fingers to deftly smooth tobacco into a cigarette paper, crumbling pieces of grass expertly into the mix, handing it to me with a smile. Then when he was thirty he suddenly gave up smoking, became a hypochondriac, and berated me ever after for my inability to shake off this dirty little habit. Then there was the moment when Tom realized for the first time that, far from being a good listener, as I gazed into his eyes and listened to his problems with one of his building projects, I was actually in a world of my own. None of us are what we seem.

"Lucy, Lucy, stop doing that, you're making the hole bigger," says Tom, interrupting my train of thought. I have absentmindedly been picking at the hole in the side of the sofa, and suddenly the money that Sam has been collecting there shoots down onto the floor. I have won the jackpot.

Emma yawns loudly.

"I'm so tired," she says.

"Have you got a work crisis?" Tom asks, hoping to return the conversation to safe territory and resisting the urge to tell her to take off her kitten heel boots when she is lying on the sofa. If he can show self-restraint with her, why can't he with me? I wonder.

"No, actually I was up half the night having phone sex," she replies with her eyes shut.

"I cannot imagine how anyone with a wife and four children has any time to spare for phone sex," I say.

"He only does it when he's away, or he's working late, but that's most of the time," she says.

"How do you have phone sex? Do you put it on vibrate?" I ask. Snorts of derision are interrupted by her phone beeping.

"He's insatiable," Emma says. "I'm going to ignore him. Boyfriends are so demanding." She opens the text message and throws me the phone.

"I don't know if technically you can call him a boyfriend if he's married," I point out. She ignores me.

"Can I go and have a quick peek at the children, Lucy?" she asks.

"Of course," I tell her. I know better than anyone the regenerative powers of this pastime.

She disappears upstairs and I ponder the technological advances made since Tom and I started dating. Back then there was enough suspense involved in waiting for phone calls. Now there are BlackBerries, cell phones, satellite navigation. For the first time since Norfolk, I feel those waves of relief that I am married and read the message.

"Want you in my office, bent over my desk, secretary in very short skirt about to walk in . . ." I drop the phone in shock.

"Whatever happened to foreplay?" I ask. Cathy comes over and takes a look.

"I hope he's put the photo of his perfect family in the drawer before he starts this," I say.

Tom announces that he has decided to go to the pub to watch football and will be out for the rest of the evening.

"There's only so much I can take," he whispers in my ear as he leaves. "I might meet this man one day."

I unthinkingly pick up Cathy's phone and suddenly find myself composing a message back. **"How short exactly?"** I write, and before I know it some primeval urge has prompted me to send it back.

"God, Lucy," says Cathy, reading the message over my shoulder, "since when have you learned how to send texts?"

The phone beeps.

"So short you can touch her arse," it reads. I'm completely out of my depth already.

"Why does he write it all longhand?" asks Cathy. "No wonder they're up all night. It must take forever to get to the end." Once upon a time, middle-aged men blew their cover by calling trousers "slacks" and referring to all women under sixty as girls—now all it takes is writing a text message in longhand.

"Do you do this text-sex thing, too?" I ask Cathy in the manner of someone inquiring whether lavender bags are an appropriate way of ensuring sweet-smelling wardrobes, as I compose a message back to him.

"Sure," she says. "Although I prefer the real thing."

"Want your sexy wife to come in, not secretary," it reads, and I send it back.

"Lucy, that is so naughty," says Cathy, just as Emma comes back into the room. Her phone beeps again and Emma strolls over to take it from me.

"Keep my wife out of this," reads the message.

"Lucy, what's going on here?" asks Emma, retracing the steps of this virtual conversation. She hectically types in another message but receives none back.

"I can't believe that you did that." She shoots me an annoyed look. "It really stresses him out thinking about his wife."

"Precisely," I say. "That is how it should be. Why should he have a guilt-free relationship with you?"

"Some people have massages to wind down. He has me. Home is not a serene retreat from the world for him, it is a place where children clamor for attention and his wife makes unreasonable demands about holidays in the Caribbean and expense accounts at Joseph. Her monthly budget is more than my monthly salary."

"But of course his home is stressful, he's got four children who all want attention from him because they don't see him enough, because when he's not at work he's with you. Home is never serene once you have children. And of course she wants some compensation, that's the deal with bankers, she's had four children, now it's payback time. Anyway, you should stop talking about yourself as though you are an aromatherapy treatment whose raison d'être is to soothe a man with a stressful job. You could have anyone you want, there must be loads of available men in your office. I think you're addicted to the secrecy."

"Lucy, actually I am quite serious about this man. I want to get domestic with him."

"What does that mean?" I ask incredulously.

"You know, do the dishes in yellow rubber gloves while he dries, cook recipes from Nigella Lawson, iron his shirts in the morning."

"You are deluded. He's married with four children. You're just a diversion for him."

"Then why has he rented a flat for us in Clerkenwell with a six-month lease?"

Cathy and I stall, because that is not where we imagined this discussion was leading, and Emma lies back on the sofa with the satisfaction of someone who still manages to pull rabbits out of a hat.

Then I say, "Because it's near his office? In fact, I can't imagine why he would want to rent a flat in Clerkenwell when you already have a place of your own."

"Maybe he has old-fashioned views on having a mistress?" suggests Cathy.

"We've been together for over a year," says Emma. "He doesn't like coming to Notting Hill in case he bumps into someone he knows, so I have decided to move east and sublet my flat. He's going to pay the rent, and we've already bought a bed together."

For some reason, it is the last detail that impresses me most. Buying a bed together is more than a simple transaction. It is one of those subtle defining moments that present themselves when you are least expecting them. The width of the bed, always a bone of contention, usually entails some degree of speculation about whether the couple is planning to have children, dogs who sleep on beds, or, even more radical, sleepovers with third parties. The price defines the degree of commitment. The more expensive the bed, the longer the guarantee.

"How much did it cost?" I say.

"Do you mean the rent?" asks Emma.

"The bed, was it expensive?"

"Vi-sprung, nine thousand springs, twenty-five-year guarantee, super-king, four figures with a three in front." Then I know he is in deep.

"But wasn't there a chance that someone might spot you in a bed shop? I thought bankers were all very risk-averse," I ask, imagining them bouncing up and down on mattresses in the John Lewis bed department.

"He did it over the phone," she says. Then I know he has bought exactly the same bed that he has at home with his wife. I bet they lived in Clerkenwell before they moved to west London.

"Look, I really want you all to meet him, then you'll see what a lovely man he is. He's trapped in this situation. His marriage was over long before he met me. It's just a formality. They only had sex about twice a month."

"Twice a month." I sputter on the Little Bear chips. "That's not bad going with four children and a proper job."

"But it was something perfunctory, there was no meaning left in it. She would suddenly remember something she had forgotten to tell the housekeeper in the middle of it all and stop to write 'Book Coco the clown' or something like that."

I am about to admit that I have done that, but some things are best left unsaid, even to close friends.

"Anyway, Lucy, I think you are being a little hypocritical, given your confession last time we were out."

"That is completely different," I say, putting my drink down rather too heavily on the table beside her. "I was playing to the gallery, trying to manufacture something tantalizing to keep up with both of you."

They look at me bemusedly.

"Actually, we're becoming friends," I insist.

"So, in the interests of friendship, tell us what this Sexy Domesticated Dad is like?" asks Cathy. Emma lethargically pulls herself into a sitting position and leans against some cushions in anticipation, and I decide that, given her efforts, she deserves something a little spicier than the rather bland reality of our exchanges so far.

"Well, he has none of the bloated self-satisfaction of men whose self-esteem is defined by their annual bonuses, he's not bald, and there's not a hint of Crew clothing about him," I start.

"Don't tell us what he isn't, tell us what he is," insists Emma.

"Tallish, darkish, definitely brooding, as long as he doesn't speak, because then he ruins it by saying something like 'Brown granary bread is infinitely preferable for a child's lunch box, don't you think?' and obviously, even with a lot of imagination, it's difficult to misconstrue something like that."

They are unmoved.

"Have you talked to him more?" presses Cathy.

"He thinks that I should stand as class rep and says he'll help me," I say.

"I don't think you can read too much into that," says Cathy, "although I suppose it would give you lots of excuses to spend time together."

"He asked me out for coffee on the first day of term," I say. Emma makes an effort to sit up on the edge of the sofa.

"On your own?" asks Emma. I nod in assent, enjoying the rapt expression on their faces.

"You never told us that," she says.

"That's because it didn't happen," I say mysteriously.

"You mean you turned him down," asks Cathy.

"No, it was more complicated than that," I say.

"God, Lucy, I don't know how you could keep quiet about all this," says Emma, holding her hand over her mouth.

"What happened, every detail, now," says Cathy.

"When he saw I was wearing pajamas under my coat he withdrew the invitation, not indefinitely but temporarily, and there has been no mention of it since."

"Lucy, that is so lame." Cathy laughs. "No one can get away with wearing pajamas outside the house, unless they are over seventy or have locked themselves out."

"Well, he shouldn't have been looking," I say. "Anyway, desperate times call for desperate measures. You can't imagine what it is like getting to school on time in the morning, day in, day out. Have you ever tried getting a temperamental almost-three-year-old dressed? It's like trying to play football with a jellyfish. I'd rather be grilled by John Humphreys or forced to wear a bikini to go to the supermarket or have an affair with David Blunkett or . . ."

"We get the picture, it can't be that bad," says Emma, pausing for a moment. "Perhaps you should think about putting Fred to bed already dressed."

And I smile to myself because this reminds me of an evening a decade ago, when I came home from work late one night to find Tom fully dressed in bed. Caught in the raptures of a deep sleep, he lay on his back with his white shirt and the buttons of his jeans completely open. I ran my hand from his neck down to an area below his belly button, still tanned from the summer, and then down inside his jeans. This was back in the days when there was no need to stoke the fires of passion with anything more than a lingering glance. Even in his sleep, the quality of his breathing changed. I tried to work out whether he had fallen asleep with his clothes on or whether he was dressed, ready to catch an early train to Edinburgh the following morning for a site visit. Then I saw a note on the pillow on my side of the bed telling me that he had found my credit card in the fridge. This was a period of our relationship when there was a gratifying harmony between my losses and Tom's searches, as though it was a sign of our essential compatibility.

But I knew that I had examined the fridge thoroughly for my credit card before I went to work in the morning and it hadn't been there. I wondered momentarily whether he was hiding things so that he could please me by finding them, so I went to the kitchen to investigate. The fridge was a little fuller than when I left it that morning, but on its own, on a shelf at the bottom, was a large, plump chocolate cake. It looked handmade. I got it out of the fridge, and when I switched on the kitchen light saw that in the middle there was a silver ring with four tiny stones in different colors. And beside the ring a message written in icing that said, "Wake me up if the answer is yes." I licked the ring free of chocolate, put it on, and it fit perfectly.

Tom was standing by the kitchen door, watching my face. "It took a lot of willpower to resist you upstairs," he said.

๑๏

"Lucy, Lucy, you've gone all dreamy again," Cathy says, nudging Emma. "She must be thinking about Sexy Domesticated Dad."

"Oh, no, I was thinking about when Tom asked me to marry him," I explain.

"That's good," says Cathy. "I was reading just the other day that the lines that define infidelity have become much more blurred, and that even having a flirty friendship with another man constitutes betrayal. Anyway, you and Tom are the most solid couple that I know, and this is the most comforting household. It's like visiting my parent. There can't be anything wrong, otherwise I would notice. What would we do if you split up or even went through a bad patch?"

But shouldn't it be about me? I think to myself.

"Well, there's been no impropriety," I say imperiously. "It's just a harmless thing going on in my head. A welcome distraction. He clearly adores his wife anyway."

"How do you know that?" asks Emma.

"Because he had told her about the pajama thing and the knickers thing."

"What's the knickers thing?" So I give the abbreviated version and they laugh so much that any tension is diffused.

"You'll probably end up being really good friends," says Cathy.

She is interrupted by the beeping of my own cell phone. I eye it suspiciously, because receiving a text is still somewhat of a novelty for me. But before I can open it, Cathy has picked it up and is reading the message. It's from Sexy Domesticated Dad. He must have got my cell phone number from the class list. **"Class rep election next Monday evening,"** it reads. She punches in a few letters, holds it up for me to read, but before I can protest, she presses send. **"And then what?"** she has written.

Within minutes the phone beeps again. This time I grab it quickly. **"How about a drink?"** Sexy Domesticated Dad writes back. I switch off the phone in awe.

"Cathy, what have you done?" says Emma.

"Nothing is certain but
death and taxes."

We are about to go out for dinner in Islington with Cathy and an architect from Tom's office, for, having made the promise to set Cathy up less than a week ago, Tom has identified an appropriate single man in his office and arranged for the four of us to meet with barely any consultation.

It is unusually peaceful for the time of day, because the babysitter arrived early and offered to put the children to bed, so I am lying in our room, watching in wonder as Tom packs his suitcase, even though it will be another three days until he leaves for Milan. He carefully counts pairs of pants, socks, shirts, pajamas, and trousers, placing them in neat little piles. Then underneath he lines up a toothbrush, toothpaste, dental floss, deodorant, and a razor, each equidistant from the next. I know that when he arrives at the Hotel Central (he has already given me the details) they will be taken out and arranged on the glass shelf in the bathroom in exactly the same order.

We no longer share toothpaste, after a run-in over how exactly a tube should be squeezed. I prefer a more freestyle technique. Years ago, I adopted the tall upstanding containers to avoid further debate, the subject, to my mind, having been exhausted. But Tom persists in buying tubes and squeezing the toothpaste from the far end, carefully rolling them up from the bottom to ensure that none is wasted, and occasionally worrying about what he will do when the tubes are finally declared obsolete. He whistles through his teeth with contentment as he stands back, hands on hips, satisfied with the job at hand. I admire an expert at work, wishing I could find similar gratification from such activities.

There might be big changes in the world by Monday morning, but Tom knows exactly what color pants he will be wearing to embrace them. He is, after all, a constant man. Until recently, I considered myself to be someone largely constant in my inconsistencies. I can be relied upon to lose my credit card on average six times a year, to leave crumbs of toast between the keys of the computer keyboard whenever I look at my e-mails, and to reduce the price of any clothes that I buy by one-fourth when Tom asks how much they cost. These days I am more uncertain in my uncertainty, which on reflection is probably even worse than being certain about it.

"What are you thinking about?" asks Tom, looking at me out of the corner of his eye while still fully engaged in the lines-and-piles process.

"What do you think about Emma's affair with this man?" I ask. "I never thought she would get involved with someone who is married. She likes everything to be so defined, and, whatever the outcome, this is all going to be very complicated."

"I think that you have to let people live their lives, Lucy," he says, pulling a suit carrier out of the wardrobe and getting a towel to dust it. "Anyway, it all sounds quite compulsive, snatched sex in his office, in elevators, in the back of cars. Clandestine encounters are a great aphrodisiac."

"How do you know all that?" I ask.

"She told me while you went to check on Fred. She can't stop talking about it. God, I hope you never talk about me so explicitly."

I ignore this and instead say, "But what about his wife?"

"Well, she's probably too wiped out. You can only do that kind of stuff with a relative stranger," he says.

"That's not what I meant. It seems so unfair that she doesn't even realize she's engaged in a battle for hearts and minds. I mean, if she knew that there was a rival, she might try a bit harder," I say.

"In what way?"

"I don't know, wax her bikini line, go to the gym, cook nice dinners, consider new sexual positions, make a fuss of him when he comes home from work."

"Maybe you need a rival, then," he jokes. "If those are the kinds of things that matter, then it's not a very substantial marriage, is it? Perhaps she does all that and more and it's still not enough. What I really can't understand is why he wants to set up a flat with her. Domesticity is the death knell of that kind of passion."

"Not if you only get to be domestic in prescribed hours. I can't see where it's all going."

"I think all this has got more to do with you than her, actually, Lucy."

"What do you mean?"

"I think you're overempathizing with other people's situations, and that unsettles you," he says.

Just as it gets interesting, Fred comes running into the bedroom and in one impressive leap from the floor lands in the middle of his father's arrangement and jumps up and down. A rabble of clothes bounces around, shirtsleeves embrace underpants, socks become separated, and the contents intended for his wash bag scatter over the floor. The razor never makes it to Milan and joins the splinter movement under the bed. Toddlers are natural-born anarchists.

"Fred, you are meant to be asleep," shouts Tom, grabbing him and carrying him under his arm like a rugby ball back to the bedroom, his little legs pedaling wildly in the air. Children always sense when you are abandoning the front line and leaving a duty officer in charge.

But Polly, the babysitter, the youngest daughter of one of our neighbors, is now too busy writing an A-level philosophy essay to worry about what is going on upstairs. I go down into the kitchen to give her a list of numbers in case she needs to contact us, glancing at her computer screen. "Socrates believes that people do wrong not because they are inherently evil but because they are unclear about what is best for them." Discuss.

"Would you like me to try and tackle the laundry once the children are asleep?" Polly asks. The overflowing baskets are in the same corner of the kitchen as they were last time she came. The clean and dirty piles joined forces a couple of weeks ago and instead of twin peaks, there is a small mountain with a sort of plateau of pants and bras on top. She is clearing a small space on the kitchen table to spread out more books. She carries plastic mugs in garish colors half-filled with milk, plates with crusts of toast and eggshells that have been sitting on the table since tea, and starts efficiently sweeping food into the bin and then putting everything in the dishwasher.

"Sorry, it's always such a rush if you are going out," I say, companionably loading the dishwasher beside her and hoping that Tom won't come in, because Polly is randomly piling plates into the bottom compartment and mixing the knives and forks together in the cutlery rack.

"I was going to clear up after I bathed the boys, but then Fred cut his lip in the bath and Tom was making endless calls to Italy. If you have time for the laundry, that would be great." I glance at her stomach as she stands up beside me. She is wearing a pair of Seven jeans that must have cost more than a hundred pounds and a multilayered vest top that keeps riding up as she bends down to put things in the dishwasher, revealing an effortlessly flat stomach and belly-button ring. It is unimaginable that she might one day be pitched against rebellious piles of dirty laundry and multiple midriffs, befuddled by flat packs and school timetables, holding conversations with her husband about the best way to stack a dishwasher. And yet once I was like her.

I wonder what she thinks of me. I see her looking at the to-do list on the fridge. Gym shoes Joe. Hairdresser. Christmas presents, underlined three times. Call plumber. Nit shampoo, because once again the children have lice.

I know that she won't sort out the clothes now. Not because she is lazy or her offer is insincere, but because she will conclude that perhaps if she works a little harder for a little longer on her essay, she might get good enough grades to guarantee a future far removed from my own.

As we load the dishwasher, I ask about her future plans.

"I want to do a history degree," she says.

"Oh, that's what I did at Manchester," I reply enthusiastically. She looks slightly perturbed but has the good grace to blush.

"So, did you work then, before you had children?" she asks tentatively, not really wanting to know the answer. And there is a part of me that wants to lie, to tell her that she will have different choices and that everything will be easier.

"Yes," I say. "And then I tried part-time after Sam was born, but because Tom was working unpredictable hours, I had to find a nanny who was prepared to stay until midnight. Then I got pregnant with Joe."

"Were you doing shift work?" she asks.

"Something like that," I reply, picking bits of pasta out of the sink.

"What exactly did it involve?" she persists.

"I was a producer on *Newsnight,*" I say.

"But that's terrible, that you had to give all that up," she says.

"When you have children, you are never truly free again," I say, "and that is both a terrible and a wonderful thing. At first, it felt as though the role I had prepared for my entire life had been taken from me, just as the curtain went up and I discovered that far from being the lead part, I was fourth spear bearer. But it was terrible never really seeing Sam. It's funny, if the thought of time with your children fills you with dread, it is probably a sign that you are seeing too much of them, and if you wake up early on a Saturday morning and get up to pack in a trip to the zoo and a museum and make pancakes for breakfast, you undoubtedly aren't getting enough time with them."

"But surely there must be a happy medium."

"Well, a really rich husband helps, because then you can buy your way out of a lot of the more tedious tasks," I joke. "But then you never see him. And there are some jobs that are more compatible with motherhood. Or you could find yourself a househusband."

"I think that I will try and have children when I am young and then build a career after that," she says thoughtfully.

"I think that sounds like a great idea." I lie because there is no point in trying to explain the incompatibility of motherhood with all that has preceded it. "Anyway, you don't need to worry about any of this at the moment, just enjoy yourself. What did your mother do?"

"She's a corporate lawyer," Polly says. "We joke that she's a mole because we've never seen her in daylight hours. I know that I never want that."

I hear shouting and run upstairs to investigate. Fred is out of bed again and the two elder boys are in the middle of a favorite new game, inspired by an episode of *ER* that Sam watched with us a few months ago. It involves carrying out operations on each other, each more grotesque and bloody than the last. This time it is Fred's turn to be pinned down on the floor. They have taken tomato ketchup from the kitchen to simulate blood, and it is all over the duvet cover. It warrants a row, but the prospect is too exhausting, so I simply pick up the ketchup and give Sam, who as the eldest should show more responsibility, a look that I hope conveys a number of emotions, including disappointment, rage, and exasperation.

"We're doing a brain transplant, Mum," says Sam.

"It's so he remembers how to count to twenty," says Joe.

"Do you want one too, Mum?" asks Sam.

I go into our bedroom searching for Tom, catching sight of a lopsided curtain that Fred pulled down during hide-and-seek, revealing a stain from where the gutter overflowed last year.

The whole house needs painting, I think to myself. But like the dream of a toy cupboard filled with identical plastic boxes with names stuck on the side to indicate where things will be located, painting the house is not a first-division priority. Then I start to wonder just what is. Finding a new cleaning lady, perhaps? Sorting out Sam's birthday party, for sure? Having sex with Tom, definitely? Resolving my ongoing crisis, absolutely?

One thing beyond question is that uncertainty is a breeding ground for more uncertainty. I attempt to chart the course of my recent loss of faith. Tom is right. The seeds were probably sown more than a year ago with a phone call from Cathy just after midnight, asking in the kind of shrunken voice that comes after hours of crying whether she could come around and see us and stay the night. She said she would tell us everything when she arrived with Ben, who was then three years old, but we knew what had happened. The fissures had been obvious for some time. There had been the sessions with a Relate counselor, when the bitterness was already so deep that even the air around them tasted sour, and the stand-up row at my brother's fortieth birthday party when Cathy had forgotten to tell her ex-husband that she needed to work over the weekend, which meant he had to look after Ben and cancel his shiatsu massage. "Look, if I don't work, we don't have enough money," she shouted.

"My therapist says that I have to have space to think and find my inner child," he brayed back.

"I think you need to find your outer adult first," she retorted.

"What is so awful," said Cathy, over several bottles of wine, after we had settled Ben upstairs, "is the fact that he is so far ahead in the decision-making process that there is no hope of reconciliation. You think that you know what someone is thinking, and then they tell you that they're not sure that they ever even loved you, and you start wondering about the truth of your own feelings and losing all faith in them."

We nodded sagely. At that time I had never questioned the strength of our emotional fusion. Tom went upstairs and found her a handkerchief. When he handed it over, she cried even more at his kindness.

"You're so reliable, Tom. If only I had married a man who arranged the spices alphabetically," she sobbed.

"If only I had married a woman who appreciated that quality," he joked.

"I thought that because we were married we would try to make it work even if it looked as though everything was stacked against us. I'm sure that he's involved with someone else because he's incapable of making a decision like this on his own."

When we went to bed that night, Tom said, "Well, that's the end of those Wednesday-evening sessions with him watching football at the pub." And then he fell asleep. And that really seemed to be the extent of his regret. "Things change, people don't, life moves on, Lucy," he said the next morning. "And actually Cathy will probably be better off without him. He's never going to evolve."

❦

"Lucy, Lucy, come on, we're going to be late," Tom says, sweeping into the bedroom and putting on his jacket and a scarf.

As we close the front door behind us, I get that feeling of lightness that comes with assuming the rear guard for a few hours, and Tom, buoyed by similar thoughts, puts his hand out and I take it. Time alone is a precious commodity, and the thought of simply being, rather than doing, is a sensation that we both relish. For a few paces we walk along in silent harmony, and I feel a surge of optimism that my disturbed equilibrium could be restored if only we had more time alone together. For perhaps as long as a minute I reconnect with a time before children, when it was just Tom and me, when we could stay in bed on the weekends, read all the newspapers, and go on mini-breaks. Then I realize that the car has disappeared.

"Oh, God. I left it outside school this afternoon, because the boys wanted to walk home. I'm really sorry," I tell him, trying to anticipate how long I might pay for this infringement, a rough calculation that involves judging to what extent his forthcoming trip compensates for his absence to make introductions at the restaurant, a detail that he would consider important but not crucial. I decide on balance that the library in Milan favors me. And I am right. Time alone in harmony is a commodity he recognizes the value of.

"Don't worry, I'll run and get it, you start walking toward school," he says, setting off at a sprint that I know he'll find unsustainable after about a hundred meters.

I think about Polly doing her essay. Where has all the information gone that I retained during that intensive period from school to university. I wonder. Is it lost forever? For sure the decline began in the childbearing years, when whole new areas of specialist interest opened up. Strollers, for example. A few years ago, I could have written a long essay on strollers. Securing our first took longer than buying a car. It required more viewings than buying our house.

I remember a conversation in my office with a couple of male colleagues who were having babies at the same time I was pregnant with

Sam. Fed up with weekends spent in baby shops, baffled and befuddled by the sheer variety of strollers, we sat down together in a meeting room with various catalogs, hoping that between us we had collated and analyzed enough information to come to some conclusions. But after half an hour, we were still involved in hefty debate over issues such as weight, forward-folding designs versus collapsible options, sporty or rural. The statistical analysis required was beyond us.

Then, when Sam was born, medical expertise became the new priority. It became crucial to know exactly how to use a glass to distinguish between viral and meningococcal rashes; it was useful to know that digital thermometers gave readouts that were always slightly too high; and it was humbling to discover that the anti-inflammatory powers of savoy cabbages and frozen peas made them much more than vegetables. Now the specialist subjects have widened further. Schools top the list. The depth of knowledge required to dominate that particular area is worthy of a Ph.D.

I look up and see Tom running toward me, waving his arms.

"It's not there," he shouts.

"God, it must have been stolen again," I say. At least this time I know that I haven't lost the spare key.

"Are you sure that you left it at school? I'm going to go inside and ask Sam if he remembers," he says, immediately taking charge of the situation and running toward the house again. Within minutes he is running out again. There is something comical about all his rushing around, as though he is living life in fast-forward while I meander along on play and rewind, and I start to giggle.

"I don't know why you find this funny, we're three-quarters of an hour behind schedule," he shouts, this time in anger, because his face is so close to mine that there is no reason to raise his voice. "Sam says that you left it outside Starbucks." But the angrier he gets, the more I giggle.

"It's strange because as I was running back I saw a blue Peugeot on the corner of that street, but of course I didn't realize you had parked it somewhere completely different."

So we set off running together. Past the same trees and houses that I walk by every day on my way to school, waving to the nice man with the black Labrador walking in the opposite direction, noting that one of the streetlamps is broken, past the new Tesco metro, hurdling the legs of the homeless man who always sits outside.

Although our pace is evenly matched and we run in time, and to the people we pass on the pavement, there must be a satisfying physical symmetry in our movements, we could not really be farther apart. We do, however, find the car.

"Lucky this happened tonight and not on a school morning," I say.

"It's nothing to do with luck, Lucy, and everything to do with poor planning," says Tom.

I would like to continue the conversation we were having earlier, but I know that all my energies must now be invested in lifting the mood that has settled over the evening.

Tom drives silently, gripping the steering wheel in quiet fury, silence being the greatest punishment of them all. I am grateful that there is no moon tonight. I am grateful that we are going on ill-lit back roads through the underbelly of north London. Most of all, I am grateful for the fact that Tom is not in the passenger seat. All because the car is still in a state of unmade bed, and I am aware that the seat and I are as one because the chocolate buttons down the back are slowly melting and sticking to my coat, and that when I move, even with the gentlest movement, old crisp packets and bits of paper from school crackle underneath. I pick out a couple of apple cores from under the hand brake and hide them in my handbag when he turns right onto Marylebone Road.

The traffic is at a standstill. So slow that no one even bothers to use their horn. So slow that some people have switched off their engine and are standing around the three-lane highway, discussing what might have happened. There is no way forward and no way back. And neither of us wants to be the first to break the silence.

I am reminded of a journey home the previous summer from my brother's fortieth birthday party. I was driving on this same road and Tom had fallen asleep in the passenger seat minutes after we left Mark's house in west London. There was an inexplicable midnight traffic jam just off the Westway, and I was left alone to roam around conversations I had had with various people at the party.

Some way into the evening, Emma said that she wanted to tell me something and led me by the arm to a quiet corner in the corridor by the front door. I balked at her timing, because I was in the middle of a conversation with my brother about why the death of my father-in-law a couple of years earlier might have sparked Tom's mother's obsession with clearing out her house.

"It is probably a way of letting go," Mark said. "Every time she gives something away, she reviews all the memories that surround that object and then moves on. Either that or she is preparing for her own death."

"Well, that leaves a lot of scope," I said.

Then Emma came over. There had been some unfinished business between her and my brother years ago—I didn't want to know the details—and there was a brief but awkward exchange before she led me away.

"I've met this man," she said, her voice dropping to a whisper. "But you mustn't tell anyone, because he's married."

When Tom and I moved in together about a year after we first met, one of his first observations about the inner workings of my life was the magnitude of confidences that I inspired. Some men might have found this irritating, since it often involved long phone calls at inconvenient moments and bottles of wine over the kitchen table late at night. But Tom said that it was much more interesting than the kind of conversations he had with his friends, and wondered how the surfaces of people's lives belied what lay underneath. Coming from a family in which emotional honesty held no currency and was largely viewed with suspicion, this was a new world to him.

Emma explained how she had met this man at a dinner for executives from her news organization and a handpicked group of senior bankers. She told the story slowly and precisely, as if each detail was significant. It was quite different from the way she usually spoke about relationships, trying to downplay their importance by deflecting any serious questions with humor, and viewing any attempts at emotional engagement with distrust.

"I normally don't have any interest in these types. They don't actually have much to talk about beyond business. They work so hard, there's no space for anything else in their life, not even their family. He sat next to me, and we hardly spoke during the meal. It was as though we both knew it wasn't a good idea. At least that's what he said to me later. There was definitely a connection, not just a lust thing, because at that stage I hadn't really examined him closely. It was more a feeling of being drawn to someone."

"When they brought around the coffee, my mobile phone rang, so I bent down to get it from my handbag. At the same time, he knocked a spoon off the table onto the floor with his left hand, and as he tried to pick it up his finger touched my own—in fact, it was less than a touch, more the sensation of something brushing past, but I felt something inside me stir and so did he. We both knew as soon as we looked at each other. It was as quick and simple as that. Like an electrical current."

"That sounds amazing. Has he done this before?" She looked at me askance, because people always like to consider their own situation unique, so I bravely continued. "Tom has a theory," I told her, "that affairs happen not because people find each other attractive, because that happens all the time, but because people allow themselves to get into situations where they can thrive. And after you've done it once, it can become a habit that's difficult to break."

"Well, he certainly created the situation, because on Monday morning he phoned and asked me to go out for lunch. He didn't even pretend that we were going to talk about anything related to work. We didn't get beyond the first course, there was too much tension, and so we went to a hotel in Bloomsbury. In the lift on the way up, we stood apart. I don't think we even talked. He locked the bedroom door behind us, and that was the first time we had touched since we met at the dinner."

"How did you know about the hotel?" I asked.

"Lucy, you always have such an offbeat line of questioning," Emma said. "But to sate your curiosity, I had been there before. He hadn't, and judging by his paranoia about his wife finding out, I really think this is the first time he has played away. You can tell men who make a habit of it. Anyway, it was amazing, all-consuming. We've met every day since then. And we've talked a lot more."

❧

As we sit in traffic I think about the prospect of a trip alone to a pub with Sexy Domesticated Dad looming on Monday evening and I realize that, actually, I don't really want to go. Although my more recent musings over Sexy Domesticated Dad have evolved into the kind of daydreams that you don't share with friends, involving, as they do, tussles in alleyways in Soho, where having sex in the street is more common than in the suburbs, they remain a fantasy. I decide I am dealing with my inner toddler, having a tantrum over something I can't have and then rejecting it out of hand when it is offered to me on a plate. It dawns on me halfheartedly that having a fantasy does not necessarily mean that you want it to become a reality. I know I am probably ahead of myself at this point, because there is no earthly reason why I shouldn't be able to go out for a drink with one of the parents from school without it being any more than a simple social engagement. A drink and perhaps more banter about his book, and how exactly he is going to help me in my imminent role as class rep.

Part of my petulance is because as far as Sexy Domesticated Dad is concerned, it was I who made the first move in sending the enigmatic text. "And then what?" It is strange how the juxtaposition of three innocuous words can amount to something approximating a proposition. As the facts stand, he will be looking to me to manage the situation, since I was the one who created it.

There is no way of getting out of it without making it look as though I am turning down the invitation because of doubts over the spirit in which it is intended. I am pretty certain that his suggestion amounts to no more than a friendly gesture. And therein lies the rub. I realize with sudden clarity that I don't really want to become friends with Sexy Domesticated Dad, because to do that will detract from the possibility of the fantasy.

Apart from old male friends, it is years since I have done anything on my own with a relative stranger. In fact, apart from sleeping, I have probably spent no more than four hours alone at any given stretch since I gave up work. Really, I shouldn't be allowed out on my own at all. With Fred starting nursery and the eldest two at school most of the day, it is becoming apparent that I need to rejoin the adult world and relearn basic social codes.

"By the way, my mother has said she will babysit for you on Monday night so that you can go to your school meeting. She's going to come and spend the day with you and stay the night," says Tom, shattering the silence. The deadlock is broken.

"Great," I say, "thanks for sorting it out."

"You aren't planning to be out too late, are you? You know how she worries that she might fall asleep and then not hear the children if they wake up."

"No, I might go for a drink with some of the mothers afterward. Just to be friendly," I say. "Right now, I think I should call Cathy and warn her we're going to be late."

"Good idea," he says.

Over the years, I have become an expert in domestic shorthand. This involves swift and exquisite analysis of situations where it is incumbent to be economical with the truth to protect harmony and deflect arguments. So I do not consider my response to be a lie, but more a partial truth. A gray area.

"I still can't really understand why you want to do this class-rep thing, Lucy. I never saw you as the committee type, and, to be perfectly honest, I don't think your great strength is organization," he says, tapping the steering wheel with his fingertips.

"What do you think are my great strengths, then?" I say.

"I think you are a wonderful mum, maybe a little short-tempered sometimes, but always there for your children. And on those rare occasions when we are both awake at the same time and there are no children in our bed, I still really like having sex with you," he says, looking straight at me. "And you're good at drawing." I'd forgotten that one.

Then he decides to put on a CD. I feel the blood coursing through my veins, because I know the CDs are all muddled up. He picks up an album by The Strokes and finds *Best of the Mr. Men* inside.

"I'm not going to say a thing," he says.

"When I take a CD out to put another one in, I generally put the one I have taken out in the case belonging to the one that I have just put in," I explain, in an attempt to derail a potential crisis.

"Why don't you put it in the right one?" he says.

"Well, because that one has got the one that I took out to put the new one in," I say. He looks confused.

"Fish in a tree, how can it be," he mutters, quoting Fred's favorite line from Dr. Seuss.

"Coldplay will be in the *Goblet of Fire* case, because that is what it replaced," I say. And I am right.

"So where is the *Goblet of Fire*?" he asks.

"In *The Best of Bob Dylan*," I say confidently.

"And where is *The Best of Bob Dylan*?" he says. "Actually, I don't want to know. It's a bit like playing 'I packed by bag.' "

"Exactly," I say. "There is a logical system. It just requires a little reverse psychology. Tell me what you are looking for, and I will be able to find it."

"David Gray, *White Ladder*," he says. I think for a moment.

"That will be in *The Lion, the Witch and the Wardrobe*." And it is.

This could have been much worse. He is lining up cases on the dashboard and putting piles of CDs on his knee. But it is good displacement activity when stuck in a small space, unable to go out for dinner because of a traffic jam on a Friday night. I look at the clock. It is almost twenty to ten. We have been here for three-quarters of an hour. And, actually, I think we are behaving pretty impeccably.

Tom peers out the front windshield as the driver of the car in front switches on his engine. Then other people start to wander back to their vehicles. As mysteriously as it knitted together, the complex web of cars packed bumper to bumper as far as the eye can see unravels, and everyone slowly drives away back to the drama of their own existence.

"Shall we go home?" he asks tiredly. "By the time we get to the restaurant, they'll be shutting down the kitchen."

So I call Cathy again to deliver what I anticipate is further bad news. Blind dates are a thorny enterprise at the best of times, and at least if we had been there, we could have filled in the silences.

"I'm so sorry, Cathy, I know we're really landing you in it, the traffic was dire. We've been at a standstill for the past hour and we might as well head home," I say. "Hope it hasn't been too torturous with Tom's architect."

"Look, it's fine. In fact, it's better than fine," she says. "In fact, it's so fine, it's probably a good thing that you're not here. There's a lot of heavy flirting, and it would be embarrassing to have witnesses. He's in the loo at the moment, and we're about to go to Soho House together."

"That's great, just as well we didn't come, then. So what's he like?" I ask.

"Great. One of those coke-and-pope types," she says.

"Sounds very wholesome, apart from the caffeine, of course," I say.

"Lucy, you need to get out more. What I mean is that he enjoys the party lifestyle but then gets guilty about it afterward. It's a heady combination. I've met these types before. Anyway, he's gorgeous—say a big thank you to Tom, won't you? Look, he's coming back. Don't call me too early tomorrow morning. I'll let you know what happens," she says.

"How's it going?" asks Tom, looking slightly worried.

"Fine. Better than fine. I think they are probably going to sleep together," I say.

"Well, there's an idea," he says. "It's been nice spending time alone, anyway."

"Not what I'd describe as quality time," I say. "I mean, a night out in the shadow of the Westway is not what I'd choose."

"No, but I feel as though we have reconnected. Sometimes it feels as though you are drifting away from me, Lucy, into an impenetrable world of your own. By the way, I think you should text Cathy and tell her not to sleep with him on a first date."

"That's a bit hypocritical, isn't it?" I say.

7

"The bread never falls but on its buttered side."

I never appreciate Tom more than when he is away. Without him, the domestic pressure cooker is perpetually pitched at the boiling point. I miss his ability to simultaneously pour cornflakes and milk into bowls at breakfast, the way he lines up three coats, each with a packed lunch on top, by the front door, and his uncanny ability for locating my keys. Today it is the latter that I miss most.

Tom left for Milan very early this morning and, as instructed, reluctantly double-locked the door behind him.

"It is unfathomable to me that the same person who left her keys in the front door not once but twice this week can be so paranoid about early-morning break-ins," he said, whispering in my ear as he bent over the bed to kiss me good-bye. "Good luck with the vote. If you win, at least you will have scored so many points that the school has to let Fred through the door." Then he reconsidered. "Of course, if you are a disaster, the reverse might prove true. There's a good incentive."

At ten past eight, ten minutes before the usual deadline, I line the children up by the front door, feeling quite self-congratulatory. Not bad. Library books. Check. Shoes. Check. Coats. Check. House keys. Nowhere to be found. At the outset, I refuse to panic. After all, it seems thus far in the day that the augurs are favorable. I search in the usual places: coat pockets, handbag, kitchen drawer. They yield nothing. "Don't forget to look in the fridge," Joe shouts downstairs. "That's where they were last time, Mum, remember?" The fridge is bare.

"Maybe you should look in your hippocampus," says Sam. "That's where your memories are stored."

"How do you do that?" I ask, suitably impressed.

"We need to open up your brain," he says.

I make the children turn out their pockets and question Fred closely, because he is the natural culprit. He looks down at his feet and shuffles them guiltily. The children follow me downstairs into the kitchen and I tip the rubbish bin out over the floor in case he has disposed of them there. It wouldn't be the first time.

The smell is overwhelming. The stench of rancid meat and the sickly sweet smell of rotting fruit compete for supremacy. The children put their hands over their mouths and stare in shocked silence at the sight of their mother scrabbling though the detritus of the past few days, shaking a malodorous chicken carcass upside down in case the keys are stuck inside, sorting through moldy bits of bread and fruit that disintegrate in my hands. I hold my breath for as long as I can and then run over to the stove, exhale, and then breathe in again and return to the fray. My hands are covered in damp tea leaves from a broken tea bag.

"Do you know that in poor countries, children pick through rubbish on enormous dumps, looking for bits to sell and food to eat?" I say, looking up at the three pairs of eyes watching me. "We are very lucky." They don't look convinced.

"Mummy, can I ask you something?" says Sam. "When we die, can we all be buried in a mausoleum, like the Egyptians, then we can always be together?"

"Sam, that's a very interesting concept. Do you mind if we talk about it later?" I say.

"Then we could make a special place for the keys," suggests Joe.

I stop the search and sit for a moment on my haunches, the bits of rubbish scattered around me like some sort of still life. I have to face up to the realities of the situation.

My house keys are lost, and because Tom has double-locked the door, I am incarcerated inside with the children. I say it several times, out loud, like a mantra, holding the sides of my head, hoping for divine intervention.

In desperation, I phone Cathy for advice. "Climb out the sitting-room window," she says. "Phone the school and tell them you are going to be late, because you have forgotten something. That is credible. This isn't. Don't elaborate—that's always a giveaway."

"What happened with the architect?" I ask. "Just the abbreviated version." I have resisted phoning her for two days.

"We went back to his flat and I ended up spending the whole weekend with him, but I am feeling dreadful today. I don't think I've slept more than about eight hours the past three nights, all chemically fueled. Also, I'm worried about having er, exotic sex on a first date." There's one detail I won't pass on to Tom, who, through the weekend, was still pontificating on the benefits of abstinence for the first month.

"I'll give you the gory details later," Cathy says.

"Actually, I think I've heard enough already," I say, retrieving the spare car key from the kitchen drawer.

The children are very excited to receive orders to climb out through the sitting-room window, this being exactly the sort of game usually outlawed by parents. I hope that no one is watching, particularly opportunistic burglars, because I have to leave the window open until I come back from Fred's nursery. The same goes for the neighbors, who have children at the same school, because this is not behavior befitting a highly organized stay-at-home mum who is about to be elected to play an important role in the running of the school and by definition a minor role in the future of education in this country. I'm never more than one step behind the bigger picture.

"This is better than *Mission Impossible*, Mum," says Sam, sliding through the narrow gap at the bottom of the window down onto the grass. They stand in the front garden, all holding hands, because they sense this is one of those rare occasions where family really needs to pull together, and watch me struggle to slide through to the other side. I have pulled my shirt and T-shirt up around my ribs in order to reduce the area

around my middle. I wriggle through in slow bursts, stopping periodically to suck in my stomach.

"We should have rubbed butter around your tummy, Mummy," says
Sam, pulling my arms. "I've seen them do that on *Blue Peter*."

"To get mummies through windows?" asks Joe.

"No, to help beached seals off the coast of Scotland," Sam says
thoughtfully, as I scramble through into the flower bed.

Feeling elated at my cool head in a crisis, I agree to play *Best of Bond*
theme tunes very loudly in the car on the short journey to school. We will
hardly even be late. At around fifty meters from the playground, my luck
runs out and the car grinds to a halt in the middle of "The Man with the
Golden Gun." We are stranded. The gas gauge is on empty. Traffic starts
to back up from the front and behind. I have one of those out-of-body
experiences, where I feel as though I am an observer watching someone
else's life.

"Mum, you can't pretend this isn't happening," says Sam, sensing what
is going on. So I phone Tom on my cell phone and coolly explain the situation to him.

"What do you expect me to do about it? I'm on my way to Milan," he
yells down the line.

"What would you do in this situation?" I plead.

"I wouldn't be in it," he says.

Impatient drivers, including Yummy Mummy No. 1 two cars back,
start hooting rhythmically. I get out of the car, pointedly open the Peugeot's hood, and start poking around the engine. "Must be a flat battery,"
I shout to no one in particular. "Anyone got any jump leads?"

I would be good in a war zone. I would be great doing front-line medical interventions. I would be brilliant at dealing with natural disasters. I'm
just not good at the small stuff, I think to myself, as I take a few plugs off
the engine and clean them with a duster. Unfortunately, it is these small
details that now define my life. I search in my pockets for something that
might qualify as a sharp object, because at this particular juncture, pierc-
ing the engine is an option I am considering. Anything to avoid admitting
that I have run out of gas.

Sexy Domesticated Dad appears, strolling down the road, away from school. His arm is out of plaster. "Got a problem?" he says, coming over to peer into the engine, walking like a cowboy in that way that urban men do when they sense a rare chance to show off manly qualities. He is even wearing a plaid shirt. This is northwest London, not Brokeback Mountain, I want to say. Words like gasket, spark plug, and carburetor trip off his tongue. But his hands remain firmly in the pockets of his jeans, which are so loose that I can spot a hint of gray underpant spewing out the top. We both peer under the hood.

Yummy Mummy No. 1 joins us the other side, leaning over the engine to reveal perfect cleavage, firm but not pneumatic.

"That's unnatural," I say, unthinkingly.

"What is?" says Sexy Domesticated Dad.

"Lucy, I will say just three words," Yummy Mummy No. 1 replies, staring straight at me over the engine. "Rigby and Peller."

"Is that a law firm?" says Sexy Domesticated Dad, looking puzzled. He seems unmoved by the view. Then he starts to get down and dirty, pulling rubber caps off bits of the engine. I'm still unconvinced that he knows what he is doing, but at least he is offering good cover. He passes something oily to Yummy Mummy No. 1. Her perfectly manicured hands are smeared with grease.

"It's a bit like one of those Micheline Arcier paraffin-wax oil treatments," she says, looking down at them dubiously.

Alpha Mum approaches. She is trying to twist her features into an expression of faux sympathy, her eyebrows furrowed and her mouth slightly open, but she can't smother her underlying smugness. "Oh, poor you," she says, looking up and down the road at all the traffic. "Of course, you live so close that you could easily walk."

"But then you can't wear high heels," says Yummy Mummy No. 1, clicking the heels of a pair of Christian Louboutin boots together in irritation.

"How do you drive in those?" asks Alpha Mum.

"I don't. I wear a pair of cashmere slippers and put the boots on when I get here," says Yummy Mummy No. 1.

The headmistress appears to investigate the noise and general chaos, and begins to order cars to reverse back down the road in both directions. "Hello, Mrs. Sweeney," she says. "I recognize your car from the other day."

"What are you doing, Mum?" yells Sam, winding down the window. I have forgotten that the children are in the car.

"I've found the keys to the house hidden down the back of the seat. That's good, isn't it?" yells Joe from the other window.

"Wonderful, darling," I shout.

The road is filled with the sound of "Nobody Does It Better." "Say, 'Baby you're the best,' " Joe shouts back.

"What helpful children," says Alpha Mum drily. I can tell she is making a mental inventory of these incidents.

"Turn the music down, we can't hear ourselves think," I shout in forced jolly fashion.

"But you don't need to think, you just need to go and get a can of gas from the garage," insists Sam, who is nothing if not rational.

They all stop in their tracks. "You mean you've run out of gas?" says Sexy Domesticated Dad, holding his head in his oily hands.

"This is exactly the kind of thing I was talking about," says Alpha Mum, her voice laced with sarcasm. "It would be disastrous to have her as class rep. Unsafe."

"Look, I'll take the children into school," says Sexy Domesticated Dad.

"Thank you," I mumble as Sam and Joe cheerfully climb out of the car.

"And I'll take you to the garage," says Yummy Mummy No. 1.

"And I'll organize people to push the car into a space on the side of the road," says the headmistress.

"And I will go and plan my victory speech for tonight," says Alpha Mum, walking away, nose in the air, leaving the rest of us standing in the street.

"Well, you still get my vote," says Yummy Mummy No. 1, as I bundle Fred into a car seat in the back of her vehicle. "School life would certainly be a lot less boring with you in charge." It's one of those double-edged compliments, but I am too busy absorbing the full range of activities in the back of the car to mind. First of all, there are television screens on the back of the seats and a range of DVDs, each stored in the correct case, in a small compartment at the back of the hand brake. Also, on the back of each seat is a transparent storage unit with pockets in various shapes and sizes. One contains pens. Another paper. Then there are age-appropriate books. It is all straight lines and symmetry. Very pleasing to the eye. "It's more Piet Mondrian than Tracey Emin, I think," she says, smiling at me as I climb into the front beside her. "Actually, it's all my nanny's work."

I shut the door and there is silence. It is like entering another universe—even the air smells different. I breathe in deeply and shut my eyes. It's not even nine o'clock.

"It's a mixture of rosemary and lavender," she says. "I get them made up specially to suit my different moods. This one is called Cup of Aromatic Tea on the Road to Marrakech." I snort with laughter, but she isn't joking.

She then hands me a Bach Rescue Remedy from the glove compartment. If she produced a pot plant or plate of sugared jellies from that Aladdin's cave I wouldn't blanch.

"Although, I don't think there is any known antidote to that woman," she says.

Then we drive to the garage, I buy a can of gas, and she drops me off back by the car. It is quite simple, really. If only I had someone to organize me, it could all be so different.

⊙⊙

Later that day, I repair to the bathroom to prepare myself for the evening ahead. I consider how this morning's disaster might impact events. On the one hand, it has given ammunition to Alpha Mum's whispering campaign, not that there was any need for more anecdotal evidence of my perceived incompetence. On the other, it makes me human, a quality that is distinctly lacking in her.

When Tom is away, it is my turn to wallow in the bath. I have spent so long soaking in the lavender oil that Yummy Mummy No. 1 kindly handed to me this morning, saying, "Your need is greater than mine," I feel as though it has impregnated my skin and that if I were to sweat, it would be sweet instead of salty. Downstairs, my mother-in-law, Petra, is tending to the children.

Tom has arrived in Milan. He sounded bright and cheerful on the phone when we spoke as I was running the bath. He had made a site visit, and contractors had finally begun digging the foundations for his library. He told me that he was reading a short story by an Argentinian writer that one of his colleagues had given to him. "It's very exciting because it's about the idea of a library being a universe made of interlocking hexagons, and that is how I have conceived the building."

I made an effort to follow that analysis, partly because I hadn't heard Tom so enthusiastic about a project for ages, but mostly because it might prove useful in conversation with Sexy Domesticated Dad.

"Has it been made into a film?" I asked hopefully.

"No," said Tom, clearly surprised by my sudden attentiveness. "It's a short story, and the main character is a library. Anyway, good luck with it all tonight, Lucy, if you are sure that is what you want," he says.

I am momentarily unnerved, thinking that he is referring to the drink with Sexy Domesticated Dad, and I don't know what to say.

"Look, I'm sure that whatever happens, it will be memorable," he says. "Must go now, we're going to raid the minibar before dinner."

Whenever I start to worry about what lies ahead, I put on the hot tap with my foot until it becomes so unbearable that any worries dissipate. My skin is shriveled, and the stretch marks on my stomach become so red that I take on the mottled quality of a melted Stilton. I disowned my stomach long ago, confining it to a twilight existence, forever banished from the public eye. I now understand why old ladies used to enshroud themselves in complicated undergarments with zips and ties to imprison unruly elements.

My breasts bob underwater with pleasing elasticity. I regard them as reliable old friends, trustworthy allies who can be called upon on special occasions to engender confidence and feelings of youthfulness but perhaps are a little unwilling to accept any loss of status over the years. The rest of my body is in a state of rebellion, always threatening to break away from me. It would take years to suppress those revolutionary elements, to rein them in and bring them under my control. A more likely scenario is a slow erosion of my authority. Occasionally, I struggle to regain the upper hand and lose a few pounds, but to stamp out the soft edges would require a degree of self-control that I simply don't have.

When I emerge from the bath and glance at Tom's electric clock, I realize there is less than half an hour to get ready and get to school. The electric clock looks lonely and abandoned sitting on the bedside table on its own, rejected in favor of the battered metal clock with a rabbit's face and frayed ears that Tom took with him. There is a shiny oval space amid a sea of dust where it usually stands, and I imagine it incongruously installed in a minimalist hotel room in Milan. Tom will never think to hide it in the wardrobe when his colleagues come to his room. They will most likely conclude it is sweet for a middle-aged man to be traveling with an alarm clock belonging to his eight-year-old son. Especially those young single women he mentioned the other night.

It is one of life's great puzzles that the equation of men plus children invariably amounts to something greater than the sum of its parts, enhancing the qualities of both parties, whereas the juxtaposition of women plus children generally leaves you in arrears. It is mostly aging, unsexy, and messy.

It might sound ingenuous, but I have never worried that Tom might be tempted to stray during such a trip. To ponder on such eventualities seems a hopeless indulgence, when there are so many more immediate worries to focus on. Besides, he is generally so absorbed by the project in hand that anything extraneous is viewed as an unwanted distraction. The devil is in the detail, he always says. Plans need to be fine-tuned, taking into account the opinions of structural engineers and clients, whose desires are all too often diametrically opposed. He is never more impassioned than when he is involved in a big municipal project like this. A few years ago, double-story glass extensions and loft conversions afforded similar satisfaction, but for an architect like Tom, size definitely matters, and now nothing less than a whole house really holds his attention.

I wish the daily rhythm of my own life afforded me similar satisfaction. Perhaps a little responsibility will engender a renewed sense of purpose.

Three minutes have elapsed, and I need to reach a conclusion about what to wear. The floor is covered in clothes, and the black long-sleeved V-neck top that was first to be tried and is now my favored option has gone missing. I crawl around the floor wearing a black bra and knickers until I find the elusive top under the bed, pull on the jeans that I was wearing earlier, and decide to put on makeup on the way to school.

Petra calls up: "Lucy, you're going to be late." I come down the stairs two at a time and she stands reproachfully at the bottom with the three boys. She disapproves of her daughter-in-law going out at night without her husband, even if it is for a school meeting. I'm glad I didn't put on any makeup.

"Would you like me to try and marshal that laundry?" she asks. "I'm going to iron a few of those shirts, too. What does Tom do if there isn't a shirt ready for him in the morning?"

"Well, he either does it himself or, if time has really run out, he has been known to buy a new one on the way to work," I say unthinkingly. "And actually it would be great if you could tame the laundry pile. I can't remember the last time I saw the bottom of the basket."

"Lucy, I think you might find that if you elect a day for washing and a day for ironing, all your problems would be resolved," she says. An interesting theory but not one likely to be put into immediate practice, I think to myself.

"She's got a point, Mum," says Sam, trying to be helpful.

"I'll stay tomorrow morning, if you like, and help you sort it out," she says, opening the front door and pushing me out into the cold night air. "Good luck. I think it's laudable that you're going to take on new responsibilities, although I'm a little concerned that you are overextending yourself."

I decide to drive, partly to prevent me from drinking when I go out with Sexy Domesticated Dad but also because the car has a mirror that I can use to put on a quick sweep of mascara and lipstick when the traffic lights are red.

I walk through the heavy front door of the school behind other parents from our year and stop in the hall to look at some self-portraits by the children in Joe's class and find the one that he has done. I am struck by the fact that, unlike the other children, who have painted heads that are disproportionally large to the small stick bodies with flaying limbs underneath, Joe's self-portrait is tiny, probably half the size of the others. The detail is astonishing, however—there are freckles, teeth, and nostrils, hundreds of curly, pencil-drawn hairs on his head, red lips, and even a small mole that he has on his chin. But the head is tiny. What could this mean, I wonder? It must be related to his fears about shrinking. He isn't significantly smaller than the children in his class. I must speak to his teacher and maybe call Mark and ask him what he thinks. Children aren't his specialty—he hasn't any of his own yet—but he never resents a meander around the subconscious of his nephews.

My phone beeps and I open up a text message from Emma, requesting an urgent conversation about a new imbroglio in her overcomplicated love life. She has obviously forgotten the significance of the evening for me, which is a little galling, since she was present when Cathy added a whole new stressful layer to an already difficult moment.

"You know I am poised to become a pillar of the community," I whisper into my phone, warning that a long chat is out of the question in my newfound role as respectable mother of three.

"I'm really sorry, Lucy, I don't know how to handle this one," she whispers back. I imagine her standing in the corner of her office with her back to her desk. Although she has her own glass bubble, the door is always open, and she is convinced that journalists who are naturally adept at reading papers upside down on people's desks are also imbued with an innate ability to lip-read.

I retreat to the children's toilet through a door with a low brass handle at the far end of the entrance hall, ready for crisis talks. It is freezing. The windows are half-open, but it is not enough to overcome the potent smell of bleach and urine. The urine has the edge, I decide. I go into a cubicle with half-height walls to offer my best advice and sit on the edge of a tiny toilet, using my foot to keep the door shut. Outside, I can hear the other parents file into the classroom for the vote.

"Lucy, do you remember me telling you that Guy has these fantasies about having sex with two women?" Emma whispers.

"Is that the name of your banker?" I ask. She has never referred to him by name before. Another sign that their relationship is moving into a new phase. She ignores the question.

"He stopped talking about it for a while and moved on to sex in public places, but he's suddenly become obsessed again," she says.

"It is every male fantasy to have sex with two women"—I bend over further to whisper into my phone—"especially for a married father of four, but it doesn't mean that he actually will go through with it. You should never have agreed to do it, even in the heat of the moment."

"Well, I thought it was only that, a fantasy, and I was happy to go along with it," she says. "But he's called me to tell me that he's booked a girl that he's found on an Internet site to come around tonight. He's told his wife he's in Paris. He says that she's really gorgeous. What should I do?" She is utterly panicked. I think for a moment.

"Tell him that you had a Brazilian and it's given you a rash. That will win you time, and then gently let him down at a later date, unless of course you decide to reconsider," I say. And then, in case I look too prurient, "At the very least you should check out the girl. You might even fancy her. I'll call you later."

I click the phone off and sit for a moment to recover my composure. Then I hear rustling at the sink. I know immediately that there is someone else in the room with me. I hesitantly stand up to full height to peek over the half-height door. Not only am I not alone, but Sexy Domesticated Dad is removing his cycle helmet and cycling shirt to reveal the full glory of slightly tanned and toned midriff a mere two meters in front of me. Luckily, the shirt is over his head at the point at which I look over. I gasp involuntarily and my hand covers my mouth in shock, and then I duck back down behind the door again.

I decide to stand on the toilet with my legs bent so that he can't see my feet underneath. In less than a minute, my legs are aching so much that I have to put my clenched fist in my mouth and bite my knuckles in an effort to displace the pain emanating from my calves and upper thighs. I pray for redemption from this Lilliputian nightmare. I don't deserve this, I think to myself. I try to work out exactly when he came in. If I am lucky, and luck wouldn't seem to be on my side right now, it might have been at the end of my conversation with Emma.

I glance over the top again, meaning to duck down immediately, but he is in the middle of removing his cycling trousers to put on a pair of jeans. He is in fact standing there in the same pair of gray underpants that I glimpsed this morning. I look long enough to appreciate that all the cycling has given him strong, firm buttocks. I duck down again but the motion makes me fall from my perch in shock. Sexy Domesticated Dad comes over and warily pushes the door open.

"Lucy, for God's sake, what are you doing? Are you all right?" he asks, bending over me and grabbing my arm to pull me up. He is using his other hand to hold up his jeans and his shirt is completely undone and my face brushes his stomach as he hauls me out of the tight space beside the tiny toilet. It is a very intimate moment, but I feel nothing but fear and embarrassment. It is more short circuit than current or connection.

"I was practicing my victory speech," I say, brushing down my jeans and trying not to stare at his underpants.

"And it was so good, it knocked you sideways?" he says.

I breeze out of the toilet and walk outside into the playground to take much-needed air.

When I go into the classroom, the meeting is well under way and the only seat left is a children's chair in between Yummy Mummy No. 1 and Sexy Domesticated Dad. Eyes follow me as I slide into the seat, but I can't really see what is happening at the teacher's desk at the front of the room.

Sexy Domesticated Dad looks down at me with a nervous smile. "You've missed the vote, Lucy. She got in by a whisker. You've been nominated secretary, and I'm the treasurer," he says, looking worriedly at Alpha Mum. "She's terrifying."

Yummy Mummy No. 1 leans down to confirm that she voted for me. "Just for the fun value."

"Please, can I have the attention of all of you," says Alpha Mum, looking at us. "Lucy, you might want to take notes for the record," she says, passing me a pen and paper.

Then Sexy Domesticated Dad leans over to me and whispers, "Never mind, Lucy, I've heard cozy threesomes are a common male fantasy. Do you still want to go out for that drink? I really need one after all this."

"Stretch your arm no further than your sleeve can reach."

This is not the outcome I imagined. This is not the evening I imagined. Actually, this is not the life I imagined. When the meeting ends, Sexy Domesticated Dad makes a point of leaving the school alone. I am not unduly concerned, because I know he will be waiting for me somewhere in the street, so I lazily pick up my bag, chat with other parents, and make my way outside.

Somewhere along Fitzjohn's Avenue, I find him lurking underneath the branches of a ceanothus bush that had drifted from its plot in a safe suburban garden to sprawl in rebellious arches across the pavement. It's only up close that the light of the streetlamp highlights a pair of trousered legs and familiar Converse trainers underneath the branches, and I inwardly congratulate him on finding an evergreen shrub so willing to participate in our intrigue.

He steps out from underneath a branch and says, "Lucy Sweeney, I presume," and I laugh a little too eagerly, brought up short when I realize that his surname has completely escaped me. I know that it's a type of fish, but I can't recall which one.

"Robert Cod, Robert Haddock, Robert Hake, Robert Dory," I whisper to myself, trying out different possibilities. I know it is one caught in the North Sea.

"Robert Bass," he says to me. I am shocked to realize that I must have said some of this out loud. I pause for a moment.

"I'm illustrating a children's book," I hear myself say.

"That's very exciting."

"Those are the main characters, it's an allegory about the decline of fish stocks in the North Sea."

"Is there a baddie?"

"Crawford Crayfish," I say. "An American import." Then I fall silent. I am at once horrified and impressed by my ability to lie on demand. I know truth is subjective at the best of times, but nevertheless I am entering whole new realms of deception.

We stroll the short distance to a noisy pub that we remember walking past on the school run, exchanging a few platitudes along the way. I notice that both of us shrink into our coats and look shiftily down at our feet when a car passes. The pub is on a quiet residential street. There are benches and tables outside on the pavement. A couple of patient dogs of the long, hairy variety are tied to table legs with leather leads wound in complicated knots. They stand up to greet us hopefully. Robert Bass tentatively opens the door, and I know that he is doing a quick sweep of the room to check that there are no other parents from school. He seems well versed in the dark art of subterfuge.

The strands of a hundred conversations and nasal tones of an early Oasis song almost knock us backward. The last time I went into this pub, about six years ago, it was an unappealing blend of grubby carpet and beige walls with a generous coating of yellow nicotine on top. If you scraped your finger down the flock wallpaper, it left a white trail behind. A cloud of smoke hung permanently at ceiling level, and the benches that followed the outline of the wall were covered with long, lumpy cushions. It was all roll-ups, red tops, and scampi fries.

Now wooden floors have replaced the ugly brown carpets with brash geometric patterns. There are hard benches and straight-backed wooden chairs. The bar serves olives, cashews, and chips made from vegetables. It is pared-back and simple but much less cozy. The demise of soft furnishings means noise has nowhere to go. It bounces from one hard surface to another like an echo chamber. People, even those under thirty, cup their ears to hear conversations.

I spot a couple leaving from a small, round table in the corner and lead the way to a bench that might have spent the previous couple of centuries in a small country church in East Anglia. It is as out of place as we are. The back has carved figures of saints wearing robes, with carefully sculpted folds that dig painfully into the back of our heads. It is shallow, narrow, and deeply uncomfortable, and it compels us into immediate physical intimacy. We rest against each other like a couple of old trees who over the years have been forced into a relationship of unwanted physicality to prop each other up. The only problem is that once we are in this position, we can't move. When he crosses his legs, I lose balance and lean toward the table, and when I bend forward and move my shoulder away from his, he lurches into the vacuum.

Robert Bass says that he hardly ever goes to pubs because he can't stand the smoke. I concur, using my foot to push the packet of John Player firmly to the bottom of my bag. In fact, it has evidently been so long since either of us has been in a pub that we sit for a while, just staring.

"I suppose we could tell Alpha Mum that we're not going to be involved," I say, while scrutinizing a coaster. "It's all too absurd. She's one of those women who should never have given up work, she's got far too much restless energy."

"Actually, the headmistress cornered me afterward and said, completely off the record, of course, that she would be very grateful if we would do this so that we can 'curb the excesses'—her words, not mine," explains Robert Bass, building a complicated structure with the coasters on his side of the table. "She said it would be an exercise in damage limitation. She voted against her. She wanted you."

"So we have to go through with it?" I say, trying not to sound hopeful.

"Yes," he says. "She's called a meeting at her house next week to decide about the Christmas party. Perhaps we could go together." He is smiling slightly, a half-smile, with his lower lip pushed out as though he is trying to stop himself from laughing. I don't dare to look at him because there are too many undercurrents and if I stare into his eyes I might get pulled under. Instead, I start to tear the corners off a coaster. I know that he is watching me and can feel the heat of his face burning the side of my left cheek. To turn toward him requires little more than a twenty-degree rotation of the head. Quiet movements are sometimes much more significant than grand gestures, especially when they involve married folk. I look around and meet his gaze, and we stare at each other without saying anything for a little too long. Then we both start to speak at once.

"I think that if we both lean forward at the same time, we could take off our coats without one of us falling over," he says. And so we rid ourselves of layers of thick coats and scarves, and I know that when we sit back, our bare arms will touch and then anything could happen.

"I think I should go and get us a drink," I say. He says that he has to phone up his au pair to warn her that he will be late back. His wife is still at work. "She is hardly ever home before ten o'clock, and she is out the door again by seven-thirty the next morning. Sometimes I don't see her for days and we communicate by e-mail and notes left around the kitchen," he says. There is no trace of bitterness. It is a statement of fact. A proper postmodern virtual relationship.

The coaster lies in tatters on the small table. It has been split in half, torn into tiny pieces that flutter onto the floor when people walk by. I remember other times, long ago, when shredding coasters into tiny jigsaws became a useful displacement activity during difficult conversations.

I get up to walk over to the bar and decide that I won't phone my mother-in-law. She is probably already in bed, because despite all her protestations that she never sleeps until we get home, we have never yet found her awake on the rare occasions that we have missed our curfew, and besides, a phone call to reiterate what I have already said, even if it involved the tiniest change to the agreed plan, is liable to provoke a disproportionate reaction.

I struggle through the crowd at the bar to create a space for myself at the front and then wait there like the hopeful dogs outside. I bob up and down, stand on tiptoe, wave, and then perch on the brass rail that runs around the bottom of the counter, gaining about half a foot in height. But I am still invisible.

A girl comes up beside me. She looks about twenty and is wearing a silver minidress and knee-high boots without any tights even though it is winter. Her long, dark hair is draped around her face in a way that looks relaxed but probably took a long time to achieve. The barman immediately comes over and takes her order. Beside me, a man is having a conversation on a cell phone and ordering drinks at the same time. I glance back toward Robert Bass, and he looks at me with a quizzical expression. I shrug my shoulders and continue with my quest, standing at the bar, thinking about the last time I ripped up coasters with such passion in a pub.

How is it that I cannot manage to assemble even the bare bones of what happened yesterday, and yet something that occurred more than a decade ago returns to mind with such a wealth of detail? It was exactly eleven years ago. Tom and I had recently moved into a flat in west London together. I was coming home from work one night in the early days of this new arrangement, at about eleven o'clock, and I was slightly drunk. Actually, I was earlier than usual. I had to get up the next morning to go to Manchester, so my colleagues had pushed me into a cab and told me to get an early night. Tom had said that he was going out with friends. Nothing specific. Our lives were so busy that we sketched the outlines and filled in the details later.

When I reached our road, it was blocked by a police car. There had been a holdup near the Uxbridge Road, and we were directed down a parallel street. So I shouldn't have been there at all. But as we maneuvered slowly down this road, I saw a couple kissing. The man was half-sitting on a low wall outside a small terrace house, and he had pulled the woman between his legs so that their upper bodies were pressed against each other, pushing back into a hedge that was growing behind the wall. I knew, even before I saw the man's face, that it was Tom. There was a familiar economy of movement in the way one of his hands was drifting up and down the woman, a finger lingering to trace small circles on the nape of her neck and then drifting around to the front of her V-neck T-shirt. She leaned back in pleasure and he kissed her.

I told the taxi driver to stop, because I needed to make a phone call. This was in the early days of mobile technology and the phone was so big that it hid most of my face. I shrank down in the back of the taxi and called Cathy.

"It's me," I whispered, even though there was no possibility that Tom could hear me.

"Are you all right, Lucy?" she said, because I had paused.

"Fine, I think. I'm sitting in a taxi, watching Tom getting quite intimate with another woman, very intimate, actually, if you consider that he is in full public view less than a hundred yards from our flat as the crow flies. . . ."

"Lucy, cut to the chase. Tell me exactly what you can see," she demanded.

"Well, I can see him kissing a woman. At least, it's a woman, I suppose, because the alternative would be too awful, because I think that women can be properly bisexual but men who swing both ways are definitely gay, although there are exceptions. . . ."

"Lucy, I know it's hard, but please stick to the story," she said.

"Well," I started again, "I can see him kissing a woman with short, dark hair. She's wearing a denim miniskirt with buttons down the front, a little top, and flip-flops. There's not much left to the imagination. The downside is it's the kind of kiss that is definitely a prelude to something more intimate. On the upside, you only kiss people like that when they taste new and exciting, so it can't have been going on for too long. They're going into the garden of the house and I think they are behind the hedge. I can only imagine the rest."

"Are you sure that it's him? You know how shortsighted you are," she asked.

"Of course I am. I'm so close that if I opened the window and leaned out I could almost touch him."

"That's awful. What a shit, Lucy," says Cathy.

"The other thing is, apart from the fact that she is everything that I'm not, I think I recognize her," I said. "I'm fairly sure that she was at Emma's party the other weekend. I think she works with her."

"Did they talk at the party?" she asked.

"Well, I did notice him talking to the same woman for a while, but I didn't think anything of it."

"So what are you going to do? Do you want me to come over?"

"No, don't worry, I'll work something out, I wanted to tell you because it helps to absorb it. I'll call you tomorrow." I continued staring at the hedge for a few minutes, knowing that Tom and the woman were behind it. There was an overwhelming temptation to get out of the taxi and stand by the garden gate until they noticed me. But I knew, if I actually heard what was going on, I would replay the whole scene with sound incorporated, and there would be no going back from that. Overhearing someone have sex is much worse than watching it with the volume turned down. So this is what I did, although I never told anyone, because through the months that followed I played the role of aggrieved girlfriend with some aplomb, and I felt that I could hold everything together as long as I had a secret to sustain me.

Instead of going home, I told the taxi driver to take me back to work and wait outside for twenty minutes. Everyone was still drinking cheap wine in the greenroom, a tatty, tired, and airless function room in the basement below the studios. We ended up here every night after *Newsnight* finished, with guests who had come on to the program, eating flabby vol-au-vents and curled sandwiches that had been sitting around for hours. My colleagues weren't surprised to see me again, and one in particular I knew would be quietly pleased.

Since this man is now a relatively well-known filmmaker, it seems unfair to mention him by name. But incredible as it sounds now, at that time we were both senior producers at the BBC with one of those professional relationships that teetered between open competition and brazen flirtation. That evening had been particularly stressful. I had successfully delivered my tape about illegal immigrants found dead in the back of a lorry in Kent at ten twenty-eight, two minutes before the program was due to air, beating this man to the top news slot and earning myself rare and therefore very sweet praise from the lovely Jeremy Paxman.

I stepped back into the greenroom in a reckless mood, feeling strangely euphoric, although with hindsight I realize I was probably in a state of shock. The man came over to me and we resumed the conversation we had left hanging in the air less than an hour earlier. He was leaving the next day for a week in Kosovo. "I know it's probably a bit left field, Lucy, but you don't want to come home with me, do you?" he asked minutes after I reappeared. It was that simple. There was no preamble. We kissed and fumbled as best we could during the taxi ride home, aware that the taxi driver was watching in his mirror, and sneaked into his house so that his flatmates wouldn't see me. He had a girlfriend, whom he has subsequently married, but they weren't living together at the time.

We had sex several times. It was invested with all the passion of months of unrestrained flirting and the knowledge that it wouldn't ever happen again. Then he told me he thought he was in love with me, and I told him that he loved all women and that he would get over me quickly when he was reacquainted with his Kosovar translator. He looked taken aback, because he had forgotten that he had told me that, and I decided that was a good moment to call another cab home.

When I finally got back to our flat, Tom was in bed pretending to be asleep. His shirt lay neatly folded on the chair, and as I leaned over to sniff the collar I inhaled the sickly smell of Opium, the olfactory backdrop to so many relationships of the nineties. He greeted me effusively and then we ended up having sex. Neither of us asked where the other had been. I spent the next three weeks worrying that I could be pregnant, that Tom might not be the father, that someone would find out. I promised myself never to get into this kind of situation again, because, unlike Emma, who was often involved in love affairs with complicated shapes from triangles to hexagons, I couldn't carry it off. Monogamy suited me, I decided.

The next day I looked through Tom's pockets and found a phone number scribbled in childish handwriting on a piece of paper. It had the same prefix as Emma's number, so I called Emma, explained the situation, and she told me the woman's name. Joanna Saunders. She said that she worked on the commodities desk. And this is when I realized that it isn't difficult to hate someone you have never met.

Emma, who was already destined for greatness and a good few rungs higher up the ladder than Joanna Saunders, arranged for her to go out for lunch with me, saying I was a derivatives trader who might prove a good source for financial stories.

I came in the pub with a fixed smile that I had been practicing in a mirror on the way, and went and sat down opposite her at a small round table. Even before she gave me her hand and confirmed her name, I could smell the perfume. It made me feel sick. I cut to the chase, there being little need for small talk in these situations.

"I'm Tom's girlfriend," I said. I have never seen anyone look more astonished. Her face split into different bits, registering so many emotions in such a short space of time that I thought it might never reconfigure.

"There isn't much point in lying, because I saw you the other night, so tell me what's going on. I don't want to make a scene, and I'm sure you don't because there are a lot of your colleagues here," I said, waving to Emma on the other side of the room.

Joanna told me that they had met at Emma's party.

"I'm sorry, but that's not enough detail," I said.

"That was the first time we met," said Joanna Saunders. I found myself admiring her skin; it was pale and English, and her lips were plump and full as she sucked Diet Coke through a straw. Her hair was cut in a messy bob, and she kept pushing straggly bits away from her face. She was wearing a pea-green coat with a pink silk lining, and it took a lot of self-control to avoid asking where she had bought it.

"Did you know that he had a girlfriend?" I asked, gripping my glass of wine so hard that I thought it might break.

"Yes, he told me that you were living together and that you would probably get married," she said. That was unexpected.

"Have you slept together?" I asked.

"Yes," she said without looking up. "He called me up a few days after that party and we went out for a drink at a pub near my house and then he came back and stayed until about three in the morning." I tried to remember when that might have been and resisted the urge to get out my diary then and there to pinpoint it.

"How many times did you have sex?" I asked. Although it might seem masochistic, there was something reassuring in establishing all the facts, as though it might make sense of everything.

"I can't really remember," she said. "Do you really want to know all this?"

"Did you have sex the other night?"

"What are you talking about?"

"I saw you in the street just beyond the tube station," I said.

"No, we wanted to but the owners of the house interrupted us and Tom said he had to go because you were going to arrive," Joanna Saunders said. This time a more defiant look had entered her eye, the sort of look that a woman gives to another woman when she knows she is holding some of the cards.

Then I picked my handbag up off the floor, took out my cell phone, and called Tom.

"I've got someone here who wants to speak to you," I said, my tone giving away nothing as I passed the phone to Joanna Saunders, who was now very pale. "Speak to him."

"Hi Tom, I'm, er, having lunch with your girlfriend," she said. "I think you'd better come right now because I can't handle this."

About ten minutes later, Tom arrived at the pub from his office. Emma came over and kissed him hello and led him to the table where I was sitting with Joanna Saunders. I poured him a glass of wine from the bottle I was drinking.

"Lucy, I think we should talk about this somewhere else, on our own," he said, looking pale, knowing he was cornered.

"I think we should talk about it right here, right now. All the central characters are present," I said. "Besides, if you are ever tempted to have sex together again, this moment will always come to mind, and it will definitely temper your appetite, I think. Happy endings need good beginnings, and this wouldn't qualify."

Joanna Saunders shrunk back into her chair, and I sat there ripping up coasters.

"Lucy, I'm so sorry," Tom said, looking desperate. "It meant nothing. It was a moment of madness. It will never happen again." I remained silent. "You've been away filming so much. We've been drifting—don't tell me that you've never been tempted."

"I have, but I've never acted on it. That's the big difference. Infidelity has no gray areas." I think that was the biggest lie I had ever told, and I knew one day that I would have to pay for it. I just didn't want to settle the account right then. But the right moment to engage in such a confession never came up, and as time elapsed and everything returned to normal, it seemed ridiculous to rock the boat. Besides, I had grown accustomed to Tom trying to make amends. It is much easier to play the role of victim than villain. And if I hadn't had my greenroom moment, then perhaps I would never have forgiven Tom.

∞

"What do you want, young lady? Excuse me, do you want a drink or are you decorative?" says the barman. Then I remember, the key to getting served in a London pub is to look nonchalant, like you don't really care. No noise, just a few subtle hand gestures.

"One glass of wine and two pints of beer please," I say, pleased at my efficiency and wondering how long it has been since someone called me young lady.

"What kind of beer?" he asks, not unreasonably.

"What have you got?"

"Well since you ask, bitter, lager, or stout."

"What do most men order?" He looks at me blankly.

"Well, it's a question of taste. We've got Adnams, IPA, Stella, you name it we've got it. What does your boyfriend normally have?"

"He's not my boyfriend," I say frostily.

"Well, your husband then," he says, looking at the ring on my finger.

"He's not my husband, either," I say. He raises one eyebrow.

"Is he a lager man?" he asks patiently.

"I'm not sure what kind of man he is," I say, sighing. "Just give me two pints of that, please," I add, pointing to the closest tap.

So I return to the table holding three drinks against my chest, contemplating the moment when I will sit down and we will touch. Flesh against flesh. It is inevitable because the seat is so narrow. The anticipation is akin to staring at a delicious plate of food when you are really ravenous, holding out as long as possible for that first mouthful, knowing that no subsequent one will taste quite so good or be quite so satisfying.

"Thanks, that's very generous," he says.

I put down the drinks, walk around the table to the bench, and sit down, cross my legs, place my left forearm along the length of my thigh, and lean back, bumping my head against the sharp pointed foot of one of the little carved figures on the back. It is Saint Eustace, the patron saint of difficult situations.

Robert Bass is involved in sorting out his two beers. For a moment I worry that he is lining them up, checking the distances between each glass, in a way that reminds me of Tom. Not because Tom's manias bother me, but because I don't really want to think about him right now.

It looks like a serendipitous arrangement. Then I realize that actually he is moving them out of the way so that he can pick up the glass with his left hand. And I can gauge by looking at the slightly superior muscle tone in his right arm that he is definitely not left-handed. Which means that the ensuing combination of movements that leave his right arm parallel to my own is premeditated. I marvel at the subtlety of all this. There is a visceral need for contact to be made, as though we can only relax when we have crossed this hurdle. I can feel the heat radiating from his arm and am aware of the slightest motion. I can even measure the rise and flow of his breath. I wait for him to exhale because then the hair on his arm gently brushes the sensitive flesh of my lower arm and there is a sense of loss each time he breathes in and away from me.

Neither of us should be here. Now that I am sitting at this table, I know with absolute certainty that there is no space in a marriage that allows for late-night drinks with virtual strangers at a location that you have both agreed upon because you implicitly understand that there is little likelihood of bumping into anyone else that you know. I am in unchartered waters, recklessly swimming away from shore, but it's not an unpleasant sensation.

"So, how is the book going?" I ask, nervously pulling a thick strand of hair over my top lip to rub the tip of my nose, a habit that evolved years ago during revision for exams.

I must try and think of other subjects for general conversation, but at least this one guarantees a degree of loquaciousness.

"Don't ask," he says, looking down at his beer. "I've resolved the other crisis, but now I'm mired in a new one."

"So, what shape has this new crisis taken?" I ask.

"Are you really interested? I promise I won't be offended if you aren't," he says without waiting for me to respond. "I'm writing a chapter about how political upheaval in Latin America informed filmmaking in the eighties."

I remain silent because his arm is now firmly resting against my own and I worry that if I say anything he might move it. I wonder if he is as conscious of this proximity as I am. Yet he might be thinking about whether Arsenal has scored against Charlton tonight, or the aesthetic values of the handlebar mustache as worn by the central character in Zapata Westerns. Hot, crowded pubs suddenly seem filled with endless possibilities. I struggle to concentrate.

"There were also a few really well-known Latin American films like *The Official Version* that actually won Oscars, which I obviously need to mention. It was about a woman who discovered that the baby she had adopted had been stolen from a mother disappeared by the military. Then, of course, there were mainstream Hollywood hits like Oliver Stone's *Salvador,* which is particularly interesting, given U.S. involvement in Central America. My dilemma is whether to include analysis of how European and American filmmakers were also inspired by these same events, and their different cultural and political approaches to the same subject matter."

"Very interesting," I say distractedly. The air is heavy with silence again, and I decide to head for high ground and go back to the bar to buy some chips.

When I return, I notice that a stool has appeared on the other side of our table. I am already feeling proprietorial about the territory we have marked out as our own and wonder where it came from. Then I spot a familiar sheepskin coat lying on top.

"We're not alone," says Robert Bass.

Yummy Mummy No. 1 appears and sits down on the stool. I note that her bottom is so small that there is no overhang and that she is wearing a button-down white shirt that highlights her perfect cleavage.

"In answer to your question, I think that you should definitely include both, you'll widen your audience for the book, and given what's going on in Iraq at the moment, it would be a timely reminder of other U.S. foreign policy blunders," I say. What a great response. I feel proud of myself.

"I will, then," he says, smiling at me. "I needed someone to endorse what I was thinking. Thanks."

"A meeting of minds, I see," says Yummy Mummy No. 1, staring at our arms. "Well, this is fun. Very cozy."

I do my best to shift away from Robert Bass.

"I think I might order champagne," she says.

"I'm not sure they do champagne by the glass in pubs," I say. Although the pub might be a moderately hostile environment for us, we are at least capable of fading into the background. For Yummy Mummy No. 1, it is an entirely foreign affair.

She waves people over to try and order drinks and then offers the young girl in the silver dress a tip to take her coat to the cloakroom. I shrink with embarrassment.

"Actually, I was thinking about a bottle," she says excitedly. "I mean, I know, strictly speaking, there is nothing to celebrate, but perhaps we should commiserate in style."

She gets up to go to the bar.

"Safety in numbers, I guess," says Robert Bass.

"Not for the sheep," I say, pointing to the coat, and he laughs.

"She said that she was driving home and saw us going into the pub and decided on a whim to come and join us." He shrugs his shoulders.

"She was really rooting for you during the vote. When Alpha Mum said that you are the kind of person who would give a Snickers bar to a child with peanut allergy, she stood up and said that there are a lot of things that could be said about you, but no one could ever accuse you of being an inattentive mother, and that you had changed more nappies than she had eaten sliced bread," he says.

"Well, that's definitely true, because she's been on a wheat-free diet for years," I say. "What did you say?"

"Well, actually, I didn't say anything," he says.

I must look disappointed, because he adds, "I thought it might look as though . . ." Then he stops, and I stare at him, willing him to finish the sentence because otherwise I will spend the rest of the night and the next week trying to fill in the blanks. "I thought it might look as though I was . . ."

But like me, he is transfixed by Yummy Mummy No. 1. We watch in wonder as the crowd parts seamlessly to allow her passage to the front and a barman comes over instantly and asks for her order. They recognize an exotic creature in their midst. She comes back to the table empty-handed, and I commiserate.

"That nice man is sorting everything out," she says. And sure enough a few minutes later the barman solicitously comes over to the table with a bottle of champagne, which he flamboyantly opens, and a packet of cigarettes.

"I hope you don't mind me joining you. After that whole debacle, I really needed to unwind. Have you called your friend with the crisis back? We all owe her a drink. If you hadn't disappeared, it would have been a hung vote," she says.

Robert Bass shifts uncomfortably in his seat and a gulf opens up between our lower arms. It is impossible to gauge how much he has revealed, so I opt for a skeletal response.

"She's going to call me later," I say, trying to resist any further elaboration. Although Yummy Mummy No. 1 is one of those women who reveal only the most tangential details of her own life, she has this uncanny ability to inveigle other people into terrible indiscretion and then disapprove of their emotional incontinence.

She is not unfriendly. In fact, she is generally unerringly polite and attentive, although I suspect she has little interest in many of us. She is probably competitive, but I am neither rich, posh, nor thin enough to qualify as a legitimate rival. Nor am I sufficiently versed in the rules of engagement, which include complicated concepts such as wearing exactly the right proportion of Top Shop, designer, and vintage.

I couldn't say whether she is certain of the ground beneath her feet, because I don't really know much more about the machinations of her life now than I did when I first met her a year ago. There are few hints of a more complex interior dialogue. Maybe her life simply has an easy script. No bleak moments. No doubts.

I used to hang on to the few crumbs she threw my way, looking for clues that might reveal a dark crisis lurking within. But there were only so many questions that you could ask to calculate whether her need for ever more extravagant home improvements might reflect an inner crisis about the quality of her happiness.

Tonight, I notice that she has a large plaster and dressing on the palm of her left hand. Her hands are small and bony, almost childlike in their proportions, and the flesh has a translucent quality so that you can see the bone structure beneath the surface. They make you want to pick them up and stroke them.

"How did you do that?" I ask, hoping for clues that might hint at some hidden drama.

"It's slightly embarrassing," she says conspiratorially, and I lean forward toward her, because there is definitely the promise of intimacy.

"My husband has to go to Brussels for a couple of nights," she says, "so he took me out to dinner at The Ivy and while I was trying to sever a particularly stubborn joint on the leg of my lobster, the scissors slipped and cut open my hand."

She laughs loudly. I try to disguise my disappointment.

"How unfortunate," I say. "How was your day?"

"Busy, busy, busy," she says. Yummy Mummy No. 1, I notice, often repeats words three times, especially adjectives. It is a trait I have discussed with Tom. Although he conceded that such a tic could be an effective strategy to deflect questions, he was unwilling to analyze further.

"She's got a great arse, that is all I need to know about that woman," Tom had said.

"What exactly, exactly, exactly did you do?" I persist. Sexy Domesticated Dad suppresses a smile.

"I was rushing around all day, hitting deadlines, tying up loose ends, keeping all the balls in the air," she says, and then, when she sees that I am still dissatisfied, she continues. "I did a kickboxing class with the gorgeous personal trainer, had lunch with a friend, and then went to a flat that we have bought as a rental investment to check that the interior designer was on track."

This was more like it. Of course this woman has an enviable existence. Perhaps what Yummy Mummy No. 1 represents is the logical evolution of the 1950s housewife, I think to myself in a moment of sudden lucidity. She embodies all those old symbols of homemaking: Her house is immaculate; the sheets crisp and ironed; and rosy-cheeked children sit round the table eating home-baked meals. She simply pays other people to achieve the effect and watches it all happen around her. She is a spectator to her own life.

Delegation, that's what it's all about. And the small matter of sufficient income to support the lifestyle. Money can't buy you love, but it can buy you time and youth. Trips to the gym, forays to Selfridges, aromatherapy treatments. I would be good at that. Naturally, there would be some sacrifices. No more chocolate, for example. But it would be a small price to pay.

"So, did you call your friend back?" asks Robert Bass, turning round to face me again. "That was quite a conversation you were having. You make a lot of assumptions about married men." I move my arm swiftly away from his, annoyed with him for sharing the details of my conversation in the toilet with Yummy Mummy No. 1. Partly because it underlines a depth of friendship with her that I haven't really managed, but also because I know the vicarious pleasure she will get from accessing the grimy undercarriage of someone else's life. Then I start to wonder whether her arrival was all part of a plan instigated by him to avoid spending time alone with me.

"Actually, it's a complicated situation," I say, trying to steer the conversation back into safe territory, because surely there has to be a middle ground between the topics of three-way sex and a day in the life of Yummy Mummy No. 1. Somewhere safe between gritty and saccharine.

"She's having an affair with a married man," I say.

"How married?" asks Yummy Mummy No. 1.

"Marriage is a black-and-white issue, isn't it?" I say. "There shouldn't be degrees." But even as I'm saying it, I'm not sure that I agree with my own hypothesis. My moral compass is wildly unsynchronized.

"But for the record, one wife, four children, more than a decade of marriage," I say.

"Just like me," she says, smiling. "And you. Albeit with one less child. Does his wife know?"

"I don't think she's got any idea. Actually, I feel sorry for her. She's probably so wound up in her children that she has put her husband on the back burner to retrieve at a later date, when she is less tired," I say. "Don't you sometimes feel like calling up one of those missing-persons hotlines and reporting your disappearance? 'Help, I don't know where I've gone, I got married, had children, gave up my job, made everyone around me happy, and then disappeared. Please send out a search party.' "

She looks at me in astonishment. "Always a bad idea to neglect your husband. Men can't stand being sidelined. They stray. That's why we have two weeks alone in the Caribbean every year. Everyone should do it," she says emphatically.

"Perhaps," says Robert Bass diplomatically, "not everyone has the financial capacity or the child care to do something like that."

"When you've got children, husbands drop further and further down the pecking order," I say. "Even below pets. Even goldfish." Robert Bass has fallen silent. The circle is complete; we are back at the beginning, talking about fish.

"Of course, infidelity could be construed as an act of fidelity to oneself," says Robert Bass without looking up.

"That's a radical concept," I say, staring at the empty bottle of champagne.

"Shall we call it a night? I can give you both a lift home if you want," says Yummy Mummy No. 1, looking at us suspiciously, as though she realizes there is a hidden undercurrent to the conversation that she is unable to access.

9

"A guilty conscience
needs no accuser."

The Sound of Music is playing on the video in the sitting room, and the children are arguing because Joe wants to rewind to the scene where the Nazis try to capture the von Trapp family.

"Joe, nothing is going to change," I hear Sam shout at him with frustration. "It's always going to be the same, they always escape. Even if you watch it a hundred times, everything will happen exactly the same way."

"But the color of their shorts has changed. They used to be dark green and now they are definitely light green," says Joe, defensively hugging the television screen so that Sam cannot turn it off.

"That's because Mummy sat on the television controls and changed the settings," shouts Sam.

"So things do change. I want to watch one more time, just in case this time the Nazis get them," Joe insists, chewing the sleeve of his pajama top. This is a recently acquired habit, but already the cuffs of all his school shirts and sweaters are in tatters.

"If the Nazis got them, then the film wouldn't be suitable for children and Mum wouldn't let us watch it," says Sam, trying to soothe him with logic rather than brute force. "No one will betray the von Trapps."

Fred is hiding behind the sofa. He has been quietly engaged in a game with his tractors and trailers since I came into the sitting room. Although

I know that a silent toddler is akin to an unexploded bomb, I decide that whatever he is doing, it is worth taking the risk so that I can deal with weeks of unopened post that has accumulated in the top drawer of my desk. I'll deal with the consequences later.

To avoid unsettling Tom, every few days I pick up the envelopes that collect on the small table by the front door and stuff them into this drawer until it is full. Then I tackle the backlog. It is not a system that Tom would approve of, but its simplicity has some merit, especially since it allows me to censor anything that might prove contentious.

I wonder whether I should intervene in the dispute at the other end of the room. The issue is whether to indulge Joe's neurosis and allow him to rewind, or force him to capitulate to Sam. I know that any involvement in peacekeeping will trigger further demands on my time. Pleas to play games, read books, wrestle, or do role-play as Shane Warne. I am due for dinner at Emma's new apartment in less than an hour, so I ignore them. If I could disappear for two hours a day, I would achieve so much.

I sit at my desk at the other end of the sitting room, trying to impose order on the chaos of unopened bills, bank statements, and anonymous envelopes before Tom arrives back from Italy later tonight. It is an enterprise born of contrition. Since the drink with Robert Bass earlier in the week, I am suffering from bouts of unresolved guilt. I haven't lied to Tom. But I have economized with the truth. If he asks about what I did on Monday evening, what will I say? That I created a situation where I could sit close enough to a man I find so attractive that the hair on my arm stood on end when our flesh touched? That I am going to see this same man again later this week? That I have vivid dreams about these feelings being reciprocated? I have dismissed Robert Bass as a fantasy, a welcome distraction, as harmless as a plant that offers color through the gray tones of winter in London. But I realize that to compare him to the witch hazel flowering in our garden is disingenuous. And then there are the children. My mind races, as it is prone to do when unpleasant emotions take hold, and I imagine them grown up, telling friends tales of their mother's treachery and how it has affected their ability to form lasting relationships with the opposite sex, and how it will affect their children and their children's children until it is carried through the generations in their genetic code.

Unable to resolve this dilemma, I force myself to concentrate on the task at hand, arranging three large piles of papers. The first has mail specifically for Tom, the second bills that need to be paid immediately, and the third is a nonspecific pile to be dealt with at a much later date, possibly never. The latter goes back in the drawer. I smile to myself, anticipating Tom's elation at discovering his post in a neat, orderly pile. Then I immediately feel guilty again, knowing that such a simple act will give him such pleasure. In many respects, he is easily pleased. He could have had a very harmonious marriage with a different kind of woman. If he had married his mother, for example.

I am stuffing envelopes that I most definitely do not want Tom to see in a drawer at the bottom of the desk. They include a couple of forgotten congestion charges, parking tickets, and credit-card bills. I now have seven different kinds of credit-card debt. This is not a source of pride. However, I have found myself surprisingly adept at juggling these bills and trawling the Internet to find the best deals. Zero percent finance for the first twelve months. Small print to make your heart sing. When I walk home from school after a particularly busy period of debt exchange, I find myself giving Fred a status report. "Move AmEx to Visa, move Visa to MasterCard, move MasterCard to AmEx," I sing out loud, changing music according to my mood, "Jingle Bells" being the tune of choice at the moment. I feel like a heavy hitter in the city, trading debt on the international market. Buy. Sell. Hold.

The traffic fines remain a blind spot. Last month, a bailiff arrived at the front door with a summons for a fine that I received about two years ago. Tom happened to be at home, working on architectural plans. The bailiff, a tall, well-built man, was wearing an ill-cut gray suit made of such cheap man-made fiber that when he pulled a pen out of the top pocket for me to acknowledge receipt, small sparks flew.

He was not an unpleasant man. In fact, he was surprisingly placid, a characteristic reinforced by his eyelids, which turned down at the ends, like a friendly bloodhound. There was no evidence that he had absorbed any of the aggression and stress that must accompany his job. His face was almost serene. Mine, on the other hand, was furrowed with worry. It was not the fear of prosecution but the fear of Tom uncovering my trail of financial deception.

So when I heard Tom coming upstairs from the kitchen to see who was at the door, I persuaded the bailiff to pretend he was a Jehovah's Witness, a bluff that he went along with surprisingly obligingly. He seemed completely at ease with this deviation from his job description.

"Come Armageddon," he said loudly, peering across my shoulder at Tom, who was still dressed in a pair of pajamas, "only the chosen will be saved. As a sinner you can repent, but only if you have resolved any outstanding parking issues."

Tom looked vaguely bemused and scratched his head, making his dark hair stand on end.

"Surely there are many worse sins," he said. "In any case, the statistical probability of one of the chosen being a traffic warden is infinitesimal, so no one would be any the wiser."

"It's best not to engage, otherwise he'll never leave," I whispered to Tom, pushing him back downstairs. "I'll deal with this. You get on with your work." I went back to the front door and signed for the summons.

"It is not for me to say," said the bailiff, "but I really think, Mrs. Sweeney, that you should try and sort out all of this. It must be very stressful, having to hide this kind of thing from your husband."

"Oh, don't worry about that, I do it all the time," I said nonchalantly. "Women are very good at juggling deception. It's part of multitasking." He shook his head, opened up a battered leather briefcase, and stuffed my papers inside before snapping it shut and clasping my hand.

I know that one day I should consult someone practical like Emma, who never even runs an overdraft, for advice on how to resolve this. Or at least I should add all the credit-card bills and parking fines together, to assess exactly how much I owe. But I simply can't face up to the situation. It's been so long since I actually accrued the debt that I can't even remember what impulse purchases caused this catastrophic chain of events. They were probably thrown out years ago.

"Mum, is it really true that the Nazis will never take Maria?" Joe anxiously calls from the sofa.

"It is; she smells far too sweet," I shout from the other side of the room, hoping this will seal the dispute.

"Mum, do you think that one day I could make a pair of shorts from the curtains in my bedroom?" he says.

"Of course, darling," I say distractedly, hiding envelopes at the back of the drawer and then covering my tracks with a pile of catalogs.

"Perhaps Joe shouldn't watch this film anymore," says my mother-in-law. I am unaware that she has come upstairs from the kitchen. I shut the drawer a little too firmly and note her looking at it suspiciously.

"He has the same issues regardless of what he is watching. Even if it's something totally benign," I say, standing up and moving away from the desk. "He's just a very sensitive child."

"Who is this Major Tom that he keeps talking about? Is he a friend of your parents'?" she asks.

She is still staring at the bottom drawer, her hands stuck deeply in the pockets of Tom's dressing gown. It has been washed and has changed color from a sort of dirty orange to pale yellow. It is so big on her tiny frame that she has to tie it behind her back. Her feet and head, still red from the bath, poke out the end like jam oozing from a fat Swiss roll.

Petra has been here all week, and there is no sign of her imminent departure. Each day she becomes more embedded. This is a familiar pattern. I will have to wait for Tom to come home to broach the subject of when she might leave. Whenever the situation threatens to become intolerable, for example, when I open the wardrobe and discover that she has organized his pants into neat color-coordinated piles, I resolve to ask her to go. She knows that she has overstepped the mark, and tries to rein herself in for the rest of the day, but her compulsion for organizing overrides everything else. She tries to compensate by asking me exactly which area of the house would benefit from further precision tidying, and offers free babysitting, which she knows I will never turn down. For the most part, this bribery quells the waves of panic. The laundry mountain is now the size of a decent hill, still undulating but less imposing. Tom's shirts are all ironed. Socks that lost their partners years ago have been reunited, and those that missed out on a happy reunion condemned to the dustbin.

"I was wondering, Lucy, whether we could have lunch together next week," she says, nervously fiddling with a string of pearls round her neck as I am trying to leave the house. Tom is due back later tonight, but there is no sign of bags being packed.

"But Petra, we've had lunch together almost every day this week," I say, feeling slightly panicked and reaching out for my coat to signal my imminent departure.

"There is something important that I need to talk to you about. It has to be said somewhere neutral. Perhaps we could meet in John Lewis, and combine it with Christmas shopping? I need to get something for your parents." She pauses without looking up from her cup of coffee. "Please don't mention to Tom that we are meeting. I'm sorry you lost your election the other day, by the way. Perhaps it's for the best, given everything else you've got on your mind."

Although I have already started toward the front door, I stop in my tracks. My assumption is that somehow over the past week my inner turmoil has reached the surface and has started to bubble through my pores, so that I now smell of self-doubt and uncertainty. My mother-in-law has many foibles, but intrigue on a grand scale is not one of them. In the twelve years since I first met her, this is her most significant overture to me, and I know it must be serious because she has a natural aversion to emotional honesty. Still, at least I have a few days to prepare a plausible defense. Later that evening, installed in the cathedral-like space that is Emma's new home in Clerkenwell, drinking expensive wine with her and Cathy, I start to relax. Obviously, my mother-in-law has made the decision to intervene because she is fearful for her son. On the other hand, she never likes to hear the truth if it is too unpalatable or unsettling. I imagine layers of emotional deception compacted against each other like bands of sediment, in colors that start to run into each other over the years, so that it is impossible to examine any single part with clarity.

The walls of Emma's loft are very white, almost clinical. Some slide into each other on invisible runners to create new rooms and spaces. These are the kinds of optical tricks that appeal to Tom. I, on the other hand, find it all quite disconcerting. I don't want my home to be a movable feast. So when Emma shows Cathy and me how the sitting room can be turned into a spare bedroom and how the bedroom can double in size, it makes me feel slightly seasick.

I'm not sure for whom this flat was built. Certainly not for families or anyone suffering from depression. There are treacherous drops from the balconies that run around the edge and large flowerpots filled with fashionable grasses that cut your skin if you brush past them too closely. It is, however, a great place for parties.

I recognize a few belongings from Emma's Notting Hill home, including a couple of Patrick Heron prints, and a kitsch white vase with big flowers stuck around the rim that I gave her on her thirtieth birthday. They are dwarfed by the space. The lift from the ground floor opens up impressively into the sitting room, but it takes two of us to pull back the heavy iron grilles, and I wonder how Emma manages to get in and out on her own.

We are unusually silent. Emma is struggling with a murky bucket of mussels. She is angrily scrubbing them.

"I've had a bad day," she says finally. "I had to phone the parents of one of our correspondents in Iraq and tell them that their son was killed in an ambush. I don't want to talk about it. These mussels are a bitch to clean, they are so beardy."

"Maybe something bigger than a toothbrush would make it easier," Cathy says gently.

Emma's bad days are always on a grand scale compared to my own, involving, as they often do, significant events on the world stage. Anything from tsunamis to civil war. Impressive problems. Discovering that my mother-in-law has organized my husband's pants into a color-coordinated scheme without asking whether she can go in our bedroom hardly competes.

I look around the kitchen, taking in the Gaggia coffee machine, KitchenAid mixer, and twin dishwashers. Only one of the dishwashers has been used. It is all conceived on such an enormous scale that Emma looks as though she is in Brobdingnag, standing on steps to open cupboards beyond the reach of mere mortals, peering into a huge American-style fridge that is empty apart from lots of bottles of white wine—Puligny-Montrachet, it says on the labels—and a packet of shriveled rocket. She looks even tinier than usual and quaintly domestic in an apron, gripping a wooden spoon in her fist like a toddler holding a fork for the first time. I can't remember ever eating a meal cooked by her before.

"What are we having?" I ask.

"Mussels followed by pan-fried scallops with pancetta," she says, frowning at a Jamie Oliver cookbook and lining up brand-new Le Creuset saucepans on the granite counter. What is it about people who never cook, choosing recipes that even a professional chef would find challenging? She puts everything in the oven and shuts the door a little too hard.

"Let's sit down and have a drink. It's hard work being a domestic goddess. I don't know how you manage to hold it all together, Lucy," says Emma, walking to the other end of the room and slumping in an oversize sofa. Her kitten-heel boots make a disproportionally loud noise on the poured-concrete floor.

I have wasted many hours explaining to Emma the grounds on which I fail to qualify for domestic goddess status, and finally realized about a year ago that maintaining this illusion is important to her. As she scrolls through news stories on her screen in her glass bubble, I know she imagines me in a floral Cath Kidston apron, removing cupcakes that I have made with the children from the oven, and drawing up plans of how they should be decorated, a complicated endeavor involving different-colored icing, little silver balls, and sprinkles.

Emma likes to invest her friends with traits that bear little resemblance to reality, but they're always positive, which is what makes the habit tolerable. So in her mind I am a glamorous, thin mother of three, with a healthy bank balance, tidy home, and cooperative children. It is a picture painted in primary colors because the idea that any of us might lead an anemic existence is anathema to her. It is also a way for her to avoid confrontation with the underbelly of life. And sometimes it is easier to believe the myth, because it makes me feel good.

"So how is living apart together?" I ask her, anticipating a rosy account filled with witty observation and funny anecdotes.

"Well, the bed finally arrived, which is bliss. Sometimes I wake in the night and Guy is lying beside me and I'm so excited that I can't get back to sleep. I don't want to disturb him because I don't want him to go, and yet I'm terrified that if I don't send him home, his wife will find out. Other times I feel a bit like a songbird trapped in a cage," she says, kicking off her boots and undoing the top button of her jeans. "And we're still going to hotels at lunchtime, because it's an addiction that's hard to break. I spend too many evenings waiting for Guy to call, because I hardly know anyone who lives in this area. I avoid making other plans in case there is a chance that he can escape work and make an excuse to his wife. And then as soon as he arrives I forget how I felt and cook elaborate recipes from one of these books, drink lots of wine, and have fantastic sex."

"That all sounds amazing," I say, because largely it does and that is what Emma wants to hear. She won't want us to dwell on the songbird image. But there is a touch of uncertainty in her voice. She sounds vulnerable.

"But I can't help thinking it's a relationship that's stunted from the start. A runt relationship that's never going to grow into something else," she continues. "We only exist within the confines of this flat. The rare moments when we are together outside of this space, we can't even touch each other. Although that makes it more charged when you can. Let's eat. It must be ready. I can't bear the sound of my own voice anymore."

We move to the kitchen table to eat the meal that Emma has prepared. She has laid each place with a complex arrangement of knives, forks, and spoons, and two glasses, one for water and one for wine. A basket of bread cut into delicate slices sits in the middle, already going stale. There is something poignant in this effort, as though she is trying to mark out new territory that doesn't really belong to her. Everything is borrowed from someone else's life.

The mussels still have sand and bits of beard in them, and the scallops are dry and rubbery because Emma put them in the oven instead of frying them over a hot heat for a short time. So for a few minutes we sit there in companionable silence. I chew a scallop in my right cheek until the muscles beg for mercy, and then swap sides. When we discover that they are resistant to all attempts to break them down into a more manageable consistency, we swallow them with gulps of red wine as though we are taking a vitamin supplement. Still, we compliment Emma on her nascent culinary achievements.

"You don't have to pretend, I know I'm a crap cook," she says, laughing, as though she is relieved that one of her most long-standing attributes hasn't changed. "Actually, Guy does most of the cooking. At home, his wife doesn't let him near the kitchen."

The kitchen table can sit fourteen, possibly sixteen. It is so new that I find myself yearning for the pockmarked imperfections of our own table with its paint stains and tiny trenches made by my children with small spoons and forks. It might be grubby, but at least it has history.

We are huddled at one corner, and it feels a little lonely. I can't imagine Emma eating on her own, although she must have breakfast here every morning. There are views out across London if you happen to be sitting on the side that backs onto the stove. Perhaps that is some compensation.

"What a great place to have a party," says Cathy.

"That's what it is designed for, but we'll never have one together," says Emma, putting down her knife and fork. "We won't even have mutual friends around for dinner or slob around in our pajamas on a Saturday morning, although I'm hoping that during the Christmas holidays, when his wife goes to their country home with the children, we might manage a weekend together. Second homes are a great thing. We had such a good summer when his wife was in Dorset."

I bite my tongue and remember Tom's advice about allowing people to live their own lives.

"You could have people around for dinner. You could have us, and I can invite my new boyfriend," says Cathy enthusiastically. "I'm desperate for you to meet him."

"That would be nice. Perhaps I can try and persuade Guy," says Emma. "The thing is that his life is so compartmentalized. He likes to keep me for himself. He doesn't want to share me. Going out with friends is something he associates with his wife, not me. I am not most of his life. I'm just a fraction."

"But you can't measure the depth of fractions, only the breadth," I say, trying to be reassuring. She sounds uncharacteristically dispirited.

"Maybe he'll leave his wife," I continue, wanting to offer a morsel of hope.

"He won't, because ultimately he is someone who plays safe. A woman with a career is the last thing that he wants. He was the one who persuaded his wife to give up work as soon as she got pregnant. I merely give a little diversity to his portfolio," she says, periodically running her nails up and down the back of her head and scratching furiously.

"Well, he is having his cake and eating it," I say, viewing this conversation as progress of a sort. It is the first time since Emma began this relationship more than a year ago that she has shown any sign of self-doubt. Her certainty has been unnatural and a little disturbing.

"I suppose what I really want is some evidence that he wants emotional evolution. He seems so satisfied with the status quo, and that feels like a betrayal," she says.

Betrayal takes on many forms, I think to myself. It can creep up on you slowly, an accumulation of self-deception and small white lies, or descend suddenly like a mist. The treachery of Emma's banker is not in what he says. He has promised nothing more than he can deliver. It is in what he doesn't say. It is in the empty gestures, the way he gets his secretary to send flowers on his wife's birthday, the way he punctiliously deletes his text messages from Emma each evening on the doorstep of his home and then kisses his children with the scent of his mistress still fresh on his breath.

Then I hold myself up for comparison. My drink with Robert Bass might seem small beer compared to the situation between Emma and Guy, but it is betrayal all the same. The time I have spent thinking about him, engineering fantasies in my mind, has already diluted my relationship with

Tom. Like a ship approaching shore after a long period at sea, I find myself feeling happier the closer I come to our next meeting. Of course, unlike Emma and Guy, my flirtation with Robert Bass will never be consummated. But what started as a harmless distraction from my other preoccupations has now hijacked a space in my head that would be much better occupied with pastimes appropriate to a millennial mother. Like, for example, putting together the IKEA shoe-shelf kit that has sat beside the front door alongside a jumble of shoes for the past two years, or mastering the espresso machine given to us for Christmas last year by Petra, or engaging in depilation befitting a woman in her late thirties.

"Lucy, Lucy, are you listening?" says Emma. "What do you think?" I realize I have missed crucial sections of Emma's moment of self-doubt and start feeling remorseful for that.

"I wonder whether you ever feel guilty for his wife?" I blurt out, and Cathy stares at me, looking slightly shocked, although whether it is because the question is inappropriate to what has preceded it or just plain inappropriate is unclear. If I was more sure of my own feelings, then I would tell Emma that it is less judgment and more self-absorption. The question hangs in the air for a while, and Emma scratches her head thoughtfully.

"Last month, he was with me one Friday evening and forgot that he was meant to be going out to dinner with his wife and some friends, because he had switched off his cell phone. She couldn't get hold of him until about one in the morning, when we finally crawled out of bed and then he turned his phone back on to discover there were all these messages from her. She had gone to dinner on her own, lying to their friends that he had to go abroad suddenly. He felt awful, and I felt bad because of that. But I think, because I don't have children and my own family life was fucked, my ability to feel guilt is limited," says Emma in a rare moment of brutal self-honesty. "He tells me that he stays with her because he has me, but I know that isn't true. However deep my self-delusion, I know that I'm not saving their marriage. Quite a lot of the time I feel contemptuous of her for failing to realize what is going on."

She looks up as she says this, knowing that it won't rest easily with us.

"Nothing is going to change. This is it," she continues, waving her hand around the room. "He's never going to leave his wife and children, and I'm not sure I want him to. Relationships that start like this are unlikely to end well. There are too many fault lines from the outset. His wife would invest all her energy into making sure it would never work, and his children would always hate me. Anyway, I would never want the responsibility for ending his marriage."

"There's no such thing as a good divorce, that's for sure," says Cathy, who is still swimming in the wake of her own, wrangling over money matters, access to Ben, and how to divide furniture. A universal formula for mutual unhappiness. The armory of failed marriage might not have very sophisticated weapons, but that doesn't make the battles any less bloody.

"Two weekends a month without any children sounds quite good to me," I say glibly, hoping to lift the mood that has settled.

"That's because you don't go out to work," says Cathy. "Handing over Ben every other weekend, when I don't see him enough during the week, makes me feel physically sick. His father's new girlfriend is trying so hard to curry favor with him that it makes me want to scream. I don't want her to even touch Ben."

"And how is Tom's architect?" Emma asks Cathy, signaling an end to any further self-analysis.

"He is fabulous," she says. "The light at the end of the tunnel. In every way. Almost. He's clever, funny, we have great sex, amazing sex. I owe Tom big-time for this one. The only downside is the man he shares the house with, who also happens to be his best friend," she says.

"Do you want to move in already? Don't you think that's a little rash?"

"Lucy, I'm never going to live with someone again," she says. "I'm never going to expose myself like that. I've got my life organized now, I'm earning good money, Ben is settled at school. I never want to rely on a man again financially."

"Well that's a little extreme," I say. "Although it's true that most architects live in a constant state of economic uncertainty."

"What I mean is that this man he lives with seems to be jealous of me in some way," she says.

"Is there an underlying sexual current between them, do you think?" shouts Emma in a muffled voice from inside the fridge, where she is getting another bottle of white wine. I count the bottles on the kitchen table and realize that we have already drunk close to one each.

"I haven't talked to him about it, because although it seems really obvious to me, he seems oblivious, but there is nothing so far to suggest any latent homosexuality," Cathy says. "Except perhaps a penchant for anal sex."

"So, how do you know he is jealous?" I ask, intrigued.

"Well, at first it was small things. If I call him at home, for example, he never passes on the messages, and a couple of times he has said that Pete isn't there when I'm sure that he is. I was happy to overlook that, but then the few times that I have actually met his roommate, he has behaved really strangely. The first time I had dinner there with both of them, which is a little odd in itself, Pete was cooking in the kitchen and he sat in the sitting room, telling me that Pete was a classic commitment-phobe who would never be able to connect permanently to anyone. He said he was like a magpie, always coveting his friends' girlfriends, constantly dissatisfied with his own, leaving a trail of misery in his wake."

"Maybe that's true, and he was trying to warn you not to get in too deep, because he knows you have already had a bad experience," says Emma.

"I was happy to give him the benefit of the doubt over that, too," says Cathy. "Then, the other night, I thought I was having text sex with Pete and discovered it was someone else."

"But how can you possibly know that?" I ask.

"I laid a trap," she says, smiling wickedly. "I replayed something that Pete and I had never done together as though it was something that had actually happened, and he took the bait."

"So what was it about?" I ask.

"I pretended that Pete and I had been to a party where we had sex with another woman in the bathroom. Took him right through it all as though we had actually done this together, and then at the end he said it was the best erotic experience of his life and that he really wanted to do the same thing again. I'm sure it was his roommate. Who else would have access to Pete's phone at night?"

"What is it about men and threesomes?" I ask.

"It's not really threesomes, is it," says Cathy. "It's about having sex with two other women, and it's not about the women having sex with each other, it's about the man having two women all over him. There's nothing democratic about it."

"What did you do about Guy's plan?" I ask Emma.

"I took your advice about saying I had a rash from a Brazilian, got a Brazilian, to make it authentic, which was about the most painful experience of my life so far, and got a rash. He's now switched fantasies and it's all about having sex in his office, which is far less complicated to indulge and actually very exciting because there is such a risk of us being caught. I blame you for that one, Lucy, it was after those texts you sent him."

"So what else has the saucy roommate been up to?" I ask, turning to Cathy again.

"Well, the other night I got there before Pete, and he started flirting with me in a really obvious way," she says.

"What did he do?" I ask, because since my drink with Robert Bass, learning to read these kinds of signals suddenly seems very important. But there is nothing subtle about what she says next.

"He came up behind me when I was opening a bottle of wine in the kitchen, and ran his finger down my spine," she says. "It was almost imperceptible; he started at the top and slowly meandered down the back of my T-shirt and stopped when he reached the skin below and then took his finger away."

Emma and I gasp.

"What's awful is that although I should have found it creepy and put an immediate stop to it, I let him go on because actually I was really tempted. He's very attractive, too, in a smooth metrosexual kind of way," she says.

"Maybe they like to share girlfriends," I proffer.

"Who knows," she says. "I don't want to say anything to Pete, because it might conflict their friendship, and we'll probably implode anyway before Christmas. I'll just see where it all takes me. The other thing is that Pete always wants to bring him out with us. It's as though they are married. They've lived together for eight years."

"Very intriguing. I'll have to ask Tom for any insights," I say. It seems incredible that he spends every day with this man and yet has never mentioned anything like this about him.

"He's definitely sexually open to all kinds of stuff," says Cathy. "He's really uninhibited, takes me to places where I forget who I am."

"That sounds good from where I'm sitting," I say, trying to rouse her from her introspection.

"I've had enough good sex to know it doesn't mean love," says Emma quietly. "And actually, I think I need to remember who I am. The best thing I could do is end it all now. The trouble is that desire is organic. You are never sated. And each day that goes by I lose a little more control. I'm never at the point where everything becomes routine and domestic, I'm in a state of perpetual lust."

"That doesn't sound such a hardship," I say. "You know, if Sexy Domesticated Dad had made even half a move the other night, I don't know how I would have resisted. The feel of his arm against my skin was exquisite. Sometimes I think that I can't live without that sensation just one more time before I die."

"Oh," says Emma, looking slightly shocked. "So you went out for a drink alone then? That's quite intense."

"It was Cathy who organized it, if you recall," I say defensively. "And we weren't alone for long because another mother came along."

"I didn't really think it would happen," Cathy says. "I would never want to be responsible for doing anything that might jeopardize your relationship with Tom. If you fail, what hope is there for the rest of us?"

"Maybe there isn't any hope for any of us," I say.

"Couldn't you rewind to the beginning of your relationship with Tom and regenerate some of that passion?" she asks curiously.

"That's like trying to start a fire again once you have put it out. The problem is that although it is the sex that makes the children, it is the children that kill the sex," I explain. "There's never any time, and we're constantly exhausted. And our sexual clock isn't synchronized." They look confused. "Women like having sex at night, and men's sexual desire peaks at eight a.m. It's nature's contraceptive."

"We never got far enough with our marriage to reach that point, so maybe you should consider it an achievement," says Cathy.

"Besides, we're never alone in bed," I continue. "Sometimes it's like musical chairs. We wake up in the morning and none of us are in the same bed that we went to sleep in."

"Can't you put them back in their beds?" asks Emma.

"You can, but often we're too exhausted to get up, and besides, they are wise to that one, so they sneak in and lie at our feet so we don't notice them, like dogs."

"What about trying something different, like tantric sex?" says Emma.

"Takes too long. Whatever we do, it mustn't take longer than twenty minutes," I say. "It's top of my long-term to-do list, though."

"What is?" asks Cathy.

"Having sex with Tom," I say.

"What else is on that list?" asks Cathy, looking incredulous.

"Well, there's the issue of my credit-card debt," I say. "Finding a cleaning lady who can actually do the washing and ironing. Inventing a part-time job. And scattering my grandmother's ashes at her birthplace. I forgot to do it when we went to Norfolk."

"So where are they now?" asks Emma.

"In the airing cupboard," I say. "It seemed like a good place to keep them. Cozy and safe. Like her."

"But those all sound like priorities," says Emma, momentarily distracted from her own problems. "Death, debt, dirty clothes, no sex. No wonder you're unnerved by your own existence. And actually, they are so easy to sort out."

"But if I sort them out, then what will be left?" I ask. They look at me in genuine confusion.

"What I mean is that if all those things were resolved, then I might discover that actually they are the glue sticking everything together and that everything just disintegrates," I say. "I'm trying to be counterintuitive."

"That's so irrational, Lucy," says Cathy. "You might feel more in control if you sorted them out."

"Maybe I want to be out of control," I say recklessly. But when I see the worried expression on their faces, I relent. "Or just out of control for a defined period of time, to remember what it feels like."

"What sort of things are on your short-term list?" asks Cathy. I hand them my diary and point to a couple of grubby pages at the back. The pages are worn through. The corners are missing and the ink has soaked through from the other side. It looks like hieroglyphics with strange words written in different-colored pens.

"Is this a kind of code?" asks Emma. I start to read down the right-hand page.

"Nit shampoo, birthday party Sam, toothbrush Fred, MMR, smear test, bikini wax . . ."

Emma is scratching her head again.

"It's because it says Nit shampoo. If you have a suggestible personality, simply seeing those words can make your scalp itch," I say.

"Why do you need a bikini wax in the middle of winter?" Emma asks.

"That has been on the list since May," I say.

"Don't try and distract me, I know your tactics for avoiding a conversation," says Emma, counting the number of things on the list. She stops when she reaches twenty-two.

"I can't understand how it can all be so complicated. Surely you could do one of these things each day, and then within a month, it would all be over and you could turn to the long-term list," she says.

"Every day there are new things to add to that list," I say. "There's another list on the fridge with other, even more urgent, things. And you're not including the things that need to be done routinely, like making packed lunches, cooking industrial quantities of Bolognese sauce, doing homework, washing . . ." I am about to mention the mess that I have left behind in the sitting room when I see that she is beginning to look bored.

Just before I left, I discovered that I had paid a heavy price for those ten minutes spent sorting through the post, because Fred had taken all the puzzles and games from the toy cupboard and was using them to load up his collection of trailers. His trucks were filled with pieces from a combination of Monopoly, Scrabble, and Clue. Hundreds, possibly thousands, of pieces that need sorting. Hours, even days, of work that won't even make it onto a list. Devastation on a grand scale, all generated in less than ten minutes. Does this qualify as two steps forward and one backward, or does it leave me with negative equity? I wondered as I pushed everything under the sofa before walking out the door. This is why I will always be one step behind.

Sometimes during my early-morning insomnia, I make lists in my mind of The Lost Things. The current one includes a plastic hammer from Fred's tool kit, the battery cover for a remote-control car, an extra-large die from Chutes and Ladders, and a rook from the chess set.

I imagine myself, like a forensic pathologist, covering every inch of ground in the house, searching down the back of chairs, underneath wardrobes, inside shoes, even underneath floorboards to locate all these things and restore order. It will never happen, partly because there is never enough time but mostly because I know that within a few days the chaos ante will rule once again.

One of the telephone handsets has also gone missing, and a key from the door into the garden, but I haven't mentioned this to Tom yet, knowing he will hold me responsible. He doesn't spend enough time at home to realize that children are like ants without a system, constantly on the move, carrying things from one room to another and secreting them in places invisible to the adult eye.

If Petra hadn't been staying, I would have resorted to one of those larynx-aching rants that purge me of my anger and make Sam refer to the NSPCC ads that tell you that shouting is tantamount to child abuse. Whoever devised those should be sent to come and clean up the carnage.

Fred came over to nestle in my lap, hoping for clemency, and my eyes stung red with the effort of neutralizing my anger. For Fred had done this before, less than two weeks ago. I imagined the vessels in my brain, bulging with the pressure of the blood coursing into my head, struggling not to burst their banks like tiny riverways during a heavy rainstorm. All it would take is one tiny point of weakness and my brain would flood like the Okavango Delta in the rainy season, leaving my children motherless. I shut my eyes and breathed in the smell of the soft skin of Fred's neck, the soft fleshy part underneath the long curls at the back of his head that I can't bear to cut because they represent the last vestiges of his babyhood. He giggled, because it tickled, but allowed me my moment of wistfulness. He smelled of a sweet blend of clean pajamas, soap, and the unsullied pureness of recently washed toddler, and I felt myself melt. Waves of nostalgia for the baby he will never be again swept over me, and for a moment I thought I might cry. Sometimes it is a question of getting through the days, but then from nowhere come those moments that you want to preserve forever.

"I think, Lucy, that you might have lost sight of the value of certainty in your existence," says Cathy. "You might lose out on the extremes, but they're not all they're cracked up to be. You don't realize what a privilege it is to be sure of things."

"My eighteen-year-old babysitter told me the other day that we are too fixated on the idea of happiness as an end in itself," I say, suddenly remembering a conversation with Polly. I am poring over my diary, struggling to decipher my own lists. "She said that our dissatisfaction is based on the belief that we have a fundamental right to be happy, and that if we could accept that anything beyond vaguely awful is a bonus, we would all be more content. So maybe I need to acknowledge that it isn't possible for a relationship to contain everything."

"God, I hope you pay her well," says Emma.

"Perhaps the key is to embrace the gray areas and view extremes with suspicion," says Cathy.

"I mistrust anyone who believes anything too much," says Emma. "That's why I'm going to a funeral next week. Tony Blair and his divine belief that he is right. We're all paying for that. It's a long-term debt."

She gets up from the table and heads toward the three enormous sofas at the other end of the vast room. We follow, then all sit bunched up on a single sofa with another bottle of wine and drunkenly settle into a game that we invented years ago, which involves holding up pages of shoes from glossy magazines and seeing who can identify a pair of Jimmy Choo shoes from around three meters. Although I have never possessed a pair of Jimmy Choos of my own—even when I worked full-time I was in the trainer league—I have always managed to beat them at this particular game, and tonight is no exception.

We are on the third round, and I have opened up a substantial lead, even though I have no peripheral vision because I am once again wearing my faithful National Health glasses.

"Lucy, this is a particularly difficult conundrum," says Emma, holding up a page from *Vogue*'s party-season issue. "I'm not going to say anything more than that."

Cathy is looking in the fridge for yet another bottle of wine for us to open. "It's the pair on the far right of the bottom row," I say, pushing the glasses high on the bridge of my nose and looking long and hard at the nine pairs of shoes. "And there's another pair, top row in the middle," I crow triumphantly.

"How do you do that?" asks Cathy, impressed as always.

"It's a mathematical skill. There is an exquisite relationship between the heel and sole, an indefinable ratio, that makes them truly elegant. I can only do it with Jimmy Choo," I say, lying back on the new sofa, precariously balancing a full glass of wine in my hand and wondering how my self-esteem has become dependent on such a useless endeavor. "Unfortunately, it won't make me my fortune."

"Just out of curiosity, Lucy, what has Sexy Domesticated Dad got that Tom is lacking?" asks Cathy.

"I suppose he's unfamiliar, so there's a lot left to the imagination," I say. "And I think he's probably wild at heart. Irresponsible." And then I feel disloyal for saying that.

10

"Hope is a good breakfast
but a bad supper."

When I finally get home it is almost two o'clock in the morning. I am regretfully counting how many days it will take to recover from the evening's excesses, an equation that involves adding up the glasses of wine consumed and subtracting the number of consecutive hours of sleep I manage to clock herein.

To my surprise, Tom is sitting downstairs at the kitchen table, staring into the distance at the portrait of his mother. The radio is on. He is listening to a program on the World Service about a Mexican architect called Luis Barragán and doesn't hear me coming down the stairs.

A model of his library in Milan sits on the kitchen table and he has a proprietorial arm around its side, like a man with his hand resting on the buttock of a new girlfriend. He is dressed in a pair of blue-striped pajamas that he must have bought in Milan. They are so stiff that they remain static when he moves his body. The collar is sticking in the air so that it looks as though he is wearing a ruff. The overall impression of Elizabethan courtier is exacerbated by the fact that he hasn't bothered to shave for the past week and now has a fair covering of black beard, making it difficult to gauge the expression on his face.

I look at the portrait from the bottom of the stairs and try to imagine what Tom might be thinking. In an effort to steady myself, I particularly focus on Petra's hair. There has been no evolution in her hairstyle since I first met her. In fact, her overall appearance has barely changed. The color palette of her uniform of neat twinsets and sensible flat Russell and Bromley shoes might have become less muted, but the sensibility is the same.

Her hair has been permed to oblivion in the same style every week for so many years that it no longer moves, even when she bends over. I have never touched it, but I imagine it would have the same quality as a wire brush. Even in a brisk wind, it remains as still as a bed of artichoke heads on a frosty morning, unchanged since the day she married Tom's father.

Yet in this picture, painted less than a year before she got married, her face is framed by long brown hair that falls in lazy waves like a pair of curtains on either side of her beautiful limpid blue eyes. Her expression is soft; every tiny facial muscle is relaxed. She looks languorous, like treacle. Then in a moment of drunken lucidity it comes to me. She is sated.

"What's wrong, Lucy? You're staring at me as though you've seen a ghost," says Tom, interrupting my reverie. "I've only been away for five days."

"It's that picture of your mother," I say. "Did you ever meet the man who painted it?"

"He was a professional artist. She posed for him way before I was born, you know that," he says, getting up to come and plant a slightly resentful kiss on my cheek. The beard tickles, and I rub the spot where the bristles scratched my cheek and then I sneeze. Perhaps I'm becoming allergic to my husband.

"But why would he give her the picture, then?" I ask, rubbing my nose, struggling to appear sober.

"I've got no idea. It was up in the attic for years. The first time I saw it was when she arrived here with it. Why are you asking all of these questions? I thought you might be interested in my library," he says, sounding slightly hurt. "I was hoping you might be here when I arrived, actually."

There used to be a time when we would sit in silence, and then, when we spoke, we were both saying the same thing. We were synchronized. Of course, old clocks never keep the correct time. Perhaps I should be content that we agree more than we disagree, although it would be better if there was less up for discussion. But perhaps if you agree about every-thing, then any discrepancy seems even more insurmountable.

"I went to see Emma's new loft. Your mother offered to babysit, and I needed to get away from her," I say. "Sorry. I didn't think you would wait up."

"She's going tomorrow morning," he says. "She's acting a little strangely. She kept saying that she didn't know when she would be com-ing back. I hope you haven't had an argument."

"No, I was remarkably restrained," I say, hoping to avoid a discussion about Petra.

"It all looks really tidy," he says. "Apart from this." He is pointing omi-nously at crumpled curtains from Joe's bedroom that are inexplicably lying on the windowsill. Even from the other side of the room, I can see there are coarsely hacked holes in the middle of each one.

"My mother found Joe trying to make a pair of shorts from his cur-tains. He said that you had given him permission. He was in his room alone with a huge pair of scissors," he says, raising an eyebrow question-ingly. "Actually, he's done quite a good job. He's gone to sleep with the shorts." He goes over to the window and holds up the two curtains with shorts-shaped holes. Narrow strips of material lie on the table.

"Those are the straps for the lederhosen," he says. We laugh. Me drunkenly, leaning against the banister to support myself.

"Anyway, with the money I'll make from this library, I think we can stretch to a new pair of curtains," he says. "Let's go to bed. Sorry about your election, by the way. Maybe it's for the best."

I am thinking of next Wednesday and the prospect of another evening in the company of Robert Bass. I should simply cancel the meeting on the grounds that it inflates my mood.

When we go into the bedroom, Tom opens his wardrobe and spots his underpants. Neat little piles of gray, white, and black. They have all been ironed and folded in half. His shirts are hanging in a blend of shades like a Dulux color chart.

"You've got tears in your eyes," I say accusingly.

"I didn't marry you because I thought you would fold my underpants," he says.

"That's why I married you." I laugh.

Then he grabs me and we fall on the bed, kissing recklessly. He pins me down with his hands and kisses me on the neck just below my ear. With his beard and ruff, he looks so different from the man who left a week ago that I imagine I have suddenly found myself in the room with a stranger. And that is exciting. His hand is already inside my trousers, and my shirt is completely undone. His fingers might be large and unwieldy, but when the same lightness of touch that makes him so good at drawing is applied to my body, I feel myself become liquid. Are all architects similarly skilled? I wonder. I must remember to ask Cathy. I shut my eyes and stop thinking about the Robert Bass dilemma.

"I really missed you," he whispers breathlessly in my ear, before moving his attention to my left breast.

But just as it looks as though the sexual famine is ending, Joe comes in the room, rubbing his eyes sleepily. He is holding two bits of material clearly identifiable as shorts.

"Daddy, what are you doing to Mummy?" he asks suspiciously. Tom climbs off me and lies on the bed, breathing heavily.

"We're wrestling," he says.

"Well, I hope you're not being too rough," Joe says, sounding exactly like me.

"Mummy, can I make a pair for Sam and Fred, too?" he asks. "So that we look like the von Trapps." He is half-asleep, and I lift him up and take him back to his room, and he eventually goes to sleep clutching the two bits of material as though someone might steal them in the night. When I finally go back into our bedroom, Tom is in a deep sleep. Another missed opportunity. If parents were allowed to finish conversations, life might be so different.

Then I notice that in an echo of his middle son, he is clutching a small cream box with a dark green ribbon in his hand. I prize open his fist, which is already stiff with sleep, and open the box. Inside is a small card.

"To Lucy. From Tom. For services rendered." It is a silver necklace with stones and charms around the bottom. It is so beautiful that I bite my lip to stop myself from crying. I try to wake him up to say thank you, but he is somewhere unreachable. I put the necklace back inside so that he can give it to me another time and I can feign surprise. But it doesn't reappear for weeks.

෨෨

December starts inauspiciously. "Mrs. Sweeney," says Joe's teacher on Wednesday morning, when I take him into his classroom. "Can I have a quick word with you, please?" When it comes to children, the language of fear is universal. And this is one of those sentences designed to strike dread into the hearts of parents around the globe.

It crosses all cultural and religious barriers. A tightening of the throat, a quickening of the heart, mouth dry, muscles alert. I struggle to stroll rather than race over to her desk.

There is much routine and repetition in the day of the average mother, but we all know that the thread that holds all this together is as a fragile as a spider's web. All around us are stories of random disaster: the child who climbed into a tumbler drier and suffocated, the boy who choked to death on a cherry tomato, the girl who drowned in a paddling pool filled with two inches of rainwater. Life and death in our own backyard. Every time I read one of these stories in the paper, I promise to be a more tolerant parent.

Yesterday morning, I woke up and resolved to face the minefield of early-morning disasters with equanimity. When I realized there was no cheese for sandwiches for packed lunch, I improvised with jam. When I discovered that Fred had unraveled and stuffed an entire toilet-paper roll into the toilet, I put on rubber gloves and unblocked the u-bend. Even in the hours of mad intolerance before six o'clock in the morning, when I discovered that the boys had all woken early and dragged all the pillows and duvets from their beds to build a ship on the staircase, eight years' worth of stuffed animals on board, and chocolate handprints from biscuits taken illicitly from the kitchen on the walls, I promised the children that I wouldn't clear it up, so that they could play the same game when they came home from school.

Then I forgot to tell Tom that the ship was still there. He came home after midnight, drunk and tired from work drinks, tripped on the oversize panda on the bottom step, and fell so heavily that he cut open his lip. I found him lying there, face-to-face with the panda, blood pouring from his mouth, muttering something about booby traps. It is difficult to look out for everyone, every minute of the day.

I see the teacher tidying her desk, and open and shut my mouth like a goldfish in an effort to force my face to look relaxed, a trick I learned from watching television presenters before they went on air. Then out of the corner of my eye I see Fred taking advantage of this unexpected diversion and heading for the corner of the room. In a matter of seconds, his trousers and Bob the Builder underpants are round his ankles and he is peeing in a small dustbin in the corner. He looks over and smiles, secure in the knowledge that I can't make a fuss. My tolerance levels start to dip dangerously. I change my route to sidle innocuously to the other side of the room and place the offending bin in my oversize handbag, then nonchalantly continue my trajectory, holding Fred's arm a little too tightly. I can feel Robert Bass watching me, and for once the attention is unwelcome.

I go over to the teacher's desk. She leans forward and I follow suit until our foreheads are almost touching. This must be bad. I run through a few scenarios in my head. Joe has hurt someone. Joe has been hurt by someone. They have made an official diagnosis of obsessive-compulsive disorder. They blame me. It is my chaos that has caused his fixations. They have uncovered a pedophile scandal. They have noticed my flirtation with Robert Bass, who is now on the other side of the classroom, helping his son get books out of his schoolbag and glancing over at me.

"It is inappropriate for parents to engage in conversations of the flirty variety," I imagine her saying. "We deal with the fallout from this kind of short-term pleasure-seeking among parents on a daily basis. Four detentions, Mrs. Sweeney."

I decide that I am becoming overly self-obsessed, placing myself at the center of my world, when really I should accept periphery status. Of course, this has nothing to do with me. I also hold on to the fact that Joe's teacher is probably ten years younger than me. Nevertheless, I find it impossible to avoid reverting to bolshie adolescent and stand hand on hip, in the classic teenage posture of defiance.

"Should I phone my husband?" I ask worriedly.

"There's no need for that. It's a minor matter, Mrs. Sweeney. We found these in the side of Joe's schoolbag," she says with a smile, handing over the half-smoked packet of cigarettes. I must have hidden them in there when I got home from Emma's last Friday evening.

"My husband must have left them there," I reply.

"You are over sixteen. No need to hide behind the bike sheds anymore," she jokes, and I smile weakly.

I open my bag to put in the cigarettes and see her scrutinizing the contents.

"Is that my dustbin you've got in there?" she asks warily.

"No, it's a portable potty," I hear myself say.

"It looks very much like one of my dustbins," she says. I realize that she is not one of those people who are able to skate over something like this. She wants the whole truth and nothing but the truth.

"I found it in the playground on the way in," I say, forgetting Cathy's advice about never dressing a lie with detail. "I think someone has urinated in it, judging by the color and the aroma. A little person, I mean, not an adult. The volume of urine would suggest a little person." She looks really baffled. "So I was going to take it to the toilet and clean it out and then return it to the playground."

I look across the room to the gaping hole where her dustbin used to stand and see Robert Bass stroll across and undo his jacket to reveal an identical dustbin purloined from another classroom. He waves at me and puts the bin down.

"Look, your bin is over there," I say.

The teacher turns around and sees her bin in situ.

"I am so sorry. I've never seen one of those, er, portable potties before, it looks very much like a dustbin," she says, in a classic volte-face. "That's very public-spirited of you, Mrs. Sweeney. We need parents like you at school."

I leave the classroom with Robert Bass, who follows me into the corridor, and fan myself with a packet of wet wipes.

"Thanks," I say, gripping Fred's hand. "You got me out of a tight corner."

"No worries. I was wondering whether you would give me a lift to this meeting tonight," he says.

"It's the least I can do," I hear myself say, all resolve to avoid him withering in the face of this overture. It is the first time that Robert Bass has initiated an arrangement with me. I justify my weakness by arguing that it would be churlish to turn him down and that, in any case, it involves nothing more dangerous than driving him to a meeting at Alpha Mum's house to discuss school Christmas-party arrangements.

There is something irresponsibly teenage about the possibilities of forced proximity that cars afford. An image of clumsy maneuvers, the handbrake digging into Robert Bass's stomach as he leans over to kiss me and pull me across onto his lap, comes to mind in stunning clarity. Even with the chair on full tilt, my head would hit the roof. Then I think about the state of unmade car—the moldy apples on the floor of the passenger seat, the sticky handle of the glove compartment, and the chocolate compacted down the back of the seat. I resolve not to clean it up, because it will curb temptation.

"That would be great, Lucy," he says. "Until then, watch out for the little people." Then he throws his head back and laughs so loudly that people start to stare.

After dropping Fred at nursery, I set off for my lunch appointment with my mother-in-law. It is one of those cold winter days where the sky is brilliant blue and the sun all the more welcome for weeks of absence. I sit in a bus on my way to John Lewis on Oxford Street, lean my cheek against the cold window, and shut my eyes against the glare of the sun, feeling something close to contentment despite the difficult conversation that lies ahead. It is mid-morning, no one sits in the seat beside me, and the driver takes corners gently so I don't bang my head against the window. Being on my own is as luxurious to me as a session at Micheline Arcier is to Yummy Mummy No. 1.

My mother-in-law believes in John Lewis like some people believe in God. She says that there is nothing worth having that cannot be bought within its stolid walls. When Selfridges reinvented itself, it merely served to reinforce her belief in John Lewis's unalienable stability. Although she has been vaguely contemptuous of attempts to modernize the furniture department and introduce new ranges of clothing, her long love affair with the department store has been generally faithful and uncomplicated, despite a brief liaison with Fenwicks shortly after Tom and I met.

As I enter the shop, I walk through the haberdashery department. There is something strangely reassuring about the rows of different-colored wools and threads. There are boxes of tapestry with kitsch designs of kittens and dogs hanging on the back wall. I imagine myself in the evening sitting beside Tom on the sofa, doing tapestry and drinking Horlicks, all thoughts of Robert Bass banished in favor of unerring devotion to family.

Knitting and sewing have been rehabilitated as acceptable pastimes for fashionable mothers, so perhaps I can put tapestry back on the map as well. I could repent of my sins and do some kneelers for the local church. I sit on a chair opposite the sewing machines, shut my eyes, and breathe in and out deeply. I feel utterly relaxed.

"Lucy, Lucy," I hear someone say. I look up and my mother-in-law is gently shaking my shoulder. "Were you asleep?" Petra asks.

"I was just meditating," I say. She is wearing what she would describe as her best coat, a navy blue wool affair with gold buttons and wide shoulders that has an eighties feel about it. There is a gold brooch on the collar, a long, thin bar with a ribbon on each end. She smells of soap and Anaïs Anaïs perfume.

We go up the escalator. I stand on the step behind her. She holds herself upright, her heels together and feet apart, like a grenadier guard. In the self-service restaurant we both order a prawn salad with slices of avocado on brown bread. It is the natural evolution of the prawn cocktail, I think to myself, as we head for a table by the window with views down toward Marble Arch. We look into the square below and stir our cappuccinos a little too vigorously. The introduction of what she calls "exotic coffee" is one change that she has welcomed.

"You have probably been wondering what all this is about," she starts off gamely. She is still wearing her coat, with the top button done up, and it reminds me so much of Tom that I have to resist the urge to laugh. There must be a buttoned-up gene.

"I think I know," I say, hoping to wrong-foot her with my proactive approach. She looks at me, a little surprised.

"I've noticed you watching me," I say.

"I know. I have been wanting to say something for ages," she says, eyeing me apprehensively. "But I've been putting it off, and now things have got to a point that if I don't say something, I think it will cause even more damage."

"It's not always easy being married," I say, deciding to deal with the situation head-on. There isn't time to saunter through this, because in less than two hours I have to pick up Fred from nursery. "You go through different phases, complete compatibility doesn't really exist."

"Indeed," she says. "Often, the very things that attract us to someone end up being the things that we find most difficult to live with. Compatibility is something to work toward." She has a mouthful of cappuccino and takes an unnervingly long time to swallow. When she looks up, there is a thin line of froth above her upper lip.

"Very true." I nod in assent. "It's not always easy to be tolerant."

"You are very intuitive, Lucy," she says. "And honest. Marriage is indeed a series of compromises, and women are better chameleons than men. You might see it as the burden of being female, but actually it is liberating rather than restricting because it allows the possibility of loving many different people."

"That doesn't make it any easier," I say. Ten minutes earlier, it would have seemed inconceivable to have such a conversation with my mother-in-law, and I am struggling to absorb this unexpected change in the parameters of our relationship. She, on the other hand, has adjusted with apparent ease.

"But I think that if you can compromise with one person, you can do it with another," Petra says. "The idea that people roam the world in search of their perfect mate has always seemed absurd to me. I think we are capable of finding many different people attractive and that if we have that chance, then we should exploit it."

She sits back in her chair, looking slightly relieved, as though she has been searching for these words for months, practicing this conversation in her head late at night. I, on the other hand, am stunned by her directness and am at a loss to know what to say. This is not what I was expecting. I desperately try to recall moments over the past six months that I have allowed her such unqualified access to the inner workings of my mind. Although I know that she has disapproved of me, perhaps in some depth, over the previous decade, I am surprised that she wants to dispose of me so easily. It seems as though she is giving me carte blanche to have an affair. I actually feel a little hurt that she considers our marriage to have so little value.

"I always thought you believed in monogamy, Petra?" I say, astonished. The shock of the conversation has made me raise my voice, and I look round to find dozens of pairs of eyes watching us. This is not the right backdrop for this kind of discussion. Nor the right audience. These are not reality TV fans. They are *Gardeners Question Time* Radio 4 types who want quiet chat about the best kind of lawn mower.

It is as though she has swept the ground from beneath my feet. Any assumptions that I have made about my mother-in-law are now open to question. She must be familiar with the concept of key parties, but to learn that Tom's parents might have had an open marriage is too much to contemplate.

"Of course I believe in monogamy," she says, looking a little shocked at the turn in conversation.

"But you are talking about loving different people," I persist. "Do you mean in a platonic way, no sex involved?"

"Well, I think that sex might be on the agenda," she says, looking very uncomfortable. "Although sex drive unwinds with age." She undoes the top button of her coat and starts using a menu to fan her flushed face. "I don't think I am explaining myself very well," she says.

"I think you are being unusually explicit," I say. People are purposefully staring at menus and spooning food into their mouths, but I know that all their efforts are concentrated on following our conversation, because they have stopped chewing and their cheeks are full, like hamsters.

"Lucy. What I am trying to say, in a nutshell, is that I have met a man whom I once loved many years ago, and I am moving to Marrakech to live with him."

I try to work out whether the sudden realization that this conversation has been all about her and not me is equal to the shock of my mother-in-law telling me that she has fallen in love with someone else and is moving abroad. I sit there, staring at her for an uncomfortably long time.

"Is it the man who painted the portrait of you?" I ask, in a moment of inspiration.

"It is," she says, looking shamefaced. "I don't know how I'm going to tell Tom. I've known this man for years. All the time I was married to Tom's father, we never saw each other. He sent the occasional letter, but I never wrote back. I was unerringly faithful. Then, a couple of years ago, he came to London and called me and we went out to lunch. He's about twelve years older than me. I was only twenty when we had our affair. It's just I have been offered this chance of happiness that I turned down fifty years ago, and I don't want to let it go again."

"But why didn't you marry him then?" I ask.

"Because he was unreliable. He drank too much. He would have never been faithful, and we would have lived in penury," she says. "We had a grand passion. I never told Tom's father. It wouldn't have been right then, but it is right now."

"But didn't you keep thinking about what it might have been like?" I ask, wondering at the willpower she must have invoked to turn off the current with her artist and switch it on when she met Tom's father.

"Of course I thought about him, and there were parts of the relationship that were never possible to switch off, but I adapted to someone else," she says. "I was trying to tell you earlier that I think it is possible to love many people. I loved Tom's father, he was more lovable really, and he loved me. He gave me the kind of stability that I yearned for. Jack would have caused misery and pain, and that would have destroyed anything good."

"Did he ever get married?" I ask.

"He's had two wives and six children, one by a woman he was never married to. He says that if I had stayed with him, this would never have happened, but I knew that there was no single person who would contain everything that he needed to sustain him. He liked clever women, and I was never clever in that quick-witted, intellectual way. He was attracted to women who were dangerous. He liked damaged people because they were exciting. I was too homely. Naturally, I drank and partied, but nothing like him. The only appetite that we shared was for sex."

A gasp ripples around the John Lewis restaurant and I am relieved, because although this perestroika in our relationship is welcome, this is one subject I don't really want to consider in depth.

"I want you to tell Tom, if you don't mind, Lucy," she says. "I can't face it."

"I think you should do it," I say. "He won't mind nearly as much as you think. He understands the need to be loved and the fear of being alone. We all understand that. Why don't you come around this evening? I'm going out for a parent-rep meeting."

"If you are sure that is the best thing to do," she says.

"I am," I say, leaning back and considering how little we really know about the people closest to us. "We'll really miss you."

"The free babysitting and cleaning?" She smiles. "Not to mention the interfering. I'll miss that, too. You must come and stay in Marrakech. It's a very exciting city, and I think the children will enjoy it."

"Will you get married?" I ask.

"No," she says. "We'll live together in sin. I'm leaving in the new year so that I can spend Christmas with you all. If that still suits your parents."

"Absolutely. They would love it," I lie.

"Shall we go shopping? I'll treat you to something. Now that I'm selling the house, I'm feeling quite flush. Let's get you out of those jeans and into something pretty."

"Actually, I have enough trouble getting into my jeans. And I don't really do pretty. But thanks anyway. Why don't we look for presents for the children instead?"

We head off to the toy department. The combination of strip lighting, lumps of plastic in garish colors, and the number of Christmas presents still outstanding makes me feel nauseated. I would like to sit down on my own and digest everything that she has told me, commit the conversation to memory, because although I know that it marked something significant, at the moment I am not sure exactly what that might be. But Petra is glowing with the relief of unburdening herself and wants to move on to more prosaic matters.

That same evening, I leave my mother-in-law and Tom having dinner together and find myself driving to pick up Robert Bass, with a damp copy of *The Economist* casually lying on the front passenger seat. I am hoping to restore some intellectual footing to our relationship and have decided after a quick glance at the magazine in the bath that conversation during our short drive to Alpha Mum's house should focus on world affairs and other safe subjects. It might sound a bit contrived, but I have decided to take control of events rather than allow them to happen around me.

On the other hand, the fact that it is so damp that the pages have become stuck together might suggest to him that I have been reading it in the bath and therefore naked, which might make him think of affairs of a different kind. Men are very suggestible. All you have to do is say something like "butter" and they think of *Last Tango in Paris*.

Although this is the first time that I have driven to his home, the route is committed to memory. A few weeks earlier, I spent a few minutes on the computer one evening trying to trace his most logical itinerary to school using the AA route finder. I have the map, blown up to the largest size possible, on my knee.

Outside his house I wait in the car for him to appear. It is a classic early Victorian white stucco-fronted building with a newly painted blue front door. I can see down into the basement kitchen over a low white wall. Someone is washing dishes. A woman with an unforgiving gamine haircut is idly scouring saucepans. They cannot be clean, I think to myself as she stacks them precariously beside the sink. I see Robert Bass go over to her and put a hand on her bony shoulder. She turns around to kiss him on the lips. She is wearing skinny jeans and Ugg boots. It must be his wife. In the background I can see the small shadow of a toddler playing with trains on the floor. I sit back, leaning against the headrest in shock. I have never seen his wife before. I had imagined someone far removed from myself, a hard-edged city type in full makeup and wearing an Armani suit. A woman with a steely smile and carefully coiffed hair. Instead I am presented with this image of perfection. Of course, close up there will be the inevitable incipient crow's-feet, a hint of slackness around the stomach, and perhaps a shadow that all is not perfect in her eyes, but from a distance she has an enviable silhouette. I am staring so hard at her that I don't notice Robert Bass leave the house. He opens the car door and sits down on top of the magazine.

"Lucy, this is very kind," he says. We drive off, and each time he moves, I notice a little more of *The Economist* escape from beneath him, until finally it wriggles its way onto the floor. He leans over as though he is going to pick it up but decides to ignore it, lifting up the papers that lie on the floor to examine something else.

"What is it?" I say, trying to concentrate on driving.

"It's a pack of butter," he says, looking at me bemusedly. I jump and must have gasped because he says quickly that he has never met anyone who has a phobia about butter.

I know that he is thinking about Marlon Brando and I would like to take credit for my insight into the male psyche, but clearly this is not the moment.

"Your car is a source of wonder to me, Lucy," he says.

"Some people have second homes, I have my car. Do you mind stopping for gas?" I ask.

"I think that would be advisable, given your recent debacle, don't you?" he says smugly. He is looking through the CD cases in the glove compartment.

"Why are they all muddled?" he asks. "Actually, I'm not going to say any more."

"In answer to your earlier question, there are many worse things than running out of gas on the school run," I say.

"Some, but not many," he replies. When I get out of the car to go and pay at the garage, I feel annoyed with him, partly because his criticism stings but mostly because of his beautiful wife.

I wait patiently in the line, still distracted by the image of this woman in the basement, fumbling in my coat for my credit card. There is a hole in one of the pockets, and eventually I find the card at the bottom of the lining. People behind me start to shuffle impatiently. All seems to be going smoothly until the woman at the counter says something about a "small problem" in that way that people do when they mean the exact opposite. She says, leaning over the counter so that everyone starts to stare at us, that she needs to call the manager and advises everyone to join the other line.

"I'm afraid we have been asked to retain this card," says the manager, his chest puffed out with self-importance, making his badge that says "manager" loom even more prominently. "It has been reported stolen."

"Look, I can explain everything," I say, immediately realizing my mistake. "You see, I thought I had lost this card, so I reported it stolen, and now I have suddenly found it in the lining of my coat. I am the person on the card. I am Sweeney, Lucy Sweeney. Simple." I smile to engender feelings of trust. He looks dubious.

"Let me go to the car, and I'll find another one that will work," I tell him calmly.

"We have procedures to follow," he says. "Besides, you might do a runner. We know your sort."

"What is my sort? Are there many of us on the run?" I hear myself ask. "Do you really think there is a movement of mothers, distracted to madness by a combination of sleep deprivation, financial worries, and overflowing laundry baskets, who find an outlet for their frustration by engaging in small-scale credit-card fraud? Of course, if there is, we will be held to account because mothers are such an easy target."

I stop in mid-rant, because everyone is looking at me and I can see Robert Bass peering out the windshield in the garage forecourt.

"Besides, we're waiting for the police to arrive," the manager continues, staring at me with a more worried look in his eye. Bad, bad, bad, and getting worse. Robert Bass comes in to the shop, looking exasperated, running his hands nervously through his hair.

"We're going to be late," he says.

"Is this your accomplice?" says the manager, looking him up and down.

"Something like that," Robert Bass says with exasperation. "What's going on, Lucy?" I explain to him.

They make us sit behind the counter on a wooden bench.

"It's a bit more comfortable than the one we were sitting on the other night," I say, trying to inject a little lightness into proceedings. But he sits beside me holding his head in his hands, nervously ruffling his fine head of hair.

"I promise it will all be all right," I say to him, my hand hovering in the air somewhere near his shoulder.

"Don't talk, and keep your hands in your lap, please," says the manager. "You might have a weapon."

Half an hour later, a policeman arrives, wearing a bulletproof vest. Surely not for our benefit. He tells the manager not to waste his time and to phone my bank. The bank tells him that I have lost eleven credit cards so far this financial year and advises him to cut this one up and let us go.

We get back in the car in silence.

"I don't know how your husband deals with all this," Robert Bass says weakly. He tilts the seat back as far as it will go and shuts his eyes. An image I had imagined many times earlier in the day, but not under these circumstances.

"On the surface, your life looks so routine, but actually underneath it bubbles and backfires like an anarchic Central American country. Nothing is predictable," he says, his eyes still shut. "I can't imagine how he copes."

"Well, I don't tell him most of it," I say.

"You're good at keeping secrets, then." And he doesn't speak again until we reach Alpha Mum's house.

"You make up an excuse, it's your specialty. I don't have the energy," he says, sighing as I switch off the engine.

Alpha Mum opens the door looking smart-casual, a look that has always baffled me.

"You're rather late," she says. "I suppose that was to be expected. Still, I have printed an agenda so it shouldn't take too long."

"Sorry," I say. "Something came up."

She leads us into the kitchen and asks whether we would like a drink. I nod and am about to request a glass of white wine when she directs me to a drawer filled with teas for all occasions. It's going to be a long evening.

"What do you fancy?" I ask Robert Bass. "Sublime Dreams, Renewed Vigor, or Tension Tamer."

"The last one sounds good," he says weakly.

A bookshelf of parenting manuals catches my eye: *The 7 Habits of Highly Effective Families, Positive Parenting from A to Z, Going to School: How to Help Your Child Succeed.*

"Which parenting philosophy do you subscribe to, Lucy?" she asks.

"Slow mothering," I say, making it up as I go along. "It's part of the slow-town, slow-food movement, aimed at producing free-range children."

"Oh," she says, trying to mask her surprise. "I haven't heard of that one."

On the wall beside the fridge is a wall chart of weekly activities that is as tall as me. While the kettle is boiling, I go over to inspect. Kumon math, Suzuki violin, chess, yoga for children.

"It must be difficult keeping on top of all that," I say, pointing to the wall chart.

"It's the o-word, Lucy." She smiles knowingly. "Everything flows from there."

"Oh . . ." I mouth, my mind wandering.

"O for organization," she counters sternly and calls for the meeting to convene. "Let's begin with our mission statement," she says, looking at us both. This is what happens to successful professional women if they give up work and don't have enough to do. McKinsey mums, too much time, too much energy, too little instinct, I think to myself, trying to maintain a frozen expression of enthusiastic interest.

"I want my term in office to be remembered for the intellectual rigor introduced to school events," she says. Robert Bass looks taken aback. "So, at the Christmas party, before Santa and his little helper hand out presents, I am proposing a short concert of ancient English Christmas carols." She hands us copies of three she has chosen from a book of the same title.

"Don't you think it should be about having fun?" says Robert Bass, skim-reading the words to "Wassail, Wassail All over the Town," "Bring Us in Good Ail," and "As I Rode Out This Enders Night." "The children will be very excited about Santa Claus arriving. Besides, they are only five years old. It's unrealistic to think they can learn these," he protests.

"Precisely," says Alpha Mum, "which is why *we* are going to sing them." He chokes on his tea.

"But I can't sing," he says weakly.

"That doesn't matter, because no one will recognize you. You will both be in costume." We look at her blankly. "Santa and his little helper," she says, pointing theatrically at each of us.

"No," groans Robert Bass.

"I expected some resistance from Lucy over this, but not from you," says Alpha Mum frostily.

But I am entranced by the sight of Robert Bass undoing his shirt-sleeves and rolling them up. What is it about forearms? Alpha Mum seems unmoved.

"That all sounds wonderful," I say dreamily.

"Traitor," he mouths across the table.

I am a little taken aback. But it is not until I offer him a lift home, when the meeting finishes an hour later, that I realize the toll the evening has taken. "No thanks, Lucy. I think it's safer that way." In a different world, he could be referring to the danger of our smoldering attraction spinning out of control. Sadly, the truth is more pedestrian: I cause him too much anxiety of a nonsexual kind.

֍

So it is with some surprise a couple of weeks later that I arrive at school for the Christmas party to find Robert Bass dressed as Santa Claus, enthusiastically waving a hip flask at me from the children's toilet.

Since the failure of the evening at Alpha Mum's, my lustful feelings toward him had begun to deflate like a slow puncture, especially after he spurned my offer of a lift home. I could no longer indulge in the fantasy that I was secretly irresistible to him, and as this reality gained currency, my infatuation seemed ridiculous. Reason started to seep back.

"Quick, I've managed to escape her," he says theatrically, referring to Alpha Mum.

"Dutch courage. I made it myself. It's completely organic." He looks out to see if anyone is watching us before pulling me by the arm into the toilet. Leaning firmly against the door, he pulls his beard down around his neck, and takes a slug of sloe gin.

"Don't you think you should slow down?" I say. He seems more reckless than usual.

"It's the only way I can deal with that woman. She's dressed as the Fairy Queen. She's covered in flashing lights. Like Oxford Street," he babbles. He offers me a drink and I take a gulp to show solidarity and immediately start to overheat.

"Why don't you take your coat off, Lucy," he says, taking another slug. "It can't be that bad under there."

But it is. Underneath the ankle-length coat that Tom has lent me, I am wearing a bespoke elf costume, hastily fashioned for the occasion by Alpha Mum. Although she told me proudly that it was inspired by an ice-skating outfit, it is aimed, I suspect, at causing maximum humiliation. It comprises a short green felt dress, cinched at the waist, with a pleated skirt designed to maximize the size of my bum.

"What do you think?" I ask nervously.

"Ho, ho, ho. That might just get me through the day. You look like some gorgeous overripe fruit, like a greengage," he says, stepping backward and crashing into the sink. "There has to be some upside to this." I have never seen him like this before. When we had gone to the pub together, his drinking habits were notably restrained. I go over to pull him up.

"Sorry, I haven't had anything to eat," he said.

"How's the book going?" I ask, in an effort to restore a semblance of normality.

"Awful," he says. "I'm stuck. It's crap. And I've missed two deadlines."

Someone starts banging at the door.

"Santa, it's the Fairy Queen, and I order you to come out. Are you in there with the elf?"

"No," he shouts. "Just coming, I'm adjusting myself." He pulls up his beard. The opening where the mouth should be is by his right ear.

"Why did you lie?" I hiss to him. "Now it will look as though we have been doing something illicit if we come out together."

"Climb out the window," he says, breathing sloe gin fumes all over me. The opening is tiny, and I climb out headfirst. This is the second time in less than two months that I have found myself doing this, and I have learned nothing from the previous experience. All goes well until my bum gets stuck. The skirt of the dress is up around my shoulders, and I know that the only thing shielding my buttocks from Robert Bass is the pair of woolly tights. I squirm and wriggle, and Robert Bass pushes, and in different circumstances this might count as pleasure. I look up and see Yummy Mummy No. 1 approaching down the road.

"I'm not going to ask," she says, as I stretch out my arms toward her and she starts to pull me out.

"We need to roll her slightly on her side," she shouts to Robert Bass, clearly enjoying the challenge.

"This cork is going to pop," she shrieks gleefully.

Robert Bass manhandles me into position and I slide out onto the pavement, my dignity in tatters.

"We're just practicing," I tell her. "It's the same size as a chimney."

Later that night, I considered that incident. A certain familiarity had entered the equation, more Laurel and Hardy than *Love Story*, and for a short while the idea that we might become friends, as Cathy had suggested a couple of months ago, took hold. I felt relieved. I could now take Tom's necklace, when it reappeared, in good faith.

11

"You should know a man seven years before you stir his fire."

I know that Christmas is going to be a study in diplomacy when my father answers the door on Christmas Eve, wearing a woolly hat. It is one of those brightly colored Afghan affairs with earflaps. It could be an affectation to provoke Petra, who frowns on this kind of sartorial rebelliousness. Most probably he is wearing it because it is so cold in their farmhouse on the edge of the Mendips. I hug him hello, holding him tightly, out of genuine affection, but also to calculate how many layers he is wearing. It's a better augur of what lies ahead in terms of temperature than any thermometer.

"Don't think I don't realize what you are doing, Lucy," he whispers in my ear. "The answer is three, not including my vest." The subject of heating in my parents' home is older than me. The general consensus is that the house is poorly insulated, the radiators inefficient, and the double-glazing woefully inadequate, because it was bought cheaply from someone doing phone sales in the mid-seventies. My parents are famously fond of a good bargain.

The wide Inglenook fireplaces, which promise so much warmth with their stone seats on either side of the hearth, blow down cold air and suck up the heat remorselessly. Many times over the years, I have seen guests arrive and go into the sitting room, take off their coats and sweaters when

they see logs crackling on the fire, only to spend the rest of the visit surreptitiously replacing those layers to avoid offending my parents. They
have come to enjoy the spectacle and have been known to place bets on
who will cave in first.

It is a cruel deception, the warmth and coziness of a fire without any
heat, like a loveless marriage. At least from a distance it is possible to
maintain the illusion of comfort. If you get too close, the realization that
there is no hope of getting warmer somehow makes you feel even colder.
So we learned long ago to huddle together on the two sofas in the sitting
room. These are soggy beasts with geometric patterns that date from our
childhood. In a classic piece of improvisation, my mother has placed a
couple of pillows underneath the main cushions to compensate for the
worn springs. Even those with generous buttocks are known to wince if
they sit down too heavily.

The underlying truth of what Tom has dubbed The Cold War is that
my parents have a Presbyterian view on comfort derived from their experience as children during the Second World War and have never really
abandoned the idea of rationing. Even though my father swears that he
doesn't switch it off at night, all through the winter, after the ten o'clock
news, the heat is mysteriously sucked from the radiators amidst a great
deal of gurgling and rattling, and any nocturnal visits to the bathroom are
a teeth-chattering experience.

It is almost six months since we last came to visit, and the distance
means I view my parents with unwonted dispassion. So I note that my
father looks a little older and shabbier. My mother has cut his hair, and it
hangs in great gashes along the edge of his frayed collar. When he lifts up
an arm to hug me, I notice a gaping hole in his sweater. Long black hairs
poke from his ears and nostrils like unpruned bushes.

He has put on a tie to please Petra, who believes a man isn't really
dressed unless he is wearing one. In combination with the hat, however, it
somehow looks like another attempt to irritate her. Of course, once I tell
him that she is running away to Marrakech to live with a former lover, he
won't feel the need to poke fun at her. It is the kind of action of which he

approves but would never engage in himself. Like me, he enjoys living vicariously.

Tom braces himself for one of my father's firm handshakes. He has kept on a pair of leather gloves as a precaution. He now stands a good half head above my father and puts his left hand on my father's shoulder in an effort to weaken his grip.

My mother lurks in the background. For reasons I find impossible to fathom, she engages in all kinds of domestic brinkmanship with Petra. I notice that the wooden floor in the hall is polished, but when I move a china plate on the stone windowsill to make room for the car keys, a ray of sun shines in and highlights layers of dust. She will have changed the sheets in the spare bedroom but forgotten to clean the bath. The larder will be its usual muddle of old newspapers, plastic containers that she is resistant to throw out, and piles of laundry in black bin bags sitting in exactly the same spot as the last time we visited.

Since she met my father while she was teaching at Bristol University and still has a part-time job in the English department, she has an excuse for the anarchy. I, on the other hand, having chosen a different route, have no similar plea bargain. The fact that I gave up work not long after Joe was born was a source of discontent to my mother, who couldn't believe that I abandoned the job I loved to stay at home with my children.

"You're going to become a housewife," she said with barely veiled horror, closing the door of the larder so that Tom couldn't hear us. There was no shade on the light, and the draft that blew underneath the door from the kitchen caused the bulb to sway gently. Shadows danced around the walls, making me feel dizzy.

"Stay-at-home mum is the more politically correct term," I told her. I knew this would be a difficult conversation. Because although my mother professed her liberal parenting credentials at any opportunity, she was actually very prescriptive about how my brother and I should live our lives.

"It's Tom, isn't it," she said. "He wants a meal ready on the table when he comes home. He wants to turn you into his mother, imprison you in twinsets."

Since she was wearing a wool turtleneck sweater underneath a long dress with loud, blousy patterns that someone unkind might call a caftan, I ignored her comment about Petra's wardrobe.

"We don't really cook much in the evening unless he does it," I said. "Compared to a lot of men, he's actually quite helpful, and he knows that I am genetically challenged on the domestic front."

"Are you criticizing the way I run my home?" she said. I couldn't help laughing. For all her vociferous disdain of anything that smacked of domesticity, she was always defensive at any suggestion of deficiency on that front. I think she took it personally, as a slight on her own decision to keep working. No matter how many times I've told her that thirteen-hour shifts until eleven-thirty at night were less compatible with bringing up children than her own brief absences to go and deliver lectures on D. H. Lawrence, she still returns to the subject with disarming frequency.

Returning to the house where you grew up with your husband, children, and mother-in-law in tow is a discombobulating affair at the best of times. On the one hand, there is a reassuring familiarity in the surroundings and the repetition of ritual. The knowledge, for example, that you must take a paper clip upstairs if you want to have a bath, in order to get the plug out of the tub. Being woken up at six a.m. by the noise of my father making early-morning tea on the Teasmade in my parents' bedroom. Knowing the exact level of force needed to make the downstairs toilet flush. On the other hand, memories bump into you without warning, jostling for position, forcing you backward in time. Although mostly benign, there is a feeling of loss of control over their ability to hijack your thoughts at any moment. None of this has any emotional resonance for Tom, the children, or Petra, who are likely to view everything with a critical eye.

On this particular visit, however, my childhood memories are colliding with something that happened much more recently during the much-anticipated trip to the aquarium in the last week of term. In that short space of time, so much has changed that it feels that what came before happened years ago. Since then, the five o'clock insomnia has evolved into something more oppressive. Instead of giving me time to indulge in medium-term mental freewheeling—where to go on holiday, for example, or how to persuade Emma to give up on Guy—I am now filled with a creeping anxiety that insinuates itself into every tiny muscle, sinew, and tendon. The only positive repercussion is that I have exploited this nervous energy to get up at six o'clock in the morning to clean, tidy, and buff our house to perfection. Tom is getting suspicious. It seems incredible that life can pivot so much in such a short space of time.

We hear a loud bang through the ceiling in the hall, and my father winces. I tell the assembled company that I am going up to deal with the children, who raced up the narrow wooden staircase almost as soon as they came through the front door, heading for the bedroom that used to belong to my brother, Mark. But at the top of the stairs, instead of turning right to go down the passage to the children's room, I turn the other way and creep along the landing into my old bedroom. I need to be alone to digest events of the final week of term, even if it is only for ten minutes. And I have to formulate a strategy for forthcoming dealings with Robert Bass.

The room remains a shrine to Laura Ashley, with its matching curtains and wallpaper in familiar floral designs. The only nod to my married status is a small double bed that used to be in the spare room. I lie down, knowing before my head rests on the pillow that the mattress is so soft that my feet will be higher than my head and we will wake up every morning with horrible headaches and Tom will start to worry that he has a brain tumor. If I survive the week, at least I will know that the blood vessels in my head are made of stern stuff.

I crawl between two cold sheets, pull up three heavy woolen blankets and a bedspread in a different Laura Ashley print on top. It feels reassuringly heavy, and slowly my body stops resisting the weight of the blankets. For the first time since the trip to the aquarium, the catalyst for this anxiety, I feel the tension leave my body. Underneath me I can feel another scratchy wool blanket. But sleeping on sackcloth for a week might assuage some of my guilt.

I should be using these precious moments alone to focus on Christmas, to wrap the presents that I bought for Tom during a guilt-fueled spree, organize the children's stockings, or help my mother gain the upper hand over Christmas dinner, a challenge that she is usually unable to rise to. Instead I lie here, endlessly running through things, looking for clues that might have forewarned me about what happened.

The school trip to the London Aquarium began on a low note when I saw Alpha Mum board the bus with a *Dorling Kindersley Guide to Aquatic Life*. Joe's teacher looked askance. She does a very good line in subtle looks that manage to conjure a number of emotions in a single gesture. Withering, dismissive, and faintly impatient is her favorite blend when dealing with Alpha Mum.

"I have done a little quiz so that the children don't get bored on the journey," Alpha Mum said, standing at the front of the bus beside the driver and waving sheets of paper. "And I thought that we should also record all those with allergies, just in case the packed lunches get mixed up in transit. Also, I have brought a comprehensive first-aid kit, including Adrenalin."

Then she walked down the aisle a couple of paces and sat down beside me. Joe went to the back to sit with his friends. I noted that in spite of his neuroses, he seemed quite popular, and proudly pointed me out to his friends. Please don't let her start the conversation about how she is worried her toddler might not get into the right nursery and therefore miss out on early promotion at Goldman Sachs. Although I have transgressed, I don't deserve this, I thought to myself.

Robert Bass followed close behind her. He shrugged his shoulders when he saw that the seat next to me was taken. I sensed a hint of relief in his expression, but as became apparent later, this was a misjudgment. Had Alpha Mum not taken the seat, I would have been able to more accurately gauge his mood by assessing whether he chose proximity or distance, and that might have altered the ensuing course of events. It had been a few days since our last encounter, which had marked what I thought was a renewed intimacy in our relationship.

Alpha Mum opened her handbag and put the papers into a file, and then smoothed down the front of her neat, tailored trousers.

"I'm worried about nurseries," she said. In front of us sat a herd of Yummy Mummies, including Yummy Mummy No. 1, who was discussing exactly how many staff to take to the Caribbean at Christmas and whether a full-time or part-time cook was optimum. I was not deemed worthy to participate in this particular debate, although I would have come down heavily in favor of a full-time cook.

Worries are very subjective. Mine included concern that there wouldn't be a bottle of wine waiting for me when I got home, worry that Tom was going to discover the cigarettes hidden in the wardrobe, and alarm that I had taken both sets of car keys with me. If only that were still the extent of my troubles.

And it was still an hour to the aquarium.

"The one where we have got a place has no interest in encouraging pencil grip," Alpha Mum said. "I didn't breast-feed for a year, give up work, and cook organic meals every day for my child to end up at a sub-standard nursery."

I must have looked confused, because then she said, "Breastfeeding raises IQ by an average of six points."

"Perhaps you need to relax a little," I suggested. "Have some fun, regain perspective. It's easy to lose sight of yourself in all this."

"I refuse to let my children fall by the wayside," she said.

"The thing is," I told Alpha Mum, "there is no point in worrying about things that are simply out of your control." She looked intensely at me.

"The thing is, Lucy, that what you put in you get out," she said.

"Why would you want four neurotic overachieving children competing with each other and displaying attendant personality traits?" I said. "Is that a recipe for happiness or self-fulfillment?" And for once she fell silent.

Then my phone beeped. Robert Bass was texting me from two rows behind. Daring.

"The thing is, Lucy, that there's a seat beside me," the message read. I looked behind me and he waved.

I should have been more alert to this overture, but I had been too distracted the previous weeks by the repercussions of Petra's decision to move to Marrakech. Despite his initial calm acceptance, Tom had become convinced that her artist was a drifter who was going to live off the proceeds from her house sale. I was trying to persuade Tom that he should give him a chance before he passed judgment.

Curiously, as my feelings toward Robert Bass subsided, my concern that Petra was misjudging her situation increased.

So when it came to the only interactive part of the trip to the aquarium, my mind was wandering far from Robert Bass.

"Who wants to tickle the stingrays?" shouted Joe's teacher.

"Me," I shouted back enthusiastically.

"I thought we might let the children have a go first, Mrs. Sweeney," said the teacher, eyeing me warily. "And then we will take them for lunch to give the parents a little break."

So when the children melted into the background to go and eat their packed lunches, I stood on the step that surrounded the tank of stingrays and put my left hand in the water. It was unexpectedly icy, and my sleeve immediately got wet. My fingers ached with cold, but touching one of these strange, flat fish had become imperative. I wriggled my fingers slowly to keep them warm and to try to attract a fish, because that is what I had seen other people doing. Each time they came tantalizingly close, then turned just as I was about to touch them, showing off their shiny white underbellies and silently opening and shutting their coat-hanger-shaped mouths. By this time, my sleeve was wet up to my elbow, but I didn't care. In my head, having physical contact with a stingray had become inextricably linked with my state of mind. If I could touch one, I reasoned, then everything would be fine. Forever.

A pump forced the water round the large tank so that when I looked down at my hand, the fingers rippled involuntarily. It was impossible to keep them completely still. I concentrated on another stingray that seemed to be swimming on my side of the tank, not letting him out of my sight, willing him to come over. He was the largest one there, the kingpin, and the edges of his fins were threadbare with age. He moved toward me with his long nose haughtily poking out of the water, like a dolphin performing tricks, and then flipped onto his front, exposing his back and stopping in the water right in front of me. He felt cold and smooth, and I ran my fingers up and down his back. He flapped his fins in apparent pleasure and struggled to stay still, swimming against the pressure of the water. Then as I continued to stare, I was aware of another hand approaching my own under the water. For a moment I felt annoyed. I had waited patiently to commune with this old man of the sea, and now someone was trying to insinuate themselves into my moment.

This hand, however, was making no attempt to tickle the fish. Although through the water the perspective was distorted, it was obviously much larger than mine, and I watched in a detached kind of way as it slowly glided to where my own hand was tickling the stingray and then, for a brief moment, it gripped the back of my hand and a voice said, "The thing is, Lucy, I think I'm out of control."

I looked up. Of course I knew it was Robert Bass. He stroked the back of my hand underwater for what seemed like ages but was probably no more than a few seconds, and I was annoyed to feel a familiar stirring within. I was so close to his face that I could examine the pockmarks thoroughly, and suddenly they gave him a weathered look that was very attractive. He stared at me and, for a moment, I thought he was going to try and kiss me. Then he simply took out his arm and walked away. I stood there aimlessly, trying to absorb what had just happened. Then I noticed Alpha Mum watching me from a bench in a dark corner on the other side of the room. Her sleeves were rolled down around her wrists and her arms were crossed disapprovingly. She couldn't see what happened underwater, but there was no doubting the intensity of our gaze, nor our physical proximity.

Now when I am not feeling anxious, I am feeling guilty. I try to rationalize that nothing actually happened. I didn't initiate this scene, nor did I respond in any obvious way. Yet I have to accept that I did play a role in events leading to this entanglement. I had engineered after-hours encounters with Robert Bass, indulged in inappropriately lustful daydreams and minor flirting.

I'm now scared of what I might have precipitated. I had never imagined even in my wildest fantasies that my feelings might be reciprocated, or that there would be any real temptation to respond. What I failed to contemplate with respect to Robert Bass was that our feelings weren't synchronized and that my subtle withdrawal from our flirtation after our awkward evening at Alpha Mum's only served to foment his interest. In short, I had forgotten how well men respond to a bit of cold shoulder. I had discovered too late that there is nothing more innocent or diverting than unrequited lust. I wanted the fantasy of Robert Bass, not the reality.

I feel annoyed with him because the aquarium incident occurred just as I had found some renewed equanimity, although of course that imploded the moment he touched me. Mostly I feel annoyed because, suddenly, the stakes are higher. There is a heightened reality to my dreams about hotels in Bloomsbury that is disturbing rather than pleasantly distracting. The bed is unmade, empty bottles lie on their side on the floor, and the room smells of stale smoke. The colors are sickly.

"This is how affairs happen," Cathy tells me firmly when I phone her for advice, still hiding under the Laura Ashley bedspread with my cell phone, in case anyone is listening outside the door. "If you felt any urge to reciprocate, stay well away. Even if he is just playing a game, it's a diversion fraught with risk."

"I'll try to avoid him," I say.

I tell her about a recent full-blown nightmare, in which my tummy played the lead role.

"Sexy Domesticated Dad was lying naked on the bed and I couldn't get out of my jeans without a struggle," I say. "Then, when he saw my stomach, he started screaming. I think he thought it had separated from the rest of my body."

"Well, just hold that image in your head if ever you feel tempted," she says. "At least you can forsake a new-year diet to save your marriage."

"But what if Tom feels the same way about my stomach?" I ask.

"He's had time to get used to it," she says.

I hear footsteps outside the door. My mother is showing Petra her room. I take the opportunity to get out of bed and slip down the corridor to go and see the children. I can still hear them jumping from the bed onto the floor. I don't mind because at least it will keep them warm. I bathed them and put them in pajamas and dressing gowns before we left

London, because I knew that there would not be enough hot water for everyone to have a bath here. Sharing bathwater was an unquestionable backdrop to my childhood.

I open the door of my brother's bedroom. The walls are mauve, painted by Mark during the term of his mock A levels after he read somewhere that red would incite passion and decided it would make a good setting to practice his seduction techniques with girls from school, mostly my friends. In the corner is an avocado sink unit with slatted doors that are painted mauve.

I go over to this cupboard and open it. A bottle of Old Spice has fallen on its side and stained the shelf. There are half-bottles of shampoo, a toothbrush with splayed bristles, a half-full pot of Brylcreem, a couple of old copies of *Playboy* from the late 1970s that I remove and put on top of the wardrobe, and, bizarrely, there are my old copies of *Jackie* magazine that my brother must have purloined in his efforts to get to grips with the female psyche.

A poster of Bo Derek has faded, and the area where her nipples once stood out so proudly has been rubbed into oblivion. Still, Sam is impressed.

"Bosoms," he says, pointing at the wall.

Then he points at another poster on the back of the door. They have hung their Christmas stockings just below a poster of a woman shot from behind, wearing a very short tennis dress. She is casually lifting up a side of her dress to reveal that she isn't wearing any knickers, her head turned back across her shoulder to look directly at the camera.

Looking at the stockings hanging just underneath the tennis player's left buttock, I can't help smiling as I vividly recall an argument between Mark and my mother about this poster. It must have been the summer of 1984, at the height of the miners' strike. We were in the sitting room, watching the news, when extraordinary images of a pitched battle between police and miners somewhere in south Yorkshire flashed on the screen.

"Why do you hang all those posters of half-naked women on your walls?" said my mother, as the police ran at the miners, holding their plastic shields.

"What would you like to see on my wall, Mum?" said Mark, who was always much better than me at holding his own in an argument. I always tended to see the other point of view too quickly.

"What about Nicaragua, the antiapartheid movement, something more issue-based?" my mother said. We all winced as a policeman struck a miner in the head with his baton.

"Arthur Scargill doesn't really do it for me, Mum," Mark replied.

"I think you should take that poster down. It shows a lack of respect to women," she persisted.

"I have nothing but respect for her," Mark argued.

"You have no interest in what is going on in her head; you're fixated on her body," she then insisted.

"Of course he is," my father said, looking up from the newspaper. "He's a teenage boy." We all stared at him, because my father, a quieter, more pensive character than my mother, had learned early in his marriage that it was more tactical to keep his own counsel when she showed some sudden conviction in a new cause.

"I thought you believed in freedom of expression, Mum," Mark argued, sensing he was close to victory. My mother said nothing and wandered off into the kitchen.

∽

The bedroom door opens, and the woman with the bottom disappears momentarily, until Tom shuts it firmly behind him. He is adopting a positive attitude toward the heating problem, taking every opportunity to draw attention to the cold, which is a little exhausting, but facing the challenge with relish, like Scott in the Antarctic. He is still wearing a hat and gloves. This excitement will turn into resentment as the days go by and he can no longer resist the urge to criticize.

It is the coldest December since 1963. There is snow on the ground, and the windchill factor has been a news item for more than a week. It is a great time for those who like numbers, like Joe, who has been plotting the rise and fall of the temperature on a graph each day, applauded for his efforts by his father.

"I wanted to check those toes for early signs of frostbite," Tom jokes, making the children line up for inspection.

"That one looks a little black, Joe," Tom says, lifting Joe's foot until his toe is level with his eye. Then, when he sees the worried look on Joe's face, he tries to backtrack, but it is too late.

"My toe will fall off in the night," Joe says.

"If it does, can we dissect it, Mummy?" asks Sam.

"Daddy's just joking; it has to be below freezing to get frostbite," I say calmly.

"The thermometer in the hall says that it is eleven degrees inside the house," says Tom.

"I think I might add that to my weather chart," says Joe, distracted by talk of numbers.

"Bottom, Daddy," says Fred, pulling Tom's arm and pointing excitedly at the poster. "No pants. Like me."

"Dad, would you describe her bottom as sexy?" asks Sam thoughtfully. He has been listening to too much Christina Aguilera.

"What does 'sexy' mean, Sam?" Tom asks him, in a classic attempt at deflection. He uses the same tactic in discussions with me.

"I don't know, really," he says. "I think it's something to do with fruit. If a bottom looks like a peach, it's sexy, I think."

The children always stay in this room, and it never ceases to be exciting to them. Although there is a single bed, they prefer to all lie on the floor entwined with each other like puppies in a basket, and since it is generally cold, I encourage this habit. Fred, who usually has to be read stories into oblivion, is always wedged in the middle.

"I can see my breath, Mummy," he now says proudly.

"You're smoking," says Sam. "Like Mummy."

"I don't smoke," I protest.

"Well, why do you keep those cigarettes in your boot?" Sam asks.

"They're just for special occasions. What are you doing looking in my wardrobe anyway?" I say.

"I wasn't," he says. "Granny told me."

"I can't believe you are so devious, Lucy," says Tom.

"That's half the fun," I say. "You should be happy I still have some sense of mystery."

"Will Santa Claus know that we are here?" asks Joe, sensing an argument brewing. "Because it's so cold, he might think there isn't anyone living here. Do you think he has those heat-seeking glasses?"

Sam is dragging Mark's record player from the wardrobe and searching for his old singles and LPs. He picks out David Bowie from the pile and puts it on. I get into Mark's old bed with Tom and pull the duvet up to my nose and listen to "Scary Monsters." When Joe starts to chew his sleeves during the chorus—"Scary monsters, super creeps, keep me running"—I ask Sam to carefully lift up the stylus and move it on to the next song and tell them that I will come back in twenty minutes to switch off the light. I resolve to tell Tom everything that has happened. But when I come back all of them are asleep, including Tom.

12

"A little knowledge is a dangerous thing."

Over the next few days, allegiances are made and broken with alarming frequency. There are no outward declarations of war, just an undercurrent of tension that culminates in periodic bouts of verbal jousting. My brother, Mark, who arrived late last night, without his girlfriend, says that he is grateful for such family gatherings because they provide a flurry of patients for him in January.

When I go downstairs into the kitchen on Christmas Day, I sense a chill in the air that is unrelated to the weather. Petra is standing by the large pine table in the middle of the kitchen, struggling to stir a bowl of icing for a naked Christmas cake. I know this cake began the day dressed in the smooth, clean lines of an industrially iced factory cake, and I try to work out just what is going on.

Tom is on the other side of the room, busy taking a large dose of prescription painkillers that my brother has given him for a bed-induced headache.

"Don't drink too much with these," says Mark.

"Just run through the classic symptoms of a brain tumor again," says Tom between gulps of water.

"Headaches, usually worse in the morning, dizziness, nausea," says Mark, without looking up from yesterday's paper.

"Do you think I should see a specialist?" Tom persists.

"No," says Mark. "It's the bed. It's always the bed. You always think you have a brain tumor when you come to stay here. Why don't you go and do something useful like organize the spices? It's a great displacement activity. The kind of occupational therapy I prescribe on a daily basis."

"If they go on, will you arrange a brain scan for me?" asks Tom.

"I can recommend someone in neurology, but we both know the headaches will disappear as soon as you stop sleeping in that bed. Just make sure you avoid any activity that might induce a sudden rush of blood to the head." Mark laughs uproariously. I wonder if he is more reassuring when he deals with his patients. Since he has just been promoted to head the psychology department of a big London teaching hospital, he must be doing something right.

Petra looks over disapprovingly, because this is what Mark expects of her, but she has always been surprisingly benevolent toward my brother. When she speaks to him, she uses an irritating high-pitched girly voice that teeters on the edge of flirtatiousness.

"So, tell me about your African adventure, Petra," says Mark indulgently. "When do we get to meet your lover?" He says "lover" slowly, with emphasis on the first syllable.

Petra is dressed in the same double layer of cashmere twinset that she was wearing yesterday: pale pink atop cream, like a marshmallow. She ignores his question and blushes. I look over worriedly at Tom, who is still having difficulty coming to terms with the fact that his mother has a boyfriend.

Fred lies underneath the table in the dog basket, contentedly licking a wooden spoon.

My mother tells Petra that she made the cake weeks ago. I know this is a lie, because I found the packaging in the pantry last night. She must have picked off the original icing early this morning in order to engage in this deception.

"I think you'll find that if you add a teaspoon of lemon juice to the mixture, then it makes the icing easier to squeeze," Petra says to her in a clipped voice.

"I have always made my icing with water and icing sugar," my mother replies confidently from the other end of the table. "Just keep stirring until it softens up."

"I think you'll find that the more you stir, the harder it will set," Petra says firmly, but she doesn't put down the spoon.

She is using some effort to get the stiff icing sugar to move round the bowl and removes one of her outer layers of cardigan. I notice that she places the heels of her shoes firmly together and turns out her toes in that gesture of defiance that only those who have known her for many years would observe.

"So, Petra, where are you going to live?" asks Mark. Tom and I have spent weeks trying to muster the courage to pose such questions, and I admire the ease of Mark's direct line of inquiry. Since the infamous John Lewis lunch, a chill has once again set between us. Because although she managed to tell Tom of her plans, she opted for the most skeletal details and they have not mentioned the subject since, except to deal with organizational issues relating to the sale of her house.

It is as though the only way that she can make the guilt tolerable is to avoid all but the most superficial discussions. Perhaps she fears that any depth of communication might make her change her mind.

"John owns a house in the Medina," she says. "But he has also bought somewhere up in the Atlas Mountains, and we'll spend part of the year there, when it gets too hot for Marrakech. He likes to paint there. He also has a house in Santa Fe. He's American, you know, he's quite well known in the States." Tom and I look at each other because we didn't. She stops stirring for a moment and stares wistfully out of the kitchen window at the frost-bleached landscape. Everything is a different shade of pale. A herd of huddled sheep stare back at us from the field that marks the end of the garden. Occasionally, they start bleating as though gossiping about what they are witnessing.

Nothing like an audience to curb the worst family excesses, I think to myself, glad the sheep are enjoying their own Christmas special.

I struggle to assess whether this sudden flurry of disclosure makes the situation better or worse. It is difficult to read Tom's expression. He is standing on a step opposite the stove, studiously ignoring the détente between our mothers. Instead, he has followed Mark's advice and is organizing my mother's herbs into alphabetical order.

"Do you think I should put the black pepper under B or P?" he asks Petra.

"I think you'll find that it's better to put it under P, followed by dried peppers and then white pepper," she says. This kind of exchange represents some deep communion between them.

I think sometimes that it is this die-hard belief in domestic routine that has helped Petra to cope with the death of Tom's father. Standards were never allowed to slip, even in the awful early days when he left her stranded following a massive and fatal heart attack. I remember a couple of weeks after he died, Petra asked us to go to the house they had lived in together for the previous forty years to help clear out old clothes belonging to him. The gesture seemed a little premature. But from the moment of that terrible phone call in the early hours of Sunday morning, Petra had been unnervingly dignified in her approach to the loss of her husband. There was no hysteria. No self-pity. No emotional outbursts.

"She won't cry in front of us," said Tom. "It's not her style. She will save it all for when she is alone."

So when I came down into the kitchen one morning during a bout of insomnia to find her weeping silent tears as she ironed underwear belonging to Tom's father, which she had obviously washed the previous evening after we went to bed, I was almost relieved. Her shoulders heaved, and great pools of tears fell onto pairs of white pants and string vests. Why didn't her washing ever go gray, I wondered? How could she cry so noiselessly and gracefully? I considered my own emotional meltdowns, a salty mixture of water, snot, and spit that left me looking bulbous and red. I needed a man's handkerchief to mop those up. Petra, on the other hand, dabbed at the corners of her eyes with a small lace affair with embroidered roses.

In the corner were three large black bin liners, one neatly filled with striped shirts that her husband had worn for work. He was a man who considered himself daring for sporting brightly colored socks with his sober suits and ties. Accountants are meant to be bland, he always said.

No one wants an eccentric accountant. There were jackets from an era when smart-casual involved precarious decisions over whether other guests would opt for a blazer with big brass buttons or the more relaxed sport jacket, or even put on a lounge suit. A pair of large black Wellington boots lay felled on the floor.

"Are you all right?" I asked her, gripping her elbow until she put down the steaming iron.

"It's not easy, Lucy," she said, sniffing delicately.

"Why are you ironing these clothes?" I asked gently.

"I couldn't possibly send them to the charity shop with creases," she said, looking at me with a shocked expression on her face. "If I did that, the whole thing would unravel."

Petra continued to wash sheets once a week through that dark period. Her underwear was always ironed. And the freezer remained filled with home-baked food, albeit in small, sad tinfoil portions for one person instead of two. They were rarely eaten. I hold on to this image to engender feelings of sympathy toward her that were seriously compromised when I opened my Christmas present late last night. She had bought both my mother and me a copy of *What Not to Wear* by Trinny and Susannah, handing them over with great excitement. "I thought I should give these to you now, in case they come in handy over the festive period," she said. My mother looked at the book blankly. Apart from the news, she hasn't watched much television since the early 1980s. Trinny and Susannah have not registered on her radar.

My mother strides over from the fridge. She has clearly not yet examined the book, because her Christmas look consists of a curious ensemble involving a skirt with a broken hem that hangs down at the back, and a petticoat visible both from the neckline of her unbuttoned shirt and the uneven hemline. Her shirt, a striped number that I remember her wearing when I still lived at home, is done up wrong. Everything is lopsided.

More cart horse than Thoroughbred, I think to myself, comparing her unfavorably with Petra. My mother has even applied makeup. But she is out of practice and probably using products bought more than a decade ago. The foundation is thick and unctuous and nestles in the wrinkles on her forehead and around her eyes, so that if she laughs, a small stream oozes out. Her lips are painted in a strong orange color, her cheeks berry-red with rouge.

My mother's insouciant attitude to her personal appearance used to be an endearing eccentricity. Now she just looks disheveled and old. I feel a sudden need to protect her from unforgiving eyes. This is a sentiment new to me and, for the first time, I realize that the balance in our relationship is shifting and that I will be called upon to take more and more responsibility. I start to feel breathless with the weight of what lies ahead.

My feelings toward my mother are fairly straightforward because she is generally uncomplicated. There is no emotional blackmail. No passive-aggressive behavior. No criticism of my parenting techniques, beyond the inevitable disbelief that her daughter chose to disengage from her career. Her belief system has barely evolved since I was a child, and over the years her strong opinions have become comforting in their predictability. Most belong to a different era. Her feminism is cast from the Betty Friedan mold, her Labour party allegiance more Neil Kinnock than Tony Blair. I know that she hoped that I would grow up with my compass set along the same lines, but nothing has ever seemed certain to me. I still find it too easy to see the other person's point of view. To believe anything too much seems almost reckless. Her fear that having children might shackle her to the kitchen and jeopardize her hard-won freedoms meant that she spent much of our childhood running away from us. As though everything would be fine as long as she kept moving. She feared giving into maternal urges, in case they might prove irresistible. She was often physically around, it was just that her mind was engaged elsewhere, mostly in some book or other. My brother blames his inability to form long-term relationships on this emotional distance.

"You're behaving like someone in therapy, blaming your parents for your own inadequacies instead of taking responsibility for your own destiny," I told him during our most recent argument about this, shortly after he had finished his last two-year relationship.

"If I'm behaving like someone in therapy, that might be because I *am* in therapy," he said, because psychologists have to learn to take it as well as give it. "You just haven't reached the level of consciousness required to realize that our childhood was blighted."

"All parents are flawed," I told him. "There is no such thing as a perfect parent. What parents should aim for is being good enough."

"You've been reading Winnicott," he said accusingly.

"I don't know what you're talking about," I said.

"That is Winnicott's theory," he said. "The good-enough mother . . . starts off with an almost complete adaptation to her infant's needs, and as time proceeds, she adapts less and less completely, gradually, according to the infant's growing ability to deal with her failure."

"Well, good on Winnicott then," I said. "It's people like you who have undermined mothers. You have created a chain of command with experts at the top and parents at the bottom. That's why those poor women got locked away in prison, falsely accused of killing their babies, on the basis of flawed evidence from a scientist they had never met. It's the Guantánamo approach to mothers; you're guilty unless you can prove your innocence."

Now, I'm not denying that my mother has flaws. But there was nothing, even as a teenager, that I couldn't have discussed with her if I had chosen to. She was nonjudgmental and practical. Unlike Tom's family, where I struggled to decipher conversations and interpret looks, like someone on their first French exchange, finally realizing after several years that things that were said were often the opposite of what was meant, there was little hidden in ours. There were long, rowdy discussions late into the night and half-drunk bottles of wine that were cleaned up the following morning. Most arguments were inconclusive, and there was a lot of verbal incontinence, mostly on my mother's part, because my father had a more evidence-based, less instinctive approach to debate, but at least everything was up for discussion. There was nothing repressed. My brother is less forgiving of our childhood, but I think that is because I understand what women are up against.

"Perhaps you would like to try?" I suddenly hear Petra say in a frosty tone. She is handing the wooden spoon to my mother, waving it in front of her face like a sword. The icing on the spoon is set as hard as the expression on Petra's face. She does up the top button of her cardigan. The battle lines are drawn.

My mother, never one to turn down a challenge, struggles to get the white mass to shift, using her not inconsiderable strength. It moves slightly, and in this subtle movement she finds vindication, but it is one great bowl-shaped mass, with the consistency and form of a Viking helmet. If the willpower of my mother cannot shift the icing, then nothing short of an ice pick will.

"I'm going to slice it in half and put the bottom bit on top of the cake," my mother says, defiantly pointing toward the knife drawer. I open it. I want her to win this battle, because the odds are stacked against her. The knife drawer is stiff and cumbersome to open, and when I finally manage to pull it out, there are many things inside but no sharp knife.

"We haven't had one of those since the early eighties," my father says unhelpfully, looking at me, then down at the paper again, blissfully unaware of the drama unfolding at his kitchen table. Petra leans over my shoulder and peers into the drawer. I can see her dissecting the contents. Old bills, stray playing cards, corks, plastic lids, an obituary cut out from the *Guardian,* rusty icing nozzles in various sizes, bits of string in different colors, grains of rice, porridge oats, and other unidentifiable debris that has found its way in over the years. Outside, the sheep bleat loudly as if discussing this display. They sense the buildup of dramatic tension.

"Would you like me to sort this out?" Petra asks eagerly. Without waiting for an answer, she takes out the drawer and immediately starts the process. "How are the children going to get the reindeer and Santa Claus to stand up on the icing? It's set hard as concrete, no one will be able to bite through it," she says, efficiently lining up objects into intelligible categories. "Why don't you let me start from scratch?"

"Because this is the way that I have always done it," says my mother fiercely.

I doubt whether she has ever made icing before, and it is bewildering to me why she engages in this pretense. It is simply not her area of expertise, and both women would be happier if Petra was left to take over everything relating to Christmas food.

"Shall I get on with the roast potatoes?" asks Petra, who at the moment has the diplomatic upper hand. "I think you'll find that if you sprinkle them with semolina rather than flour before you put them in the oven, they will have a crunchier edge."

She is moving toward the fruit bowl, and I know even before she reaches her destination that she will be unable to contain herself from throwing away the moldy apple that I spot on top.

My mother goes into the pantry that leads off the back of the kitchen, and I follow close behind.

"B is for bastards," she seethes, and I shut the door to have one of those hold-it-together conversations.

"This is a difficult time for them," I explain. "The more anxious they are, the more they tidy up. Just try and enjoy it. Don't take it personally. Petra prides herself on her domestic capabilities; they are integral to her sense of self. You have many other things in your life, so be generous."

"It's a difficult time for me, having both of them here at once," she says, sitting down on a stool and accidentally setting off a mousetrap with the tip of her shoe. "I thought the decision to move to Morocco might have loosened her up. I can't believe that she can be engaged in something so impetuous and still be obsessing about the consistency of icing at the same time."

"She draws comfort from the repetition of these rituals, just as you do from delivering that introductory lecture on D. H. Lawrence to first-year students every year and seeing the expression on their faces when you say 'cunt'," I say. "I think it is because she is moving to Morocco that you want her to get worked up over the icing. So that she conforms to your expectations. I think that you are resentful of this late blush of freedom in Petra's life, so you are trying to force her back into her corner. Anyway, she's got a point about the icing."

"Why would I be jealous?" she says. I am surprised at her use of adjective, because I hadn't actually considered that my mother might be envious of Petra's existence.

"Because for the first time since you have known her, she is doing something more exciting than you," I say. "You're not used to her taking center stage."

This explanation seems to satisfy her, and I sense her moving on to new territory.

"So, Lucy, when are you going to get a proper job?" she asks.

"I have a proper job," I say. "Looking after children is a proper job."

"It is unpaid hard labor," she says.

"I couldn't agree with you more," I say. "But I would have thought, given your political leanings, that you would be the last person to judge a person's worth based on the size of their paycheck. Just because I don't earn any money doesn't mean what I'm doing has no value."

"I can't believe that a daughter of mine has chosen to be a housewife," she says, her mouth twisting as though the word has a bitter taste.

"Actually, Mum, part of the problem lies with feminists like you, because in overemphasizing the importance of women working, you totally devalued domestic life," I say. "In fact, you're indirectly responsible for the current schism between working and nonworking mothers."

She looks a little taken aback.

"Fred is at nursery now, you must have more time on your hands," she persists.

"But then there's the holidays," I say. "Do you know how much money I would have to earn to pay for child care?" She ignores that argument.

"What I mean is, when are you going to do something that involves using your brain?" she says.

"Well, that's a different question. I do use my brain, only in a less obvious, more lateral way," I say. "Anyway, it's not that I left work, work left me. If I could find something part-time that was compatible with having children, I would do it."

"It's such a waste," she says, warming up to the subject with familiar zeal.

"Did you know that mothers with children who are out of the workforce for more than five years are less employable than Eastern European immigrants who can't speak English?" I say. "Didn't you see that in the paper last week? No one wants to give us jobs, at least not the kind that I would enjoy. There's a dilemma for you and your feminist cronies to debate in the pub."

"But do you feel fulfilled, Lucy?" she persists. "Is it satisfying?"

One of my mother's most endearing traits is her infinite curiosity about what motivates people, especially if their choices are at odds with her own. Her persistent line of questioning might appear critical, especially since she is a woman of strong opinions, but there is a childlike innocence to her approach, an unquenchable desire to really understand where someone else is coming from.

"At the end of the day, I often feel as though I have achieved nothing," I say to her. "A successful day consists of maintaining the status quo. I have managed to get three children to and from school and nursery without significant mishap. I have cooked three meals, bathed three children, and read them all bedtime stories. When I compare that to what I was doing before, it seems absurd, especially since I don't seem to get any better at it."

"But you are at ease with your children. I don't think I ever felt that." She sighs.

Something in my pocket starts to beep.

"What's that?" says my mother suspiciously.

"Joe's Tamagotchi," I say, taking out my son's electronic pet and pressing a few buttons. "It needs feeding. I promised him I would look after it while he watches *The Sound of Music.*"

In the corner of the pantry, I spot a large shape covered with tinfoil.

"What's that?" I ask her.

"Oh, God, it's the turkey. I've been so distracted by that woman that I've forgotten to put it in the oven," she says, removing the foil to reveal the huge, loose-skinned, bald bird beneath. Its color and texture match her arms. "She's won again."

"Why do you get so competitive with Petra?" I ask wondrously. "Your culinary disasters are usually feted. It's not as though anyone has any expectation of anything else."

"It's difficult to explain," she says. "I suppose I measure myself against her and find myself lacking as a homemaker. Then I wonder if I did the right thing by my children."

"Of course you did," I say. "We're no more than averagely fucked up. In fact, we're slightly less than averagely fucked up. That's a good outcome. Average is good. It prevents extremes."

The door opens and Mark wanders in. He is eating a bag of chips. "I'm anticipating a late lunch," he says.

"More criticism," says my mother, flouncing out of the pantry and back into the kitchen carrying the turkey.

Mark sits down in the chair that my mother has vacated and immediately steps on another mousetrap.

"Shit. That hurt," he says, rubbing his big toe. He is wearing a pair of thick hand-knitted socks that Petra made him for Christmas. The trap hangs limply at the end.

"How are you, Lucy?" Mark asks. "I've hardly had a moment to talk to you properly. You seem a little preoccupied," he says, taking off his sock to rub his toe.

"Is that your professional assessment?" I ask him. "Or are you simply trying to deflect attention to avoid any difficult questions about the whereabouts of your girlfriend and your lack of Christmas presents?"

"They got left in London," he says, looking guilty.

"The presents or the girlfriend?" I ask.

"Both," he says. "But not in the same place. And that is significant. I got some trashy stuff for the boys at the service station. Anyway, let's not talk about me."

"But I'm sure your stories are more interesting than mine," I say.

"Do you want me to tell you what I think about Joe?" he asks suddenly. "I promise I'm not trying to avoid awkward issues. I just thought that might be what you are worrying about."

"It's one of a multitude of things on my mind," I say, softening. Mark has been an unerringly good and faithful uncle to our children. "Tell me what you think."

"I think that although he is displaying certain neurotic tendencies, there is little of the repetition and ritual that is the classic manifestation of obsessive-compulsive disorder," Mark says.

"But what about all the worry during *The Sound of Music* and the shrinking?" I ask.

"That is a symptom of anxiety, of a deep-seated desire for things to stay the same, for predictability and routine in his life," says Mark. He has got up from the seat and is wandering around the pantry, lifting the lids off various containers and peering inside to see what lurks within. "The shrinking is more complicated. I think it has something to do with a desire to retreat from the world to a place where everything is safe and makes sense. He's an unusually sensitive child. He'll probably end up doing something creative."

"You don't think it's my fault? That my chaos has made him neurotic?" I ask.

"No, better to veer on the side of chaos than be too controlling," he says. "Behind an anxious child there often lurks a neurotic parent. Being a good mother depends on defining the right dose of devotion. Too little and the child wilts, too much and it is stifled."

"So you don't think I need to go and see someone?" I ask.

"Basically, I think you need to accept that he is his father's son," he says.

Mark is busy throwing out a maggot-infested container of rice that he has found on a shelf. Something beeps in my pocket again and I get out the Tamagotchi. But it is asleep, so I pull out my cell phone from the back pocket of my jeans to check my messages and am shocked to see that there are three from Robert Bass, all sent much earlier this morning.

"Want sex. Where are u?" they all read.

This is hardly a logical extension of the approach made at the aquarium. I drop the phone in astonishment and it slides across the greasy floor toward my brother.

"Just as well Mum didn't serve this rice up to Petra," he says, bending down to pick up the phone. I rush over, but he is too fast. He can't resist a peek at the screen and holds the phone high in the air, exploiting his height to advantage. Privacy is an alien concept to Mark. As a teenager, I had to hide my diary underneath the floorboards in the bedroom to prevent him from reading it.

The expression on his face immediately darkens. He squints at the message, reading it again to be sure that he hasn't misunderstood. Then he fiddles with the phone to look at the identity of the sender.

"Who the fuck is SDD?" he asks.

"I don't know," I say weakly.

"He's on your contacts list, otherwise his name wouldn't come up," says Mark, looking at me suspiciously.

"If you must know, it stands for Sexy Domesticated Dad," I say defensively.

"Is he from one of those cleaning services where the men come and tidy your house naked?" Mark asks.

The idea is so preposterous that I start to laugh.

"Is that what's putting you off married life in the suburbs?" I ask him, giggling so much that I have to cross my legs.

And then, because I am so nervous about the message and my brother's discovery, I find it difficult to stop, and each time I try to start a serious explanation of what is going on, I laugh even more. I suddenly feel very much like his younger sister again, a feeling that hasn't occurred very often in our relationship since I became the one with the husband and children and he became the serial dater, unable to make up his mind about which girlfriend he should marry.

Then the phone rings and Mark drops it on the floor. We both stare at it, and I pick it up to answer the call.

"Lucy, it's me," says Robert Bass. "Look, I'm really sorry, I meant to send those texts to my wife, but I must have put in your number by mistake. I hope you didn't think, er, that, er . . ." he splutters.

Trying not to sound too relieved, I say, "To be honest, I prefer a more subtle approach."

More spluttering. "You must be on my mind." He laughs weakly. He's right. I can't help feeling a little flattered. Then the line goes quiet. "Hello, hello, are you there?" I ask.

"Who are you speaking to?" I hear his wife ask. "Who is on your mind? You might as well tell me, because all I have to do is look at your phone." The line goes dead. I have little time to consider the implications of this interruption, because my brother is standing over me with his hands on his hips.

"Are you having an affair?" asks Mark.

When we were younger, my brother's attitude to my boyfriends ranged from dismissive, when the flirtation was unrequited, to surreptitiously protective when I embarked on a new relationship. He basically operated on the assumption that all men were as indiscriminately promiscuous as he was.

"It's because my mother is a feminist and we had too many au pairs to sleep with. I'm engaged in a kind of Oedipal revenge," he used to say. "Just remember, Lucy, men might talk the talk, but that doesn't mean we'll walk the walk."

And then, against all better judgment, I find myself clearing a space on the windowsill, moving empty jars of coffee and dirty old milk bottles and sitting down to tell Mark in detail the saga of Robert Bass. The innocent flirtation that ended in a flat kind of pass being made on a school trip. I can hear how ridiculous it all sounds as I tell it from beginning to end. He doesn't interrupt and looks at me intently.

"It's not really a big deal," I say. "Nothing has happened."

"Do you find him attractive?" he asks.

"Yes, in the abstract," I admit cautiously.

"Then it is a big deal, because he obviously fancies you."

"Do you really think he does?"

"Don't be so naive, Lucy. To believe otherwise is to engage in self-deception on a grand scale. You are deluding yourself to allow a situation where an affair can flourish. Frankly, I'm really surprised."

"Do you think I'm having a midlife crisis?" I ask him. "I thought that was a male prerogative."

"No." He laughs. "You have disconnected from Tom, and rather than mending that short circuit, you are looking for a new connection with someone else. But the answers won't be found with this man. They lie within you."

"Don't you think I could just have a small affair and then leave it all behind?" I ask him.

"Women are useless at that," he says. "And I don't mean that makes it a negative quality. Women's inability to separate emotion from sex is not a weakness, it is a strength. It fosters connection and mutual understanding. I have never understood why women view one-night stands and an ability to binge-drink as a sign of social progress. Why is it positive to adopt traits more commonly associated with men? Men would do better to become more like women. I'm speaking as someone who has found that particularly elusive."

"So what should I do?" I ask.

"Tell Tom," he says. "By allowing other people into the fantasy, you will minimize the possibility of turning it into reality. And if you don't tell him, then I will. You might be chalk and cheese, but largely your relationship works, and life is about much more than short-term pleasure-seeking, especially now that you have children. That's why we are all so miserable. We're obsessed by the quick hit, a couple of lines of coke to improve a party, a dirty fuck with a married woman. But this separates us from who we are. It destroys our spirit rather than elevating it. Do you know the biggest growth area in my profession? Dealing with adolescent boys who have spent so much time surfing Internet porn that they are completely unable to relate to women sexually or emotionally. If you thought the men of your generation were fucked, then you should take a look at these kids. Being brought up on *Playboy* was an age of innocence."

"I don't really see how this relates to me," I say tentatively. I am shocked at Mark's outburst, not because of its content but more because he generally tries to stay one step ahead of anything that might be construed as a belief system for fear of sounding like my mother. "Look, I'll try and avoid him."

"What I am trying to say is that you need to be the author of your own destiny, Lucy. It is one of your worst traits, allowing things to happen around you as though you have no involvement in their outcome."

"That's why I'm eating so much," I say. "The more I eat, the fatter I will get, and then it will be impossible to have an affair with anyone."

"That's not quite what I meant," he says. "But it could be interpreted as a small step in the right direction."

My phone beeps again. He eyes it with renewed suspicion, but this time it is a message from Emma, inviting Tom and me to dinner with her and Guy at her new home. She says that Guy finally agreed today because he felt so guilty about not being able to spend any time with her over Christmas.

"It's Emma," I say. "She wants us to meet her boyfriend." Mark looks interested.

"A serious relationship?" he asks dubiously. "I thought Emma's specialty was keeping all emotions at arm's length."

"They have moved in together," I say defensively.

"But then why haven't you met him before?" he asks. Then he smiles knowingly. "He's married, isn't he? That was always going to be her fate, to find someone she couldn't possibly have."

"I think he's quite keen on her, actually," I say, then change tack, because Emma and my brother are an awkward subject. "Mum thinks I should go back to work."

"There's no panacea for man's condition," he says. "What good would it do your family if you go off to Iraq to chase a story?"

"Or if I was stuck in London, jealously eyeing up my colleagues' ability to go abroad at the drop of a hat. But perhaps I would be more involved with the bigger picture."

"Human existence is the sum of our relationships. We all want to connect with people," he says. "And we never stop fancying people. Just consider Petra. She's going to be having more sex than all of us, and she's in her sixties, or 'sexties,' as we say in the age of Viagra."

"Just don't go there," I plead.

The door opens. Tom peers tentatively around the door.

"It's a shame to come all this way and then spend all your time in the pantry," he says.

"I'm looking for a couple of chickens. We've decided to abort the turkey and eat it tomorrow." I pick up the cell phone from the windowsill and put it deep in my back pocket, making a mental note to delete those messages as soon as I have a moment.

Later that night, I lie in bed beside Tom, filled with good intentions to tell him what I said to Mark earlier in the day. We sit there reading books that we gave each other for Christmas. For him: Alain de Botton on architecture. For her: a biography of Mrs. Beeton by Kathryn Hughes. And guess what. It turns out that Mrs. Beeton was as much of a domestic fraud as I am. I wish I had given this to Petra.

It is so cold that I have done up the top button of my tartan pajamas. We are both dressed in thick fleeces, and Tom is wearing hand-knitted socks made by his mother. He has cleverly raised the back legs of the bed on piles of books purloined from my bookshelf. For the first time we are looking down rather than up at our feet.

The children are in bed, asleep in their nest of duvets in the middle of their room, favorite presents scattered around them. Joe is hugging his fingerprinting kit. I turn to Tom and take a deep breath, but he puts up a hand to indicate that he wants to say something first. He carefully marks his place with a bookmark and then puts it in the middle of the bedside table, fiddling around until he is sure that it is exactly in the center. I rest mine facedown on my knees, making him wince.

"You'll break the spine," he says gently, taking Mrs. Beeton from me and carefully placing the flap inside the cover to mark the end of the second chapter.

"I know what you are going to say," he says. "And I blame myself. I have been totally preoccupied by my library. Obsessed even. I forget that looking after the children is even harder work because you aren't permitted the luxury of focusing on one subject. I also know that my compulsion for tidiness and order is irritating, but when I am around my mother, I know that there is no hope that I will be able to change. It is my genetic destiny. Your brother says that there is no distinction between the personality of my buildings and the inside of my mind. Mind you, it would have been worse to be married to John Pawson."

"But you have always been the same. Even during your loft-conversion period, you were always absorbed by what you were doing. You are the same man that I married; the problem must lie with me," I say.

"We just need more time on our own together," he says. "It's difficult not to be possessed by this library. It is the most prestigious project that I have been involved with, and it's taken over my life. I have been resentful of anything that has distracted me from it."

Then I realize that he doesn't really know anything. Tom thinks that it is all about him, a noble sentiment in the sense that he is not trying to shirk responsibility for the situation. Nor is he trying to blame me. But he isn't looking outside of himself for answers, and I find myself resenting this. He is just skimming the surface, giving the problem a light sand, when I need someone to plane back my emotions, to peel back every layer until the core is exposed.

Before I have a chance to explain that he is wrong, that I have lost my equilibrium, that I can see where I have come from but can't see where I'm going, and that I need him to help me recover my balance, he reaches under his pillow, pulls out a present, and hands it to me, smiling. I adopt what I hope is an expression of delighted surprise and open it up, expecting to see the necklace. Instead, there is a pair of Spanx pants. I unfold them. They are the color and texture of a sausage skin and probably perform a similar function. There is a large hole around the crotch for peeing.

"I got them in Milan," he says proudly. "The woman in the shop said even Gwyneth Paltrow wears them. They iron out every lump and bump."

I groan loudly and sink under the duvet.

"I got you something else, too," he says, peering underneath to hand me a familiar cream box. "I was looking for the right moment to give it to you. I had it made while I was in Milan."

I open the box and then quickly hug him, because it is a strain maintaining the pretense that I have never seen the necklace before. We are so thickly layered that we grasp onto each other, holding only layers of fleece between our fingers. The force of this movement causes the bed to fall off its books, and we hit the floor with a loud bump. It would be good to have sex. But sometimes it is just too cold. Tomorrow we will eat turkey. Tomorrow I will wear my new necklace. Tomorrow I will tell Tom about Robert Bass.

13

"The road to hell is paved with good intentions."

Back in London, the new year comes and goes. Drifting by. I find that there is never much to cling to at this time of year and make a few resolutions to give some structure to the uncertainty that stretches before me. I can never understand why people want to celebrate the beginning of another year. How can they be so sure that what lies ahead will be better than what has passed? Beyond the age of thirty, it takes some bravado to assume that the future holds more promise than the past. Surely there is more that can go wrong than can go right. By the end of the year, there will be more global warming. More chance of a bird flu pandemic. More dead in Iraq. More chance that I will have an affair with Robert Bass, thus irrevocably harming my marriage and giving my children a lifetime of blame and therapists' bills to heap on me.

In order to combat all this, I have decided that this must be the year in which I finally inspire gravitas. This will help me overcome the feelings that possess me and impose order upon my life. By the end of the year, credit-card debt, mold in the car, and anything else that speaks of domestic sluttery will be a distant memory.

When I woke at five o'clock this morning, despite all my good intentions, I felt heady with the anticipation of seeing Robert Bass again, after the three-week hiatus over the Christmas holidays. I ran through what I might wear on the school run, a catwalk involving jeans with tops in various shades, knowing that I would inevitably end up dressed in the same outfit that I had on yesterday, because a wardrobe crisis is an impossible luxury on a school morning.

I indulged in a couple of my favorite fantasies, involving mostly clothed fumbles against walls on dark streets somewhere close to Greek Street, promising that this would be the last time I allowed my mind to wander so far, and justifying my intemperance with the thought that it will soon be too light in the evening for anything like this to actually happen. In the interest of gravitas, I also forced myself to think up neutral subjects for conversation, should the need arise, starting with the disappearance of Greenland and ending with the relative benefits of Polish au pairs over those of other nationalities. Not that we have room for an au pair, but it is a good subject to master.

Then, when Tom woke up, he offered to take the children to school. I fought hard to hide my disappointment.

"I thought you would be really pleased," he said.

"That's great, a real help," I said unconvincingly.

"Honestly, sometimes women are incomprehensible," he said, pulling himself out of bed, eyeing the piles of clothes on the floor suspiciously. "Dressing up for the school run?" he asked rhetorically. "Are you turning into a yummy mummy? Or is there someone you're trying to impress?"

"I am becoming a mother with gravitas," I said.

"Please don't go neurotic on me," he pleaded.

I still have not confessed to Tom about my infatuation, although I have told Mark that I have, which makes me feel as though I have almost done it. I don't like to think I am lying to my brother, more that the truth hasn't yet caught up with itself, as though he is living in a different time zone, some hours ahead of my own. After all, he never comes to me with a problem unless he has harvested all of its pleasures first. I resolve to tell Tom later this week.

I wonder whether Alpha Mum would allow herself to indulge in such wild abandon. She would undoubtedly have the self-discipline to contain the fantasy, to shut it firmly in a small box in one of those tidy kitchen drawers, alongside the one marked "cards for all occasions." It is easy to imagine some women having sex with lots of people. Take Yummy Mummy No. 1, for example. Even though I have never met her husband, I can imagine her entwined with her personal trainer, meeting the challenge of sexual positions that require the athleticism of a twenty-two-year-old with dedicated enthusiasm. I can even imagine her entwined with her nanny or, for that matter, with Tom. Alpha Mum is a more elusive case, an obsession with germs, cleanliness, and orderliness being less earthy preoccupations.

I rein myself in to remind myself of my new year's resolutions: (1) to become one of those mothers who gets asked advice on matters educational (specialist subject schools in north London), (2) to never forget details like picking my children up from school, and (3) to regularly depilate with an emphasis on eyebrow plucking and dyeing. Tom welcomed the first two resolutions when I unveiled my strategy last night but was less sure about the latter.

"I don't see how that will make a difference," he said. I presented him with a picture of Fiona Bruce torn from a magazine to show him.

"It's all in the eyebrows," I told him. "If I looked like that, then people would take me really seriously. And I would take myself more seriously."

He looked doubtful. I kept quiet about resolution number four: to stop having inappropriate thoughts about Robert Bass (already broken) and to avoid ever being alone with him.

I decide that my initial focus must be on the third resolution, and to that end buy a rudimentary eyebrow-dyeing kit from a pharmacy after I drop Fred at his nursery.

"Is there anything that can go wrong?" I question the girl behind the counter at the chemist.

"Not if you follow the instructions," she says lazily, closing her magazine to look up at me. "My mother slept with my boyfriend," "I discovered my brother was my father," "My dad ran off with my sister," read the headlines on the cover. Straightforward extramarital affairs are so last century.

"Do you enjoy reading about that kind of thing?" I ask her with curiosity.

"I just skim it," she says, fiddling with a belly-button ring. Her stomach is not an obvious asset, and I wonder why she has chosen to highlight its burgeoning power in this way. "Unless it's really unusual."

I stop myself from asking her to define "really unusual."

"Have you ever read anything about people coming to harm from botched home eyebrow-dyeing kits?" I ask.

"Never," she says emphatically.

So when Fred falls asleep in the stroller on the way home from nursery after lunch and I have an hour to spare before I set out to pick up the other two boys from school, I decide to forge ahead with the eyebrow experiment. I race upstairs to get a mirror from the bathroom. It is the one Tom uses for shaving and it magnifies everything. I stare at my face, like someone who has just had cataracts removed and is seeing herself clearly for the first time in years.

Every flaw is highlighted. The crow's-feet around my eyes have deepened to become channels that I imagine will one day be capable of directing tears down the side of my face. New trenches have opened, some in curious crisscross fashion with vertical drops. I experiment with a few grimaces to work out exactly which facial expressions might have caused these. I finally happen upon an unlikely combination that involves my mouth being wide open and my eyes being scrunched up until they are no more than small slits. Surely I cannot be unconsciously making this expression on a regular basis, unless I am doing it in my sleep.

My nose looks sharper and more pointed. Forever growing, I think, trying to envisage what it might look like in twenty years' time. The skin on my neck looks slightly ruched. Still some way until I turn into a lizard. Or my mother. On my chin I have a small spot. By what curse do women suddenly develop adolescent acne in their thirties, I wonder? What potion of hormones is responsible for this betrayal? Still, a fine pair of eyebrows will compensate for all this and distract attention away from my flaws like a beautiful fireplace in a room with peeling paint. Then I discover that I have lost the instructions.

Not to be thwarted, I decide to press on. It all seems very straightforward. Women around the world do this kind of thing every day. I mix the dye and the hydrogen peroxide with the satisfaction of someone doing a GCSE chemistry experiment. This simple motion makes me feel as though I am already regaining control of my life. I brush the dye on my eyebrows and wait for cosmetic alchemy to take place. When nothing happens after five minutes, I decide to repaint both eyebrows.

Then I start to search the house for tweezers, ready for the second part of the process. I lie flat on the floor in our bedroom to look under the bed, kicking away rejected pairs of trousers from this morning and, sure enough, the tweezers are there. So is the die from Chutes and Ladders. And a credit card. These are the kinds of indicators that point toward a positive change in my fortunes, I think. Then I catch sight of Tom's rabbit clock. It is already past three o'clock, and if there is any hope of arriving at school on time, I will have to run most of the way.

I set off at a jog, pushing Fred, wondering how new year's resolutions can so quickly conspire against each other to pervert the course of natural justice. We are almost at school when Fred wakes up. He takes one look at me, shrinks back into his stroller with a look of fear, and starts howling loudly. I stop running for a moment to get a packet of sunflower seeds from the pocket of my coat, healthy snacks for children being part of my Great Leap Forward. My hands are slippery with sweat, and it is difficult to open the packet. Finally, I tear it open with my teeth and the seeds spill over the pavement. I make what I hope are soothing noises to prevent one of those cantankerous moods that can settle on an almost three-year-old following an afternoon nap, when the only incentive to smile is a half-full packet of sunflower seeds.

He throws them angrily on the ground. Parents who have already collected their children walk by and stare at us as I kneel in front of Fred, trying to comfort him. The expressions range from empathetic smiles to poorly disguised disdain, according to the amount of exposure they have had to their own children, the mothers with the most staff falling into the latter category.

"Hairy monsters," he cries, and I assume that he has had a nightmare about the David Bowie song that made Joe so afraid at Christmas.

"There aren't any scary monsters," I say to him repeatedly, but he keeps pointing at my face. I feel a tap on my shoulder, and I know before I turn round that it will be Robert Bass, because even though Fred is in the midst of a tantrum, I feel a shiver wander down my body to settle somewhere in my groin.

I try to remember what Mark told me about voles. The prairie vole is monogamous and mates for life. Meadow voles, on the other hand, are promiscuous. Partners mate and move on. But the only real difference between them is hormonal.

"You are a prairie vole, Lucy," Mark said. "I am a meadow vole."

"But I can empathize with the meadow vole's position," I said.

"That doesn't mean that you need to act on those feelings," he said. "You might think you're having nothing more than a casual conversation with this Sexy Domesticated Dad, but actually there is a complex chemical process taking place in your body, and if you feel there is a connection, then most likely there is. Science has proven that we are drawn to people with a particular set of genes, mainly through our sense of smell. Mates with dissimilar genes produce healthier offspring. This is what sexual chemistry is. Are you on the pill?"

"Er, no," I said, unsure where all this was heading. "That's good, because women on the pill have the opposite instincts and choose mates who are not genetically suitable," he said. "But that's an aside. What I am really trying to say is that if you find each other attractive, it's probably because an attraction exists. During intimate conversation, you release hormones, which create a bonding feeling with someone. In fact, there is empirical evidence to prove that the more you look into someone's eyes, the more you find them attractive. So first and foremost, you should stop chatting to this man, to prevent the biochemistry of love taking over. And if you can't do that, you need to remind your rational self that you have the willpower to stop yourself from crossing the line."

"What is the line?" I asked him.

"You'll know when the time comes to decide whether to cross it. But my advice would be to step right back now, before you even come across it."

๑๑

"Happy New Year, Lucy, good Christmas?" asks Robert Bass in jolly fashion. I feel myself jump.

"I am a prairie vole, I am a prairie vole," I whisper to myself in between Fred's wails. It is a tricky dilemma. If I release him from the stroller, he is likely to prostrate himself on the pavement and turn himself into a dead weight, a secret weapon used by toddlers when they sense they might lose an argument. I decide to use my own secret weapon and pull out a packet of chocolate bears from my pocket. The cries immediately subside.

"Did you just say that you are a prairie vole, Lucy?" asks Robert Bass, eyeing the chocolate bears with disapproval. He is definitely more of a sunflower-seed man. Which probably makes him a meadow vole, sunflowers not being native to prairies.

"Fred finds it comforting," I tell him.

Then I turn around to speak to him, still trying to avoid eye contact. I am not breaking resolution number four, because Fred is with me, but I feel immediate guilt that my youngest child is unwittingly acting as a chaperone.

"Yes, sorting out schools for Sam, getting on top of everything. The usual," I say with conviction. This is not so difficult.

"Oh my God," he says, ignoring what I have said. "Where did they escape from?" His face comes so close to me that I can feel his breath, warm against my cheek, a not unpleasant mix of coffee and mints. I fleetingly wonder, despite the presence of scores of parents from school and Fred, whether this is The Moment. Far from engaging my rational mind, I seem to have accessed ever more murky regions of my subconscious. This is what happens if you spend too much time talking to psychologists.

From the dim recesses of my memory, an incident of unreasonable passion filed away years ago elbows its way to the forefront in stunning detail. But it is not the detail of what occurred, rather the feeling of guilt that it engendered that grips my stomach first. Then I feel even more contrite, because this last moment of unreasonable passion was truly wicked, involving as it did a married man, and I thought I had condemned it to a part of my brain never to be accessed again.

Shortly before I married Tom, sometime in the winter of 1995, just before the end of the Balkans War, the same colleague who had unwittingly provided solace during Tom's infidelity found himself waiting for a cab home at the same time as me, in the early hours of the morning after a long session at *Newsnight*. We had never mentioned our fling the previous year, and although we continued to circle each other with flirtatious enthusiasm, it was less meant than before, because we knew it should not be repeated, lest it turn into a habit. Besides, now that he was recently married and I was due to be married in a few months, our colleagues viewed such lapses less indulgently. .

I had returned from two weeks filming in Sarajevo. I knew that he missed me, because whenever I called, it was he who wanted to discuss details of what time I had set up my satellite feed, whom I had interviewed, whether I had remembered to wear my BBC-issue flak jacket and helmet, which I hadn't because there was a flap designed to protect the male anatomy which made me walk uncomfortably like a penguin.

That night, we all got drunker than usual after the program finished. There had been a glitch in a feed from the U.S., and the presenter was left improvising for about thirty seconds until we managed to make the connection. Iain Duncan Smith was in the studio answering questions about Srebrenica, and he always liked to stay late after the show, drinking in the greenroom into the early hours. And I was relieved to be back in London because I was getting married in four months and needed to find something to wear.

"Can I share your cab?" asked the colleague. I must have hesitated, because he added, "I'll sit in the front in case you can't resist." I smiled. Somehow this tacit acknowledgment of what had come to pass reassured me. He made the prospect sound absurd. Then he got into the back of the car.

We set off through the back streets of Shepherd's Bush, heading toward my flat. Before we reached Uxbridge Road, his hand had crept toward my own until he was gently stroking it with his middle finger. I knew that I should move away from him, but every nerve ending on the back of my hand craved further attention and my willpower ebbed away until I felt that time pivoted around this small movement.

"Come back to my flat, Lucy," he leaned over to whisper in my ear.

"What about your wife?" I heard myself say.

"She's away," he said. Then we started kissing, fumbling around in the back of the taxi like teenagers, his knee pressed between my legs, his hand ever deeper inside my trousers. I tried to push him away when I saw the taxi driver—they were all Bosnian or Serb at this company back then— vicariously enjoying the situation in his mirror. But it was impossible to resist, and I allowed myself to enjoy the moment.

"Change of direction?" asked the taxi driver, in a thick accent.

"Yes," I said, reciting his address off by heart. And we spent the night together. Soon after that, he wrote his first script for a film and left *Newsnight.* I was relieved. He promised to keep in touch, but I knew that he wouldn't and I didn't see him again for years. The trouble with the memory of good sex is that, like a favorite restaurant, there is always the temptation to go back and try the same dish again, to see whether there is room for improvement. If Mark knew about this, he might feel more dubious about my status as a prairie vole.

So when Robert Bass reaches out and touches my eyebrow, I wonder what might happen next. Fortunately, eyebrows are a less erogenous zone and, besides, he is staring at my face a little too intently. This is where Mark's theory about eye contact breaks down, I think, relieved.

"Forget Lucy Sweeney, it's Denis Healey," he says in wonder. I bend down to look in the sideview mirror of a nearby car. My eyebrows are no longer a whiter shade of pale. They have reinvented themselves as bushy black caterpillars. There are salty streaks of dye mingled with sweat running down my face. How will this react with hydrogen peroxide? Will I be left with streaks? I imagine the woman in the pharmacy avidly reading a piece about me under the headline "Home dye experiment left me looking like tiger." I rub my eyebrows frantically and they look even more wild and unruly. The black dye comes off on my hand.

"Definitely more Southern Hemisphere. I'm thinking jungles of Borneo," says Robert Bass wondrously.

Yummy Mummy No. 1 crosses the road to greet us, but as she closes in, she stands stock-still, her hands frozen in the air.

"I'll have to bleach them," I say desperately.

"I wouldn't do that," says Robert Bass. "Then you'll look like a leopard. Or an albino lion. Or—"

"I get the picture," I say.

"No more homespun solutions, Lucy," says Yummy Mummy No. 1, taking control of the situation. "Think 1930s. Think pencil skirts. Think Roland Mouret. Scarlett Johannsen. Think elegance is the new bohemian." Robert Bass listens, agog. "Think Marlene Dietrich and narrow, arched eyebrows by my discreet home plucker. She does Fiona Bruce. Come to my house next week."

Robert Bass and Yummy Mummy No. 1 walk protectively on either side of me along the road to school, with their respective offspring a few steps behind, like the Praetorian guard. They meet bemused looks with patronizing smiles. I will have to revise my position on Yummy Mummy No. 1. Despite her natural inclination to herd with her own kind, she shows the right instincts in a crisis.

When we reach the queue of parents waiting to pick up year-one children, there is a flutter of excitement in the air that is mercifully unrelated to my eyebrows. Parents would usually have left school long ago.

"What's going on?" I whisper to Yummy Mummy No. 1. "Is everyone late?"

"Haven't you heard?" she says conspiratorially. "A celebrity parent has joined our ranks. That's why we're thrilled by an excuse to come back to the playground."

Just as January looked bleak and gray, Celebrity Dad has joined Joe's class. Or rather his son has. I can't reveal Celebrity Dad's true identity for fear of encouraging paparazzi to lurk outside the school gates, but suffice to say that he is an American actor, a dark and brooding sex-in-the-lift kind of man and, if you believe the tabloids, a notorious womanizer, despite the presence of wife number three.

"I anticipate children's parties involving home cinemas, indoor and outdoor swimming pools, a chance to mix with the rich and famous in a casual Issa dress kind of way," says Yummy Mummy No. 1.

I feel immediate sympathy for Celebrity Son, because he will always live in the shadow of his parents, and even if he manages to overcome that setback, he will never feel that he has done it under his own steam. Pheromones hover above the playground. I notice that Yummy Mummy No. 1 has pulled out all the stops and is carrying a white Chloe Paddington bag and wearing a fake fur coat, rock-chick fashion.

I have to confess that I don't recognize Celebrity Dad on first viewing, because he looks quite different from the photos I have seen in magazines. Also, I am only wearing one contact lens. A blurry scene unfolds something like this.

"Mum, Mum, Fred is about to pee on that man's foot," says Sam, as we wait outside the classroom for Joe to appear. Fred has discovered this is a unique way of grabbing parental attention away from his older siblings. Before I can intervene, his trousers are around his ankles and Fred pees on the man's foot.

Celebrity Dad bends down to examine an expensive-looking trainer. I rush over and start mopping his foot with *The Times*, because I am not the sort of mum who carries wipes for all eventualities.

"Fred, that is so naughty," I say, admonishing my youngest son. "Say sorry."

"Sorry," says Fred, smiling proudly.

"No worries," says Celebrity Dad, wanting to appear laid-back but looking very worried. "Actually, I think the print will stain it." Too late, the print has stained the limited-edition trainer. I know it is limited, because Yummy Mummy No. 1, who is watching all this, tells me in hallowed tones later that "it is the trainer equivalent of the Chloe Paddington. You can't put a price on it."

Robert Bass comes over and gives him wipes, because he is the sort of father who carries wipes at all times. He hovers but then walks away, because there is no excuse to hang around.

"I'm really sorry," I say to Celebrity Dad.

"It really doesn't matter," he insists. "Actually, it's quite nice to have someone talk to me. Everyone has ignored me apart from that woman over there. I guess that's an English thing?" He points to Alpha Mum. "She has asked me to join a committee to organize a party for parents."

"But we're not having a party," I say.

"But I agreed," he says with a puzzled expression.

"Maybe it's just you and her, then," I say quizzically.

"What happened to your eyebrows?" he asks.

"Home dyeing disaster," I tell him. Close up, even half-sighted, I can appreciate the overall gorgeous effect. Celebrity Dad collects his child and walks off. Mothers rush over to me.

"What did you talk about?" asks Yummy Mummy No. 1.

"His marital problems, whether he should change agents, why he doesn't have a nanny, the inside story," I tell them nonchalantly.

"He is in one of the films that I am writing about," says Robert Bass. But no one is listening to him. His position as dominant male has been usurped. He looks at me with an unfamiliar look in his eye, one I haven't encountered for many years. Jealousy.

I decide that the conversation with Tom can wait for a couple of weeks. Robert Bass's loss of control is greater than my own, and that puts me in a position of strength for the moment. The new term has kicked off very promisingly. I might not be able to avoid the line, but at least I am the one unlikely to cross it. And that seems an enviable position to be in.

◎◎

Later that week, I announce to Tom that I am going to retire to the office to send an e-mail. **Subject: "parent/teacher drinks evening,"** which Alpha Mum, in her role as class rep, has just asked me, in my role as her secretary, to help organize.

"I can't understand why you put yourself through this," says Tom in a muffled voice. "It's destined to end in disaster."

Without looking, I know that he is in the midst of his biweekly audit of the fridge.

"Look," he says, triumphantly holding two half-eaten jars of pesto sauce. "How did this happen?" He is consulting a typed list of fridge contents that is stuck to the door. This was Petra's legacy to us during her last weekend in England.

"I think you'll find that it is much easier to organize shopping if you tick each item off as you use it up," she said. I nodded obligingly, because I knew that she wouldn't be returning for some time.

I try to be patient with Tom, because his mother's departure has left him adrift.

"There is no record of the second jar of pesto leaving the fridge," he says.

"Maybe it's having an illicit affair with the spaghetti," I say. He mutters about systems, and I firmly close the kitchen door and go upstairs to begin composing an e-mail to the parents on the class list.

But no sooner have I started than I quickly become bored. I decide instead to first write an e-mail to Cathy, who I know is still in her office, with details of an even more significant event that took place under our roof earlier this week.

"The time for fasting is over," I tell her. **"The sexual détente has been broken. Hurrah!"** I explain in some detail that, last night, I bumped into Tom in Fred's bedroom at around three in the morning.

"What are you doing here?" I said to him.

"Looking for the tiger," he replied wearily.

"That's a coincidence," I said. "So am I. But where is Fred?"

"He's asleep in our bed," he explained.

So then, I asked, why are we both awake in the small hours, looking for a tiger? It's unusual, but then these are desperate times, I tell Cathy. And so the months of famine ended, and then we retired for the rest of the night in Fred's single bed under a Thunderbirds duvet, with Tom exploring one of his favorite postcoital subjects.

"If you had a gun at your head and were forced to have sex with any parent in Joe's class, male or female, which one would you choose?" he asked.

"Why Joe's class?" I asked.

"The parents are better-looking," he said, looking at me intently.

I protested tiredness and then he said, "I quite fancy that mum with the perfect arse." He meant Yummy Mummy No. 1, I tell Cathy.

"But she's so vacuous," I objected.

"No more puddlelike than Deep Shallows," he responded witheringly. "All that careful dishevelment is too mannered. I bet you, underneath it all he probably topiaries his pubic hair with a pair of nail scissors. And the way he puts on that tortured writer act is risible."

"Who on earth are you talking about?" I asked, already knowing the answer. I press the "send" button and potter around for a bit, procrastinating about writing the school e-mail. A few minutes later, my heart leaps when I see that Robert Bass has sent me an e-mail. For the first time ever. Since this doesn't break any of the rules, I feel quietly elated.

"Very glad to hear good news," it reads, **"but puzzled why you want to share this with the class, unless you are considering a party with a seventies theme involving car keys. Can only assume that I am the puddle. This not very good for my self-esteem."** I stare at the screen in shock, but there is no time for reflection because a message from Yummy Mummy No. 1 follows almost immediately. **"Dear Lucy, rather too much information for my taste. Can only assume I am the woman with the perfect derrière. Ciao, ciao."**

Then Alpha Mum writes: **"I can no longer tolerate your cheap attempts to sabotage my rule as class rep and wish you to consider your position."**

Forget puddles and shallows. I'm in deep water. The e-mail has gone to everyone on the class list. I leave the sitting room feeling a little shaky. Tom has already gone to bed. I watch *Newsnight* until it finishes and decide that nothing that ever happened to me at work was as frightening as what has just come to pass.

The early-morning insomnia regresses into a night spent tossing and turning. The darkness has a terrible way of exaggerating fears. My stomach churns with nerves. At two-thirty, I think I hear noises and creep down-stairs, carrying a *Star Wars* lightsaber. "May the force be with me," I say to myself.

In the sitting room, I decide to raid Sam's secret sweet supply, promising to replace everything I eat the following day. I bring a Cadbury Creme Egg up to the bedroom and force myself to eat it slowly. First I lick it like a lollipop, until it starts to melt. When the white cream becomes visible, I allow myself to nibble the sides, counting twenty seconds between each mouthful. Then I throw caution to the wind and stuff the rest of the egg in my mouth and munch it loudly with my mouth open. This is much more satisfying, but my nerves are unassuaged. The urge to unburden myself to Tom is irresistible. I poke him in the ribs. He groans.

"There aren't any burglars, and I'm not getting up to look," he mumbles. "The dog will get them."

"But we haven't got a dog," I say, my mouth full of chocolate.

"Visualize one and then you'll get less scared," he says.

"It's worse than that, Tom," I tell him.

"Has the boiler burst again?" he asks sleepily and immediately falls into a heavy slumber. I wake him by running my left toenail up the side of his calf.

"Lucy, have mercy," he says, closing his eyes again.

"Tom. I have sent an e-mail to every parent in Joe's class telling them everything that happened last night," I say. Now that I am describing the problem out loud, it seems even worse.

"What happened last night?" he mumbles.

"We had sex and discussed which parent was most beddable, and you said that you favored Yummy Mummy No. 1 because of her perfect bum," I say.

"Are you trying to seduce me?" he asks, sleepily rolling over onto his side with a hopeful look in his eye. "God, what's that in your mouth?"

"A chocolate egg. I'm trying to tell you that I have done a terrible thing," I say, licking my lips.

"People like you don't do terrible things, Lucy," he says. "Go back to sleep."

"But we do," I say, pleading with him to listen. "Not by design. By accident. Not that I am trying to absolve myself of responsibility for my actions, because I know that is one of my worst traits."

"What exactly have you done?" he asks, sighing and closing his eyes again.

"I thought I was sending an e-mail to Cathy about rekindling our sex life, but instead I sent it to the class list," I say.

He sits bolt upright. He understands.

"You fucking idiot," he says slowly, holding his head in his hands and rocking backward and forward. "I have done my best to maintain amicable relations with these parents over the years, a carefully balanced strategy aimed at being neither too friendly nor too unfriendly, and now you have revealed the inner workings of our sex life. I'll probably be impotent from now on, because forever after I will associate sex with fear."

"I'm really sorry," I say. "I think Yummy Mummy No. 1 was actually quite flattered. She doesn't see much of her husband; it's probably good for her ego." He groans. "I think the stay-at-home dad was a little more insulted."

"Did you say that I called him Deep Shallows?" he asks weakly.

"Yes," I say.

"Actually, I think he's quite a nice bloke. I was just trying to wind you up because I think you fancy each other," he says. "Why were you telling Cathy about this anyway?"

"Because she knew that we hadn't had sex for ages," I say weakly, ignoring his first comment.

"Do you really have to share this kind of detail with your friends?" he says. "I've got to sit next to her at dinner soon."

"I know. But on the good side, that's one thing you don't have to worry about, because she never got the e-mail," I say.

"You are such a Pollyanna," he says. "I'm never doing the school run again. By the way, did you say that we had sex twice?"

"No," I say.

"But that's the most impressive detail," he says regretfully and then falls into a deep sleep again.

I used to find Tom's ability to sleep through a crisis reassuring. It diminished the magnitude of my worries, reducing them to dust. Over the years, it began to pique me, as I always seemed to be the one stumbling around the house, dealing in a maddened state of tiredness with whatever the darkness chose to throw at me. I was the night watchman for crying babies and then for children with fevers that always rose in the night. I saw the night breathe life into common or garden niggles, turning them into exotic problems. Tom, on the other hand, slept through all this beside me, immune to the driftwood of life washing up in our bedroom, occasionally complaining if I disturbed him when I finally climbed back into bed, exhausted but with little hope of going back to sleep.

The following morning, giddy with fatigue, I walk away from school alone. I decide to stop for a coffee to gather my thoughts. "Hello, Lucy, would you like to join me?" says Robert Bass suddenly from behind me in the queue. "I don't have any topiary appointments this morning, and I promise I won't talk about my book." I jump.

Given the e-mail, it seems impolite to turn him down, even though I know that I am breaking several resolutions all at once. I stare resolutely at the ground. Avoiding eye contact is not difficult on a morning like this.

"I'll have a double skinny latte Frappuccino," I say breathlessly at the counter.

"Doesn't exist," says the waitress.

"Do you want me to order for you?" asks Sexy Domesticated Dad. "Why don't you go and sit down over there." He is pointing to a small table for two in the most discreet corner of the café.

He walks over carrying two mugs of coffee and sits down opposite me.

"How are your eyebrows?" he asks, as if inquiring about a family pet. "They didn't respond to the call of the wild?"

"They're fine," I say, gritting my teeth and rubbing my forehead absentmindedly. "I'm just a little tired."

"I'm not surprised, after all your, er, activity," he says.

We sit there for a few moments in companionable silence, sipping coffee and staring out the window.

"I'm really sorry about my message on Christmas Day. Technology obviously doesn't agree with us," he says. "I'd be grateful if you didn't mention that to anyone. Not that I think you are meaningfully indiscreet, it's just after that e-mail last night, I got worried in case you inadvertently revealed to the world my own impropriety."

"I won't say a word to anyone," I say, trying to remember who I have already told. "I've learned my lesson from this mistake."

"Actually, it was quite reassuring to my wife," he says. "After my, er, setback on Christmas Day, she became uncharacteristically suspicious of you. She said there are lines in relationships that shouldn't be crossed. When I showed her the message last night, she realized that you're still at one with your husband, if you know what I mean."

"I do," I say, nodding so vigorously that coffee spills from my cup.

"If you know there's a line, then it's more difficult to cross it," he says slowly, as if searching for the right words.

I'm not sure exactly what he is talking about, and I look up. He puts out his hand and grips the fleshy part of my arm below the elbow. I anticipate pleasurable sensations but instead he holds it so tightly that I can feel the blood start to pound in my fingers. He looks over to the other side of the café, and I follow his gaze.

Out of the corner of my eye, I notice Alpha Mum and indeed most of the other mothers from our sons' class sitting round a table in the opposite corner. A deathly hush falls over the café as the entire group turn around to stare at us.

With great clarity of mind, I suddenly remember this was the day for our mothers' coffee morning. Even Robert Bass pales.

"We got here before you." I wave cheerfully, knocking my coffee over him. "We weren't expecting such a good turnout. Do you want to come and join us or should we join you?" I shout, mopping steaming coffee from his lap with my scarf. He winces.

"No gain without pain, I suppose," he whispers conspiratorially, recovering his composure. I get up and stride purposefully toward the table and sit down beside Yummy Mummy No. 1. Robert Bass sits on the other side of me. I admire his attitude.

"Never apologize, never explain, that's my motto, Lucy," whispers Yummy Mummy No. 1. It is unclear what part of my life she is referring to. "Anyway, I have something much more important to ask you. Can I count on your discretion? I don't want any e-mails to the class list about this."

I am intrigued but a little wary, knowing that her revelation will inevitably prove a letdown.

"My husband has nits," she whispers in disgust. "Not just eggs. Fully blown nits."

"Did he catch them from the children?" I ask.

"No," she says. "I got the nanny to check them. Not an egg in sight. He says that his secretary caught them from her children and gave them to him. Anyway, I wondered, given that your children introduced them to the school, whether you could recommend the best method of eradication."

Alpha Mum clears her throat disapprovingly. She is wearing a power suit from her McKinsey days and carrying a laptop computer, which she switches on. "The less said the better, I think, about Lucy's e-mail last night. She has overstepped the mark and is reconsidering her position," she says, looking serious.

"Sounds as though Lucy was considering a number of positions," says Celebrity Dad, who has just arrived late. He asks Robert Bass to move up so that he can sit next to me, despite a spare chair next to Alpha Mum. Coffee mornings have suddenly become much more exciting.

"Where's the tiger?" he whispers in my ear. I sit there with a fixed smile.

"If anyone is interested in replacing Lucy, please let me know. This class-rep thing is becoming a full-time job," she says, laughing heartily. We all smile weakly.

"I've never been to a mums' coffee morning," says Celebrity Dad to me, saying "mums' " with an English accent. "Great e-mail, by the way. Schools in the States were never so much fun. Certainly puts me in perspective. For which I am very grateful. So I'll definitely come to the party. Hope it lives up to expectations."

"Are there any issues anyone wants to bring up?" asks Alpha Mum, trying to draw the attention of the group back to her and clearly hoping there are none. Yummy Mummy No. 1 puts up her hand. "I am really worried about the nylon content of the school sweaters," she says. "They don't allow their bodies to breathe." Alpha Mum duly types in her concern on a spreadsheet.

"I have a few new ideas that I want to throw around," says Alpha Mum. I wince inwardly and can sense Robert Bass doing the same. "We have to think out of the box," she says, and proposes that we start making plans for the summer fete.

"Perhaps it would help if you tell me what you did before you had children, so that I can assess your strengths and weaknesses as a group," she says, staring at me when she says "weaknesses." "What did you use to do B.C., Lucy, or were you always a stay-at-home mum?"

"Actually, I used to be a producer on *Newsnight*," I say. Stunned silence.

"Moving swiftly on, the headmistress has asked parents to please stop parking on double yellow lines when they are late in the morning, and remember there is a child in the class who is very allergic to nuts. A parent, who shall remain nameless, sent their child to school with a Walnut Whirl," she says, staring at me.

"You did that?" says Robert Bass loudly.

"I said she was dangerous," says Celebrity Dad.

"Look, you've got me completely wrong," I start saying to him.

Alpha Mum vigorously taps another button on her computer. "Parents' party list," she says smugly. But instead, a luscious naked brunette astride a blonde in a very compromising pose flashes up on the screen.

"Game set and match, Lucy Sweeney, I think," says Yummy Mummy No. 1.

14

"There's many a slip between cup and lip."

On the way up to Emma's apartment a couple of weeks later, Tom and I stand in silence. We are positioned stiffly on opposite sides of the generous elevator, in front of full-length mirrors, so that when Tom eventually speaks, I can see him from both the front and behind. He is scratching his ear with one hand and slips the other in and out of his back pocket, a gesture that he adopts when feeling nervous. His lips look smaller and paler, because they are pursed with tension. I feel a sudden surge of affection for him. I am probably the only person in the world who can access every element of this hidden language. It takes years to build up such an extensive vocabulary of someone else's behavior. I can gauge the exact degree of nervousness, anger, curiosity, and tiredness. I know how much is systemic and how much is provoked by tonight's dinner. I take a couple of steps forward, put out my hand, and run it down the side of his face, and he leans in to me and closes his eyes.

"You were the one who told me to live and let live," I say gently. It is not meant as recrimination.

"Tolerating an affair is not the same as confronting its reality," he says. "I am happy for Emma to talk incessantly about this man, although not in the kind of detail you favor, but I don't want to meet him. It's not a moral judgment, it's more that the situation makes me feel uncomfortable, and that is not my idea of a fun evening out with my wife."

"But you understand why we have to go?" I ask. He ignores the question.

"I suppose the good thing is that it makes me supremely grateful that we lead such an uncomplicated existence," he says, yawning. "I cannot imagine a scenario where I am giving a dinner party with a woman who is not my wife, meeting all her friends, knowing that my family is at home in bed. It's too much of a head fuck."

"Neither can I," I say. And I can't. I wonder whether the fact that I can't entertain this fantasy reflects the shallow depths of my feelings toward Robert Bass—it is, after all, a single-issue relationship—or whether this cozy domestic scene is simply the antithesis of where I want to escape to.

"I know it's going to be a bit of an endurance test. Just say the word if you want to bail out," I say.

"The code is 'Deep Shallows,' " he says teasingly. "Have you seen him again?"

"I have, a couple of times," I say truthfully.

"Did he studiously ignore you?" he asks.

"No, he was quite attentive really," I say, and he raises an eyebrow. "Actually, his wife has been around a lot more. Celebrity Dad is a big pull. Adds a bit of glamour to all our lives."

"How is Joe getting on at school?" he asks.

"Apart from going to bed in his school uniform in case we wake up late, I think it's all fine. Do you know he watched the whole of *The Sound of Music* without rewinding to the Nazis once?" I say. "He's also got a girlfriend but says that they haven't yet discussed the m-word."

"But surely he knows that we have two alarm clocks. We'll never sleep in. What's the m-word?"

"Marriage," I say. "He takes these things quite seriously."

"Have you called the builder about that leak in the bedroom?" he asks.

"Yes," I say.

"Did you renew the house insurance?" he asks.

"Yes," I say.

"God, Lucy, how uncharacteristically organized of you. If I didn't know you better, I'd say you had a guilty conscience," he says.

"You know me too well, then," I say, but the lift has stopped and he doesn't hear.

The doors open, and we struggle to push back the iron grills. Such an entrance favors those who are already there. Opening, as it does, into the large sitting room, it is designed to wrong-foot new arrivals, who are left stepping from darkness into light, narrowing their eyes to adjust to the glare. The grills make such a noise that it is impossible to arrive unnoticed. Pairs of nervous eyes look at us as we make our entrance, but we are robbed of any opportunity to assess the configuration of characters scattered around the room or mark out territory that we can occupy. We are too involved in trying to escape from the cage.

Emma's banker, sensing our discomfort, steps forward and puts out his arm to shake hands with us, pulling Emma along with him. His other arm is firmly coiled around her. I stare at this arm, tracing it from the top down to where it comes to rest somewhere just above her left buttock, the tips of the fingers actually tucked down the back of her low-cut jeans.

Emma's arse is one of her best features. That was decided years ago. And he clearly concurs. They are entwined in a way that suggests that separating to opposite ends of the table over dinner will be difficult.

"Hi," she says, leaning forward to kiss us and then resting her head on Guy's shoulder before staring at us inanely, waiting for one of us to say something. She has that dreamy, faraway look that women get when they either are pregnant or have just had sex. He has that slightly smug air of a middle-aged man who has recently discovered that his touch can still reduce a woman to rubble.

"I'm Guy," says the banker confidently. I feel Tom recoil beside me. I am relieved for Emma's sake that Guy has decided to play a proactive role in hosting this party and embrace the occasion in all its awkwardness alongside her. At least this is one situation she won't have to face alone. Already I feel annoyed with him and to a lesser degree with her. Then I feel guilty since as far as I can remember, this is the first dinner party that

Emma has ever thrown. They want us to enjoy their happiness, but I am obviously finding it more difficult to forget that he has a wife than they are. I don't know what I had anticipated, but I thought they might be a bit reticent, or a little shy, or at least sensitive enough to realize that other people might find all this disconcerting. It feels so fraudulent.

Because I am immediately called upon to fill the uncomfortable silence that lies between us, I have little chance for anything more than a cursory assessment of the man who stands before us. He is dressed in a fine interpretation of smart-casual that I imagine Emma has put together for him. A pair of True Religion jeans, a striped Paul Smith shirt, and a pair of trainers so shiny and new that I doubt they have left this building. I wonder what he wears at home, but that would depend on whether his wife wears Boden or Marc Jacobs. Husbands always end up resembling their wives. He is smaller than expected, not short but small enough that Emma is wearing a pair of flat gold ballet shoes. Attractive, although in a less obvious way than I had imagined, and younger-looking than his forty-three years, because judging by the flat stomach under the slightly-too-tight striped shirt, he is a man who goes to the gym. I wonder when he has time for this. Having two of everything is an exhausting prospect. Two women; two super-king-size beds; two wardrobes, one filled with clothes chosen by his wife and one with clothes chosen by Emma, and he needs to remember exactly who bought him what. At least he doesn't have two sets of children. Yet.

"Nice to meet you at last," I say.

"I hope so," he says. "It's unconventional, I know."

When he smiles I can understand what has drawn her to him, because despite the blustery confidence, there is an openness to his face that suggests someone who is less certain about the lot he has drawn in life than he should be. And I can relate to that. He stares at me for a little too long, and I don't begrudge him assessing me in the same way that I have just done. Given that we are complete strangers, we both know much more about each other than we should. I wonder exactly what Emma has told him about me and whether we are so different. He might have crossed the line, but I'm not so far behind. I am close enough to see him on the other side.

I spot Cathy sitting on the sofa between two men, neither of whom I recognize. She looks at me apologetically and shrugs her shoulders to indicate that she has brought the roommate with her. But from my vantage point on the other side of the room, it is not immediately apparent which man is her boyfriend. She is sitting on the sofa, barefoot, her legs curled underneath to one side so that her knees rest against the man on the left. But he looks like the metrosexual one, I think, a little confused. His hair, short and spiky, requiring at least a monthly trip to the hairdresser, definitely has product applied. He is laughing loudly. The man on the other side is fiddling with her hair, pulling a few stray strands away from her face. It is like an old painting where you have to try hard to work out all the relationships between the people pictured by looking for clues in the symbolism of the objects littering the background, except in this apartment almost everything is new, which makes it all the more confusing.

Tom pulls me along by the hand as though he is leading a slightly recalcitrant pony.

"Great place. Generally speaking," he says. "I'm not sure about the mechanism for sliding the walls along, looks a bit cheap to me. Let's get another drink." He is heading toward a bottle sitting at the end of the island in the kitchen area. I am alarmed to notice that he has already finished one glass of champagne.

"Which one is Cathy's boyfriend?" I whisper as he fills up my glass.

"The one on the right," he says proudly. "I thought they might be a good match. Pete seems a decent bloke. He's never been married, got no children as far as I know, and I think he's pretty good-looking, although obviously that's difficult for me to tell. I do know that he's the office heartthrob."

"How do you know that?" I ask, squinting at him across the room.

"I canvassed some of my female colleagues for opinion," he says.

"The trouble with matchmaking is that it isn't something methodical," I say. "It's more chemical." But as we get closer, it becomes clear that

Tom is right. This man is gorgeous, even though he is dressed in the architect's uniform of black shirt, black jeans, and jacket. He is also tipping toward forty and unmarried, and there are always questions that need to be asked about that.

"By the way, I forgot to tell you that you look really great. I love that dress," says Tom.

"Oh, thanks," I say, appreciatively. It is a wraparound dress with a long sash that used to do up at the side, but as I have become more voluptuous, it does up farther and farther around my waist.

Tom's colleague waves at us to come and sit down. He looks relieved to see us and unfurls himself from the sofa to stand up and introduce himself, holding out an improbably long arm to shake hands. He is tall and lanky, and leans over us both.

"This is Pete," says Cathy excitedly. "And this is his roommate, James."

"Great to meet you, Lucy, of course, I recognize you from the photo that Tom has of you and the kids on his desk," Pete says. This disarms me slightly, because I had no idea that Tom had taken a photo of us to work. It seems on the face of it to be a sweet gesture, a show of family pride. After all, from a distance family life looks so neat and tidy. But I would normally demand picture approval if I was going to be on such public view.

"Which photo is that?" I ask Tom.

"It's that one of you holding Sam and Joe when you were about to give birth to Fred," Tom says, looking down at his glass because he knows that this is a big faux pas. For some reason he always loved that picture. Perhaps because it underlines his virility. But I am horrified, and he knows it. I have that doe-faced expression common to women in the latter part of pregnancy, and my features have melted into the soft folds of my face and neck. I look like a dog with a litter of puppies clinging to me. I will need to resolve this later, although it is too late because it is that image that will stay with people.

"You look amazing, like a potent Aztec fertility symbol," says Pete.

I am speechless. It is not the look I am aiming for. I am sure that Yummy Mummy No. 1 never gets compared to ancient fertility symbols. Her last pregnancy, with her fourth child, went unnoticed for the first six months, and even then there was debate over whether she was simply gaining weight.

I note with relief that Emma hasn't been left to her own devices in the kitchen. Guy seems to be in charge, pointing to plates to indicate exactly how much arugula should be placed on each one, and in what order the prosciutto, feta cheese, and walnuts should be applied. The whole process takes some time, because every few minutes they stop to kiss each other.

"If they keep that up, they won't make it through dinner," says Pete, looking indulgently at Cathy and leaning over to kiss her on the lips. "We might not, either."

"I suppose if I thought this might be the first and last time I would ever give a dinner party with the man I love, then I might be like that," says Cathy. Pete puts his arm proprietorially around her.

"We can have as many parties as you want," he says.

"I'll help with the cooking," says James.

"He's a great cook," says Pete. "Isn't he, Cathy?"

"Very good," says Cathy, looking at me and rolling her eyes. "I'm going outside for a cigarette. Do you want to come with me, Lucy? Just for company."

"I know all about her smoking habit," Tom says dismissively. "The children told me."

We open the doors onto the balcony outside. It is warmer than anticipated, and we sit down at a round table and chairs, surrounded by small bulbs peeking from flowerpots. Inside, I can see Tom and Guy in animated conversation. I light up a cigarette from Cathy's packet of Marlboro Lights. I have tried to make my own last, because as long as I don't buy another one, I feel as though there is no serious intent to my habit. I have even smoked half a cigarette, stubbed it out in the garden, and finished smoking it a couple of days later. I feel that if I can keep this under control then somehow I will be able to keep everything else in order.

I try to explain this to Cathy, but she looks dubious.

"Lucy, however you try and rationalize things in your head, I know that you are on a collision course," she says. "Your brother is right. You should stay away from that man, especially now that you know your feelings are reciprocated."

"Just because you think about something doesn't mean that it will happen," I say. "Besides, he's helping to lift my mood. I'm having a lot of fun."

"If both of you are thinking the same thing, there is more chance that it will," she says. "Especially because you show no appetite for disengaging."

I would like to continue this discussion, but at that point James comes outside and it all becomes a little confusing, because he puts his arm around Cathy in a way that suggests much more has come to pass between her and him than between Robert Bass and me. He looks me straight in the eye, while his fingers wander up and down Cathy's side. She tries to move away from him, less because she wants him to stop and more because she can read my mind. Why, I am thinking, is she so concerned about my moral rectitude, when she is obviously sleeping with both of these men? The second question that I want her to answer is whether Pete knows about this, but there is barely time for this to ferment in my mind before he comes outside, and when Cathy and James make no attempt to disentangle, I realize that this is more complicated than I had anticipated.

"Dinner is ready," Pete says, and the two men wander inside.

"What's going on?" I ask her firmly.

"I'm not sure," she whispers. "I know it's a little weird. It's not a gay thing with them. I think they fought over the same women so many times that they eventually decided to share. Then neither of them is under pressure to commit. It's unconventional, I know, but it's quite good for my ego."

It strikes me that everyone I am close to, and that includes my mother-in-law, is in the midst of a big adventure. It makes a dalliance with Robert Bass seem trifling. I am realistic enough to know that my body will betray me in many more ways over the next decade, and suddenly it seems reasonable, even advisable, to take up the opportunity of one final fling. I am sitting in the Last Chance Saloon. Consider Madonna. Four hours of exercise a day. Strict macrobiotic diet. Fighting the ravages of time beyond the age of fifty is a full-time job. Tom, on the other hand, has another twenty years ahead of him to attract young women to his side. If Robert Bass and I slept with each other once, and made a pact not to let it happen again, then we could control the shock waves. The key is not to let things advance any further. Like the smoking. That way I can control the fallout. It's a decision made on the hoof, perhaps, but I resolve that while I am not going to do anything to pursue the relationship, I am not going to take any steps to prevent it from happening, either.

For the first time in six months, I have clarity.

"Do you disapprove, Lucy?" Cathy asks. "You look very animated."

"No," I tell her. "I just wonder whether it has legs."

"Of course it doesn't," she says. "There isn't a ménage à trois lobby that has made it an acceptable format for relationships."

"But if it was, would you consider it?" I ask.

"If I didn't have children, perhaps, but it would be difficult to explain the concept of three daddies to Ben, I think." She laughs. "Really, it's just a way of moving forward away from all the awfulness of divorce, to get beyond the hatred."

"I thought things were a little easier?" I ask.

"I think it would have been easier if one of us had died," she says. "At least then we would have been left with a few positive memories. Now I wonder why I ever married him, and that makes me mistrust my judgment on all other relationships. Notwithstanding friendship, of course. You and Emma have always been there for me."

We get up to go inside. I stand up so quickly that I cut my leg on a pot of pampas grass. I run a finger down the scratch and look at it. It has drawn blood. Guy waves me over to the table.

"I wanted to sit next to you, Lucy," he says, pulling out a chair for me to sit on. "You feel very familiar." You have no idea, I think to myself, struggling to repress the image of them having sex in his office.

"How long have you and Cathy known Emma?" he asks.

"We were a threesome long before I got married," I say. I feel myself blush. He is staring at his salad, critically assessing the ratio of walnut to fig, and I can't see the expression on his face.

"We all met at university. We lived together in the last year and partied a lot together. The three of us. As a threesome," I say. I have now said "threesome" twice within the space of a minute.

"What else could you have meant?" he asks bemusedly. Deep shallows, deep shallows, I want to shout to Tom from across the table.

A label with £110 written on it hangs down from his shirtsleeve, and I point it out. He has the good grace to look embarrassed and asks me to remove it, undoing the button and pulling up his sleeve to reveal his forearm. I look at it. It is insubstantial, weak-looking, almost womanly. The hairs are downy and so pale that you can see the freckles underneath. His wrist is so thin that if I made a circle with my middle finger and thumb I could almost hold it in my grasp. I note the simple gold band on his index finger.

"Emma endeavors to get me to look the part." He smiles. I am struggling to break the small piece of plastic that holds the label to the shirt. When finally it breaks in half, my hand shoots away from him so fast that I knock my glass of wine over him. He tries to push himself away from the table, but it is too late, his shirt is soaked.

"God, I'm sorry," I say. I can see Tom staring at me in wonder from the other end of the table.

"Is this some kind of test?" Guy asks, but he is smiling benevolently. "Don't worry. I've got another shirt in my briefcase. My secretary always keeps one in there for me. I don't know what I'll do when she retires."

"But isn't she too young to retire?" I ask unthinkingly. I consider whether I have developed a form of Tourette's that involves imbuing all conversation with sexual innuendo derived from my knowledge of their relationship.

"How would you know how old my secretary is?" he asks suspiciously, mopping himself with a dishcloth that Emma has handed to him. She listens to his question and frowns at me.

While he changes his shirt, I give myself five minutes to settle on a benign subject, but it isn't easy. I take deep breaths to steady myself. It is a difficult call. Talk of wives, children, schools, and anything domestic is strictly off-bounds. I try to remember the last film I saw.

The Squid and the Whale. All about the breakup of a marriage. What else have I seen? *Syriana.* But I can't possibly talk about that because I couldn't follow the plot even when I was in the cinema. Was it set in Dubai or Qatar? Then it comes to me: Iraq. We must talk about Iraq, so many opinions that can be canvassed. No room for talk of affairs, threesomes, or secretaries.

Besides, it says a lot about someone to know where they stood on Iraq before the war, although obviously people now deny that they supported it. I establish that Guy was in favor of intervention but only with UN approval. I ask him whether there is any political context to his job, and he says that there isn't. And then I ask him exactly what he does.

"I create mechanisms for exchanging foreign debt on the international market, basically," he says. I look blank. "Don't worry. Even people at my bank don't understand what I do. Emma does, though." He looks proudly down the table at Emma, who smiles back at him.

Then he tells me about a recent dinner held between prominent members of the business community and Gordon Brown, and how Gordon Brown couldn't tell jokes, and this made people suspicious of him.

"Do you miss being at the heart of all this?" he asks. "I know all about your past." This is said in a way that indicates he is not merely referring to my job.

"Sometimes I miss the adrenaline rush, because that kind of job is all-consuming, and I really miss my colleagues," I say, wanting to bring the conversation back to conventional territory. "But I'm glad that when disasters happen I no longer have to suppress that surge of excitement and can relate to them with unadulterated sympathy. Revealing you are a stay-at-home mum just doesn't do it for people in the same way as saying you work on *Newsnight,* although mostly people wanted to know what Jeremy Paxman was like."

"So, what was he like?" he asks. I stop myself from sighing.

This is often the first question that people ask me when they discover that I worked on *Newsnight* for seven years. Some amble around the subject with well-chosen questions that they hope will impress upon me their serious interest in the subject of the process of making a news feature and therefore elicit some never-before-revealed insight into Jeremy Paxman. But I know that before long they will want to ask about him.

"He is a really great guy. Very brilliant. Everyone adores him," I say, hoping that is enough to satisfy him. "Mostly, though, I struggle to recall what life was like before children." He laughs.

"Well, we all struggle with that," he says.

"Do you enjoy your job?" I ask.

"I used to," he says. "In my twenties, I had things to prove to people, and I worked like a dog. In my thirties I became a managing director of my bank, and I still worked like a dog. I made more money than even my wife could spend. When I hit forty, I began to lose interest. I don't mean to sound arrogant, but there was no longer any challenge. I can do it with my eyes shut, and making money is no longer a strong enough incentive."

"Only someone who has no financial worries can say something like that," I say. A few days earlier I had sat down at the desk, removed my credit-card bills from their hiding place, calculated the total of my unpaid parking fines, and came up with a figure that left me gasping. Twelve thousand seven hundred and sixty pounds and twenty-two pence. The initial debt was probably half this amount; the rest had accumulated as the bills were left unpaid and the interest payments soared.

"Also, I began worrying about my own mortality. I wonder, when I step off this treadmill, whether I will be able to look back and consider my life well spent," he says. "Your husband is a lucky man."

"To be married to me?" I say, delighted at the compliment.

"I wouldn't know about that," he says. "What I mean is that he is doing something he feels passionate about. The only thing I feel really passionate about is Emma. She has filled a void, breathed new life into me. I have been unhappy in my marriage for a long time now."

"But don't you think that's just an argument to justify your deception? Perhaps you should just learn to live alongside your midlife crisis," I say, leaning toward him. "You can't just use Emma as a short-term antidote."

"She might be a long-term antidote," he says, leaning back toward me.

"People having affairs always like to think their situation is unique, as though their feelings are somehow more powerful than those of anyone else who has lived through a similar experience. But actually it's a cliché. You are just one of thousands of middle-aged men going though this," I say, knowing before I have finished my diatribe that I should have stopped after the first sentence. "My brother, who is a psychologist, says that men are driven by sex, that they are not designed to be monogamous, they are designed to spread their seed, and that those who avoid this kind of situation are higher up the evolutionary scale. And what about your wife? Does she have any idea about what's going on? Doesn't she deserve to have a chance at understanding what is going on in your head? And if she doesn't, then don't you owe it to your children to try?"

Guy looks completely shocked. For a moment, he is silent. I remember Emma telling me how he doesn't like to be reminded of his wife and realize that he is angry with me. He puts down his wineglass a little too heavily and circles the rim with his finger so that it makes a quiet hum.

"I don't have to justify my behavior to you in any way, but in the interest of friendship, I want you to know that I have tried to talk to my wife about the way I feel, but she dismisses my crisis as an indulgence. I have told her that I want to downscale and change the way we live. I have told her that I am fed up with dinner parties with other bankers and their wives, where the conversation revolves around schools, children, and jobs, with an explicit undercurrent of competition beneath the chat. She says that we can't afford for me to earn less money, but what she really means is that she doesn't want to compromise on her lifestyle. Sometimes I think this is what money has bought me: a wife, four beautiful children, a home in Notting Hill, and a great girlfriend who nurtures my ego and those other places that no one else can reach anymore."

"But what about Emma? Doesn't she deserve more than mistress status?" I say. "What about children?"

"Emma doesn't want children," he says. "And if she did, I don't see why this would preclude having a child."

I'm shocked.

"And what about you, Lucy? Does your husband know what's going on in your head?" he says, still stroking the wineglass. "Do any couples know exactly what is going on inside each other's heads? Do you know what's going on in your own head?"

"But surely it would have been better to deal with your existential crisis before embarking on an affair," I say. "Lust is very distracting."

"So I have heard," he says, raising an eyebrow. "Is that what you are doing?"

"Sorry?" I say, wondering whether I have misunderstood him.

"Emma tells me that you have been grappling with a crisis of your own," he says. "We're no different, really. The thing is, Lucy, that we are compatible with many different people, and that is both a wonderful and terrible thing."

I drop my knife on the ground, and everyone turns around to look at us. Then my phone rings. It is the babysitter.

"Fred has thrown up everywhere, Lucy, he's inconsolable, I'm really sorry, but would you mind coming home? He says that he's eaten a packet of tablets that he found in your bedroom," Polly says, her voice wobbling with fear and tension.

"What sort of tablets?" I ask, my stomach gripped with anxiety.

"It says omega-three on the side," she says.

"Fish oils," I say with a certain amount of relief. "We'll come right away."

◎◎

The evening ends in the accident and emergency department of the hospital where Mark works.

"What do you think?" I ask the doctor.

"He looks a bit green around the gills," he says, smiling. "Sorry, bad joke. I've been on duty since nine o'clock this morning."

"Will there be any lasting side effects?" Tom asks.

"Well, if he starts growing fins, bring him back and we'll check him over," says the doctor.

I carry Fred in my arms, like a baby, whispering songs in his ear, and he quickly falls asleep, exhausted with the effort of so much crying and retching. These are the same rhymes that mothers have sung to children for centuries, a thread carried through the generations.

Almost exactly three years ago, we carried Fred home from this same hospital. I feel time passing like sand slipping through my fingers. Perhaps it is good that we remember only fragments of their childhood as we grow older. Otherwise, the loss would be too great to bear.

We go home, but it is impossible to sleep. Fear is a difficult thing to control once it has seeped into the bloodstream. Tom, who usually falls asleep as soon as he is placed in any horizontal position, lies awake, staring at the ceiling.

"So, what did you think?" he asks.

"I think I should have put the tablets in the medicine cabinet," I say.

"Not that," he says. "I mean, what did you think of Guy?"

"I'm not sure. I don't think he's reliable, but there was a certain vulnerability about him that I wasn't expecting," I say.

Tom snorts.

"Availability, I think you mean," he says. "He's just a type."

"What type?" I ask.

"The kind of man who fucks around and tries to justify it by making people feel sorry for him for being misunderstood," he says. "It's a great strategy to adopt in your forties. Might even get you through them. The only surprising thing about him was that he seemed familiar. I think I've met him somewhere before."

15

"It is better to live one
day as a tiger than
a thousand years
as a sheep."

When life loses its sense of alignment, vital clues get missed while others become the objects of excessive scrutiny. And so it was that I quickly forgot about Tom's sense of déjà vu surrounding Guy. Instead, I became preoccupied with an issue that affected me more directly because at the beginning of February, a time of year when every woman deserves a daily dose of sublimity, Robert Bass went to ground without any explanation for his absence.

Every Monday I began walking to school with a small spring in my step, hoping that this would be the day that he would reemerge from hiding. By the end of the week, my pace had dipped and my shoulders started to droop as another weekend loomed with expectations dashed. I looked at missed calls on my cell phone more than was reasonable and wrote e-mails to him that I never sent, because I couldn't find the right tone and was scared I might inadvertently dispatch them to the wrong person. Instead, his wife and au pair appeared at school with the children. I tried to ignore them, because I didn't want them trampling over my daydreams.

The weeks dragged by without even a sighting. Celebrity Dad disappeared to L.A. for a month to promote his latest film. Tom was in Milan for long stretches during the week. Cathy was busy being kept happy by two men. And Emma was still trying to turn her loft into a home with both furniture and husband on loan from someone else. Actually, she had stopped calling so much, and when she did there was less talk of Guy. There was mention of a trip to Paris and a new promotion at work, and once she referred to a new car but only to underline the fact that I had forgotten her birthday. I put this down to a combination of my transgression at dinner and the fact that she had entered a more settled phase in her relationship. Then I laid this to rest. Friendships, like gardens, sometimes come into bloom again when left unattended for a while, I thought. It proved another stone left unturned.

Even Yummy Mummy No. 1 had disappeared, dispatching her housekeeper to drop the children at school. My own escape route having suddenly closed down, I envied all of them for having somewhere else to go, without considering that where you go is not necessarily as satisfying as where you have come from.

I was left with Alpha Mum, who had started GCSE Latin so that she could help her eldest son with his homework. "*Errare humanum est. Ego te absolvo,*" she said one morning. "You can retain your position."

I replied, using the only Latin phrase that I could remember. "*Non sum pisces,*" I said, which means "I am not a fish." She looked surprised. "I wouldn't have had you down as a Latin speaker, Lucy."

I stopped worrying about what to wear in the morning and put Tom's oversize coat on top of hastily thrown-together outfits, so that no one noticed I was disappearing into myself. I began to think that I might never see Robert Bass again and then felt annoyed for allowing him to impact on my mood in this way, especially at a moment when I was in the ascendant. On the other hand, since he had vanished, there was no longer any imperative to tell Tom about him. He had become a historical figure. My certainty wilted and I became convinced that he was trying to avoid me, because the focus of his affections was directed elsewhere.

There were days when I struggled to recall exactly what Robert Bass looked like, although I couldn't forget how he made me feel. I could picture each feature individually but struggled to amalgamate them into a cohesive whole. I could remember his green eyes, but then his nose lost focus, or I could recall the exact tilt of his chin but then became unsure of the shape of his lips. He became a jumble of almost remembered features that didn't fuse together properly. I looked at school photos of his daughter to try and find his face, but swiftly concluded she looked much more like her mother, whose perky walk and gamine features had by this time become more familiar to me than those of her husband.

The February weather underlined what was impossible rather than what was possible. There was little rain, just endless days of damp and drizzle. Despite all indications, it wasn't the coldest winter since 1963, just the grayest. My victory over the heating lost significance. There was some comfort to be drawn from the repetition of daily ritual, wrapping cheese sandwiches in plastic wrap, pushing Fred on the swing in empty parks, stopping to stare at street cleaners using machines like giant hair driers to blow the leaves into piles, and then watching the wind dance them over the road before they had a chance to pick them up. The children asked the same questions every morning, and because the answers were well rehearsed, I could speak and think at the same time.

"Is that taking two steps forward and one step backward?" asked Sam, pointing at the men blowing leaves.

"It is," I said. "Never mind, spring is around the corner."

"And then what's around the next corner, Mummy? Is it summer?" asked Joe. Children propel you forward, and at this time of year, that is a good thing.

In the background, Fred was running through his daily inventory of road markings.

"Single yellow," he said, leaning out of his stroller to examine the pavement. Then a few minutes later, "Double yellow." Every mark on the road was deserving of commentary.

"Dotted line," he yelled in triumph, because they are less common.

Sam collected red rubber bands that the postmen leave on the ground. I thought of all the things that I didn't notice before I had children: that people are kinder to children and mothers in most other European countries, that going to the toilet is not a solitary experience, that you can't have it all.

"I don't understand why the leaves get picked up and the rubber bands dropped," said Sam.

෬

Then one Wednesday morning at the beginning of March I find myself listlessly shaking a tambourine at the Munchkin Music Group, urging Fred to wield his maracas less savagely because he is upsetting the small girl beside him. I am pondering how, in twenty years, my children will be more likely to work alongside people called Tiger and Calypso than Peter and Jane.

Although there are tatty chairs covered in faux leather around the edge of the church hall, for reasons that I have never understood, we are all required to sit on the floor on foam mats, our children perched between our legs in deference to the woman who runs the group and is entitled to look down at us from her chair. It is cold and uncomfortable, and by the end of the hour my thighs and buttocks have gone to sleep, making standing up a painful experience. But the sense of self-sacrifice and suffering for the sake of Fred imbues me with feelings of piety that generally last the rest of the day, although perhaps the headiness has more to do with breathing in a combination of bleach and disinfectant for an hour. Because as well as a meeting place for mothers, the church hall also doubles as a center for the homeless, both groups forming part of the disenfranchised.

Today, I am doubly unfortunate because I am sitting next to the woman that those of us with boys refer to as Smug Mother of Girls, or SMOG for short. On a good week, she restricts herself to deep sighs and self-satisfied comments.

"My girls are so self-contained, they spend the whole day drawing," she says, watching the boys run wildly around the hall, followed by their mothers. On a bad day, she mutters about hyperactivity and pouring Ritalin into the national water supply. At the end of the hour each week, I swear her chest is as puffed up as a turkey's.

"Is that rough boy upsetting you?" she asks her daughter, staring at Fred. I bristle and bite my tongue.

"Do you know I didn't want to have a third child, in case I gave birth to a boy?" she continues.

"That's a shame, because it might have made you less of a bunny boiler," I say, shocked even as the words spill out of my mouth. She looks at me, astonished, and shifts along the floor, opening up as much space between us as is possible when you are sharing a small foam mat. The door of the church hall opens and a familiar tousle of hair, a little longer and stragglier than when I last saw it and decidedly unwashed, appears as Robert Bass walks in with his toddler. My spirits lift and I shake the tambourine with renewed vigor. He looks somewhat taken aback to find Fred and me, because this is an out-of-context encounter.

He is late, an infringement that would normally be met with at least a searing glare from the fierce woman who runs the children's music group. But when he throws one of his winning smiles her way, I note that she blushes and urges him to come and join in, pointing decisively to a space beside her. How easily women of my age melt in the face of a little attention. We know that years of invisibility lie ahead.

Despite her best attempts, Robert Bass rejects the advances of the leader of the Munchkin Music Group and chooses to come and sit next to me and Fred, something I know I will pay for somewhere down the line. Her benevolence does not generally extend to mothers.

As I make space for him on my foam mat, I consider the fact that in the entire history of our flirtation, we have never been so physically close. Forget pubs and cafés—if you really want to get close to a man, toddler music groups are the place. Most of the right side of my body is touching him, even though the pleasure is diminished because I no longer have any feeling in my upper thigh. Thoughts of sitting cheek-by-jowl for the next hour cast endless choruses of "Wind the Bobbin Up" in a whole new light. Since this is his initiative and we are surrounded by other people, I decide that I can enjoy the moment with unadulterated pleasure, all the sweeter for the period of drought that preceded it.

Now all this is forgotten, and I am filled with born-again enthusiasm, waving the tambourine with Fred perched between my legs.

"Stop, Mummy, stop," he says, pawing at my shirt with sticky hands.

"Shh, Fred," I tell him, energetically shaking the instrument to compensate for his lack of activity.

"Mrs. Sweeney, Mrs. Sweeney," says the woman who runs the Munchkin Music Group. "There are no more green bottles hanging on the wall. You can stop now."

I look round to find everyone staring at me, including Robert Bass, who eyes me warily.

"You seem very enthusiastic, Lucy," he leans over to whisper in my ear.

"I just sometimes get carried away," I whisper back, enjoying the sensation of his breath on my neck. I am so close I can smell him. I close my eyes and breathe a tangier-than-usual mixture of raw sweat, coffee, and toothpaste. I wonder if he is doing the same and regret that I forgot to put on any deodorant. Still, this is how we will discover whether our genetic makeup is compatible.

"And how does the sheep go?" shouts the head of the Munchkin Music Group, breaking into my reverie.

"Baaah," I hear myself shriek enthusiastically. There is a stony silence.

"That one was for the children, Mrs. Sweeney," she says coldly.

"Where have you been?" I whisper to Robert Bass.

"My wife has taken a couple of months' sabbatical while I finish my book," he whispers back. "I was going to call you, but I decided that it would be too, er, distracting."

I am holding a carton of apple juice and am so surprised by this comment that I squeeze it a little too hard and a burst of liquid is propelled through the straw straight into his eye.

"Direct hit," he says, wiping his eye and the green khaki jacket that matches them so well. Tom is right. This attention to detail is not unconscious. Whether it is for my particular benefit or for womankind in general is less certain. I notice that once again all eyes are on us.

"I always forget that mixture of pleasure and pain in your presence," he says. "The agony and the ecstasy." I feel myself getting hotter.

"Can you please save your conversations for after the class," says the head of the Munchkin Music Group severely.

I open my handbag and blindly begin to search for wipes, but Fred is fed up with me and squirms between my legs. He is picking up crumbs of chocolate biscuit that have congealed on the floor of the church hall and putting them in his mouth. His face and hands are covered in a thin layer of chocolate. I hold his hands so that the trail cannot spread any farther. Smug Mother of Girls looks on disapprovingly.

Robert Bass offers to help look, and in the spirit of this new familiarity, I let him rummage in my handbag while I hold my sticky toddler. I pull Fred tight to me, reveling in the soft fleshiness of his thighs and bottom, tickling him at the back of his neck, and he rewards me with sloppy chocolate-flavored kisses. This is one pleasure that is never dulled by repetition.

Robert Bass pulls out, not necessarily in this order, one apple core, one pair of Bob the Builder underpants (clean), a couple of lollipop sticks, and then the tour de force, a cheese sandwich wrapped in plastic, black and blue with mold.

"Your bag is alive," he says. "I'm surprised it isn't playing a tambourine."

"Try the side pocket," I urge him, shaking my maracas vigorously. He pulls out a condom and turns it around in his hand as though he has never seen one before.

Oh, God. How did that make its way in there? Perhaps he thinks it is meant for him?

The music stops, and the head of the Munchkin Music Group gives us a withering look. The room has fallen silent apart from braying children.

"I keep one in case the children get bored on car trips," I hear myself say to the group of mothers and Robert Bass. "You can blow them up and they look just like balloons."

"Mrs. Sweeney," says the head of the Munchkin Music Group, "that really is the limit. I am going to have to ask you and your man friend to leave the room."

Robert Bass gathers up our toddlers and we retreat, shamefaced. We have been expelled from the toddler music group. Smug Mother of Girls is so inflated that I worry she might burst.

"Well, that was short-lived," he says outside on the pavement. It has started to drizzle again. I decide to offer him a lift home in the car, trying to recall the exact status of the mess.

"Would you like me to drop you home?" I ask hesitantly, having been turned down the last time I asked.

"That would be great," he says. "As long as we don't stop at any gas stations."

We strap our children in the back, and I notice that he holds his breath as he leans in to fasten the seatbelt and then exhales when he is outside on the pavement again.

"It's not so bad in the front," I say.

"I never know what I might find in here." He laughs nervously. "It's always a little more adventurous than anticipated. So, where are we going?" he asks.

"How about a walk on the Heath?" I suggest in daring fashion. "Or should you be at work?"

"I think I deserve a small break," he says.

He scrabbles around on the floor and asks me whether there is something to drink.

I am negotiating a difficult turn across a busy road of traffic and unthinkingly tell him to look on the backseat. Before I can say "carburetor," I see Robert Bass pick up a plastic bottle with yellow liquid inside and swallow thirstily.

He then makes a noise that is perfectly pitched between pain and disgust and spits out the drink all over me.

"What are you doing?" I hear myself shriek. "I'm soaked."

"Oh my God, what is that? It is so rank, it tastes like piss," he says, his eyes watering. All the fingers of his right hand are in his mouth in a desperate effort to remove all traces of the mystery liquid.

I immediately realize that he has picked up what we refer to as the "pee bottle." Early in the parenting experience, I discovered that we would never get anywhere on time if we stopped whenever one of the boys needed to pee. So all three children have been trained from an early age to use a plastic bottle.

He tentatively sniffs the liquid remaining in the bottle.

"It is piss, isn't it, Lucy?" he yells.

"Didn't you think it was an odd color?" I retort.

"I thought it was Lucozade or one of those electrolyte drinks," he says. "Do you think I should go to the doctor? Or A and E?"

"No," I say firmly. "Don't be ridiculous. Some people drink urine for medicinal purposes. Tito, Lady Di . . ."

"But it's fresh. There's a pint of piss in this bottle. How long has it been in here, Lucy?" he demands.

"Look, you're going to be fine," I say reassuringly, wondering if he is the kind of man who wants a woman to shower before he has sex with her.

"Just take us home, please, I need to brush my teeth," he pleads.

On balance, I decide that this has been for the most part a positive encounter.

❧

Tom arrives home late on Friday night. I am already in bed, so tired that I am unsure whether I am asleep or awake, when he stumbles into the room with his suitcase. He switches on the light and I close my eyes against the glare as he changes into another new pair of pajamas. He is in a buoyant mood. I know because he leaves all but the middle button undone.

The building work has begun on his library, he tells me excitedly. Huge concrete blocks, so big that trucks normally used by loggers have been commandeered to carry the load in a slow convoy through Milan, stopping the traffic for a day.

He has got a write-up in the local newspaper and pushes *Corriere della Sera* into my hand with the headline *"Il Genio Inglese."* And a photo of him underneath, with his arm around an attractive brown-haired woman who is looking away from the camera and up at him.

"Who is that?" I ask.

"That's Kate," he says. "She's one of the junior architects working on the project."

"She's very attractive," I say.

"She's one of Pete's old flames," he says dismissively.

"Does she go on all of your trips?" I ask.

"Yes," he says. "And before you ask me, the answer is no."

Hatred for Italian bureaucracy, which meant the project had been delayed for almost two years, has been replaced by love of cheeses from the Lombardy region. He takes a large slice of Gorgonzola, a chunk of Grana Padano, and a salami Milanese from his suitcase. He has even brought home a truffle wrapped up in kitchen roll, which he plans to shave on top of scrambled eggs every morning. He waves this round my nose, and I make grateful noises of appreciation. He unwraps the cheeses, lines them up on the chest of drawers, and shuts his eyes to sniff them with a look of ecstasy on his face.

"They've been asleep," he says.

"So have I," I say, trying not to sound grumpy.

"They need to breathe," he says, pointing at the unwrapped cheese.

"So do we," I say, reluctantly getting out of bed to take them downstairs.

It proves a fortuitous decision, because on the kitchen table I find a letter that arrived for me from Petra this morning. It is a short and formal note, properly punctuated, in her familiar neat handwriting. I glance over it again just to be sure that I haven't misunderstood what she said.

Dear Lucy,

Please read this when Tom is not around and then destroy it, because I know that otherwise you will leave it on the kitchen table. When I stayed with you in London just before I left for Morocco, I tidied your desk one morning and stumbled across a number of bills and notes from debt collectors indicating that you owe a substantial sum of money to various people. I hope you don't think that I was being nosy. The money for the sale of my house has finally come through and I am enclosing a check, which will go some way in resolving this situation. I am settling into life in Marrakech.

With love and affection,
Petra

PS: Read the book on Mrs. Beeton. None of us are what we seem,
but I would still recommend designating a specific day for laundry.

On the way upstairs, I stuff the letter and a check for £10,000 in the top drawer of my desk, feeling an unusual lightness of being. This represents a reprieve. I have already started to make a list of who to pay off first, with the nice bailiff at the top.

Tom's happiness is infectious, so when I return, I judge this to be a good moment to ask whether he would mind babysitting next week, so that I can go out to celebrate Emma's latest promotion. I know that by the middle of the following week, some other catastrophe will have befallen his project, and his mood will dip.

"That's fine," he says. "Someone is coming around to interview me for a piece in *The Architects' Journal* that night. Did I tell you that one of the Italian architects has invited us to go and stay in his house in Tuscany for two weeks?"

"How fantastic," I say, with genuine enthusiasm. "No tents?"

"No tents," he says. "A palazzo with a vineyard, no less. Although I don't think the camping provided a complete explanation for the fiasco in Norfolk."

"So what did then?" I ask.

He doesn't get a chance to respond because the phone on his bedside table starts to ring. We both eye it suspiciously, because phone calls late in the night are generally harbingers of bad news. I stretch over him to pick it up, but Tom puts his hand firmly on the receiver, waiting for it to ring exactly five times.

"Hello," he says tentatively. "Oh, Emma, do you want to speak to Lucy? I'll pass her over right away."

"She sounds a little odd," he whispers, his hand covering the wrong end of the handset. Tom's benevolence toward my girlfriends does not extend to dealing with emotional crises.

"Lucy, it's me," says Emma. She isn't crying, but her voice sounds breathless and panicky.

"Is she ill?" asks Tom, pulling at my arm. "Perhaps she is one of those high-powered women getting diseases that used to be more associated with men, like heart attack or stroke. I've read about it on the Internet."

"Where are you?" I ask her, ignoring Tom, because even when he talks about other people's maladies, he is still talking about himself.

"I'm outside your house," she says. "Will you come down?" I go over to the window, open the curtain, and see her waving up at me from the driver's seat of an old powder-blue Mercedes sports car that I haven't seen before. This must have been a present from Guy.

I consider my last birthday present from Tom, an aromatherapy candle from a High Street store, which smelled of burnt sugar and cheap chemicals when I lit it. It represented a marginal improvement on the previous year, when he had given me a manicure set. On balance, I decide that if this is the price you pay for not having to share your husband, it is a price worth paying. Then I remember how much the quality of his recent presents has improved.

"Can't you come inside?" I ask Emma.

"No, I've done something awful and I have to deal with it now," she says, slowly and clearly to underline the seriousness of the situation. "Please say that you'll help me."

"Whatever you've done, Em, it can't be so bad," I say, getting out of bed.

"Where are you going?" asks Tom.

"There's a crisis," I whisper to him.

"Will you put on something dark?" Emma says. "I can see that you are still wearing your pajamas. I'll explain everything when you come down. I'm so sorry."

Emma is not prone to apologies. In fact, I think this is the first time that she has ever said sorry to me. It is not that she doesn't realize when she has messed up. She just never likes to admit she might be wrong about anything. She is a woman of conviction.

I open the front door into the night and, shivering with a mixture of cold and fatigue, climb into the passenger seat of her car, breathing in the warm smell of the old leather seats and admiring the wooden dashboard with its dials and walnut finish. I would really like one of these. For a moment I consider the check from Petra that is sitting in my drawer.

"Are you having a Thelma-and-Louise moment?" I ask her as she starts driving down Fitzjohn's Avenue and then heads due west toward Maida Vale, following instructions on the portable satellite navigation kit that sits on top of the dashboard. "We're not going south of the river, are we?" I ask, because I have heard of people being directed into rivers by their sat nav before.

"No, Notting Hill," she says.

Emma always drives faster than I do. She keeps her finger on the gear stick at all times and changes up and down to alter her speed rather than braking. In fact, since we met at Manchester in the late 1980s, she has always done everything faster than the rest of the world. I can imagine her as a child, sighing with boredom when her four-year-old friends wanted to play with dolls instead of experimenting with makeup, then growing frustrated as a teenager when her friends spent hours applying cheap Avon products while she had already moved on to a more natural look that didn't involve foundation in shades of American tan.

I have seen photos of her as a child, and even back then she somehow looked more polished than the rest of us. A dedicated Londoner, she started university with all the apparent advantages that big-city life offers. While I bought from thrift shops out of necessity, developing a look that could best be described as baggy, with its emphasis on ill-fitting knitted cardigans and oversize coats, she was already combining cheap period pieces with items from Miss Selfridge. She knew how to snort cocaine without sneezing and blowing away the fun for everyone else. She sang in a band. Even her parents' divorce seemed exciting in all its plate-throwing recrimination. Emma made us all feel as though we had no experience of life. Back then, her wariness and cynicism made her seem cool rather than brittle. Aged nineteen, she was already weary of life. She was also the only person that I knew who was sure about what she wanted to do when she left university. In our last two years at Manchester, she worked every weekend at a local newspaper. She knew where she was going, while the rest of us had barely opened up the map.

In our final year, she came to stay at my parents' house for the weekend with Cathy. It was this weekend that crystallized my view of her. Mark had come for a couple of days to lick his wounds after finishing a relationship with his latest girlfriend. He wanted to talk it through with me. But when Emma walked into the room, his misery over his inability to be faithful evaporated.

"How can I settle on one woman when there are so many wonderful girls out there?" he said.

"But isn't there one that seems more wonderful to you than any of the others?" I asked, a hint of exasperation in my voice.

"They are all fantastic at different times," he said.

"You can't have a girlfriend to suit your mood," I insisted.

"But you can; that's the problem," he said. Even as I was having strict conversations with him about the need for a fallow period before rushing into another relationship, his responses drifted into intense glances at Emma.

By the end of the first evening, Mark and Emma were making feeble excuses to be alone together. It wasn't the first time that he had fallen for one of my girlfriends, and I was almost certain it wouldn't be the last. But it was the first time that someone failed to call him back. A few months later, Mark was facing the bitter sting of rejection. This was never discussed with me, by either him or Emma, but Mark never recovered his lost pride over the affair.

By that time, Cathy and I were used to Emma taking center stage. I was happy with my observer status. Life didn't revolve around me. I revolved around life, and that felt comfortable.

☙❧

Heading toward Notting Hill, I have that same sensation of being a spectator to Emma's life, but as she switches the engine off in a dark street just off Colville Terrace, I know that this time she requires more of me.

"Lucy, you know that I am usually a rational person who rarely loses control," she begins, turning in her seat so that she faces me. I nod, but I no longer believe it. "Well, the past month I have been in turmoil," she says. "About four weeks ago, Guy told me that he had decided to leave his wife and move in with me." She pauses for dramatic effect, and I willingly comply with a few suitable adjectives. It suddenly feels very late, and my body wants to go to sleep.

"That's amazing," I say sleepily, wondering why she had to drive all the way to Notting Hill to tell me this.

"It would be, except that he hasn't done it. At the beginning of this week, I looked at his BlackBerry and discovered that they have booked a two-week holiday in Sicily in August. When I challenged him, he said that he thought he might have one last family holiday and then tell her everything. Then, this weekend, we were meant to go to Paris together and at the last minute he blew me off because he wanted to go skiing in France with them. It suddenly dawned on me that he would always have a ready excuse to avoid telling her and that I could spend years growing old and bitter, waiting for him to do this, and that he might simply never do it. So I decided to take the situation into my own hands."

I sit up and stretch, too tired to anticipate what might be coming next.

"So, earlier this evening, I did something radical. I knew that they were away, so I phoned his home and left a message that must have filled the entire machine, giving a detailed account of our affair and everything that has gone on."

I look at her in disbelief.

"But he'll never stay with you after doing something like that," I say. "His wife will be devastated."

"Precisely," she says, her head resting on the steering wheel. "And that is why we are here. We have to get into their house and delete that message."

She sits up resolutely, opens the door of the car, and gets out, pulling on a pair of yellow kitchen gloves and handing me a similar pair.

"We mustn't leave fingerprints. Pass me that handbag, please, Lucy," she says, coming to open the passenger door and pointing at my feet. It is her favorite black Chloe Paddington. It is so heavy that I have to use both hands to pick it up.

"With or without you, I am going to do this," she says with steely determination.

I open the bag and look inside. It is full of tools. There are a couple of screwdrivers, a drill, and a sturdy-looking hammer. I shut it immediately and cling to it. Emma tries to pull it out of my hands.

"You're insane," I tell her. "I'm going to phone Tom immediately."

"I have no choice," she says. "I made a bad decision, and if I do this, I can change the course of history. I promise you, Lucy, that if you help me, I will end it with Guy. Eventually."

"But you said that you are doing this to prevent him from leaving you," I say.

"Lucy, it's not as bad as it looks," she says, ignoring my comment. "I got the keys to his house from his secretary, and I know how to disable the alarm. I'm just covering my back in case the answering machine is in a room that is locked. There is a plan. Forget the tools. There will be some in the house anyway."

She has started walking away from the car and down the road. I get out to follow her, struggling with the Chloe handbag. It is a dangerous time of night to be walking around alone, although in our dark clothes and yellow rubber gloves we are probably the ones to avoid. She starts to run at a slow jog, pulling a hat over her face.

"In case there's CCTV," she says, as though this is a familiar situation.

I struggle to keep up and eventually manage to maintain a slow trot beside her as we go through Powis Square, my tummies bouncing up and down uncomfortably. I am so breathless that I can't speak. We settle into a kind of rhythm and turn into a small cobbled mews, my chest aching with the effort of keeping up.

Suddenly, I have an epiphany. I know with absolute conviction that at the end of this street, Emma will turn first left and we will stand in front of a large, early Victorian house in Saint Luke's Road. I have never been to this house before, but I know who lives there.

Because in one of those strange coincidences that make up life, I realize with absolute certainty that Emma is having an affair with Yummy Mummy No. 1's husband. There have been many clues, but I have been so wrapped up with my own dilemmas that I have ignored the obvious.

"I know the people who live here," I say to Emma as we go up the steps at the front of the house. I am leaning over, panting, holding my legs.

"Of course, it's Guy's house," she says, looking at me from underneath the brim of her hat. "Are you all right, Lucy?"

"What I mean is that I know his wife. And his children," I say. "We're at the same school. She's somewhere between an acquaintance and a friend. Actually, we're coming to a school party here next week."

"God, that's no good," she says, but she doesn't stop trying keys in the front door locks. Every few seconds she looks nervously up and down the road to check that no one is watching. This is Emma's drama, and she doesn't really want me claiming a part of it.

"I'm really sorry to involve you in this, but I knew that you would have the imagination to help me resolve the situation. You're so unflappable."

The front door opens and we find ourselves in the hallway of Yummy Mummy No. 1's house.

"Am I?" I say, a little surprised, shutting the door behind me, forgetting how Emma always uses flattery to get her own way. She pulls out a small piece of paper from her pocket and starts to punch numbers into the alarm.

"I suppose it's because you are used to dealing with unpredictable situations in hostile environments," she whispers. "Mothers are good at that."

"You make me sound like a member of the Special Forces," I say, looking around. I don't know what I was expecting, because I didn't have the luxury of anticipation. I switch on the light and look up at a beautiful chandelier with multicolored crystals that throws different-colored light against the cream walls. Its brightness makes me blink. There is a table and bunch of flowers beside a large mirror, and in the reflection I can see a black-and-white family portrait hanging at the bottom of the staircase.

Yummy Mummy No. 1 is lying on an overgrown lawn with Guy. In the background is a house that I imagine is their Dorset retreat. Her head is thrown back in laughter. Guy looks at her indulgently. They are surrounded by their four children. It must have been taken in the summer, because the children are wearing swimsuits and Yummy Mummy No. 1 has a pair of cutoff denim shorts that show off her long legs to perfection. Emma goes over to look at the picture and sighs.

"How did I get involved in all this?" she says wearily.

"Pictures never tell you the whole story," I say, trying to be reassuring. "They're a projection of how people want you to see them."

A big vase of purple alliums, lilacs, and green chrysanthemums sits on the table.

"That's exactly like the bunch he sent me on my birthday," she says bitterly. "He must have got a job lot from Paula Pryke. Come on, let's go and look for this answering machine."

We creep into a huge double sitting room that leads of the hallway and both take off our shoes. Wooden shutters are closed over floor-to-ceiling windows. I turn on a small lamp on a table at the end of the room facing the road. The answering machine sits there, flashing to indicate that there are new messages.

"I hope they haven't picked them up remotely," Emma says, looking worried and chewing the sleeves of her black shirt. She looks small and vulnerable. I press the play button on the answering machine. Emma's voice fills the void, and in a raspy, slow tone, she gives an account of herself to Guy and his wife. I sit down on a chair in front of the desk, remove my glasses, and sleepily rub my eyes.

"Your husband is living a double life. . . ." the message starts. I want to listen to it all, but Emma comes over and presses the delete button before I have a chance to stop her. I feel slightly cheated because I think if I could hear the whole message, I might access parts of her that are normally unreachable.

"I don't want you to hear it," she says. "I sound so pathetically desperate. The rational part of me knows that I should end it with Guy, but I'm too weak to do it. I've never felt so close to anyone. I think that he means it when he says that he loves me, but what I now realize is that he is also happy when he's with his family, while my life is on hold until he comes back. I've never felt so fragile. And it was all so obvious that this would happen." Then she starts crying. "This is what happens if you become dependent on someone. You become impotent. That's what happened to my mother, and now the same thing is going to happen to me."

"Falling in love is always a risk," I say, slightly shocked to hear Emma's relationship philosophy expounded so baldly. "But it isn't a sign of weakness. You could argue it is a sign of strength. Because inevitably there will be periods of doubt and incompatibility, but when you get over those, they transmute into something even more valuable. Let's go downstairs and make a cup of tea."

She laughs weakly.

"Sometimes I wish I was you, Lucy," she says. "Everything sorted."

"Don't be ridiculous," I say. "It's all a pack of cards. Could come tumbling down at any moment."

We stand at the bottom of the stairs in the basement kitchen. I switch on the light. We are in an enormous space, staring at a kitchen island that is so long it looks like a landing strip. A kettle sits at one end, and there is a pile of papers at the other. I take off the rubber gloves and start opening and shutting cupboards, searching for tea. Emma is looking at the pile of papers, immersed in what looks like Yummy Mummy No. 1's bank statement.

"Look at this, Lucy," she says. "His wife thinks that she is getting rent from the flat where I live." Sure enough, every month a payment of £2,500 is deposited in her account under the heading "rent Clerkenwell." I look around the kitchen. Everything comes in pairs: two sinks, two dishwashers, two kettles. I start making us a cup of mint tea.

"I've just noticed that all these appliances are exactly the same as the ones in my apartment," she says, a note of despondency entering her voice again. "I'm going to take a look at the bedroom."

She rushes up the stairs and I trail behind, leaving the cup of tea on the step. On the second floor, Emma finds Guy's bedroom.

"I knew it," she says. "The bed is exactly the same. Can you believe that he chose exactly the same bed that he shares with his wife?"

"It shows a certain lack of imagination," I say. "But you always say that bankers play safe and I suppose once you have found the ideal bed, you stick with it. I think we should go now, before someone wonders why all the lights are on."

But Emma has disappeared into a walk-in wardrobe. I follow behind. I have always been curious about Yummy Mummy No. 1's collection of clothes, and I am not disappointed. Although it is more the way in which they are organized than the content that impresses me. There is a bank of shoes, each inside a shoebox with a photograph stuck outside. There are rows of color-coordinated cashmere sweaters. I take a picture with my mobile phone to show Tom.

Emma seems to be looking for something. She takes off her rubber gloves, and I am aghast to see her rifling through Yummy Mummy No. 1's underwear drawer. She pulls out a gorgeous Agent Provocateur bra and matching underwear and stuffs them down the front of her trousers.

"You can't steal her underwear," I say, grabbing a bra strap. "That's really deviant. Put it back, you're probably not even the same size."

"I want it as evidence," she says. "Do you know he bought me exactly the same set?"

"If I let go of this bra strap, will you walk out of this house now with me?" I say.

"It's a deal," she says. "There's one last thing that I want to do." She goes into the en suite bathroom and comes back holding a Rampant Rabbit.

"Two of these," she says.

"You mean she's got more than one?" I ask.

"No, he bought me the same model," she says.

I'll never be able to look Yummy Mummy No. 1 in the eye again. Emma switches it on. The noise fills the room. She then goes back into the walk-in wardrobe and leaves the Rabbit with the battery running in the pocket of one of Guy's suits.

"This will prove to him that I've been here," she says, sending him a text to tell him what she has done. Guy's weekend in the Alps has come to an abrupt end. I resist the urge to feel sorry for him. That is the trouble with being able to see everything from everyone else's point of view.

16

"There is more to marriage than four bare legs in a bed."

Sam is lying on our bed while Tom and I get ready for the school party tonight. He tells me that his next project is about the Middle Ages and wonders if we can shed any light on the subject. I am happy to be distracted. Much to Tom's astonishment, I have been ready for almost an hour, trussed up in my wrap dress with all its cleavage-enhancing and tummy-flattening possibilities. Over the past week, anxiety has become my constant companion and I have discovered that apart from its weight-loss potential, it has also turned me into a clock-watcher. Forget gravitas—under the skin of every organized mother lies a rich seam of neurosis.

I smooth my dress over my stomach. It is as familiar to me as an old friend, and reminds me of old times, of other parties, with different people brought together by something less arbitrary than the coincidence that our children share the same school. It connects me with a time before I was married, and in this sense it is a powerful dress because only I know its danger.

Sam watches me pouring hand cream onto the palm of each hand and then massaging it onto my fingers, taking special care with the backs of my hands. Their gnarled appearance, the incipient brown liver spots, and the papery surface around the knuckles remind me of my mother. Both of us have always washed our own saucepans. My mother never wore gloves because she thought they symbolized the domestic subjugation of women. I never wore them because I could never find them at the right moment. This I think sums up the essential difference between me and her: her passion and my passivity. Yet the origin of both words is the same, from the Latin *passus*, to suffer.

Around the edge of my nails, the skin is chewed and the cream stings these raw, red channels. When my hands are so smooth and oily that they shine, I switch attention to my forearms and see Sam's eyes following the motion of my hand as it moves briskly up and down my arm.

"What are you doing?" I ask him.

"I'm trying to hypnotize myself," he says, sitting very still. I stroke his hair, and for once he indulges me, nestling into my shoulder. When Sam was a baby, I remember lying beside him on the kitchen floor, before he was able to turn over on his own, trying to calculate the value of the tiny space that he occupied and realizing that there was no price that could be put on it. When I was pregnant with Joe, it seemed impossible that I would love this new baby as much. I imagined I would have to halve my affections, because surely there was a finite level of love? But that was the wonder of motherhood, the discovery that there were always untapped reserves available. And every day, despite the upheavals and the chaos, there are brief moments when that is all I feel, the unadulterated pure pleasure of love.

I have given Tom an abridged version of what took place with Emma because I knew that if he was acquainted with the whole story, he would refuse to come tonight. Of course, once we get there and he recognizes Guy, he will realize there has been a small collision of two worlds, but by then it will be too late. This is probably irresponsible, but perhaps this discovery will deflect attention from the unfortunate incident of the misdirected e-mail, a source of great worry to him. For both he and I are equally nervous about encountering Robert Bass, although for very different reasons. And I think it is enough to be worried about seeing one person. If Tom was enduring the same anxiety that I felt about also seeing Guy and Yummy Mummy No. 1, then it would be unbearable. I absentmindedly start rubbing the hand cream on my face, forgetting that I am sabotaging my makeup.

"What do you think the Middle Ages are about?" I ask Sam as I reapply foundation.

He crosses his legs, considers the question for a moment, his finger on his lips, and then says thoughtfully, "Your new eyebrows, Daddy going bald, being tired all the time, forgetfulness. Oh, and disintegration." This is his favorite new word.

"You're thinking of being middle-aged," I explain to him. "The Middle Ages is something quite different." I mention wandering minstrels, jousting, bloodletting, and the arrival of olive oil in England. Sam looks suitably relieved.

"That sounds like much more fun," he says, leaving the room to go downstairs, where the babysitter is making hot chocolate for them all.

"Do you think we are disintegrating?" I ask Tom. It is not an image that I favor.

"In the sense that more of us are dying than growing, then I suppose we are," he shouts from the bathroom. "We are heading toward middle age, even if people no longer like to describe themselves that way."

"Well, I don't really feel middle-aged," I say.

"That's because you're having a midlife crisis," he says through a half-closed mouth. He must be shaving that area to the right of his chin. "Clinging on to the last vestiges of youth."

"Define midlife crisis," I say, a little disconcerted.

"Discontent with the status quo, restlessness, questioning decisions that you made years ago, thinking you've grown apart from your husband, wondering whether happiness lies with another man, breaking into the house of a complete stranger," he says, peering around the door and waving his razor at me to emphasize the latter. "But you'll get over it."

"Why haven't you mentioned this before?" I ask him.

"I don't want to indulge your crisis," he says. "And I'm worried it might be contagious."

"Mark says that we no longer communicate properly," I say.

"That's because we're always interrupted by someone, mostly our children but sometimes your friends, and more recently my work. Lucy, I don't have time to access everything that is going on in your mind," he says. "But I have a good grasp of the overall picture, and I don't think that hours of analysis would ameliorate anything. In fact, it might make it worse. Right now, however, I am far more concerned that you remain sober enough to avoid revealing any further details of our sex life to complete strangers."

"They're not complete strangers," I say. "What's more, we will know these people for the next six years. In fact, sometimes you find that people you think you don't know are more familiar than the people you thought you did know. If you know what I mean."

"I'm not sure that I do," he says, sighing.

You will soon, I think to myself.

"Also, we didn't break into Guy's house, we had the keys," I insist.

"That's like saying the man who stole the car because you dropped the key on the doorstep was borrowing it," he counters.

"You promised that you would never mention that again," I say.

"I'm still reeling from the fact that you went along with Emma's plan," he says. "And that when you came home, you woke me up to show me a picture on your mobile phone of Guy's walk-in wardrobe as though it was the most notable part of the whole exercise."

"Well, in a way it was," I say.

Less than an hour later, we are standing on the doorstep of Yummy Mummy No. 1's house. It is now light enough in the evening to see that the steps are covered in small mosaics in white, blue, and brown. There is a wisteria growing up the side that hasn't yet come into flower. The front garden has been planted with grasses, euphorbias, and enormous wine-colored phormium. It looks beguilingly careless, but I know it was the product of meticulous planning, because it was one of Yummy Mummy No. 1's Grand Projects. The others being the Double-Height Glass Extension and the Flat to Rent, which is where Emma now lives.

Someone I don't recognize answers the door. She must be the Filipina housekeeper, I think, trying to remember the exact dimensions of Yummy Mummy No. 1's staff. I recall mention of a clutch of Eastern

European au pairs, a man and woman, "so that they don't stray," and one English nanny. Then, for a long time, there was a night nanny who was training the baby to sleep through the night using ayurvedic techniques. And the Slovakian personal trainer. That's globalization for you.

We are directed to the sitting room, where glasses of wine are being handed out. I know before I see the bottle that it is Puligny-Montrachet. Emma is right. Guy doesn't have much imagination.

I listen to a conversation behind me.

"We might IPO the MBO we did last year, and John is going to make a fortune on his LTIP," says one man in a suit to another. Tom raises an eyebrow at me. Could be a long evening, the look says.

Yummy Mummy No. 1 glides across the room. She looks even thinner than she did before half-term, wispy and papery. Even though it is a school party, she clearly sees her role as that of hostess. She is wearing skinny white jeans with thick cork-wedge heels and a top from somewhere ethnic via Selfridges. She looks fantastic.

What a waste of all those hours invested in the gym and that careful application to her wardrobe. It's like studying for exams that get canceled at the last minute. If you can do all that and still your husband strays, then there doesn't seem much point in embarking on those time-consuming, age-defying techniques in the first place. Better to have room for improvement than attain perfection. Looking at those long legs that Emma admired in the photo last week, encased in jeans cut so tightly that they taper at the knee and then expand slightly to cocoon her calf, I decide that whatever fashion dictates, I will hang on to my extra pounds and wear boot-cut jeans for the rest of my life.

I look around the room at the other parents. The other yummy mummies are dressed in variations of the same theme, and, not for the first time, I wonder how they know what each other will be wearing and what the point is in going to all this effort if everyone ends up looking the same anyway. But maybe that is the point. It's a tribal thing. Is knowing exactly which brand of jeans from L.A. is in the ascent an art or a science, I wonder? For Yummy Mummy No. 1, it has definitely been raised to an art form.

The corporate mums have suits purloined from work wardrobes that look a little formal with their straight lines and sober colors. Then there are the mothers like me, the slummy mummies, the muddlers and befuddlers, the ones who don't know what to do when a spare minute comes their way because it is so rare, wearing old dresses that have stretched with us over the years.

"Lucy, how fantastic to see you," she says, leaning in to kiss me on both cheeks. The contact is unanticipated, and we end up clumsily kissing on the lips. "And you must be Tom," she says, as though this is the first time that he has registered on her radar, although she must have seen him at school before.

I note that she is sporting that inverted-panda look favored by spring skiers. White eyes set amidst a deep-brown tan.

"Did you have a good half-term?" I ask her.

"Les Arcs, with friends," she says. "Fantastic snow. How about you?"

"Les Mendips," I say in a French accent. "With my parents. There was a fresh cover over Easter. Very unseasonal." Tom steps aside to look at me, baffled by the direction of this conversation, and shrugs his shoulders.

"I haven't heard of that resort. Is it in Bulgaria?" she asks.

"It's a bit further west," I say vaguely.

"Mark Warner? Powder Byrne? Off-piste? Tricky runs?" she asks, using verbal shorthand to indicate the imminent closure of our discussion on the merits of ski resorts. Sure enough, I see a herd of yummy mummies with identical tans waving at her from the other side of the room.

I think of the tense hour spent roaming small villages in the Avon Valley after I simultaneously forgot to tell Tom to turn off the M4 and then discovered that a key page covering said villages was missing from our British road map.

"Dramatic," I say. "We covered a lot of ground." Including arguments about (1) why our clothes were packed in plastic bags instead of suitcases, (2) how, despite the plethora of plastic bags in the trunk, there were none available for episodes of car sickness, and (3) on what grounds we ever considered ourselves compatible enough for marriage.

"Was the resort very high?" she asks politely.

"Sort of average. It was very cold, though," I say. "Did your husband manage to take any time off work?"

"He came out on the orange-eye both weekends," she says. Then, when she sees me looking bewildered, she adds, "The Easy Jet flight to Geneva that leaves early on Saturday morning."

Yummy Mummy No. 1 shifts her attention to Tom.

"I'd love to show you around, Tom, and see what you think of the house," she says. "Although I know that you parted company with glass extensions many years ago."

"Well, it was my bread and butter for a long time," Tom says. Then she calls her husband over to come and meet us.

"Guy, Guy," she peals, "come over and meet the Sweeneys. They've just got back from les Mendips; it sounds fantastic."

Guy walks over from the other side of the room. He is smiling in the manner of someone who is clearly used to being in control of situations. A man who is never short of a good anecdote over dinner, who knows how to make a woman feel as though she is the only person in the world that he is interested in, who can survey a room and spot the person most useful to his career and engage in conversation with that person without them realizing that he is networking.

It is the same smile he uses when closing a Big Deal or showing off in front of junior colleagues or meeting his mistress's friends for the first time. He lifts a bottle of wine in greeting. I watch him closely, wanting to register the exact moment when he realizes that he is no longer master of all he surveys.

It takes a few seconds longer than anticipated, because along the way he stops to greet other guests and takes the opportunity to look around the room and bask in the attention. For a short man, he has a large stride. When he is perhaps six feet away from us, the smile disappears completely and for a moment he stands stock-still in shock, his eyes flitting from Tom to me. For a moment I imagine the room is falling silent, then Guy moves forward again, a little stiffly perhaps but mustering a passable show of pleasure, although, as he gets closer and shakes my hand, I can see the muscles around his cheeks twitching with the strain of maintaining this friendly expression. His eyes, however, are not smiling. They are cold and angry.

"I'm lucky he's here. Last time we were meant to meet friends for dinner he had to go to Paris for work," says Yummy Mummy No. 1. "Work is his mistress. Isn't it, darling?" Tom tenses beside me, and we hold hands a little too firmly to reassure one another.

"Nice to meet you," Guy says, formally shaking our hands. Tom takes longer to recover, and while he manages to shake Guy's hand, he recoils slightly when he is released and slides it into his back pocket, where it darts restlessly in and out for the next five minutes.

"Lucy is on the parents' committee," Yummy Mummy No. 1 says warmly to Guy. "She helped organize tonight and managed to persuade the woman who heads it up that we didn't need to come dressed as our favorite character from a book."

"The quid pro quo is that the summer fete will have a Roman theme," I say.

Tom and Guy remain still and silent.

"She is one of my firm allies," says Yummy Mummy No. 1, looking anxiously at Guy as if willing him to say something appropriate. I try to resist being flattered, because I know she is going through the motions and that I will still be passed over in the playground if there are tastier morsels on offer.

"I've heard a lot about you," Guy says finally, putting his arm round Yummy Mummy No. 1 to steady himself. He fills Tom's glass with wine, and I notice that his hand is trembling slightly.

"Can I borrow him for a moment?" she asks me, pointing at Tom. "I really want to show him the kitchen extension. We had the same architect as David Cameron. He lives around the corner. Very exciting to be living in the shadow of the next prime minister." She moves away, one hand in the back pocket of her jeans, showing off her bottom in all its tight-arsed glory, a gesture that I know is directed specifically at Tom. He whispers in my ear as he moves away, "Nothing middle-aged about that." I know that on the way home I will run into a wall of silent reproach, but I also know that I can rely on Tom to avoid a scene.

"I'll catch up with you later, Lucy, there is something I have to discuss with you," says Yummy Mummy No. 1. This time I manage to contain the impulse to invent exciting scenarios. Still, if she wants advice about schools, then my transformation into Mother with Gravitas will be complete.

Guy and I are left standing together. I take the bottle of wine from his hand and pour myself a generous glass, then place it on the table where the answering machine sits. This time it is not blinking at me. I perch on the edge of the table, and Guy turns around to face the window so that no one can see us talking.

"Are you a Cameron fan?" I ask politely. "Or do you think that inside every Tory lurks the spirit of Norman Tebbit?"

"What the fuck are you playing at?" he asks. His voice is quiet but laced with aggression, and his face is so close to mine that I can feel the heat from his breath. "A return visit, within a week, no less? I'm minded to call the police. Your fingerprints must be everywhere."

"Don't be ridiculous," I say. "What would you tell the police?"

"Well, you tampered with my home, stole my wife's underwear, and then left that . . . device in my pocket," he says furiously. "You know it was still running when we got home."

"We wore gloves," I say.

"I know, because you left a pair in my wife's dressing room," he says. "I had to take them to work with me to dispose of them."

"I was just an observer. The only thing I did was help to delete Emma's message to you both, and I think you will agree that I have done you a favor. Consider the alternative," I say, trying to calm him with logic.

He puts a hand on the back of his head and starts rubbing it irritably. I notice that he is losing his hair.

"Look, sorry, I'm under a lot of stress at the moment. Emma is refusing to take my calls; my wife is watching my every move. I think you could have given me some heads-up," he says. "Why didn't Emma tell me that you know my wife and that our children are at school together?" He groans.

"I had to come because I helped organize this," I say, waving my hand around the room a little more forcefully than intended. "As for Emma, perhaps the question is better directed at her."

My arm hits something hard and I turn round, just as the contents of the glass of wine spill onto the striped shirt of another father from school. I look up to see if I know the person that I am about to apologize to and feel that familiar quiver of excitement grip my body as I see Robert Bass trying to soak up the excess liquid with a dirty-looking handkerchief.

"God, I'm sorry," I say, wondering how such a small glass of wine could cause such a large stain on his shirt. "Guy, this is Robert Bass, his son is in the same class as our children."

"So, you're the writer," says Guy coldly, after an inappropriate silence, and I know that he is following this trail to its logical conclusion. "Lucy has told me about you."

"Oh," says Robert Bass, looking pleased.

"We were talking about her ski holiday in les Mendips," says Guy. "And the morality of skiing off-piste when you know it could cause an avalanche."

Then he walks off without saying anything more.

"I'll go and find a towel or something," I say to Robert Bass, feeling uncharacteristically flustered by this situation.

"What's eating him up?" he asks. "I'll come with you." We walk out of the sitting room into the hall. There is no one there. Everyone is either in the room that we have just left or downstairs in the kitchen. I go into a small room beside the front door that I remember from my visit last week. It looks like a cupboard but runs the breadth of the house and is used as a coatroom and general dumping ground. At the end, overlooking the garden, is a small sink. I pick up a towel and hand it to him.

"How did you know about this room?" asks Robert Bass, soaking up wine with the towel. He picks up his glass and gulps down what is left without taking his eyes off me. He is looking at the outline of my wrap dress, where it is set against the skin at the top of my shoulder, tracing it from the hard bone of my sternum to the soft contours above my cleavage. He chews his lower lip thoughtfully and stares at me with such intensity that I have to look away.

"Instinct," I say.

"You must have good instincts, then," he says.

"Sometimes," I say.

"Well, we're definitely off the beaten track here, Lucy," he says, closing the door behind him.

There is a point in a relationship where what is left unsaid becomes more important than what is said, and I have just reached this juncture with Robert Bass. But what I should have said to him at this moment was that my intentions were noble when I offered to search for a towel, and that I didn't intend to lure him into a glorified cupboard. Instead, I remain silent. The light is on, but it is still gloomy, and we are swaddled from the outside world by layers of coats and jumpers that hang neatly on pegs on both sides of the room. It is the kind of moment that you look back on with the benefit of hindsight and wonder how things might have been had you gone down a different route. It is a time for decision-making.

He puts out his hand and with his middle finger he traces the line he burned with his eyes a minute ago, until it rests in that soft cleft in between my breasts. I hear a gasp, a noise that might be imperceptible in a less silent context, and am surprised to discover that it emanates from me. The pleasure is exquisite. It is as though my mind has separated from my body and I am observing this happening to someone else. I lean back against Yummy Mummy No. 1's sheepskin coat and tilt my head slightly toward the ceiling to give him access to the lower regions of my neck. Now I am the one chewing my lower lip. I don't want him to stop, but I don't want the responsibility of responding.

He takes his finger away, and I gasp again because every part of my body demands more attention. Then I see him lean toward me. He puts one hand against the wall of the coat room, letting it rest at the top of my arm, and the other inside my dress at the top of the shoulder, pulling it slowly down to expose most of my upper body. I shiver with the pleasure of anticipation. The risk of discovery only adds to the excitement, and I wonder how for so many years I have managed to stay away from this kind of encounter. Then he leans toward me, the same hand that was on my shoulder now pulling me toward him from somewhere above my shoulder blade, and we are about to kiss when there is a knock on the door.

"Lucy, is that you in there?" says a male voice outside. "Lucy?" The fear of discovery is slightly alleviated by the fact that it isn't either Tom or Robert Bass's wife. But the knocking is so insistent that inevitably it will attract the attention of other guests. I go to the door and open it slightly to find Celebrity Dad standing outside.

"Sshh," I say, putting my finger to my lips.

"You don't need to be quiet at a party," he shouts, pushing his way in through the door. "I knew it was you, Sweeney. I was in the garden and looked up to this window and recognized your dress."

"The garden?" I say.

"I thought you might be doing coke," he says.

"Doing coke?" I say.

"Are you just going to repeat everything that I say?" he asks.

He is now inside the room and shuts the door behind him. Robert Bass has moved to the back and is standing behind some long coats beside the sink. I can see his legs sticking out at the bottom among pairs of Wellington boots and shoes. Celebrity Dad, however, has his own agenda and pulls out a credit card and small bag of white powder from his jacket pocket. He locks the door, then, in swift succession, sits down on a small stool, takes a magazine from a pile by the door, and efficiently starts chopping up lines of cocaine. He generously passes the magazine to me but I decline.

"I have enough problems going to sleep without any chemical inducement," I say.

He leans over the magazine and snorts a line through a rolled-up twenty-dollar bill. He is so familiar to me that I wonder momentarily, through the haze of wine, unconsummated passion, and lack of air, whether I am in fact watching one of his films. Possibly one directed by Quentin Tarantino. Then I start to calculate whether it would be worse to be discovered in flagrante with one parent or assumed to be taking drugs with another, and I realize that there is not much to choose between the two and that I must get out of this room as quickly as possible.

"So, what were you doing in here, then?" Celebrity Dad asks. He is looking at my dress, hanging off my shoulder. I pull it back up but it gapes over my stomach. The only solution is to untie the dress completely and start from the beginning again. So I briefly unwrap the dress and then curl it around me, tying a tight bow above the waist.

"I'm readjusting," I say. "I wasn't expecting an audience."

"It is so great to be out of L.A. and back in a country where women look like women," he says enthusiastically. "I love all that tits and bums stuff that you get here; it is so much healthier than dealing with middle-aged women with prepubescent bodies. So readjust all you like."

"I really need to get some air," I say, when I am convinced that I have recovered dignity. "I think I'll go and have a walk around the garden."

"I'll come with you," he says. "That woman was doing my head in, asking me about what extra activities my children do, whether they are going to apply for Harvard, my views on parental discipline. She's enough to drive anyone to drugs."

"So what did you say to her?" I ask.

"I asked whether she could introduce me to those two women who popped up on her computer screen when we were in the café," he says.

We go down into the kitchen and the crowds clear, as they do when Celebrity Dad approaches. A waitress offers us a tray of tiny Thai spring rolls, and I take the opportunity to grab a handful. I wonder if Celebrity Dad notices all this quiet attention. Did this deference start overnight after that Coen Brothers film, or was it something that evolved slowly over time, so that the onset was imperceptible?

I search for Tom among the crowd but can't find him. Despite the envious looks from other mothers, he is the person that I would most like to be with right now. I go out into the garden with Celebrity Dad, aware of pairs of jealous eyes observing me. As I breathe in the night air, ignoring the drizzle, and gulp down another glass of wine, my body starts to slump with the relief that comes after an unexpected shock. I am not the kind of person who can adjust to these situations, I think to myself. That is the difference between Guy and me. He is unfaithful in a professional kind of way, while I will always be an amateur. I am already feeling racked with guilt about a kiss that never even happened. I resolve then and there never to allow myself to get into such a compromising position again.

And yet I am already rerunning the scene over and over in my mind, wondering where it would have all ended and whether, given similar circumstances, it would happen again. Because sometimes, when people have looked over the edge of the precipice, they decide they would rather take a few steps back, even though the view is great. And the more I think about it, the more I wish I was still in the coat cupboard.

"Does it bother you the way that people behave around you?" I ask Celebrity Dad, looking for conversation to distract myself from these turbulent thoughts.

"What do you mean?" he says, sniffing loudly. We have reached the end of the garden, but it has taken a good five minutes. In the corner, beside the riding mower and the kind of climbing frame you would find in a good London park, is a pristine Wendy house in pastel colors, with a small veranda and a windowsill planted with real plants. There are small lights that twinkle around the window.

He opens the door.

"After you," he says with faux gallantry. "The truth is, Lucy, that I don't often hang out with people who aren't famous. I know that sounds arrogant, but it's true, and sometimes those people have lost sight of who they are, so it is fun to be with real people. Unpredictable. Like that woman who heads the committee. She is hilarious. I am going to make it my mission to corrupt her. You can tell the corruptible types, and you're not one of them."

"How do you know that?" I ask.

"Instinct," he says.

We bend down to go through the small door, but inside it is so capacious that we can stand up straight again.

"Don't say it. I know that I am smaller in real life," he says. "Don't tell me things that I know, tell me things that I don't know."

"That's what I mean," I say to him. "You expect to be entertained, and life isn't like that for the rest of us. We have to make our own fun."

"Lucy, when I'm with you, I know I will be entertained," he says, pulling out a small, child-size chair and preparing another couple of lines of coke. I am examining a sink in one corner of the Wendy house and am astonished that when I turn the tiny child-size tap, real water spills out.

"You can't do that in here," I say, turning round and looking out through the windows, in case other parents are approaching. "Put it away. It's not that kind of party."

"By the way, I saw him in there, hanging among all those coats like an art installation," says Celebrity Dad, ignoring me.

"What do you mean?" I ask tentatively, although I already know the answer.

"I saw Deep Shallows in that room with you," he says. "But I won't say anything about your little secret if you don't say anything about mine."

"It isn't like that," I protest. There is nothing worse than being accused of infidelity without enjoying any of its pleasures. Then he stands up and theatrically says in a passable English accent: "What is it men in women do require / The lineaments of Gratified Desire? / What is it women do in men require? / The lineaments of Gratified Desire.

"Lucy, it's what the world revolves around. William Blake knew it. I know it. Where I come from, everyone is at it; it's not a big deal," he says.

"But you don't understand, for me it is," I say. "Actually, I really love my husband, in a long-term kind of way."

"Well, then, why do you want to fuck this other man?" he asks, a hint of exasperation in his voice.

"I'm not sure," I say. "I suppose I want to do something reckless, to feel alive."

"There's nothing wise about me," says Celebrity Dad. "But one thing I can tell you is that uncertainty is not a good basis for anything. I'm on my third marriage, remember? I live with a lot of uncertainty in my life. I've been with my therapist longer than any of my wives." Then he gets up suddenly.

"Maybe you should have married your therapist, then," I say.

"He's a man," he says. "I better go and mingle with the masses. I think I'll put some music on. People need to loosen up a little. Apart from you, of course. Maybe you need to tighten up."

We go back inside and Celebrity Dad puts on a Radiohead album and goes in search of Alpha Mum to ask her whether she wants to dance. I spot Robert Bass in the corner of the room, talking to Tom. They both look up at me. Robert Bass looks away a little too quickly. However you look at it, a line has been crossed. But lines are sometimes blurry and you can cross them without realizing. Mark didn't consider this.

I gulp down another glass of wine, hoping that it will have an anesthetic effect on my body. Every nerve ending is in a heightened state of alert. Reflexes are ready to be activated. I feel curiously alive, ready for detonation. Mark would tell me that my body is coursing with adrenaline and that I am in fight-or-flight mode. But explaining away feelings takes the mystery out of life.

I spot the busy headmistress briskly walking toward me.

"Thanks so much for all your hard work," she says, smiling.

"It was nothing," I say.

"Organized but not too organized. Pitch-perfect. I knew that you would have a restraining influence, Mrs. Sweeney. It's hard enough to know what to wear without the added complication of coming dressed as your favorite character. It must be a relief to be sharing the burden with Mr. Bass."

I start to choke on my mini spring roll. I stopped counting how many I had eaten when I reached seven.

"Absolutely," I say, more enthusiastically than intended. Then I cough a little more and miss the beginning and end of her next question. The middle words are, I think, "consider a fourth."

"Three is our limit. Actually, my husband is considering a vasectomy," I hear myself say. I should stop in my tracks at this point, but an irresistible urge to expurgate our bedroom secrets prompts me to mention Tom's obsession with contraception.

"He doesn't wear two condoms yet, but we're close," I say, laughing. "In fact, he still explodes into periodic rants because I once mentioned the idea of a fourth. Not a fourth condom, a fourth child I mean."

She has a fixed smile on her face. She is used to confessional parents. I sense other mothers looking on intently, no doubt wondering what is holding the busy headmistress captive for so long. Both Alpha Mum and Yummy Mummy No. 1 have come over and are listening to the tail end of this conversation.

"I think four is the perfect number, because then no one is left out on the chair lift," says Yummy Mummy No. 1. She says, in fluent banker's-wife speak, that she had four under three, or was it five under two or six under one? Impossible arithmetic anyway.

"The most difficult part is getting my five-year-old to her harp lesson, because my four-year-old has Suzuki violin at the same time," says Alpha Mum, looking for approval from the headmistress but receiving little more than a glacial smile. She persists. "Running with a harp is very hard work, when there are deadlines looming. At the beginning of every school year, I hang a timetable on the kitchen wall with all my children's and husband's activities recorded, so that nothing is ever forgotten."

She looks pointedly at me.

"Actually, what I was asking was whether you would consider staying on the parents' committee for a fourth term," says the headmistress, turning to me and nodding emphatically before moving away to join another group of parents.

"So, do you record all your activities?" I ask Alpha Mum, genuinely impressed.

"Everything," she says.

"Even sex?" I ask, wondering if this might be the solution to the dearth of activity in our household. "Doesn't that make it less spontaneous? Also, you would need a very big wall chart since five in the morning seems the only moment that both parties are free at the same time."

"It is not something that we review in advance," she says.

I say that it is strange that my single girlfriends have lots of time for sex but no one to have it with.

"I don't really have any single girlfriends anymore; we tend to mix with other couples," she says, in the manner of mothers who claim their children eat anything and everything. So I tell her she is missing out, because over recent drinks with single friends the talk was of nothing but sex and activities, which made me glad that postpartum hemorrhoids and time constraints preclude anything but sex against the clock. She says that she is very pleased with the new anti-bullying policy and then walks off.

"There goes a woman who hasn't had sex with her husband in years," says Yummy Mummy No. 1. "Lucy, do you have a moment?"

She goes upstairs into the hall and signals at me to follow. For a moment I wonder if she is going to lead me to the coatroom and berate me for my behavior, but she continues upstairs into her bedroom. This evening is turning into one of those nightmares where every awful thing you have ever done in your life comes back to haunt you, and friends and enemies and people who don't even know each other mysteriously appear at the same time to expose you. As I walk up the stairs, I consider my worst possible scenario and wonder whether my *Newsnight* colleague of yesteryear is waiting in her bedroom with Tom, comparing notes.

"Do you mind if I use the loo?" I ask her as we go in the room. I feel dizzy and want to splash cold water on my face in an effort to reconnect my mind with my body.

"Sure," she says, and I go into the same bathroom that I explored with Emma last week.

"How did you know that was the bathroom and not a wardrobe?" she asks suspiciously.

"Instinct," I say brightly.

I go inside and shut the door behind me, leaning against it to catch my breath. I make several rash promises to myself. I will never complain about life being boring again. I will behave with utmost decorum in all situations. I will never overspend on my credit card. I will never shout at the children again. I will dedicate one day a week to washing. I will do all these things, if I can just get away with everything. I look at my watch in disbelief. How could so much have happened in such a short space of time? We have been here for less than two hours.

I catch sight of myself in the mirror. My mascara has run. The water comes out cold and I wipe my face free of makeup, to try and find someone I recognize. Then I leave the bathroom and go into the bedroom where Yummy Mummy No. 1 sits straight-backed at the end of the bed, her legs crossed.

"Are you all right, Lucy?" she asks, scrutinizing my body in my wrap dress in that way that only women can. "You look a little flustered."

For a moment I consider telling her everything. What has just happened with Robert Bass, that her husband is having an affair with one of my best friends, that her house in central Notting Hill is built of straw. But I resist the urge, knowing that the relief of confession will swiftly be replaced by a whole set of new worries about unleashing some new, unpredictable chain of events. What I need now is to head for the high ground. Regroup. Eat nourishing food. Sleep for two days. Take a vow of silence.

"What did you think of Guy?" she asks, patting a space beside her at the end of the bed. The door to her walk-in wardrobe is open, and I feel slightly sick staring at the familiar rows of shoes.

"He seems lovely, very warm and friendly," I say resolutely.

"I think he's having an affair," she says. My chest tightens, and I focus on breathing in and out through my nose to prevent myself from hyperventilating.

"Why would he want to do that?" I say breathlessly. "He's married to a gorgeous woman, has a brood of fantastic kids, a perfect life. It would be illogical to risk all that."

"But that is precisely why he would. It's all too predictable," she says, getting up to go over to a chest of drawers. She pulls out a packet of cigarettes, opens a window, lights one up, and inhales deeply, then hands it to me. "We can go out on the balcony. I do it all the time."

"What makes you think he is having an affair?" I ask her.

"In increasing order of relevance," she says, grateful, I assume, for the chance to unburden herself. "First up, he has a new shirt that I definitely didn't buy him, and I know that he wouldn't have gotten it himself because it's from Paul Smith and he never shops there. Also, I have been through his bank statements and I can't find any evidence for these new clothes that keep appearing. Secondly, when we have sex, he is doing stuff that he hasn't done for years. Thirdly, for the past ten days he has been in a filthy mood, and calling out someone else's name in his sleep. Fourthly, there is the question of the little visitors."

"Is that a reference to the seven dwarfs?" I ask, because at this stage of the evening it would not surprise me if Elvis Presley made an appearance.

"The nits," she says. "I checked with his secretary, and she was insulted that I thought she had given him head lice. So if she didn't give them to him, then who did?"

"I agree, that all sounds compelling," I say, because it seems ridiculous to disagree. "But it's not conclusive." I take a deep drag from her cigarette.

"Don't pretend to feel sorry for me. I'm not the kind of person that people pity. In fact, I'm the kind of person that people hope this will happen to," she says.

"So what are you going to do about these suspicions?" I ask, resisting the urge to scratch my head.

"I have a number of choices. I could do what my mother did and overlook his indiscretion, but the trouble is that Guy is the kind of man who could easily think he has fallen in love with someone else and decide to leave me. And I am not going to risk that happening. He's not practical, and if my life is going to fall apart, then I want to be the one in charge of its dissolution. I could do what his mother did to his father and divorce him with a hefty settlement tucked under my belt. And then I would never be invited to dinner anywhere else, because women would always worry that I might steal their husband. Or I can expose the situation and try and rebuild our marriage."

"Do you love him?" I ask her.

"I love what he used to be, but I don't love what he has become," she says thoughtfully. "And I think he would say the same about me. It's a strange thing, but money can make you less sure about things because it presents too much choice. I think we need radical solutions. Actually, I have already taken action."

"What kind of action?" I ask warily.

"I'm doing a course," she says.

"A horticultural one?" I say a little too eagerly, because that is the next logical step in her life trajectory.

"Don't be ridiculous, Lucy," she says. "It's a sleuthing course. Devised for people who want to spy on other people. But popular with women in my situation. Even if my instincts prove wrong, it's a good insurance policy for the next couple of decades, until his sex drive diminishes. He is someone who needs to be kept close. He is vain, and vain men are always vulnerable to flattery."

"I'm impressed," I say, holding several debates in my mind at once. I could warn Emma about this, insist that if she is going to end the relationship, it is imperative that she should do it now, thereby ensuring there is nothing to uncover. Yummy Mummy No. 1 can put the evidence to rest, burn the Paul Smith shirt, and enjoy the fruits of a more varied sex life. If it was me, would I want to know?

"By the way, what name has he been shouting out?" I ask with faux innocence.

She angrily stubs out the cigarette, a little too close to my bare left calf. There is a long silence, in which she nervously smooths the legs of her jeans. I am rapt with attention, because I know what she is going to say.

"Yours," she says finally. And then she looks at me intently. "He says the same thing over and over again. 'Lucy Sweeney, what have you done?' And now I'm wondering the same thing. So tell me, are you fucking my husband? Where did you meet him? Is all that flirting with Robert Bass just a cover? And before you humiliate me further by lying, I should tell you that I have discovered that Guy has two other mobile phones registered in his name and that the bills from one of those numbers have endless calls made to you. And it is no secret that it was your children who started that outbreak of nits last term."

I open and shut my mouth like a goldfish, but no sound comes out. She must be talking about Emma's phone.

"Can I get back to you on this?" I ask hopefully.

"No," she says sternly. We sit in silence for a moment.

"Have you considered that the phone bill you have might not be mine, but belong to someone else who knows me?" I say finally, carefully choosing my words.

"No," she says. "But actually that makes sense, because the second phone has lots of phone calls to the first phone, and when I dialed the first phone, it wasn't you, and when I dialed the second number it was

Guy at the other end. Tell me what you know. Please. If you can't do it for me, consider my children. If you put the children first, then everything else is logical." She is gripping my knee tightly. "You can't imagine what hell it is, Lucy, going through something like this. Everything you have taken for granted suddenly seems uncertain. There are no guarantees. I am suspicious about everyone and everything. Can you imagine the humiliation when I was waiting for him to turn up in that restaurant? I kept telling people that he would arrive at any moment and endlessly dialing his cell phone and he never appeared. People knew something strange was going on, because they avoided asking the most obvious questions about his whereabouts. That's the reason I need to resolve all this now, because otherwise I'll end up hating him."

"Perhaps you should confront Guy with this?" I say.

"I'm not giving anything away until I have all the evidence. We're studying surveillance techniques at the moment. Then, when the time is ripe, I will choose my moment and act," she says. "Which of your friends do you think might be having an affair with Guy? Think about it. There will be someone obvious, probably someone he has met through work. He's always overly impressed with those clever women in suits. That's how I met him."

"I'll give it some serious thought and get back to you," I say.

"Do you promise that you don't know?" she asks.

"I have a couple of ideas but nothing confirmed," I say, wondering if this constitutes a lie.

"Let me know if you turn anything up. Please."

We hear the bedroom door open and put our heads around the corner of the balcony to see Celebrity Dad and Alpha Mum come into the bedroom. They look around the room and then shut the door behind them. Celebrity Dad puts a chair under the handle. He busies himself with chopping further lines of cocaine, and Yummy Mummy No. 1 and I look on with wonder as Alpha Mum hungrily snorts a couple and the two of them leave.

"She's definitely done that before," whispers Yummy Mummy No. 1. "There's no doubt about it."

In the cab on our way home to the suburbs, I sit in silence, trying to make sense of everything that has happened this evening. It has always puzzled me how people have such different experiences of the same party.

"God, that was boring," says Tom. "Apart from the thing with Guy, but actually I think you were right not to tell me. His wife seems nice, though. Surprisingly so. I had a good chat with Celebrity Dad, too. He says you are the most authentic person that he has ever met and wants me to take him to an Arsenal match. And I made my peace with Deep Shallows. I think he has forgiven me. So all the loose ends are tied up. Where did you disappear to?"

I shut my eyes and pretend to be asleep. The coward's way out.

17

"Old sins cast long shadows."

Sometimes during my five-o'clock insomnia, I try to send myself back to sleep by counting how many decisions I have made in a day. When we were camping in Norfolk last summer, the point at which, I now realize, the insomnia became embedded, I once got as far as seventy-one. They roamed a pyramid-shaped range, starting at the bottom with the tiniest: whether to go for another day without having a shower in the cold, muddy communal washroom on the campsite or to give in to the children's pleas to eat breakfast inside the tent because of the cold, knowing that the Rice Krispies would inveigle their way into my sleeping bag, blend with the sand and dried mud to form an uneven sandpaper that made going to sleep even more difficult than it was already, within the confines of a small tent with three restless children.

"Think of it as a free exfoliation service," Tom said earlier in the week, when he was trying to play the role of fun dad, before his mood grew gloomy. In the greater scheme of things, the consequences of these decisions were immaterial.

They then tapered into medium-sized decisions: Should we abandon the campsite in favor of a small B and B somewhere along the coast? Should I tell Tom that the missing passport, the reason that we had to forsake the holiday in France for a rainy campsite in Norfolk, had been found in the glove compartment of the car? I decided against in both cases. Then there were the big ones. To laugh or to cry? To stay or to go? And that fateful one that caused the rot to set in. One of those rogue decisions that started at the bottom of the pyramid and then erupted out of the top, when I was least expecting it.

If marriage is like a landscape, then on the north Norfolk coast that summer, I think I reached my natural home. I looked behind me from the beach and could see the marshes stretching out, and behind them a line of arthritic-looking trees, their branches bent into unpredictable shapes by squalls of wind. Ahead was the sea, looking moody and treacherous. Depending on the tide, it could carry you either mile after mile along the coast to Cromer or far away toward Holland. I could see where I came from but not where I was going. I saw myself as a piece of luggage carried on one of the huge passenger ships that drifted by on the horizon, with "destination unknown" stamped on my side.

The insides of my ears ached so much from the cold that I could feel the pain in my throat, but it wasn't unpleasant. It was reassuring. I was diminished by the elements. They allowed me to escape from myself for a while. We stood there in a row, bent forward against the wind, heads down, huddled like soldiers in retreat, Fred holding hands between Tom and me, because we had discovered that a strong squall could knock him over and Joe was terrified that he would be taken into the sky, like Dorothy in the opening scene of *The Wizard of Oz.*

"It comes in straight from Russia," Tom shouted to the boys above the wind, and even Fred looked impressed. "That's why it is so bitter." I got out another sweater from my bag and put it on.

"It's not that cold," shouted Tom over the wind. "It's worse when you don't have any underpants, that's for sure. My bollocks are a shadow of their former self."

"You promised you wouldn't mention the underpants again," I said.

"It was a quid pro quo if you stopped complaining about the weather," he shouted back.

"You're the one saying it's cold. I didn't complain about the weather, I simply put on another sweater," I insisted.

"I'm being descriptive. Putting on a sweater is implicit criticism," he said. "Put your sweaters on in a less public way."

"Where do you suggest I go to put my sweater on?" I asked, waving an arm along the deserted beach. A black-and-white oystercatcher turned its head, which was tucked low into its body to conserve heat, and looked at me inquisitively as if to wonder why I was so emotional. Conserve your energy, it seemed to be saying.

"I just don't understand how you could forget to pack any underpants for me when you have put in ten pairs for Sam, six pairs of shorts for Joe, and three bobble hats for Fred. It's all so irrational, Lucy. Didn't you make a list before we went away?" yelled Tom. Even across the wind, his voice was unnecessarily loud.

"Why don't you consider all the things that I have remembered, rather than the things that I forgot? You could have packed your own clothes," I said.

"But you know how busy I was, trying to sort out that problem in Milan," he replied.

"Well, you could get some underpants in Holt," I retorted, determined to hold my ground.

"I'm not doing that on principle," he said, a sanctimonious tone entering his voice.

"And what principle would that be?" I asked, knowing instantly that this question was a strategic error.

"The principle that it is important to learn by your mistakes and that you will never again forget to pack my underpants if I have to endure a week without them," he said smugly.

"I won't, because I will never again pack for you. You are so ridiculous, Tom, I'm not going to even grace it with a response." And then we started laughing, because it was so absurd, and the children laughed, too, without knowing why, but it was all a little shrill.

We were a family marooned. Condemned to each other's company within the confines of a tent measuring around forty-three cubic feet.

This I knew, because Tom and Sam spent a rainy afternoon with a tape measure doing the exact calculation. Things were off-kilter from the moment we left home. The future of Tom's library in Milan, a project that had already absorbed the best part of two years, was in jeopardy. Our financial situation was bleak. Tom's company had already invested too much time and money in the library. As we stood on the pavement outside our home while he packed the car, I began to consider for the first time that we might have to sell the house.

I watched him lining up the luggage on the pavement, trying to find the most perfect packing solution. He might not be able to control the vagaries of the Milan planning department, but he could impose order on the trunk of the car.

"Surely, as long as it all goes in, it doesn't really matter how it is packed?" I pleaded in the face of impatient children strapped into the backseat.

"Systems, it's all about systems," Tom muttered. "I'm trying to assess what we will need first when we arrive and put that on the top. Do you know what you'll be cooking for lunch?"

Another decision. But one that could and must wait, because determining what we will be eating for lunch before nine o'clock in the morning is a step closer to derangement.

"We'll get something there," I said. "Or on the way."

"But if we stop on the way, then that requires a different system," he said, starting to prioritize small folding chairs over gas canisters. "And will we stop at a service station or have sandwiches on the side of the road?"

"You have to accept that we need a degree of flexibility, Tom," I said, trying to circumvent another argument. "Not knowing what is going to happen can be liberating. In fact, it is the endless repetition of routine that kills the human spirit." He looked at me as though I were a creature from another planet. I closed the passenger door and opened the glove compartment, and that was when I discovered the passport. Sam saw.

"Don't say a word," I told him. He understood. Some day, Sam will make a very good husband.

Then there were the underpants. Feeling guilty one afternoon after our argument on the beach, on the only day that the sun made a consistent appearance for more than a couple of hours, I volunteered to go back into Holt and find an underwear shop. It was the kind of gesture that marked a cease-fire between Tom and myself. A bilateral peace accord.

"Are you sure, Lucy?" he said gratefully. "That's so nice of you."

"We might be hard up, but new underpants won't tip the balance. However, it is generous of me," I concurred, because I wanted to accumulate enough points to see me through the three remaining days of the holiday. Of course, there is little self-sacrifice involved in spending an afternoon in your own company, browsing through shops in one of those north Norfolk towns that sells five different kinds of olive oil and has resisted the pressure to build an out-of-town shopping complex. I was happy to be on my own and leave him on the beach with the children for the afternoon.

In Holt I quickly found a shop that boasted an underwear department with big aspirations. The breadth and depth of its selection was disconcerting for a shop of its size and location. It ranged from raunchy little numbers in pastel shades to Jockey y-fronts in colors that I hadn't seen since I was a teenager, when Mark would insist on wearing only red pants to show his credentials as a "hot lover." Then there were lacy knickers and bras that made me want to weep because they were so white and delicate and would inevitably fray and turn gray within a week in my possession. They were also very expensive, and because Tom's library project was indefinitely on hold, and my credit-card debt was out of control, I resisted the temptation to buy but couldn't leave without trying them on.

I stood there in front of the mirror and found that somehow they reduced the rolls of fat around my tummy and made my breasts look pneumatic. So, having chosen Tom a pair of sensible boxer shorts in thick, white cotton that would protect his manhood from any sea squall, I decided that I would hold on to this bra and knickers to enjoy the moment for a little longer.

I was daydreaming under a large sign that read "lingerie for him and her" with a red heart drawn around "him and her" when I realized that I was no longer alone. A man was searching through the Calvin Klein section. I was contemplating whether the male ego was affected by buying a pair of underpants in a small size, and whether I should exchange the medium-size underpants that I had chosen for Tom for the extra-large, thus currying even greater favor, when this man turned round to face me and I realized immediately that I recognized him.

Ten years on, he was a little heavier. His cheeks were rosy and full, and I could see more clearly what he might have looked like as a chubby toddler, because the extra weight meant fewer wrinkles. It added flesh to the bone. It was the look of a man who eats and drinks well. His hair was thinner, which meant his face looked disproportionably large, and underneath the first chin, I could see the hint of a second. The broad brushstrokes were the same. We ruthlessly assessed each other for a couple of seconds, and I concluded that, on balance, time had been marginally kinder to me, mainly because it was easier to hide my flaws.

"Lucy," he said in surprise. "What are you doing here? Did you follow me in?" I bristled. It was typical he should assume, even after all this time, that he was being pursued by me. The foundations of our relationship lay in mutual flirtation, leaning over a desk to look at something in the newspaper for a little too long with our shoulders touching, making each other laugh too much without letting other people enter the fray, and always ensuring that we sat next to each other at office parties. It was a pursuit of equals. But underneath his studied nonchalance, he was a vain man. In the same way that first impressions often give clarity of judgment, I was pleased to find that an unscheduled meeting after almost a decade provided similar insight. Distance doesn't necessarily lend enchantment to the view, which is just as well during the Middle Ages, when nostalgia for the past and fear for the future can prove an explosive partnership for the present.

"Actually, I was here before you, and we're both after the same thing, I think," I said, holding up my underwear display.

"I can't decide whether I am a medium or a large," he said.

"Medium, from what I remember," I said. He laughed. Sometimes when you meet a former lover, there is an ease of communication that cuts through the years. There can be a corresponding sense of loss because that same degree of intimacy can never be replicated. I was relieved to feel only the former.

"I fell into that one," he said warmly. "Do you fancy a coffee?"

I think that inviting a woman out for coffee is the twenty-first-century equivalent of a Victorian man asking a woman to come and view his etchings. It is a seemingly innocuous invitation, propelled by apparently innocent intentions, yet the underlying issue is about being alone together. So we both put down our underwear haul a little too quickly and headed off to a small café where tea was served in proper china cups on white tablecloths. Over the next hour he told me the following. That he was on holiday in Norfolk with his wife and their two children. They had rented a converted barn somewhere outside of Holt along the coast at considerable expense. He was directing an independent film set in Bradford about a love affair between an Asian girl and a white boy. He was on the board of the British Film Institute. He spent a lot of time traveling. His wife was fine. Being apart so much made it even more difficult being together, because they lived separate lives. He had never told her about us, and nothing similar had ever happened again. I wasn't sure that I believed him, but it said something about how he wanted to view himself. Typically, because I had forgotten how self-obsessed he was, he asked nothing about me until the tea in the pot was cold and it had started raining again outside.

"So what are you up to, Lucy?" he asked finally.

"Married, three children. I'm a stay-at-home mum," I said. "There's a job title that ends a conversation in its tracks. I gave up *Newsnight* a couple of years after you left. I worked for a while after our first son was born."

"Why did you do that? You loved that job," he said. "You had so many plans, so many ideas. I thought you were destined for greatness. I'd give you a job any day."

"Work-life balance proved too elusive. So I thought I'd take a year out, then I got pregnant again and then again, and suddenly eight years rolled by," I explained.

I wanted to ask him whether he could remember any of my great ideas, because I certainly couldn't, and they might come in useful now. Like all the excess sleep that I took for granted before I had children. I wished I had banked all that for future reference.

"So does it suit you being a full-time mother?" he asked.

"Giving up work is a bit like moving from the city to the countryside," I said. "Once you've done it, it's difficult to go back. I was sucked into the parenting vortex. The pace of life changes, it's wild and unruly terrain, contemporary culture passes you by, and you go to bed earlier and earlier because it's so exhausting, but you learn to live by the seasons again. And I think my children like having me around, and I like being there for them. Now I'm obviously utterly unemployable and have less status than a lap dancer."

He laughed. And we smiled at the irony of our shared aspirations and their wildly different outcomes, because feminism might have come a long way, but women are still the ones who make the difficult decisions.

"Lap dancers are powerful people," he said. Then he paused. "And how is married life?" The question hung in the air, because this was dangerous territory. I stared into my cold cup of tea.

"Fine, bumpy at times, tragicomic at others, I suppose," I said with the kind of honesty that is permissible when you are with someone you know you won't see again, the kind of honesty that traveling in foreign lands allows. "Having children pushes you to extremes, and relationships can get lost in the domestic quagmire."

"Tell me about it. I sometimes think it is easier to be in love with people before you really get to know them and they topple off their pedestal," he said. "When I moved in with my wife and saw her cutting her toes and then eating the nails, a little bit of me died. That's why those old relationships that never evolved beyond the lustful stage have such a hold on memory."

"Very true," I said blankly.

"That's what my next film is about. It's more commercial, based on this man and woman who meet each other again on Friends Reunited and end up trying to rekindle an old affair," he said. "It's got American backers, so it has to have a Hollywood ending."

"So does she stay with her husband or go off with the old boyfriend?" I asked.

"She leaves her husband," he said.

"But how is that a happy ending?" I asked.

"I didn't say it was a happy ending, I said it was a Hollywood ending," he said.

"But surely it would be more romantic if she stayed with her husband?" I persisted.

"Lucy, it would be a bit of a slow boiler if she did that," he argued.

"So what happens to her husband?"

"He ends up with someone else," he said a little impatiently.

"And what about the wife of the old boyfriend?"

"She's dead," he said, yawning. "It's more convenient that way. Old relationships don't make good films; it's the early stage, the sexual tension and the excitement that people want to see."

"I think long-term love is more about an attitude than a state of mind. It's about how much you can give each rather than what you get from each other. Actually, in some ways it is more interesting than an immature relationship," I said. "At least that's what I'm hoping."

"A slow, steady return on your investment over the years?" he asked.

"Something like that," I said.

"Well, mine is doomed then, because I am a selfish bastard," he said. "What about your husband?"

"He's very detail-oriented, which can be maddening, but actually he isn't structurally selfish," I said, "not in the way you are. But perhaps that's why you are so successful."

"The trouble with success is that you are always meeting people who are even more successful than you are. When I made my first film, I thought that would be enough. Now I realize that unless I can produce a consistently successful body of work, I will feel as though I have underachieved. There are moments of euphoria, but I rarely feel content. Contentment has eluded me."

I know that I missed obvious clues, but this man was no longer attractive to me. My curiosity was that of someone who had been there at the beginning of a story. I wanted to know what happened in the middle to work out whether there would be a happy ending.

As I glanced at my watch, I realized with horror that I had been sitting in this café for almost two hours. The shop was now shut, and I had forgotten to buy the underpants. To return to the campsite without the underwear was inconceivable. I rummaged in my bag in search of my purse. It was then that I discovered that I had accidentally pilfered the bra and knickers I had tried on in the shop. This was the first time in my life that I had ever stolen anything. I decided immediately that I would keep them. I didn't feel any remorse because the theft was not premeditated. It was permissible to engage in rash acts of dubious morality as long as they were unconscious.

"Do you know that you have always been at the back of my thoughts, Lucy? I always wondered how it might have been, if we had evolved together," he said suddenly. "Whether you might have been the answer." His teacup looked tiny gripped between his hands.

"Did you?" I said in astonishment. I noticed one of his hands moving toward my own and abruptly got up from my chair. It tipped backward until it rested precariously against a radiator. I left it there.

"I wouldn't have been. It's always a mistake to expect other people to make you happy. It helps, but it's not a panacea," I said. "I think I'd better leave now." I left a five-pound note on the table, knowing that he wouldn't have any cash because he never did. "It was really nice to see you again." He got up awkwardly and told me to get in touch, but I knew that he didn't really mean it. We had covered too much ground, and it would be difficult to see each other again.

In a sense it was a fortuitous meeting, because for me it closed a chapter. But the repercussions of forgetting Tom's underpants and stealing underwear for myself endured. When I got back to the campsite he was furious, even before I told him that it was a fruitless endeavor.

"What have you been doing all afternoon?" he demanded. "Fred fell into the mud and cried for about an hour. Joe thought he was shriveling up because the saltwater made his skin go wrinkly. And I found that passport in the car, so Sam cried because he was worried that you would think he had told me."

I looked at Fred. His hair was caked with bits of seaweed, hard dried pieces of mud, and the odd small feather. On his cheeks there were a few clear gulleys amidst the mud where I imagined pools of tears had fallen down his face.

"Why didn't you wash him?" I asked, holding his little face in my hand.

"I thought you would be home to help," Tom said disapprovingly. I looked at him, then said to Sam, "We're just going to have a small argument. Keep an eye on Fred and Joe, please."

So I told Tom that I had bumped into an old colleague. He remembered him with unusual clarity and asked whether I had ever slept with him, because he had always suspected that there was something between us. I made a bad decision. I failed to see the situation from Tom's point of view and assumed because it was unimportant to me that it would hold similar currency for him. So I told him the truth about the first encounter, because I thought that it had happened so long ago that it didn't matter and I was pleased to discover this man meant so little to me. But of course it mattered. So I didn't mention the second. And then I told Tom that he was being a hypocrite, because he was the one who had slept with Joanna Saunders and that he had done it much more and for longer than me. His account was in arrears. And all those raw wounds were reopened. Forgetting is sometimes easier than forgiving.

18

"If you can't ride two horses at once, you shouldn't be in the circus."

When I get a text message from Robert Bass a month after the party saying **"We need to talk. Can you meet me for a coffee? Have finished book,"** I recognize that whatever my reply, it constitutes a big top-of-the-pyramid-type decision. After what had transpired at the party, contact between us had become loaded with specific undertones. There was nothing impressionistic about the encounter in the coat cupboard. The attraction was explicit, which now means that I have to assume greater responsibility for my actions. It is the difference between consciously and unconsciously stealing underwear from the shop in Holt. This is what happens when fantasy spills over into reality.

I force myself to wait at least half an hour before replying, and then I write: **"Congratulations, but not a good idea, I think."** By tacitly acknowledging what occurred, I am not only curtailing the chances of anything happening again but also derailing the possibility of even a little harmless flirtation. I try to feel self-congratulatory about having made what I know rationally is the right decision. If there had been no forbidden fruit in the Garden of Eden, then Eve would never have had to decide whether to eat it, I tell myself. There is little doubt in the tone of my message to Robert Bass, but it is not written with utter conviction. Being rational is one of those long-term investments with few immediate dividends.

Although I have felt guilty, it isn't the kind of acute guilt that is alleviated by dramatic confession. It is more the chronic variety that I think might fade in time. I console myself with the fact that nothing really happened. A tangle, not even a knot, which means there is nothing to unravel and still less to confess. So no one, apart from Celebrity Dad, is aware that we were even alone together. I ignore the obvious fact that secrets give oxygen to fantasies.

A few weeks after sending this text message, the Easter holidays now a distant memory, I wander into the local café after dropping the oldest boys at school and Fred at nursery, for a meeting convened by Alpha Mum to discuss the forthcoming school fete. It is the first time since the party that I will be in such close proximity with Robert Bass, because I have, so far, successfully managed to avoid all but the most superficial contact with him.

Yummy Mummy No. 1 waves at me as I stroll through the door. She proprietorially pats a space beside her and I walk over to sit down, relieved to find that I am early and Robert Bass has not yet arrived. I am grateful and anxious in equal measure. On the one hand I fade into the scenery beside her brightly colored fifties-style tea dress and massive sunglasses, on the other, she will inevitably want to talk about Guy.

"Hello, Isobel," I say.

"That's the first time I've heard you use my name," she says, looking pleased.

I look back nostalgically, to a period not so long ago when I was lucky if Isobel threw me a few crumbs of attention, and even those were drained of any emotional content. Now my feelings toward her are composed of an uncomfortable blend of incompatible flavors, like a culinary experiment where an amateur cook throws improbable ingredients together in a hopeless attempt to produce a memorable new dish. Curry powder, sugar, and salt. Admiration, sympathy, and guilt.

Admiration for the way in which she has elected to deal with the situation, because she has carried the emotional burden alone, without infecting her children with her anxiety, and has faced the world with the same blend of humor, detachment, and impeccable dress sense. And these characteristics enhance my sympathy.

Guilt is, however, the predominant emotion. My loyalties are deeply divided. From the outset, I felt it would be wrong to betray Emma. The breadth and depth of my relationship with her are incomparable to my burgeoning friendship with Isobel. But now I feel guiltier about deceiving Isobel than I do about my own brush with Robert Bass. If I remain resolute, there will be no repercussions for me, just a return to the status quo. Her situation is much less predictable and inevitably involves a good slice of pain.

The first few weeks after the party I had several awkward phone conversations with Isobel, about the possible identity of her husband's lover and new facts that she had uncovered about the scale of Guy's deception. The fact that these calls have diminished can only mean she is closer to discovering Emma's identity under her own steam or that she feels I am part of the conspiracy, which I am.

Also, I am increasingly frustrated with Emma. I have tried to explain to her that the longer the relationship between Guy and her endures, the more entrenched the pain and anger become for Isobel and the more difficult it will be to repair their marriage. Each time I speak to her, she promises that she is close to ending the affair. She is using a method she describes as "slow withdrawal," which I have said sounds like a tantric sex technique but she maintains is part of her campaign to leave the situation in a position of strength.

It is tempting to unmask Emma, but at this juncture it is hardly likely to help the situation. Isobel's dignity has been maintained in part by her detective work, which gives focus to her anger and allows time to work out an appropriate response.

So my reserves of anger are directed toward Guy. Most surprising, I have had several phone calls from him, wanting reassurance that I won't tell his wife what is going on or persuade Emma to leave him. I wonder whether Isobel is still monitoring his calls and what she will conclude from this new clue on the phone bill.

I look at her. Worry suits her, I decide. She is glowing.

"You look like Jackie Kennedy, when she was on her honeymoon in Acapulco," I tell her.

"That is an unfortunate analogy from a number of angles," she says, peering over the top of her glasses, "although at this stage, shooting Guy is one of many options that I am considering. Particularly since I have discovered that the night of that dinner in the restaurant he wasn't in France at all."

"I was referring to your look. Anyway, JFK probably wasn't having affairs at that stage," I say, trying to be at once reassuring and direct her away from talk about her husband.

"I wasn't thinking about his affairs," she whispers tersely. "The reason I'm wearing these glasses is because I have a sports injury."

"I didn't realize that you could tone facial muscles," I say in genuine amazement. "Wouldn't that cause wrinkles?"

"Are you being deliberately contrary, Lucy?" she asks, but I know she finds this kind of conversation pleasantly distracting.

I would like to tell her that I am deeply uncomfortable with the enforced intimacy of our relationship and want to get back on to the kind of ground that we used to cover, but it is too late. We are bound together by circumstance.

She lifts the sunglasses to reveal a massive black eye extending from her left eyebrow down toward her cheekbone.

"I accidentally punched myself in the face during my kickboxing class," she says. "It's because I'm so preoccupied."

"Having such a fine arse must entail some element of suffering," I say.

"Lucy, you have two choices in life," she says, sighing. "You decide to save either your face or your bum, and I have chosen the latter."

I must look puzzled, because she continues: "If you exercise a lot, you get wrinkles; if you are overweight, your face looks younger."

"But surely your husband sees more of you from the front than from behind?" I ask. "Wouldn't it make more sense to invest in that?"

"Actually, since you ask, he doesn't see much of either at the moment. I have withdrawn all services. Besides, my personal trainer says I should focus on my unique selling point," she says. "It's an investment for the future, in case things don't work out." Her voice is a little shaky, and a small tear escapes from the bottom left-hand corner of the sunglasses.

She wipes it away, sniffing delicately.

I reach out to hold her arm. I wish that Emma could see this side of the story.

"Don't be kind to me, I can't bear people feeling sorry for me," she says. "Say something nasty so that I don't cry."

"Your dress is as blousy as a bed of chrysanthemums. Judges don't look favorably on personal trainers in divorce settlements. Your next car will be a G-wizz," I say. She smiles weakly.

Robert Bass comes over to join the group and I try to concentrate on my orange juice, sipping loudly through a straw, resisting the temptation to look up. I allow myself to examine his legs from the thigh down and note that he is wearing cutoff shorts that stop unevenly somewhere just above the knee. A hot summer is not the best time of year to banish lustful thoughts. I watch his legs walk toward a chair next to Alpha Mum. I try to find the comedy in his knees, to look for hairs on his toes, calluses on his heels, anything that might prick the bubble of desire.

To say that I haven't thought about him at least once a day would be a lie, although every time he poaches headspace I make myself think of something different, a serious subject that will underline the frivolity of my obsession. For example, I make mental lists of countries that have borne the brunt of U.S. foreign policy blunders, and then, if this isn't sufficiently distracting, I try and put them in some kind of order. Is Iraq a worse mess than Vietnam? Should one judge the situation by the number of civilian casualties or the decades that will be lost simply to get back to the point of no return? In which case was Nicaragua a bigger mess than Somalia? Sometimes my mind wanders. Would a brush with infidelity radically alter the landscape of marriage? How long would it take to return to the status quo? How many casualties would there be?

If my resolve needed bolstering, I would stop and stare at my children and feel sure that I had the willpower to resist any overtures from Robert Bass. But what I had failed to understand was that while I was trying to retreat, he was still in pursuit. My weakness for seeing situations from everyone's point of view failed me at the precise moment when it would have been useful.

Yet despite all this, I regard myself as lucky, because whenever the memory of the coat cupboard threatens to dominate my thoughts, I can simply switch attention to the other dilemmas thrown up by that portentous evening. Displacement anxiety, Mark would call these overlapping loops of worry, because he has to attach a label to everything.

Alpha Mum claps officiously to indicate that the meeting has begun and hands me a pen and paper to take notes. We all sit up in our seats, and still I resist the urge to look at Robert Bass. Celebrity Dad slouches into the café. He is wearing flip-flops, tight-fitting Superfine jeans that must belong to his wife, and a hat pulled over his head so that only the bottom of his face is visible. He asks Isobel and me to move up so that he can sit next to me. I am now squashed between the two of them. He smells of sweat and alcohol. He sits down beside me and his arm sticks to my own. When he moves it to lift a cup of black coffee to his mouth, I surreptitiously lick my wrist and conclude that it tastes of alcohol. He is sweating neat whiskey.

"What's going on, Sweeney?" he whispers throatily. I wish he would stop calling me by my surname.

"She is proposing that the fete should have a Roman theme and that we should all come in costume and speak in Latin," I tell him.

"Is this one of those weird English customs?" he asks, taking off his sunglasses.

"No, just one of those weird north London ones," I say. He looks awful, as though this is the end of a long night rather than the beginning of a new day. His eyes are so bloodshot that my own start to water. "I think you should keep the sunglasses on," I say, pointing to Isobel. "You're in good company."

"I am imploding, Sweeney," he says. He makes a sound like a bomb exploding.

Alpha Mum looks over disapprovingly.

"My wife has gone," he says. "She's taken the children with her back to the States. My youngest one asked if I was in a stable."

"What did she mean?" I ask.

"Unstable," he says. "But I'm not. I go through periods of self-destruction, and then I come back out again. It's my way of dealing with life."

"So what are you doing here, then, if you're no longer a parent?" I ask.

"I start filming in Prague in four weeks' time. I haven't got anything better to do," he says. "It's more entertaining than watching TV, and I need to keep an eye on you."

൭൦

When I have counted to two hundred and fifty in my head, I allow myself to look up and steal my first glance at Robert Bass. I notice that the sleeves of his white T-shirt are carelessly rolled up to reveal his upper arm and the first hint of his shoulder bone. His skin is tanned. He sits back in his chair, his legs stretched out in front of him. He is using the index finger of his left hand, the finger that touched me, to draw tiny circles on the dusty table. He intermittently runs his other hand through his hair until it starts to stand on end.

I recall the constellation of awkward situations that hung over the party that night, like a scientist putting together the empirical evidence to calculate the possibility of a natural disaster. I think of people in offices in Colorado, monitoring tiny movements in the Earth's tectonic plates each day, trying to predict the likelihood of an earthquake. If they applied the same science to my life, they would undoubtedly conclude that a serious incident was still inevitable. I decide I have turned into the San Andreas Fault.

I shut my eyes and breathe in, trying to stop myself from sighing. I can recall the smell of Isobel's sheepskin coat, the dripping of the tap, the way his hand felt so hot on my body that afterward I looked to see whether it had left an imprint. I consider how the material of my wrap dress stretched with the force he used to pull it down from my shoulder. It will probably never regain shape. I start to wonder exactly what he would have done next, had Celebrity Dad not interrupted us. I imagine the hand that is tracing the circle on the table inside the shoulder of my dress, moving down my body. And then I sigh loudly. Celebrity Dad nudges me.

When I open my eyes, Robert Bass is looking at me. I wonder how long he has been staring. He takes his finger from the table and uses it to stroke his lower lip thoughtfully. Then he smiles at me, a sort of half-smile, hidden in part by the finger. I'm sure that he knows what I am thinking.

"Get a grip, Sweeney," whispers Celebrity Dad in my ear. "Unless you want the whole class to intercept those hungry looks." I sit up straight in my seat, worrying that I am so transparent.

"Think dormice and denarii. Think gods and gladiators," I hear Alpha Mum say excitedly.

"Any minute now she will introduce a competitive element to the proceedings," I whisper to Celebrity Dad.

"And a prize for the parent who comes in the best costume," says Alpha Mum triumphantly.

"I love the way the English are always looking for excuses to dress up," says Celebrity Dad, "especially if there is potential for cross-dressing."

"I think it's only fair if we take a vote on something like this," says Robert Bass moodily, leaning forward. The right sleeve of his T-shirt creeps down to cover the top of his arm.

"*In vita priore ego imperator romanus fui,*" says Alpha Mum. "Besides, there was no democracy in ancient Rome. We agreed last term that all school events should have an educational component."

"But we're not in ancient Rome, we're in north London," insists Robert Bass. "Not all of us are studying GCSE Latin to help with our children's homework."

He looks even more attractive when he is angry, I think, gazing at him dreamily. It certainly beats his monologues on the importance of composting and directing children's play.

"Perhaps I can use the costume that I wore in Troy," suggests Celebrity Dad, trying to repair the frayed edges of the discussion. Robert Bass glares at him.

"Wrong era, but what a marvelous idea," says Alpha Mum, clapping her hands excitedly and opening up her laptop.

"I hope you've brought those ladies with you again," says Celebrity Dad, leaning forward toward her. Alpha Mum squirms in her seat, crossing and uncrossing her legs. Her smile is taut. But she is clearly enjoying the attention.

"Your costume, does it involve lorica and greaves?" she asks demurely.

"The whole shebang, including an Aquincum helmet with a red crest," says Celebrity Dad.

"Are you proposing that we all make our own costumes?" I ask.

"You can just run something up on your sewing machine, can't you?" says Alpha Mum impatiently.

"I don't have a sewing machine, and it took me a week to make the Barney Bear costume for the school play," I plead.

"And what are the men meant to wear?" asks Robert Bass. "Not all of us have costumes from Hollywood films."

"Something short, pleated, with strappy sandals," fires back Alpha Mum, knowing that she is in the driving seat. "I'm sure Lucy will help you. I am proposing that you run the Roman cake stall together."

"I'm not sure that is such a good idea," I say. Everyone stares at me. "Can't I do pin the tail on the Trojan horse instead?"

"Wrong era," says Alpha Mum dismissively. "Why don't you want to do the cake stall with Robert?" She looks at me and then at Robert Bass, who shrugs his shoulders dismissively.

"Are you worried about his levels of enthusiasm?" she asks. I splutter on my orange juice.

"I'll help you as well, Lucy," says Celebrity Dad. "I am Spartacus." He is doing his best Kirk Douglas impression.

"No, I am Spartacus," replies Robert Bass.

Then Isobel joins in. "No, I am Spartacus," she says. We all start laughing.

Then suddenly Isobel stands up beside me, her arm outstretched and her hand pointing in the air. We all look at her in awed silence.

"I've got it," she says. "Think Pleats Please, think gorgeous Miu Miu gladiator sandals with turquoise stones, think vestal virgin."

"We're meant to raise money, not spend it," says Robert Bass sternly.

"I'm glad that some of you can muster a little enthusiasm," says Alpha Mum. "We'll meet in the playground early Saturday morning with our contributions, all themed, of course, and in full costume." We all nod meekly.

෧෨

"Why have you made so many cakes?" asks Tom late Friday night. "Is it one for every glass of wine you have drunk this evening?"

"I just need one to be perfect," I say, slumping in the chair and wrapping Tom's dressing gown around me. "My entire status as a mother depends on producing a perfect cake."

"Don't be ridiculous, Lucy," says Tom. "How can baking have any bearing on your parenting skills? It's completely illogical. You're behaving like your mother at Christmas."

"It's a genetic condition, the inability to bake a cake," I say.

"Couldn't you have gotten Deep Shallows to do them instead?" he asks. "You are sharing the cake stall, after all."

"You must stop calling him that," I say.

"Well, I can hardly call him Sexy Domesticated Dad, can I?" he says teasingly. "Isobel told me that is how the mums refer to him. I thought baking was his specialty?"

"It is, that is the point," I say, getting flustered.

"Why are they so flat?" he says, pressing one, which immediately deflates further.

"They look like Frisbees." Then he pauses. "Why don't you pretend they are Roman discuses?"

I look at him in awe. "What a brilliant idea." I say, almost weeping with relief. I go over to hug him.

"That dressing gown is revolting," he says, putting his arms around me. We lean against each other in silence.

"Are you all right?" asks Tom. "You seem very distracted of late, even by your standards. Are you worrying about Emma? Or Cathy? Or Isobel?"

"I'm fine. I'm looking forward to the summer and going to Italy," I say.

"The library will be well under way by then, and I'll take a proper break," he says. "We can find each other again, we just need to get through the next month. I'm going to bed. Did I tell you I have to spend next week in Milan again?"

He hadn't, but to be honest, I was getting used to Tom being away. The problem is not being apart but learning to be together again. The drift set in months ago, and now it is actually easier to be on my own. I just need to get to the end of the school year. The summer holidays loom on the horizon like dry land after a rocky spell at sea. If I can get through the school fete, then I am safe. The holidays will put a proper distance between Robert Bass and myself, and, besides, after that he will be away promoting his book.

At five o'clock in the morning, I stumble down into the kitchen ready to renew hostilities. Even before I reach the basement, the acrid smell of burned cake fills my nose. By the end of the previous evening, a combination of sleep deprivation and too much wine meant I had fallen asleep on the job, condemning my last experiment, a Victoria sponge, to an uncertain future that didn't involve the Roman Empire.

I sip from a glass of wine left over from the night before to soothe my nerves, hoping that I won't get Breathalyzed on my way to school. An overwhelming sight awaits me, more battleground than domestic idyll. Every bowl commandeered into action during this late-night exercise is filled with cake mix now set unforgivingly hard. On the sideboard there is a no-man's-land of unidentifiable gunk and a couple of empty wine bottles. Dirty saucepans are stranded in pools of icing. The Magimix is partially encased in chocolate. I assess the situation with admirable sangfroid and decide dispassionately that the carefully sculpted chocolate dormice complete with string tails can be salvaged, along with one slightly overcooked chocolate sponge and three discuses.

Then I put on the radio and listen to a program aimed at people who get up early to milk cows and those caught in cake peonage. More swallows are returning to Britain after years in decline; there is a shortage of shepherds and rural vicars. This pastoral image has soothing qualities, and I start another cake with renewed vigor. As I crack eggs into a bowl, I look out of the window into the garden and see a sheet flapping gently on the washing line. Then I realize that, in my compulsion to bake cakes, I have forgotten the most crucial ingredient of the day, the handmade Roman costume. I stride decisively into the garden, buoyed by the early-morning glass of wine, and snatch the sheet from the washing line. A wood pigeon eyes the Victoria sponge that I leave on the lawn and warbles appreciatively from the end of the garden.

Nil desperandum, to every problem there is a solution, and mine is staring me in the face. A beautifully clean, if unironed, fitted single sheet waiting for its moment of glory. Using the kitchen scissors, I cut a rough circle where the head should be. Beside the shorts that Joe manufactured, it looks like the work of an amateur, but with a rope round my middle, I will pass for a slave girl or some other ancient minion. Our neighbors' curtains are firmly shut. I take off the dressing gown and shake the sheet.

I hear a noise at the window and look up to see Tom peering out of our bedroom window, looking confused. He opens the window and sleepily leans out.

"Why are you standing naked in the garden at five o'clock in the morning?" he asks wearily, as though fearing the answer. He spots the cake in the middle of the lawn. "Don't tell me you're practicing for the chocolate discus competition. I'm beginning to wonder about the sanity of parents at this school, particularly your own."

"Sshh, you'll wake everyone up," I say, cutting a slightly larger hole round the neck.

"Why have you ruined that sheet?" he asks.

"There, isn't it obvious now?" I ask.

"Not to the idle bystander," he says.

"It's my Roman costume," I tell him.

"Funny that, because it looks as though you are wearing a sheet with a hole cut in the middle," he says, slamming the window shut and muttering under his breath.

A few minutes later he rumbles into the kitchen. Glancing up at the spots of chocolate on the ceiling, he says, with a hint of desperation, "God, Lucy, just tell me again how you make so much mess? Why don't you tidy up as you go along? It's a system tried and tested over the centuries. Even during Roman times. Look at the picture of my mother, it looks as though she has a dermatological condition." He uses his finger to wipe the spots from Petra's portrait and carefully licks them clean.

I explain that at a key moment in the cake-making process, I was unable to find the lid of the blender and so, with Heath Robinson–like ingenuity, I improvised by using a piece of cardboard with a hole cut in the middle for the handheld electric whisk.

"Is that something you saw on Blue Peter?" he asks. "You realize that you could have just put it all in a smaller bowl."

I remove my final effort from the oven and tip it from the cake tin. It has conspired to be at once overcooked on the outside and undercooked in the middle.

"How can that be?" I ask him despairingly. "It's like being fat and thin at the same time." He goes to the toolbox and brings out a hacksaw.

"That worked for Joe's birthday cake last year," he says reassuringly. "Then you can cut a hole in the middle and fill it with chocolate eggs."

"But chocolate eggs aren't authentically Roman," I tell him.

"Nor is a cake stall. I don't understand why you volunteer to do something that will inevitably end in disaster. It's so masochistic." Then he stops. "It's difficult to have a serious conversation with an adult dressed in a sheet."

He goes upstairs and brings down his old tweed coat.

"I know it's hot, but you cannot walk to school wearing that. You look absurd. I'm going back to bed. I'll get the boys up and bring them along later."

In a rebellious mood, I leave the house a couple of hours later, carrying my sponge discuses and chocolate dormice in a basket. I walk toward school feeling hot and itchy in Tom's coat. Just outside the school gate, I spot Robert Bass locking up his bicycle, with a Cath Kidston cake tin under his arm. It is too late to avoid him.

"Carrot cake. All organic." He smiles nonchalantly. "My specialty."

I resolve to recall this sentence every time I think of him, because if ever there were six words designed to suppress desire, then these are them.

He is also wearing a long overcoat. I stare at his calves and notice that they are entwined in leather, in the manner of an ancient Roman.

"What have you got on under there?" I ask.

"As instructed, I am wearing a short, off-the-shoulder toga and leather belt." He smiles, gritting his teeth.

"How short?" I ask.

"Well, put it this way, we could only find a child-sized sheet," he says, opening up the coat to show me the full, glorious effect. Robert Bass is wearing a miniskirt to the school fete. I indulgently gaze at his legs, a little too hairy for my taste but finely honed. In the spirit of shared humiliation, I show him my own fitted sheet with the hastily hacked hole in the middle. He visibly blanches.

"It's Casper the Ghost," he says, retreating toward the hedge to get a better view. I am saved from further excoriation by the arrival of Isobel. She draws up beside us and her electric window winds down.

"Comparing notes?" she asks rhetorically. She disembarks, wearing a full-length cream number with perfectly ironed pleats and little spaghetti straps.

"How on earth did you manage that?" I say, genuinely impressed.

"Issey Miyake," she replies.

"I didn't know you had a Japanese cleaner," says Robert Bass.

"I got it especially," she informs me. It is then I realize that my priorities are wrong. Chocolate cakes are anonymous, but the dress code is highly visible.

Robert Bass and I walk in silence toward our cake stall.

"About the party, Lucy," he says. "We need to talk."

"There's nothing to say," I say, looking around in case someone is listening.

"You can't avoid me forever," he says, standing behind the trestle table with his arms folded.

It is difficult to imagine a circumstance that could be more engaging than the conversation that Robert Bass is trying to engineer. But the playground falls silent as a very authentic-looking centurion guard, wearing a short, white skirt, full body armor, and helmet complete with visor and crest, walks toward us.

"Hail Caesar," he shouts to us, waving his sword in the air. Celebrity Dad has arrived.

"I'm here to defend your honor, Lucy," he whispers, as Robert Bass walks to the front of the stall and starts unpacking cakes. "Unless I pass out first. It's all a bit tight. I think I have gained a little weight since I made that film. It must be the beer."

"Not the whiskey?" I ask.

"Well, that too," he says.

"Can everyone assume their positions?" shouts Alpha Mum, clapping her hands. As we stand behind the cake stall, the clouds break open and Robert Bass and I discover that, with the sun upon our backs, our sheets are rendered completely transparent.

"Those don't leave a lot to the imagination," says Celebrity Dad, looking us up and down from under his visor, his layers of skirt bobbing up and down pleasingly.

"At least you're wearing big underpants," he says to Robert Bass, putting his arm around him and poking him in the stomach with his sword.

"As long as we remain behind our stall, our dignity will be protected by the cakes. We'll have to try and hang on to them as long as possible," says Robert Bass.

"What are you all chatting about? There's plenty to do," says Alpha Mum. She theatrically unfolds a tablecloth that she has personally embroidered with Roman numerals to match perfectly formed cupcakes iced with Latin inscriptions. My carefully crafted dormice suddenly look very agricultural.

"Where are your Roman sandals, Lucy?" she asks, staring at my wedges and handing me a plate of Roman coins. "Here's the denarii. Remember, we want to make this as authentic as possible for the children."

"Well, I should have spent the night plucking songbirds and roasting dormice then," I say, pushing my chocolate cake to the forefront of the cake stall. She picks it up, staggers exaggeratedly, and maneuvers her cupcakes into the front line, tipping the front row over the edge of the table and onto the ground.

"I think that's an authentic Pyrrhic victory," says Robert Bass, lifting my cake from danger and helping Alpha Mum rescue her battered cupcakes.

"Lucy, what have you got in here?" he mutters. "It weighs more than me."

Before I can reply, Alpha Mum announces that she has a great idea and has decided to use my cake for a "guess the weight of the chocolate discus" competition.

"But they didn't do that in Roman times," I protest weakly, inwardly cursing Robert Bass.

"Nor did they have tombolas or bash the dormice, but we have to make money somehow," she says tersely.

Robert Bass looks at me apologetically and shrugs. "Sorry, she's a woman on a mission, Lucy."

"Perhaps Robert could run that competition instead?" I suggest a little too eagerly.

Isobel glides across the playground, her pleats undulating gently behind her. She is carrying a spear.

"Think vestal virgin," she says, looking Celebrity Dad straight in the eye.

"But you've got four children," I say.

"I think more Minerva," says Robert Bass. "Perhaps I can be your slave."

"Or me," says Celebrity Dad.

"You need to get into the spirit of all this, Lucy," says Isobel forgivingly to me.

"She has," says Robert Bass, pointing at my costume. "She's dressed as Casper the Ghost." They all snort with laughter, and even I smile reluctantly. Robert Bass moves away to set up his competition and I feel calm again.

The sun comes out from behind a small cloud, and I am again revealed in my full glory. Isobel stares at my groin and groans. "If you had used one hundred percent Egyptian cotton sheets with a high thread count, you could have avoided all this." She waves her finger at me.

"But it takes so much time to iron," I plead.

"I wouldn't know; not my department," she counters. "And, Lucy, polyester was inevitably going to make it clingy. Next time I would certainly wear a cotton sheet and possibly consider a Brazilian."

As other parents arrive and the playground fills up, word spreads about the intimate nature of the experience on offer at the Roman cake stall. We find ourselves inundated with parents and children who start to outbid each other for chocolate discuses and dormice. An orderly line has formed for the "guess the weight of the chocolate discus" competition.

The sun is so hot now that I am wrapped in a sweaty polyester sheath that clings unforgivingly to my body. The hastily hacked hole has frayed horribly, and the neckline has moved from demure to plunging in the space of an hour. Every time I lean over to get change from the box marked "denarii," I have to hold the front of the sheet against my chest. Holding my stomach in is becoming increasingly exhausting. Handing over a cake involves two hands, and Celebrity Dad obligingly preserves my dignity by placing a hand somewhere just above my breasts.

During a lull in proceedings he looks me up and down, appraising my body with no hint of shame or apology. "More Venus than Minerva, I think," he says teasingly. "There's nothing like a fulsome Roman woman to whet the appetite of a humble centurion."

I spot Tom approaching with the three boys in tow.

"I hear the Roman cake stall is the success story of the fete, Lucy," says Tom in disbelief. "I should have had more faith."

He looks at Celebrity Dad.

"That's quite a costume," he says. "Perhaps you should try something different when we go to the Arsenal." The sun comes out again.

"God, Lucy," says Tom. "You might as well be naked. Good job you've got a centurion guard to protect your honor."

Then he laughs for probably a minute, head thrown back, right from the stomach.

"I can see Mummy's underpants," announces Sam to anyone within earshot.

"I'll come back later," says Tom.

"There's nothing like children to bring you down to Earth," says Celebrity Dad sorrowfully. "Sometimes you don't know what you have until it's gone. Uncertain people are dangerous people, Lucy. I've sacked my therapist, by the way. I've decided he was part of the problem."

"Fire is a good servant
but a bad master."

Later that same day, I sluggishly walk up the stairs of Emma's private members club. It is one of those summer days in London when the heat burns down from the sky and then back up from the pavement so that you feel its full force somewhere at waist level. My clothes stick to me, and part of me wishes that I had stayed at home, except we are here to celebrate Emma's latest promotion. I climb flight after flight and it gets hotter and hotter until finally I reach the top floor of the building. I lean against the wooden panels to catch my breath, hoping they might cool me down, but instead they are warm and sticky and leave brown marks on my white shirt.

I think longingly of Isobel's tea dress and imagine the floaty billows of the skirt cooling me down. It occurs to me that I haven't bought any new clothes for almost a year. It took Isobel's housekeeper a day to separate her summer and winter clothes. My life has none of these seasonal boundaries. I am wearing the same pair of jeans I had on the last time I was here, ten months ago.

I feel so exhausted by my late-night and early-morning cake-making endeavors that I have one of those moments I used to have when the children were babies, when, walking along the street, I would feel a sudden jolt as though someone was trying to wake me up. Was I awake or dreaming? There was no philosophical angle to this question; it was purely a physical sensation, the product of almost two years without a full night's sleep. I consoled myself with the fact that no one has ever died from sleep deprivation, although undoubtedly it accounts for erratic behavior. I say all this because it might explain some of what occurred later. From the outset, everything had a dreamlike quality. It's not an excuse, just a partial explanation.

Tom offered to babysit because he felt guilty about forgetting to tell me that he was spending next week in Milan. But the offer was contingent on the children being in bed before I left the house so he could get some more work done before the trip. So between the fete and leaving home, I want to note that I accomplished the following: I simultaneously cooked spaghetti Bolognese for tea and tended a knee injury that Fred sustained when Joe accidentally kicked him during a football game in the garden. Joe had persuaded Fred to be Jens Lehmann. But Fred stood in front of him stock-still when he took a shot at goal, and because Joe was wearing football boots, there was blood. This was always the source of intense fascination, even for Sam, who at nine years old still hadn't tired of the dramatic possibilities of a serious injury. "Is there blood?" one of them always asked hopefully, and I could feel the frisson of excitement if the answer was affirmative, a mixture of fascination and awe. I think blood must be proof to children that they exist separately from their parents. A sign that one day the travails of life will have to be borne alone.

I then simultaneously put on a load of washing and tested Sam on his spellings; I called another mother to confirm Joe's presence at a forthcoming birthday party and mended a shelf; and ironed the pair of damp jeans that I am now wearing, while answering Joe's questions about sperm. His obsession over *The Sound of Music* has passed, and he has moved on to David Attenborough wildlife programs.

"Mum, how big is a sperm?" he asked.

"Tiny," I said.

"Even if you are a sperm whale?" he asked.

"Correct," I said, hoping that if I didn't engage, he would choose another moment to embark on this discussion. "No matter what size you are, the sperm are still tiny."

"Can I keep some as a pet?" he asked.

"They don't really survive once they have left home," I told him, knowing that this fudge will sow the seeds of confusion later, but time was simply not on my side. I was meant to meet Emma and Cathy in less than an hour.

"Dad could give you some," said Sam, trying to be helpful. "He grows them."

Joe looked at him suspiciously. Sam lives on the light side of life, but for Joe there will always be questions.

This would have been a good moment to embark on a rudimentary chat about the birds and the bees, but I just didn't have time. I had an image of Joe, age sixteen, having sex with a girlfriend, getting her pregnant, and then blaming me because I told him that sperm couldn't survive in the outside world. I concluded that, on balance, there was plenty of opportunity for this discussion before then.

"I think I'll save up my pocket money and buy some instead," he said.

"Maybe a goldfish would be better," I replied. "They have more personality. Why don't you both have a game of Top Trumps?"

It was not what I call a babysitting-plus situation, which would have given me a night off from bathtime and stories, a process that takes about an hour and a half, even using shortcuts. It was the kind of babysitting whereby you are exhausted by the time you leave the house. When I was reading to Joe, I felt my eyes grow heavy, and it was half past eight when Tom woke me up.

"I put Fred to bed," he said. "Hurry up, and you'll still make it."

I rushed out the door, mumbling thanks, but I was annoyed with him because I could count the number of times that he had babysat for me this year on one hand, while I had lost count of how many times I had put the children to bed on my own. No applause for that, and yet I know that he will think he has accumulated points for babysitting tonight that

I will never be awarded. What is it about even the most helpful men that compels them to quantify all their domestic efforts? Every minor contribution is meticulously logged, from bathing and getting breakfast to unloading the dishwasher. They want and expect acknowledgment and plaudits. I know that I will go home to find the detritus from teatime still on the table and be expected to deal with Fred when he wakes up, as he does almost every other night.

So although the thought of an evening out with my girlfriends usually fills me with the kind of enthusiasm reserved for a teenage girl meeting a new boyfriend for the first time, tonight I wish for nothing more than an evening slumped in front of the television with a bottle of wine for company.

But when Emma and Cathy wave at me from the other side of the room, my spirits lift slightly. It has been almost two months since we last saw each other together, and my last night out with Emma was memorable for all the wrong reasons. It certainly didn't involve much small talk. I have been in a slump since I decided to abandon contact with Robert Bass. Eventually, I will emerge with renewed energy, but for the moment there is a vacuum in my life.

"Here's to world domination," says Emma, handing me a glass of champagne as I sit down opposite her. "I'm now in charge of Europe, North Africa, and the Middle East." I gulp the champagne as though it is water and toast her success. Emma's ability to always look outward impresses and amazes me. She wins new territory like a colonial superpower, while I feel as though I am engaged in a constant struggle to control a tiny part of the terrain under my command. Even the laundry pile is in a constant state of rebellion.

"I suppose it's a bit like having three children," I say. "The eldest is relatively calm but prone to arguments about money, the middle one always feels left out, and the toddler is stubborn and volatile."

I sit back against the velvet sofa, pleased with my geographical relativism. "I do still read the newspaper, you know." Then the phone rings. I know, even without looking at the number, that it is Tom. If I were a

region I would be Central Africa, I think to myself, out of control, heading toward civil war, and ruled by petty dictators.

"Lucy, I can't find any nappies," he says. "And Fred will piss everywhere if he doesn't wear one at night."

"I think we might have run out. I'll get some on the way home. You'll
have to wing it," I tell him, holding the phone from my ear.

"Exactly what are you proposing?" he asks suspiciously.

"Well, you could use a tea towel and then put a big pair of pants on
top. That will buy you a couple of hours at least," I say.

"You've done this before, haven't you?" he says with exasperation. The
phone goes dead.

"I can't ever imagine a situation where you fail to come up with an
answer," says Emma, looking impressed. "You are so good at improvising.
It's a real skill."

"It goes with the territory," I say. "Three short straws and a husband
on a short fuse release your inner firefighter."

"I can't imagine that I will ever have three children to be able to compare notes," says Emma without any hint of wistfulness. "It's ironic, but
although I have had a steady boyfriend for the first time in years, I am
further than ever from the baby question. Guy definitely wouldn't have
wanted any more." She pats the huge black handbag that she used to
store tools during our nocturnal visit to Guy's house in the way a pregnant woman pats her stomach. It looks full, and I wonder what might be
inside, considering its contents the last time we went out together.

"Just as well, since he's got a steady wife, too," I say, noting her use of
the pluperfect rather than the present when referring to Guy.

"And I'll never have any more, not if my current situation endures,"
says Cathy. "I think that on balance Pete would make a better father, but
it wouldn't be an auspicious start to family life."

"But couldn't you choose one over the other?" I ask her.

"Or have a baby with one and then the other?" says Emma.

"Then I'd have three children with three different fathers," says Cathy.
"How trailer trash is that? Anyway, it's not an option. I think that the deal

is that you go out with either both of them or neither of them, although we never analyze the situation in any depth. Actually, together, they make the perfect man."

"So what do you talk about then?" I ask.

"Football, films, restaurants, where to go on holiday, books we're reading, the usual," she says. "Within its strangeness, it's all quite normal. I just find it a little exhausting. It's great having so much sex and being adored by two men, but it's a bit like eating too much chocolate. You can have too much of a good thing."

"So when Ben is with his dad and you spend the weekend with them, how do you decide whose bed to sleep in?" I ask.

"We all sleep in the same bed," she says.

"Very cozy," says Emma.

"Actually, it's a bit too hot at the moment," says Cathy.

"So at what point does the other one know that he can join you?" I ask, imagining the kind of bell system that you find in some country houses. The great thing about spending time with Cathy and Emma is that their situations are invariably more diverting than my own.

"Well, that is the only part of the relationship that has evolved," she says. I am struck by how the two men have fused. "Without entering into too much detail, it all sort of happens at the same time."

"So there is a gay element," says Emma triumphantly, because she considers her original theory to be proved.

"I don't think it's as simple as that," says Cathy. "I think they get off on seeing each other have sex with the same woman. And there's a competitive element to it all."

"There always is with men," says Emma.

"God, I'll have to tell Tom," I say.

"I want to rediscover the joys of vanilla sex," says Cathy.

"What's that?" I ask, imagining a scenario that involves ice cream, not a prospect that I would ever entertain, on the grounds that it would exacerbate my precarious laundry situation.

"I mean straightforward common or garden sex," she explains. "We never seem to get to that 'slumped in front of the television with a take-away' zone."

"There's years in front of you of that kind of stuff," I say wearily.

"And there's not much companionship. Your brother says that loyalty and a loving nature are important traits in a man and that in our twenties we tend to dismiss men who exhibit them. Then, in our thirties, those men are taken and we're left with the rest just at the moment when our priorities change."

"Does he include himself in the rest?" I wonder.

"Oh, yes," she says. "He describes himself as a classic commitment-phobe, unable to sustain a relationship with any woman beyond two years."

"Oh. Have you seen him then?" I ask, because this is not the kind of conversation that people have over the phone.

"I bumped into him a couple of weeks ago, and we've had lunch together a couple of times," she says.

A waiter comes over with another bottle of champagne.

"Would you like a ginger beer?" he asks me after greeting Emma.

It is the same waiter from my last visit, and I congratulate him for his impeccable memory and glance down enviously to review his apron. Since Petra left, the washing landscape has evolved slightly. I have found a laundry service to do Tom's shirts, and the babysitter is earning extra money sorting out the rest. Things have progressed, but it is still one of those perennial problems.

To my surprise, the apron is wrinkled and covered with stains. There are so many that it looks like a world map. I search for the outline of different countries and find a patch of red wine that looks like Australia and a series of small red islands alongside a larger stain—all formed, I imagine, from a tomato sauce—that could be mainland Greece and a few islands, possibly Crete and Corfu. He sees me looking and shakes his head sadly.

"He left me," he says. "I kept leaving the fridge door open. I came down one morning during this heat wave and everything had started to go off and that was it. Three years of starched aprons dissolved in less than five minutes over a pint of curdled milk."

He shrugs, pours me another glass of champagne, and then walks away.

"I can't believe that couples break up over such minor issues," says Emma.

"They sound minor if you consider them in isolation, but they are almost always precipitated by a chain of events," I say.

I tell Emma and Cathy about my most recent domestic row with Tom.

"After lengthy discussions, he finally gave his approval to purchase a hamster for Joe's sixth birthday, on condition that I assumed total responsibility for its well-being," I explain.

"I don't want it running loose, chewing through wires, and making a mess," he said.

"It's not as though you need to take them out for walks or anything. They are tiny little things. You won't even notice," I told him.

I explain how I went to a local pet shop with the three boys and chose an orange hamster, which they decided to call Rover, because what they really wanted was a puppy. A displacement pet, Mark would call it. Cathy laughs loudly at this.

By the time we arrived home, Rover had chewed his way out of the shoebox and was missing in action somewhere in the car. The children were inconsolable, and so we returned to the pet shop to buy an immediate replacement, which I transported home in a fish bowl strapped in the front seat of the car and transferred immediately into a high-security cage in the garden.

The next morning, as we got into the car to go out, I discovered that Rover had taken up residence there. He had found his way into the glove compartment and chewed through some red and white wires. He had eaten a broken breadstick and an apple core and left his calling card everywhere. Tom tried to put on a CD, but it didn't work. Nor did the light in the glove compartment. He peered inside and pulled out a chewed chocolate bar.

"If I didn't know better, I would say those teeth marks belong to a rodent," he said suspiciously.

"Well, Rover is safely in his cage," I said. "You saw him there."

"Who is Rover?" he asked. "I thought the hamster was called Spot."

"That's his middle name," I whispered. "Don't talk about it, because there was a fight over what he should be called."

Tom unearthed the A-to-Z on the floor behind the passenger seat. He lifted it into the front of the car, and tiny pieces of paper fluttered around. Clearly, Rover was nesting.

"Lucy, what on earth has happened to this map?" he asked. "Something has eaten half of Islington."

Fortunately, he was so busy trying to piece together the page that he didn't notice a small hamster staring at him from the back of the glove compartment. Unfortunately, the children did.

"Mummy, look, it's Rover, he's been resurrected," said Joe. Rover leapt from the glove compartment onto Tom, who jumped in his seat, swearing loudly.

"Daddy said the f-word, Daddy said the f-word," started a chorus from the back.

Rover disappeared into the back of the car.

It took us another half-hour to catch him and return him to captivity, partly because we were arguing so loudly that Rover refused to come out.

"You are useless at subterfuge," said Tom as we shut the cage door. "I suppose at least that means you'll never have an affair, or at least if you do, you'll never manage to keep it secret."

◎◎

"Well, he's right about that," says Emma. "You're so transparent."

"The point is that in three months, the hamster might be seen as a defining moment," I say thoughtfully. "The tipping point."

"What do you mean?" asks Cathy warily.

"Nothing explicit," I say. "All I mean is that it's only with the benefit of hindsight that you can see how one event impacts on another. Chain reactions."

"You mean like when Archduke Ferdinand was killed in Sarajevo?" says Emma.

"Exactly," I say. I have finished my glass of champagne, and Emma pours me another full glass.

"So what's the state of play with *Sexy Domesticated Dad*?" inquires Cathy.

"I lost interest," I say. "We became friends. It evolved from distracting fantasy to banal reality."

"What about him?" she asks.

"Not even a frisson," I say so convincingly that I almost believe what I am saying.

"I wish I could switch off the sexual current with Guy," says Emma. "It's the most difficult part of the process."

"So what's the overall prognosis?" I ask her.

"It is almost resolved in my mind, and I can guarantee that it will be completely finished before the weekend is over," she says mysteriously. "Actually, I'm meeting him later. I promise that I will give you every detail once I have done it, but I don't want to talk about it now because I might get stage fright."

"I can't go on lying to Isobel indefinitely," I say. "It makes me feel awful."

"I can't imagine how uncomfortable it must be," says Emma.

"Perhaps you should try a little harder," says Cathy firmly. Emma has ignored the fact that this is the same territory that Cathy roamed a couple of years ago when her husband left her. "If you lack conviction about Guy, you have a moral duty to finish the relationship now. Children are almost always losers if their parents split up. They grow up and get into relationships without any blueprint to follow. Look at you, you're still so affected by your father walking out on your mother that you only go out with men that never want to get domestic."

"But Ben seems fine," says Emma, after a disconcerting silence.

"He is, in part. We try to present the fact that his parents no longer live together in a positive light. I tell him he is lucky to have two bedrooms, two houses, two Christmas presents, double the amount of holidays. But even as I'm saying it, I don't really believe it."

"Look, I'm almost there," says Emma. "Every time I'm with him, I find something new to dislike, and eventually I'll feel strong enough to give him up completely. Basically, I need to find a replacement."

"Any possibilities?" asks Cathy. I am glad for her intervention in the conversation. Emma's ability to see things only from her own point of view is at its most frustrating in this kind of situation.

"I have started a good flirtation with someone at work," she says.

"So what's the stumbling block?" asks Cathy.

"He works in the New York office," she says. "But he's not married. An ocean is easier to bridge than a marriage."

Whether she knows this is an effective way of cauterizing our line of questioning or she has really come up with a master plan to withdraw from Guy is uncertain. I decide, however, that whatever happens, next week I will tell Isobel the truth as I know it.

I finish another glass of champagne. Already I feel a little shaky on my legs. The heat, the tiredness, the alcohol, and the lack of air in the wood-paneled room are a heady combination. I shut my eyes. The world has started spinning. When I open them, my brother is standing by the table.

"What are you doing here?" I ask, bemused by his unannounced arrival.

"I'm speaking at a conference tomorrow morning, and they've put me up in a hotel. So I won't be long, because otherwise I'll drink too much. Cathy told me that you were coming, so I thought I would join you. Do you want another drink?" He walks toward the bar, and I go with him. "You don't mind me barging in on your girls' night out, do you?"

"As long as you don't sleep with any of my friends," I joke, wondering just how many times he has bumped into Cathy.

"I'm too old for that," he says. "Where's Tom?"

"At home with the children. A reluctant babysitter," I tell him. "The kind that makes you wish you had paid for someone. Although, whenever we do pay someone, it sort of increases the pressure to have a good time. But he's already called twice and I only left the house an hour ago."

Mark orders a beer from the barman.

"And the library project?" he asks.

"All back on track. Unbelievable. It has become such a part of us that I can't imagine life without it. Tom's got some other good commissions on the back of it, so our financial situation suddenly looks much better than it did," I tell him.

Normally, I can't imagine anything more relaxing than being with my brother. Growing up on the edge of a tiny village meant that, for most of our childhood, we were dependent on each other for entertainment. While he purported to find me irritating when his friends came around, I knew that it was an acquired attitude to avoid losing face. Being a teenager is complicated enough on your own, without being responsible for a younger sister. I understood this, and I didn't mind because their teenage conversation was limited to three main subjects: girls, sex, and how to make that equation work for them. My brother always had girlfriends, and his friends would look to him for advice.

"Talk to them and treat them like goddesses," I remembered him telling his friends. "Then everything is up for grabs. Analyze, they love to analyze. And oral sex. That's crucial."

Mark liked women. And so women liked Mark, even if they knew that he was structurally unreliable. He made friendships out of messy relationships, because he was always willing to talk things through.

There is very little that I censor in conversation with him, and I think he would say the same. But tonight I feel uncomfortable being alone with him. He has sat down on a bar stool, his head leaning on his arm, and is clearly not planning an imminent return to our table. His chin is covered in stubble and his shirt is grubby. In the way that you intuit with family, I understand that he is here on a specific mission.

"Did you come straight from work?" I ask him.

"Mmm," he says dreamily, leaning back his head to drink a couple of swigs of beer from a bottle. He holds on to the bottle and I notice him glancing over at our table, smiling slightly and then taking another gulp of beer. "And how are my lovely nephews?"

"They're great. Overenthusiastic puppies," I say. "They roam around the house, make the most appalling mess, even when they try to clear up, wrestle and fight at least a couple of times a day, eat more or less constantly, and talk nonstop, mostly asking me questions all at the same time and then accusing me that I love one of them more than the other when I prioritize one question over another. I'm looking forward to the summer holidays."

"Why?" he asks suspiciously. "You normally find the holidays exhausting. In fact, the summer is the only time that I have heard you seriously entertain the possibility of going back to work full-time."

"Funny how people talk about going back to work as though looking after three children isn't work," I say. "Work is much easier than looking after children."

"I read an interview with John McEnroe and he said that it was easier to play a Wimbledon final than look after his children," says Mark. "Mothers beat themselves up about things much more than most other people, apart from elderly Catholic women."

"Actually, motherhood and guilt are so entwined that it is difficult to see where one stops and the other starts. The guilt just becomes second nature. Although, since I have given up work there is a guilt vacuum looking to be filled," I say, knowing that he is treating me like one of his patients, gently lobbing questions in ever-decreasing circles until the subject that he wants to tackle is finally in focus. But he forgets that I was once a journalist who spent a lot of time watching politicians wriggle away from awkward questions.

"Anyway, I've got lots of things planned," I say. "I might go and stay with a friend in Dorset, then go on to Mum and Dad, and we're going to Italy."

"Who is the friend in Dorset? Have I met her?" he asks.

"You mean have you slept with her? The answer to both questions is no. Actually, she is a mother at school and the wife of Emma's boyfriend," I say.

"That sounds complicated," he says.

"It's a difficult situation. My friend Isobel knows her husband is having an affair, and she is close to identifying Emma, but Emma doesn't want me to tell her until she has extricated herself from the relationship with Guy," I explain. "And the extrication process is taking longer than I anticipated."

I think of Isobel. I have rarely encountered someone so utterly convinced of the way her life is constructed. In all the time that I have known her, she has never demonstrated any shred of doubt. And yet her husband has spent the past year systematically drilling through the foundations so that the whole edifice threatens to crumble around her. I wonder what she will be able to retrieve from the wreckage.

"So, how's your crush?" he asks, ordering another beer and checking his cell phone for messages at the same time. Mark is one of the few men I know who can genuinely do two things at once. "You haven't mentioned him for ages. In fact, he is conspicuous by his absence."

"That's very Jonathan Ross to throw in a question like that. Whatever happened to subtlety?" I say, hoping to head off the conversation.

"You're being evasive," he says.

"He's fine," I say. "We don't talk much anymore."

"So why is that?" he asks.

"We lost interest in each other, I suppose," I say benignly. "How are you enjoying celibacy? Life alone isn't one of your strengths."

"Lucy, I don't believe that you woke up one day and found each other unattractive," he says. "You can only do that if there has been no declaration of intent."

"I don't really want to talk about it," I say, standing up.

"You've slept with him, haven't you?" he says. "You've got that air of abstraction about you." It's an outrageous provocation, and I fall straight into the trap.

"We were at a party, there was a minor tangle, we didn't even kiss, and I decided that we should put a bit of distance between us," I say. "In fact, I think I have behaved pretty impeccably."

"Did you tell Tom?" he asks. "If you haven't, then I am going to remain suspicious."

"There was nothing to tell," I say.

"If there was nothing to tell, then why are you being so cagey about it all?" he asks.

"It takes a lot of concentration," I say. "Trying to avoid thinking about someone is quite exhausting."

"There is nothing relaxing about being in a state of constant desire," says Mark.

Emma comes over.

"Are you two going to join us?" she asks, smiling, "or are you going to spend the rest of the evening trawling through family business?"

We go back to the table and sit down again. Cathy and Mark exchange a knowing smile. I am convinced that she has put him up to this, to check the veracity of my account of dealings with Robert Bass. But I'm not annoyed, because I know that both of them have my best interests at heart. This thought soothes me.

Emma questions Mark about his work.

"Do you always like your patients?" she asks.

"I'm less involved in patient care now," he says, "but when I was training, I generally found that everyone has some redeeming qualities. Actually, what is interesting is that certain groups of patients are more appealing than others."

"What do you mean?" asks Emma.

"Well, certain psychopathologies produce a commonality of personality traits," he says, "and some of those traits are more attractive than others. Anorexics, for example, are frequently perfectionist people pleasers. People with obsessive-compulsive disorder are very inflexible, and they always tidy my desk."

"Who are your favorites?" asks Cathy.

"People with sex addictions," he says, without a moment's hesitation. "Not because they always try to seduce you, which they do, even the men, but because their success depends on being utterly charming. They are great conversationalists, and they make you laugh a lot. They are intent on having a good time."

"Like Russell Brand?" says Emma.

"Precisely," says Mark.

"How do you resist their advances?" asks Cathy.

"I think about the fact that I would lose my job if I succumbed," he says. "I play out the consequences in my mind. With the men it's easier; I can't help but be resolutely heterosexual. And I see more men than women. It's a more common problem in men."

"How can you tell the difference between an addiction and an unhealthy obsession?" I ask.

"Some people might view all of these things as a form of addiction," he says. "But to qualify as an addiction, these things have to dominate your life on a daily basis, you withdraw from people, the addiction becomes your friend. There is also an element of self-loathing. You, Lucy, might be obsessed, but you're not addicted." He sits back, looking satisfied. Mark loves his job.

"Do you think I am addicted to Guy?" asks Emma tentatively.

"No," he says. "Guy could just as easily be someone else; you are simply addicted to a type of man who can never be yours. Ultimately, you fear intimacy, in case you are rejected."

I am a little taken aback. None of us ever speak to Emma with such honesty.

"So, what's the cure?" she asks, sounding less confident than she did earlier in the evening.

"You should consciously avoid this kind of man. Inasmuch as you recognize them as a type, they also recognize you," he says. "You should probably get professional help."

"What about you?" says Emma.

"Actually," says Mark, "I think I have met someone I might want to marry."

"Fuck," I say. "When do we get to meet her?"

"Soon," he says mysteriously.

Someone is tapping me on the shoulder. I assume that it is the solicitous waiter and lethargically turn toward the arm of the sofa to ask him for another bottle of champagne, because I have decided to treat tonight as though there is no tomorrow. But it is not a waiter. It is Robert Bass.

He puts his hands on the arm of the sofa and leans over to speak to me. His fingers are splayed and I note that he is scratching the velvet, leaving tiny furrows in its pile in a way that suggests a certain nervous determination.

"What are you doing here?" I say, trying to sound less startled than I feel.

"I've just finished having dinner with my editor," he says. "I saw you and thought that it would be unfriendly to leave without saying hello. What are you doing here? You said you never go out."

"I don't generally. I'm here with some friends and my brother," I say, but I make no effort to introduce him to them.

I get up from the sofa and stand in front of him, standing parallel to the table to indicate that he shouldn't sit down with us. He leans forward and kisses me once on the cheek. It is a gesture that on a superficial level looks meaningless. Neither Mark nor my girlfriends seem remotely perturbed. They assume he is an old friend—someone from my *Newsnight* days, no doubt. But the kiss lingers a little longer than it should. I feel his cheek against my cheek, his hand on my shoulder. These are knowing gestures, a continuum of the intimacy at the party. I realize that we must both have replayed the episode repeatedly in our minds. When we look at each other, I can see my own desire reflected in his eyes. I start to feel breathless. I see the front of my shirt moving up and down too fast and start to chew my lower lip. I want to make it bleed to distract myself with the pain and extricate myself from this situation. I think of Fred's tiny knee, covered in blood, and the way he cried for me, as though there was no one else in the world that could make him feel better. I think of Tom, cool, rational, certain about things.

"Lucy, you have a responsibility to talk to me; you can't pretend that nothing has happened," he whispers in my ear. "We're both complicit."

"I have a responsibility to my family, and so do you to yours," I say. "Look, this isn't the time or the place."

"Name the time and place," he says. "I can't get through this on my own. I'm really tormented." Then my brother, gregarious and friendly as always, gets up and walks toward us.

"Would you like a drink?" he asks Robert Bass. I introduce him to the table, relieved that no one knows him by any other name than Sexy Domesticated Dad. I have to get him to leave as swiftly as possible.

"Let me get a round," says Robert Bass, walking toward the bar.

I sit down, feeling slightly nauseous. But this time I can't blame the drink. I am sick with desire. It's like trying to stop a chemistry experiment when the ingredients have already been placed in a test tube, I decide.

"Who is that?" asks Emma theatrically. "He's gorgeous. He could definitely distract me from Guy. I would even forsake world domination for a share of that." It is gratifying to hear an old friend validate my taste in men, but on the other hand it makes me wonder whether Robert Bass is just too obvious.

"He's an old friend," I say. "I haven't seen him for ages. But I'm pretty sure he's married."

"Marriage is a state of mind," says Emma. "That's what Guy says. When he's with his wife he feels married, and when he's with me he feels like fucking. He says that his ideal is to be single during the week and married on weekends."

"That's because men have a frightening capacity to compartmentalize their life." I sigh. "Women could never live like that."

"So, where do you know him from?" asks Mark. "It must be a decade since you last had a job, I mean, since you decided to evolve from white-collar to blue-collar worker."

"Why blue-collar?" asks Emma.

"Looking after children is like working on a coal face, except there is never any break between shifts," I say. Then I turn to Mark and look at him straight in the eye. "He's an old contact," I say, deliberately vague. Mark raises his eyebrows twice, but Robert Bass has come back to the table. He sits on an armchair next to me, with Emma on the other side.

"So, what are you doing here?" she asks, turning her body toward him and smiling in her most engaging manner. Emma is incorrigible. Robert Bass leans on his left elbow so that his back is turned toward me. But his legs slide further under the table. I know that I should shift up the sofa to remove the possibility of any physical contact, knowing that my defenses are low and that every time we touch it sets off a terrible reaction.

But before I can put this plan into action, I feel Robert Bass's left leg settle resolutely between my knees, pushing up toward my thighs. Either he must have done this kind of thing before, because this is an accomplished piece of daring, or he is simply intent on having sex with me. Luckily, the table is so high that it screens us from suspicious eyes.

Cathy continues to talk. She is oblivious. Mark is at the other end of the table opposite Robert Bass, and I am sure that he can see nothing. I know that I should just move away, but since that might draw even more attention to what is going on, I decide to enjoy the moment.

"So, Lucy, have you made any big decisions about what to do in September, when Fred is at nursery all day?" she asks.

"You know, I think I'm going to start painting again," I say dreamily, leaning as far forward as possible, so that the area under the table is obscured from view. It is now getting dark outside, but the lights inside are not yet switched on. "I have an idea for a children's book, and I think I might start doing some illustrations for that and see where it takes me. I'm not going to look for anything full-time. I know that means we still won't have enough money to completely buy my way out of domestic chaos, but I've decided that it doesn't really matter anyway."

"That sounds great," she says. "My main aim is to turn my triangle into a straight line before it turns into a square." She looks at me enigmatically. I have no idea what she is talking about. "I want to extricate myself from this relationship and get into something more linear."

Emma gets up to go to the toilet.

She walks away, and Cathy is talking to Mark, and Robert Bass turns to face me. His expression reveals nothing. He leans toward my left ear, his breath tickling my neck.

"Imagine my hand where my leg is," he says. "And then imagine my head where my hand is."

"You are bad," I tell him.

"No, I'm not, I just know what I want," he says. "It's a beautiful coincidence that we are both here tonight. Let's take advantage of it. We can spend a couple of hours together and then forget that anything ever happened. Suspend reality for a while and then go back to our rather dull, routine lives. Come on, Lucy, live a little."

It is always tempting to read too much into coincidence. But the truth is that we attribute meaning to some events but not to others. For example, it is enticing, given the fact that Robert Bass is here tonight, when I have only been here twice in the past year, to invest meaning into this serendipity, to say that fate dealt its hand and absolve myself from responsibility for my actions. But, actually, the chances of bumping into my brother are statistically less likely, yet I have barely considered that coincidence. And what about the fact that we have exactly the same waiter? We like to find symmetry in the world around us to find meaning in its arbitrariness.

Robert Bass's hand moves onto my upper thigh, and his fingers lightly circle an area ranging from the upper knee to somewhere on my inner thigh. Of course, I could get up and walk away, but it is just so pleasurable.

I note that we are both staring into our glasses. It is impossible to speak, as though everything has been reduced to the simple movement of his hand on my thigh.

"So, how do you two know each other?" my brother asks suddenly from the other end of the table. The question makes me jump. I had almost forgotten that there was anyone else here. "You haven't got a lot to say to each other for people who haven't seen each other for years."

I shoot him what I hope is a look malevolent enough to deter him from this line of questioning. Robert Bass doesn't move his hand.

"We've covered all the ground," he says. "I'd better get home." He gets out a piece of paper, writes something on it, and passes it to me. "My address, in case you want to get in touch."

When he removes his hand from my leg, I feel an immediate sense of loss. I get up to say good-bye to him. He kisses me again on the cheek— this time it is a swift and perfunctory gesture.

"See you around," he says to Cathy and my brother.

"I hope I didn't frighten him off," says Mark. I ignore him and instead unfold the piece of paper.

"Me at Hotel Aberdeen in Bloomsbury, waiting for you," it says. I scrunch it up quickly and put it in my pocket. Emma comes back to the table.

"Has he gone already?" she asks. "I thought the party was just beginning."

I plead tiredness, and fifteen minutes later find myself catching a cab to the hotel.

20

"The journey is the destination."

When I arrive at the Hotel Aberdeen, I walk with straight shoulders and head held high toward the man behind the reception desk and tell him that I have a reservation. At first I am affronted that he doesn't get up from his stool to speak to me. Then I realize that the small man in the large suit is so short that, even at full height, his elbows barely reach the reception desk. It doesn't lend the occasion the gravitas that it deserves. I look round for someone else, but the lobby is empty. Hotels that rent rooms by the hour are unlikely to have the kind of service associated with the Sanderson, but I am surprised to see that he is sharpening pencils.

"Are you attending the anxiety convention?" he asks slowly in a strong Spanish accent, stroking his chin wisely.

"Do I look nervous?" I reply, intrigued that a complete stranger can read my emotions so accurately. He points to a board sitting on the floor beside the lifts. It welcomes guests to the third annual anxiety conference. Guest speakers will address a variety of subjects including (1) the role of deep breathing in controlling nervousness, (2) making anxiety your friend, and (3) breaking the cycle of tension. There will then be a break for anxious delegates to have coffee and tea together.

"Sometimes talking about it just doesn't help," I tell him. "And the caffeine will only exacerbate the problem." He looks at me suspiciously and puts down the pencil sharpener.

"I can find an anxiety expert for you to speak to if you are having any doubts," he says. "It happens every time. The anxious people are often anxious about attending the anxiety conference."

For a moment I wonder whether this hotel, notorious for its role in hosting illicit affairs, has become like those television channels that show harrowing dramas and then give numbers for people to call if the program proves too disturbing. Perhaps it would be a good thing to speak to an anxiety expert about my reasons for being here.

"I have an appointment with Mr. Robert Bass," I say decisively. "At one o'clock in the morning."

"Is he one of the conference leaders?" he asks.

"No," I say. "He's, er, a friend. Bass, like the fish."

"A friendly fish?" he inquires. Then he says slowly, "A nocturnal, friendly fish."

He starts to check through his reservation list, moving his hand slowly down a large leather-bound book, stopping at each name for a moment, pointing at it with his newly sharpened pencil before muttering a surname under his breath.

"Smith . . . Klein . . . Robinson . . . McMannus . . . Smith . . . Villeroy . . . Raphael . . . Smith," he says, sounding out every syllable as though he is in an English lesson, and impressively rolling his R's so they resound like volleys of machine-gun fire.

"Roderick Riley," he says with satisfaction, smiling up at me. There are two pages of names. It could take four or five minutes to get from the beginning to the end. Even reading upside down I can already see that there is no one with the surname Bass on the first page. I look nervously around the foyer of the hotel, wondering how I will explain myself if I see someone I know, then reassuring myself that their presence is unlikely to have an innocent explanation, either, unless they are attending the anxiety convention.

I look at the name on the lapel of his jacket, turning my head slightly to one side because it is not pinned on straight. He is called Diego.

When I look up, his head is facing mine tilted at a similar angle. He smiles reassuringly.

"Do you think he is using his real name?" he asks. "We have a lot of Smiths every day."

"I'm sure he has booked the room under the name Bass," I say. "I think it's *trucha* in Spanish."

"A *trucha* is a trout," he says. "Maybe you mean a *merluza*?"

"Isn't that a red snapper?" I say. "Or a grouper or something? He's more of a cold-water fish. An English fish."

"We have so many wonderful fish in Costa Rica," he says wistfully. "Have you ever been there?"

I shake my head, willing him to turn to the next page of the reservation list because I can see that someone else has arrived and is waiting behind me at a polite distance, shifting from foot to foot and trying not to listen to our conversation.

"Is he here for the adultery or the anxiety?" I joke nervously to Diego. He smiles benignly, revealing nothing.

"And manatees," he says. He senses my impatience. "Trout, trout, trout," he mutters under his breath.

"No, Bass, B-A-S-S," I repeat. "Do you want me to have a look?"

He hands me the book with a flourish and turns to the second page. I scroll down and then, when I find the name Robert Bass, I feel a sort of nauseous excitement.

"Ah," says Diego, winking at me. "He only called about twenty minutes ago. I'll show you up to your room. It's booked for three hours, but if you overrun I won't charge you."

He starts walking toward the elevator. I can't believe that Robert Bass has booked the room for so long. Won't his wife be suspicious if he goes out until four in the morning? It is strange, but it doesn't occur to me to ask the same question about Tom. I try to calculate how many times we might have sex in three hours and then feel shaky. The man who was queuing behind me at reception looks bemused as I obediently follow Diego into the elevator.

"You have no luggage, I see," he says, shutting the elevator doors behind us and pressing a button to take us to the fifth floor.

"I'm not here for very long," I say. He is looking at my wedding ring. I put my hands behind my back and look up at the ceiling.

The elevator shudders to a halt on the fifth floor. We walk down a long corridor, and he opens the door of room 507 with pride.

"This is one of our best rooms," he says. He goes toward the bed, lifts the covers, and pulls back the top quarter of the sheets so that they lie on the bedspread in a perfect sandwich-shaped triangle. I imagine Robert Bass and myself lying in this bed and put out a hand to steady myself.

Diego wants to show me the bathroom.

"The bath is enormous. Big enough for two. Or three," he says. "Not big enough for a manatee, though." No matter what he says, his voice is still sorrowful.

He goes back into the bedroom and asks whether I want room service to send anything up.

"We have Tension Tamer tea for the anxiety delegates," he says kindly.

"That would be great," I reply.

Anticipation does not necessarily heighten desire. For the professionally unfaithful, those who habitually wait for their lovers in functional hotel rooms in Bloomsbury, it might allow time to get into the mood, to make the switch between work and play, to have a shower and consider the pleasures that lie ahead. Perhaps they lie back on the carefully made bed with its cover that matches the curtains and watch the *Playboy* Channel or read a book and order a bottle of cheap wine.

I, on the other hand, sit gingerly on the edge of the bed and wonder about how clean the mattress is, given its workload. My mood of languid desire has passed, and I am starting to become all too aware of my surroundings. When I look at the door key lying on the bed beside me, I start to invest the numbers with ridiculous emotional significance. Five hundred and seven. If you subtract seven from fifty, it is forty-three, Tom's age. We were married on the fifth of July. The London underground was bombed on July 7. I wonder what time in the morning the anxiety conference is programmed to start. I conclude that it will be an early kickoff, because it wouldn't be good to allow a group of tense people to wait for too long for redemption.

There is a television, but I prefer the quiet. If the silence is overwhelming, I can always put on the radio and listen to the World Service. I wonder if Robert Bass listens to the World Service and whether I could suggest to him as a preliminary exercise that we just lie beside each other in companionable silence and listen to the radio for fifteen minutes and then go home. And then I wonder what he watches on television, what books he reads, whether he leaves a decent tip for waiters, whether his cup is half-full or half-empty, what was the last film he saw. It strikes me that I know very little about him apart from the kind of routine information that parents share. I know his children had single measles jabs, that there is no television allowed during the school week, and that they each play two musical instruments.

Would he be able to light a fire during a damp camping trip? Does he patrol the fridge for inexplicable changes in the way food is organized? Would he notice, for example, if the yogurts were on the same shelf as the chicken, if the lettuce had formed a close relationship with a half-eaten jelly, or if the milk was not stored according to its sell-by date? Does he talk in his sleep? Does he have a mother complex? Are his parents alive? Does he have siblings?

Of course, I might discover that we concur on everything. More likely, I would determine that his imperfections are different from Tom's but not necessarily any less irritating in the long term. The first time someone sleeps diagonally across the bed, their legs straying over to the other side, the desire for communion through the lonely hours of the night seems a sweet gesture. Within a week it becomes mildly irritating and painful. Ahead lies a future of single beds.

Then I consider the fact that all too often when Robert Bass has spoken, I have found what he says irritating. This is something that I have tried to suppress over the previous months, but now all his most annoying comments and habits crowd up behind each other, jostling for consideration.

The vanity of removing his cycling helmet and combing his hair before he goes into school seems ridiculous, the way he expounds his parenting techniques—no television during the week, the importance of playing with children without directing play, of never using processed food, not even a can of baked beans—becomes thoroughly irritating. Even the way he walks, like a cowboy, suddenly seems ridiculous. Everything is so mannered. The scars on his face, far from being manly, are a hangover from adolescent acne.

It reminds me of something that had happened during a summer holiday when, out of the blue, Simon Miller had called at my parents' house and asked whether he could come and see me. It had been at least two years since we last met up, and I was studying at Manchester. My parents were on holiday, and I was fully prepared that he might stay the night and we might relive the passion of our teenage years. When he arrived, I noticed that he was wearing a pair of white athletic socks, and for some inexplicable reason, this detonated a series of negative feelings toward him, culminating in his spending the night in the spare bedroom with me counting the hours before he left. When I met Tom, and he committed far worse sartorial hara-kiri, I was relieved to find that it had no effect. Even the shaggy dressing gown was endearing. Thinking of Tom makes me feel nostalgic.

There is a soft knock at the door. I'm unsure what to do. I decide that it looks a little forward to be lying on the bed, but then, opening the door might prove even more awkward, because it isn't obvious where we would both sit down. There is a small table with one chair beside the window. All routes lead to the bed. I could swear that there is a worn path between the door and the bed, like a track cut with a lawn mower through a field of long grass, trampled by people for whom time is of the essence.

"Come in," I shout. Diego comes in with a pot of tea and a reassuring orange mug. When I realize that I am relieved to see Diego rather than Robert Bass, I know that the moment is lost. That is the thing with desire, it is all so amorphous. If we had come here together, there is no doubt that by now I would be involved in an adulterous relationship with a father from the school run. The moment would not have passed.

"Shall I pour?" he asks solicitously.

"I'll do it," I say.

"Still no sign of Mr. Bass," he says. "Just phone reception if you need anything else."

It is one-thirty in the morning. How have I got here? I wonder. I look at my cell phone in case he has sent a text. There is nothing. No missed calls. No messages. The first lesson for the amateur adulterer is therefore to arrive late. The second is to close the curtains and keep the lighting low. I have already made two mistakes because, in a rare show of punctuality, I have arrived early and am now staring out of the window with its plastic panes, wondering which route Robert Bass might adopt. The third lesson is to avoid conversation with the hotel staff, but I have already fallen into that trap. I am now thinking about the flora and fauna in Costa Rica and considering its strengths as a family holiday destination when times are less lean.

I go and lie on the bed again, but, actually, what I want to do is go home. Despite the air-conditioning, the room is still so hot that my calves stick to the polyester bedcover. It is a shiny, green-and-purple mass of interlocking shapes that makes me feel dizzy if I look at it for too long. The carpet is in a different shade of green, slightly deeper, and the bedside lamps are purple. I have heard Emma talk about this hotel so many times with such affection, and yet I feel nothing of what she has described.

"It's so louche," she told us. "Like a French film. Everyone has a secret to hide; this heavy, lustful air hangs over everything. It's the ideal backdrop for uninhibited sex." But I can relate to none of this. Instead, I think of a conversation that Tom and I had after the party.

"You know, I think Deep Shallows fancies you," said Tom, just after I woke up at five o'clock in the morning. He was lying on his side, leaning on an elbow, one hand resting on my buttocks.

"You look a bit rough," he said, as I groaned. My drinking habits were getting out of control, and after Tom had gone to bed I had sat in the garden and smoked the last two cigarettes. I stuck my leg out of the bed and put one foot firmly on the ground to stop the spinning sensation.

"Why do you think that?" I asked, trying to pull myself together.

"The way he avoided you at that party, the way he looks at you, the way he always puts his arm around his wife when he sees me watching, as though he wants to underline the fact that he is interested in her," he said.

"Well, it's not true," I said a little too defensively. "He's happily married."

"Being happily married doesn't preclude finding other people attractive," Tom said, not unreasonably. "Do you find him attractive?"

"He's not unattractive," I said.

"That wasn't the question," said Tom. "Do you fancy him?"

"Do you find other women attractive?" I asked.

"Sometimes," he said. "Mostly when Arsenal win. Stop trying to avoid the question at hand."

"So, have you ever been tempted in recent years?" I asked him.

"The thought has crossed my mind on occasion," Tom said. "I'm only human. But there's a big difference between thinking about doing something and actually doing it."

"What precisely?" I ask.

"The difference between fucking someone and not fucking them, Lucy. Don't be so guileless," he said.

"Do you think there's such a thing as emotional adultery?" I asked him.

"What do you mean?" he said.

"Do you think that if you spend too much time thinking about having sex with someone who isn't your husband or wife, then you are committing a form of adultery?" I asked.

"No," he said. "That is absurd. If you spent a lot of time with someone, thinking that you would like to have sex with them, then that is more dangerous territory, because it means that both of you are looking to create a circumstance where something could happen."

"So, have you ever come close?" I asked.

"This was meant to be a conversation about you, not me," he said.

"You didn't answer the question," I said.

"Well, neither did you," he replied.

"We're allowed one question each," I tell him. "Me first. Have you ever been tempted?"

"There was a situation," he said. "In Italy. I went out for a drink one night with Kate, and when we got back to the hotel she asked me if I wanted to go up to her room."

"So, did you?" I asked.

"You've asked your question," he said. "Now it's my turn. Do you fancy Deep Shallows?"

"Sometimes, especially when the weather is hot," I said. "So, what did you say to her?"

"I told her that it wasn't a good idea," he said. "Because it isn't. And then I went to my room. Alone. To be honest, I'm glad that stage of the library is resolved and temptation is out of the way."

"But how do you resist temptation?" I asked.

"You think about all the good things about me and ignore the rest: I'm a good father, I don't play golf every weekend, I don't make passes at your girlfriends, I'm relatively solvent. You think about how you don't want to become another middle-aged cliché. Infidelity is a bad habit to get into in your forties. Otherwise, you might end up like Deep Shallows."

"What do you mean?" I asked.

"Serial adulterer. It's written all over him," he said.

༄

There is a knock on the door, a single, sharp knock that makes me jump.

"Come in," I shout a little too loudly. Robert Bass looks around the edge of the door and comes into the room. He closes it behind him and then leans against it, panting, his familiar green cycling helmet in one hand, his hair wild. I imagine he spent at least thirty seconds running his fingers through his hair to achieve this look of tousled abandon. He is eating some sort of muesli health bar.

"Slow-release carbohydrate," he says, wiping his forehead with his sleeve and smiling.

"Is something chasing you?" I ask. He smiles weakly.

"No, I'm exhausted from cycling so fast. I thought you might have left," he says. He is sweating profusely. "Sorry I'm so late. God, I'm so hot, it must be about ninety degrees out there."

He comes over to the bed and sits on the corner, on top of the triangle of blankets and sheets that Diego pulled back. His T-shirt is damp with sweat. He leans over to kiss me.

"Have you done this before?" I ask, shrinking away from him. He looks a little disconcerted at my line of questioning.

"No," he says, sitting up. "Why?"

"You seem quite professional," I say.

"What do you mean?" he asks.

"You knew about this hotel," I say.

"Everyone knows about this hotel," he replies. "You knew about it. I haven't come here for an inquisition, not from you anyway, I get enough of those from my wife," he says, wiping new pools of sweat from his brow.

"What about?" I ask. He looks at me cagily.

"The usual stuff. And then some more. Mostly about the fact that I don't earn enough money for her to cut back on work. Look, I'm not really in this for the conversation."

"Why don't you have a bath?" I suggest, pointing to the small door wedged between two wardrobes. I can't understand why hotel rooms have such big wardrobes when most people have so little luggage.

"I might just do that," he says, going into the bathroom. His head pops around the door. "Do you fancy joining me?"

"I think I'll listen to the end of this program about the life cycle of Amazonian ferns," I say. "It's very interesting." He looks at me dubiously and goes into the bathroom.

When I am sure that I am alone again, I take a deep breath and lean against the wardrobe. It creaks and wobbles precariously. I cannot believe that I am in a hotel room in Bloomsbury with Robert Bass expecting to have sex with me. Although I have imagined this scene many times over the past year, now that it is about to materialize, I am utterly disengaged from the process.

This is not what I want. For the first time in almost a year, I feel absolutely certain about something. I cannot believe that I have come this far. I put it down to a combination of his persuasive powers, the alcohol, and something more indefinable: the urge to do something reckless. Sometimes you have to get to the point of no return to know exactly where you are going. I realize that it was the illusion rather than the reality of escape that I wanted.

He leaves the door open, and when I am sure that he is in the bath, I get up to leave. I decide not to tell him, in case he manages to divert me. In any case, I don't want to see him naked in the bath.

The water stops and Robert Bass hums a Coldplay song. I switch off the radio, but outside in the corridor I hear raised voices. I go over to the door and listen. There is the noise of someone running, then a woman starts shouting, a male voice joins in, and a door bangs and then opens again. I poke my head around the door in case someone needs help.

The room opposite is open and the noise is definitely coming from inside. I tiptoe across the ugly, worn carpet and walk into room 508.

There are three people standing there. At first they don't notice me in the doorway. This gives me time to absorb the fact that I recognize all of them. They are all talking at once, in raised voices, using clumsy hand gestures to illustrate different points. When they see me standing there, they fall silent, their bodies still, even though their hands are raised in the air in awkward positions that must make their muscles ache. A triptych of ashen faces, their expressions frozen, stare at me.

"Lucy Sweeney, what the fuck have you done?" says Guy angrily, without moving from his position on the right side of the double bed. The buttons of his shirt are undone and his trousers hang around his hips, unzipped and crumpled. I hope he was in the process of undressing rather than dressing. His arms are by his side, his fists angrily clenched. The shirtsleeves fall down over his hands. He is looking for somewhere to channel his anger.

"This has nothing to do with her," shout Emma and Isobel simultaneously. But this will be the only harmonious moment during the next torturous hour that we will spend in this room.

"Lucy, thank God you're here," says Emma, as though this was something that we planned together. She looks relieved to see me. "It's not going according to plan." Obviously, Emma thinks I am here because of her. It wouldn't occur to her that my presence relates to something going on in my own life.

"I've come to the end of the trail," explains Isobel, without removing her gaze from Emma. There is a hint of pride in her voice, but she sounds exhausted. I know that she is ruthlessly assessing the woman in front of her, wondering what Emma offers that she can't deliver. I want to tell her that this is a mistake, that trying to compare a wife of ten years with a mistress of one year is a pointless debate, weighted entirely in favor of the new girlfriend. The fact that Isobel probably has a better body than Emma, who I don't think has ever been near a gym in her life, is irrelevant. Emma has novelty on her side. Time makes people more critical of each other, they lose their mystique, wives become nags, and husbands become moody.

"It's like comparing Saint Paul's cathedral with the Gherkin," I say. "One is old and familiar, the other new and exciting. The question is which one will endure?"

"Sorry, you've lost me there, Lucy," says Emma. I hadn't realized that I was speaking out loud.

"Did you know all this time?" Isobel asks, turning toward me. Her black eye has faded, I note, and she has dressed for the occasion. Her Roger Vivier sandals give her the advantage of height over all of us, and she is wearing a dress more appropriate to the annual party at the Serpentine. But, of course, all this is irrelevant, although I realize that keeping up standards is of huge psychological importance to her. She would definitely qualify for the Jerry Hall school of divorced wives, I think to myself.

"I'm really sorry, Isobel," I say. "I wanted to tell you, but I thought Emma might finish the relationship before you found out. I was put in a very awkward position."

"I understand your dilemma, Lucy. But you should have decided that, on balance, I had the right to know this." She picks up a briefcase and holds it with both hands in front of her body. I start to imagine what might be inside. For a moment, I wonder if she is planning to shoot Guy. But with her monthly allowance, she could have hired someone, I rationalize.

"Actually, you have done me a favor, because four weeks ago I wouldn't have uncovered the extent of his deception, and might even have considered some sort of reconciliation," she says. "I might not have realized that he is a compulsive liar."

She undoes the briefcase and brings out various bits of paper and photographs. She starts to list things. Some are familiar to me; others come as a surprise. She knows about Emma living in their flat in Clerkenwell. She knows that he caught nits indirectly from my children. She knows that his secretary is complicit in the deception. She even knows that Emma and I broke into their family home. She looks up at me when she says that, and I look at my feet like a contrite child.

"Sorry, I feel awful. I thought if Emma deleted the message, I might be able to change the course of history."

Other discoveries come as a surprise. Emma has met his two youngest children. She spent a weekend in a hotel near their Dorset retreat, so that Guy could come and see her when he said he was going running. Isobel even has information on another woman that he had slept with a couple of times over the past year.

"She meant nothing to me, Emma," Guy says, pleading with her to reconsider her position.

"It's too late, Guy," says Emma. "When I went to your house that night, I realized that you never had any intention of leaving your wife."

"How can you apologize to her when you have been married to me for more than ten years?" says Isobel to Guy. Silent tears stream down her cheeks and her carefully applied eye makeup starts to smudge. I offer her a dirty tissue that I find in my pocket and walk over to put my arm around her, but she pushes it away.

"I'm so sorry," says Emma. "I didn't mean for all this to happen."

"What did you mean to happen?" asks Isobel sharply, walking slowly toward Emma. "Actions have consequences."

"I think I was just enjoying the moment," says Emma, shrinking back toward the bedside table. "I thought I was in love. Guy is the one who should have felt responsible for his actions, not me."

"You have no right to fall in love with someone else's husband," shouts Isobel, who is now standing less than a couple of feet in front of Emma. "You didn't just take him away from me, you took him away from his children. You even met two of my children and felt no remorse for what you were doing. You wanted to steal someone else's family, because you have none of your own."

Isobel pulls out an envelope. "Photographic evidence," she says, banging it down on the dressing table.

Mostly Guy is too shell-shocked to speak. I wonder whether Emma had already finished the relationship with Guy when Isobel stormed into the bedroom. I glance at the bed. It hasn't been used and, following the thread of Emma's comments earlier this evening, I immediately understand that this is significant. I look more closely and realize that there are different objects and items of clothing placed on a bedcover with the same green-and-purple design as the one in my own room. They are carefully laid out. It is a little like those memory games children play when you put random objects onto a tray and then have to remember what was there five minutes later. I recognize the Agent Provocateur bra and knickers that Emma took from Guy's house, partly because the bra strap was broken during our tussle. They take pride of place in the middle of the bed. The rabbit sits vertically to the left of the knickers. To the right is an assortment of other items that I imagine were presents from Guy to Emma: a bracelet identical to the one that Isobel is wearing on her wrist, Jo Malone perfume, a novel, and a series of plane tickets from various weekends away. At the foot of the bed is the now empty black Chloe Paddington.

"I was in the middle of finishing the relationship, Lucy," says Emma, looking toward me for approval. "I told you that it would all be over by the end of the weekend."

"You said that you were in Germany," Isobel interrupts, addressing Guy. "How can you lie to me with such conviction? Do you not have any respect for me or our children?" She stands stock-still, and because she remains stationary, everyone else is rooted to the spot.

Guy looks panic-stricken. His eyes are wild. His gaze flits from one person to the other before finally resting at a neutral position somewhere in the middle distance. He is watching himself in the mirror of the dressing table.

"Our marriage was dead on its feet," he says coldly. "I was just a wallet to you. You didn't even want to consider me changing jobs because you enjoyed the perks too much. We hardly had sex. Our life was so prescribed by your endless plans that I was drowning. Suffocating in suburbia."

"Notting Hill is hardly suburbia," says Isobel.

"Suburbia is a state of mind," counters Guy.

"We had sex every two weeks, that's pretty good going," she says. "Isn't it, Lucy?"

"She's right," says Emma. "Lucy has gone for a lot longer than that without having sex with Tom."

"That's because she doesn't have any staff," says Isobel.

It is the first time that any of them have referred to me. It is strange, but although there is a weird but explicable logic to their presence in the hotel, there is none to mine, and yet no one questions what I am doing here in the middle of the night. I look at my watch and realize that it is after two o'clock in the morning. I start to worry about how tired I am going to be tomorrow and wonder how I can extricate myself from this room and get Diego to call a taxi for me to go home. Suddenly, there is nowhere in the world that I would rather be than in bed with Tom lying asleep beside me.

I remember with shock that Robert Bass is in the bath in the bedroom opposite. This seems even more extraordinary to me now than it did ten minutes ago. I am caught up in the excitement of other people's lives and have forgotten the drama of my own. This is because my own is resolved. I notice a chair by the open door and sit down. Everyone looks at me suspiciously. It is clear that no one wants me to leave.

"Should I shut the door?" I ask Isobel. "I think it would be better shut."

"No, leave it open, please, Lucy," she says.

In the corridor I can hear more raised voices. Perhaps this sort of thing happens all the time. Perhaps in another room, further down the corridor, an identical scene is being played out. Diego must be used to this kind of thing. I can hear his voice outside.

"Come this way, please, this way, the noise was coming from here. It might be some of the anxious delegates," he whispers. Still sitting on the chair, because it seems to unsettle everyone if it looks as though I am leaving, I shuffle far back to lean into the corridor to see what is going on. If it is Robert Bass, perhaps I will be able to head him off before anyone sees him. But it is another couple.

"I'm going to see what's going on," I tell the assembled company.

"Don't be long, will you?" says Guy, a note of panic in his voice. I look at him blankly. He doesn't want to be left alone in the room with Isobel and Emma. I go into the corridor. By this time, the couple has almost reached the room.

"Lucy," shouts one of them in astonishment. "What's going on?" It is my brother, and he is holding Cathy's hand.

"Keep your voice down," I say, speaking in a whisper, as though I am showing latecomers to their seats at the theater. "What are you doing here?"

"I'm speaking at the conference tomorrow," whispers Mark. "My room is on this floor. The man from reception said there was an altercation and asked me to investigate. The hotel is full of anxiety delegates."

"And what are you doing here?" I ask Cathy. "Are you one of the anxious people?"

"Only to see you," she says. "Actually, I'm spending the night here. With your brother."

She looks down at her feet in embarrassment. I am glad that I was a news hack for so many years, because I have never lost the ability to absorb information from multiple sources all at once and immediately prioritize what is most significant while simultaneously processing the short, medium, and long-term repercussions. So the downside will be the following: (1) listening to Cathy eulogize my brother, (2) dealing with them both if the relationship fails, and (3) telling Emma.

"We were going to tell you," Cathy says quickly. "I wanted to find the right moment. Besides, it hasn't been going on for more than a month."

"But he's so unreliable," I say to Cathy. "Are you sure you want to take that risk?"

"That's so disloyal, Lucy," says Mark, but he isn't angry. Actually, he has that docile expression of a man in the early stages of love.

"More to the point, Lucy, what are *you* doing here?" asks Mark.

I point to room 508 and give them a brief précis of what has happened.

"I think it is fundamental to get everyone out of here as quickly as possible," I say to Mark, trying not to reveal any self-interest.

We all go back into the bedroom. Isobel and Emma are still arguing. Guy is sitting on the bed, holding his head in his hands. His clothes are still undone. No one looks surprised to see more people come into the room. Three impartial observers should dilute the tension a little.

"I'm Lucy's brother, Mark," says Mark, shaking hands with the assembled company and giving Emma a perfunctory kiss on the cheek. "And this is my girlfriend, Cathy, whom you, Guy, have already met." He puts his arm around Cathy and smiles proprietorially, as though the real reason that we are all gathered in this room is to celebrate his new relationship. He stands there, waiting for people to congratulate him. Cathy smiles up at him happily. This could become tiresome, I think to myself, unable to resist smirking at Guy's look of perplexity.

Then I see Emma's face and realize that for her the sudden blossoming of this relationship is more uncomfortable.

"I didn't realize that you had a brother," says Isobel, politely shaking hands with Mark.

"I think we're heading home soon. Isobel, shall I drop you on the way?" I ask, but it is more command than question. She looks at me for further direction and then nods in assent. Her shoulders slump, and I urge her to pack up all the papers and photographs that she has carefully assembled on the dressing table.

"We'll take Emma home," says Cathy. I note that she is already making decisions on Mark's behalf.

"But aren't we going to spend the night here?" Mark asks Cathy, running his fingers through her hair and using the arm he has carelessly slung around her shoulder to pull her close to him.

"I don't want to go back to Clerkenwell on my own," says Emma in front of everyone. "Can I stay with you, Lucy? Just until I can move back into my old flat again. I can't face being taken home by Cathy and your brother. I had always thought that perhaps we might manage to make things work between us."

I can't quite believe that Emma has chosen the very moment that Mark has publicly revealed his relationship with Cathy for the first time to declare unresolved issues with him. Not for the first time, I wonder whether Mark is right, that she would benefit from a spell with a therapist to get things straight in her head.

"We'd be a disaster," says Mark, a little too hastily. "Anyway, it's always a mistake to revisit old relationships."

So I agree to phone Tom to tell him that Emma will be arriving home soon and staying indefinitely, while I deliver Isobel to her home in Notting Hill.

I find it easy to direct everyone else away from this hotel, but it is less clear how I will explain my own presence here when the inevitable inquest takes place later. I begin to feel quietly confident that I might get away with a blurry story about following Emma here after leaving her private members club, because of residual concerns about her well-being. As long as no one dissects the facts too closely, I might be able to neutralize any residual suspicion with this account.

But I will need to prepare for Tom's precision questioning.

"But didn't you say that you left first?" I could imagine him saying. "And how come you happened to be passing that hotel, when it is so far from where you spent the evening and not on your route home?" Hopefully, the drama of everyone else's evening might sate his curiosity and divert him from this logic.

"What about me?" Guy asks me as everyone prepares to leave. His tone is a little petulant, as though I am responsible for sorting out everyone.

"I think you might have to spend the night here or go to your flat in Clerkenwell," I tell him, perplexed that he is looking to me to resolve his accommodation problems and is unable to absorb the repercussions of what has occurred over the past hour.

"The room was booked anyway, and if this one isn't available for the whole night, I'm sure they can find another one."

"Please, can I come home with you?" he pleads with Isobel.

"I can't believe that you have apologized to her for your infidelity with another woman, shown no remorse for what you have done to me and the children, and then ask to come back and spend the night with me. What you need to understand about adultery is that it adulterates your existing relationship. It takes something away that can never be put back in the same way," she says angrily, pointing at Emma and then turning to Guy again. "You assume you have the right to do whatever you please without any repercussions. Your arrogance is your biggest failing."

"But where am I going to live?" he asks, noticing that his trousers are still unzipped and pulling them up around his waist.

"That's not my problem. You have forfeited your right to call our house your home. You can move into the flat in Clerkenwell," she says. "Come around tomorrow afternoon and we can explain everything to the children."

"But what will I tell them?" he says.

"That you have fallen in love with someone else," she says, starting to sob again, her voice rising. "I can't have him back," she addresses all of us. "There are degrees of betrayal, and Guy's is complete. I could never trust him again, especially since this woman isn't the first, and I'm sure she won't be the last. Our marriage fell at the first fence."

Everyone concurs and nods wisely—even Mark, who has rarely left a relationship without a period of overlap with some other woman. Perhaps over time she might reconsider, during a phase of cold reflection, when the emotional resonance of this evening has faded. Guy might change. The experience might humble him. Both of them might come to the realization that they had left their marriage to grow wild for too long, that marriage is more than an act of faith; it requires careful tending and pruning. I feel as though I am looking at the logical extension of my breakdown in communication with Tom, as though I have been given the chance to see what happens if the rot sets in. I resolve to go home and tell him everything from beginning to end.

Just at the moment that I am beginning to feel as though the evening is drawing to a close, Robert Bass appears, with a white towel wrapped around his waist. He comes into the room.

"I've been waiting in there for so long," he says to me, pointing at the room opposite.

Then he realizes that there are five other people staring at him. For what seems like ages, there is silence. He runs his hands through his hair.

"What are all these people doing here?" he finally asks. "Is this a honey trap? I should have known better than to involve myself with you—you're a recipe for disaster. My wife is probably in the wardrobe." We all look nervously at the wardrobe, and even I wonder whether she might choose this moment to make an appearance.

"Oh my God, Lucy," says Cathy, looking distressed. "What is he doing here?" Isobel looks stunned.

"You're all at it," Isobel sobs. "I can't believe you're having an affair with a father on the school run. It's all so corrupt."

"I thought he was an old friend from *Newsnight*?" questions Mark, closing the door.

"Don't be ridiculous. He's the Sexy Domesticated Dad," Isobel says to everyone. "They've been flirting all year. I thought it was a bit of banter. I never thought that it would transmute into a full-fledged affair."

"I can't believe that you've done this," says Emma, her hand over her mouth in shock.

"She's no better than me; it's the worst kind of hypocrisy," says Guy, animated for the first time in the evening.

Coincidence might make you feel as though there is a strange logic to life, but too many in one evening underline its essential chaos, as though anything could happen at any time.

"Nothing has happened," I tell everyone. They look unconvinced.

"He's virtually naked, Lucy," says Cathy. "It doesn't look good."

"That's because he's just had a bath," I say, as though they might find this a credible explanation.

"Lucy, no one comes to a hotel like this to have a bath," says Mark angrily. "You'll be telling me next that you came so you could listen to the World Service."

"Actually, I have been listening to the World Service," I say. "I cannot believe how hypocritical you all are. Apart from Isobel, you are all involved in infidelity of one kind or another. I have spent the past year debating what to do about this man, and we haven't even kissed properly."

"She's right," says Robert Bass. "I know this doesn't look good, but really nothing has happened. In fact, Lucy has tried to resist my advances on several occasions."

There is a knock at the door. We all stare at it nervously. It is not Diego's quiet, tentative, rhythmical knock. It is more determined and demanding.

"Who is that?" asks Robert Bass, looking at me. Everyone else stares, too.

"Who is it, Lucy?" says Mark abruptly.

"How can I possibly know who is at the door?" I say, irritated.

"You are the common thread of connection here," says Mark.

"I'll open it," says Isobel resolutely. "It might be someone from my sleuthing course."

"Let me go," I insist. "It might be Tom."

I think about what lies ahead. Months of recrimination, of doubt about the authenticity of my story, the sneaking suspicion of everyone in this room that Robert Bass and I were not telling the truth. It's not better to be hung for a sheep as for a lamb. Absolutely not. Then I consider how everyone present will use my story to detract from the drama and emotion of their own, until the rest of the evening blurs into insignificance when set against my alleged infidelity. Tom will want to believe me but will face the humiliation of all these people assuming that he is being blind. I sigh deeply, the first of what I imagine will probably be a lifetime of sighs. Tom might leave me. He might decide that I am untrustworthy and that it would be better for the children to live in a household with less suspicion and tension. He might retaliate with a proper infidelity of his own, not a half-baked unconvincing fantasy of the kind that I have dabbled with.

I turn the handle.

"Sweeney," a male voice says, pushing against the door when he feels my resistance. "Let me in. I am here to rescue you." The last sentence is said in an accent from the Deep South. The others stand transfixed as Celebrity Dad comes into the bedroom. I worry that he has finally succumbed to a partial nervous breakdown and is reliving a role he played in a Hollywood film. Possibly something set in the tropics written by Graham Greene, because he is wearing a grubby suit that probably started the week cream but has ended it in an off-gray color.

"Not him." Robert Bass groans. "My bête noire."

"Oh my God," says Emma, perking up. "Can I just say that I have seen all your films and I think you are a fantastic talent. Also, I am newly single."

Celebrity Dad looks at her appreciatively.

"What are you doing here?" I ask him.

"I am here with a specific purpose, and that is to take you home," he says. "I have a car waiting outside."

"Would you drop me on the way?" asks Isobel.

"Can I just say that you really know how to divorce in style," says Celebrity Dad admiringly. "And, of course, I can drop you."

"It's of little consolation," says Isobel, but I can tell that it helps slightly.

"But how did you know that I was here?" I ask.

"Tom called me," he says. "About three hours ago, you sat on your cell phone and dialed home. Tom has been listening to everything that has happened since then. He found my number on the class list and called up to ask if I would come and collect you."

"How long has he been listening?" I ask, nervously gripping the sleeve of his jacket.

"Since you arrived in the hotel room and started to listen to that program about ferns in the Amazon," explains Celebrity Dad. "An unorthodox erotic prelude if ever I heard one."

"So does he know that nothing happened between me and Robert Bass?" I ask.

"Absolutely," says Celebrity Dad. "He realized that you were completely out of your depth and called me up to intervene. He briefed me on everything that was taking place and told me that you had gotten yourself into a situation that required immediate resolution and that, since I knew everyone involved, and am a fellow Arsenal supporter, I was the best person to come and sort things out."

"But why didn't he come?" I ask.

"He was worried that Fred might wake up and find a drunken American actor asleep on the sofa," he explains. "Also, I know this hotel. I have very fond memories of the Aberdeen." He laughs wistfully.

Diego comes to the room.

"Your time is up," he says to me sorrowfully. "We usually charge per person."

Celebrity Dad hands him a bundle of notes.

"That should cover it. He'll pay the rest," he says, pointing at Guy, who remains sitting on the bed.

"That's like that moment in *Reservoir Dogs*," says Emma. "Or was it *Traffic*? *L.A. Confidential*? God, I can't believe he is with us here."

☙

On the way home in his car, we sit in a row across the backseat. It is clean and tidy, and the driver plays soothing music. Isobel falls quiet. Celebrity Dad pulls out a bottle of whiskey from a small cupboard behind the driver's seat, takes a slug, and offers it to her. She tips her head and drinks deeply, shuddering at its bitterness.

"It's going to be tough doing this on my own," she says. "I know I have a lot of help, but ultimately I will have to take responsibility."

"You could have been married to someone like me, and then you would be doing it on your own anyway," says Celebrity Dad.

"You might not be on your own forever," I say.

"I need to mourn my marriage for a while and try and make sense of it all. I am not without fault in all this. It is just that I am paying a heavy price for my mistakes," she says bleakly. "But I won't punish the children for the sins of the father."

"What are you going to do?" she asks Celebrity Dad.

"Actually, I have learned a lot from this whole experience," he says, slurring his words and periodically jabbing his finger in the air. "When you live life so publicly, you come to dread dealing with yourself privately, because there is such a gulf between the two. I'd like to believe the myth of myself, but every time I look in the mirror, all I see is the reality. I think I need a period somewhere remote with my wife and children, to try and find the ground again. Somewhere without a liquor store for fifty miles. When Tom phoned me tonight, I felt that I had some purpose in life above and beyond having a good time. It actually felt good to be asked to do something positive. Something real. It's also good practice. I've got a role lined up in a film about childhood sweethearts who meet up on Friends Reunited."

"What about you, Sweeney?" he asks. They both look at me.

"More of the same, I suppose," I say, with an unusual hint of certainty in my tone. "And less of anything different."

I'm not sure what I am expecting when I fumble for my keys to open the front door of the house, but I did at least anticipate a reception committee. I tried not to think about Tom's mood or the arguments that might lie ahead, because it is often difficult to read him and, from my point of view at least, the evening marked the end of something.

Instead, it is dark as I head upstairs to the bedroom. The bathroom door is slightly open, and the light is switched on. I go in to wash my face and remove my contact lenses. I can't find the case, so I put them in a coffee cup that is standing on a shelf and then hide the cup on the top shelf of the airing cupboard. Suddenly, I hear gentle splashing on the other side of the room.

Of course, Tom is in the bath. That is perfectly predictable, and I feel a surge of joy at the logic of this situation. I go over and peer around the side of the shower curtain and find him lying underwater, his hair floating around his face in pleasing patterns. I put my hand out to move a piece that has settled across his cheek when he grabs my wrist.

"Lucy," he says, smiling. "You're home."

acknowledgments

I would particularly like to thank Gill Morgan for allowing Lucy Sweeney to unburden herself in *The Times Magazine* every week. None of this would have happened without her. I am also indebted to Simon Trewin, with me every step of the way, and to Zoe Pagnamenta in New York. I am very grateful to my editors, Sarah McGrath at Riverhead and Nikola Scott and Kate Elton at Century, for their unerring enthusiasm and dedication. No thanks big enough for my husband, Edward Orlebar, for his impeccable advice on anything and everything, and for picking up the domestic mantle just when it mattered most. Helen Townshend and Henry Tricks read the manuscript and gave constant encouragement right from the start. Helen Johnston was an inspiration in every way. I am very grateful to Sally Johnston for insights into life at the BBC and to Imogen Strachan for advice on matters psychological. Thanks to my parents for so many things, but mostly the laughs. To the original slummy mummies, thank you for your friendship and, most important, for sharing trade secrets. You should know who you are, but in case not: Louise Carpenter, Carey Combe, Caroline Combe, Alexa Corbett, Sarah Dodd, Vicky McFadyen, Ros Mullins, and Amanda Turnbull. Last but not least, thanks to Lucy Sweeney, an inspiration to us all.

about the author

Fiona Neill is a features writer for the London *Times Magazine* in which her weekly "Slummy Mummy" column appears. Previously she was the features editor for *Marie Claire* and assistant editor of *The Times Magazine*. She lives in London with her husband and three children.